THE WITCH OF ELLESMERE

KIRSTY INIC

The Witch of Ellesmere
Copyright © 2022 by Kirsty Inic

First edition: January 2022

Paperback ISBN: 9780646839004
EPUB ISBN: 9780645167801

With special thanks to:
Editor; Chloe Hodge
Cover artist; Sara Oliver Design
Formatting; Lorna Reid
Illustration; Tess Pollard

Want to stay in touch? Find me at: **kirstyinic.com**
Instagram: @kirsty_inic
Facebook: Kirsty Inic Author

For my loved ones, who always believed in my magic.

One

Sitting behind the long wooden countertop at the front of my mother's apothecary, I stared out the large front windows, watching the deserted main street of our small town grow darker with each tick of the clock's hands. My eyes shifted to the large clock hanging on the opposite wall. The hands showed it was seven-thirty. Only half an hour until the other witches and warlocks of our Coven arrived for my induction. Picking up my small porcelain cup, I drank deeply, hoping that the tea's soothing aroma of chamomile and lavender would help calm the jittery feeling growing in my stomach. Placing my cup back on the saucer, I took a deep breath through my nose and let it out slowly. I began to feel my body lighten as the growing tension of tonight's ceremony drifted away like a leaf on an autumn breeze. A soft hand touched my shoulder gently, lingering momentarily before withdrawing. I didn't need to see their face to know who the hand belonged to.

"How are you feeling, pet?"

Maeve's soothing voice flowed over me like water upon rocks and I smiled as the tension in my shoulders began to ease. Maeve had been with our Coven in Pryhollow for as long as I could remember. One of my mother's oldest and dearest friends, Maeve was some years older than her and had been the grandmother I never had growing up. Coming around to stand in front of me, Maeve's bottle-green eyes locked on my own. Her long grey hair fell in a tangled and messy heap around her shoulders.

"I'm okay," I replied softly as I reached again for my tea and took another large sip.

My eyes darted to the clock once more and my heart began to beat a little faster. *Not long to go now.*

Over the years, Maeve had become adept at reading my facial expressions. I wasn't always the best at keeping my emotions off my face, and seeing through my little white lie, Maeve gave me a warm smile. Taking my teacup from me and placing it gently on the saucer, she took my hands in hers and pulled me up, placing her palms on the sides of my face.

"It's normal to feel nervous about your induction, Braelyn, but you have nothing to be concerned about. You will be fine." She gave my cheek a comforting squeeze.

While I appreciated her reassuring words, it did very little to put my mind at ease.

In the weeks leading up to tonight, I had thrown myself into the pages of any witch history book I was able to get my hands on, hoping to educate myself on what tonight would really entail. Growing up, my mother had told me about my induction ceremony—that it was a time to celebrate my coming of age and receive my true magic. That's what this was all about. Elemental magic. As a child born with witches' blood, I grew up learning the ways of Maleficia Magic. Herbalism, botany, healing elixirs and protection spells were among some of the subjects my mother taught me. She showed me the best ways to dry herbs to make teas and poultices, and what ingredients went into making only the best potions. All so I would be ready for my induction ceremony at the age of seventeen, which involved some of the most sacred of magics. To harness and use our magic, every witch and warlock draws on the four elements—Earth, Air, Fire, and Water—but each of us has one element that is more dominant than the others. On the night of your induction, it pulses through your veins and makes itself known to the Coven. This is when our real magic blooms.

Draining the last of my tea—which had now gone cold—I placed the cup and saucer in the small sink that we hardly ever used. Reaching to turn on the hot water, my hand barely touched the tap when a strong stream gushed from the nozzle. Jumping back in surprise I spun around to see Maeve giggling by the shelf that stocked our teas. It was one of her many tricks she enjoyed playing on people when they least expected it. Maeve was a water witch and could manipulate water in some of the most magnificent ways, but most of the time she simply enjoyed exploding water out of things and laughing at the shock that appeared on people's faces when they realised what had happened. Despite her age, she loved playing tricks on people. It was one of the many things I had always loved about her. The water splashed up, soaking my favourite mustard-coloured sweater and seeping through to my white blouse, leaving a dark stain in the middle of my stomach. Maeve walked over to where I stood soaking wet and threw me a small cotton towel—still giggling to herself. Catching it mid-air I soaked up the wet patch on my clothes as the soft material turned cold and stiff.

"It's about time you got changed anyway, pet. The rest of the Coven will be here any minute and you don't want to be late."

"You could have just told me that rather than soaking me," I replied, giving her a small frown.

I chucked the wet towel over the back of a nearby chair as Maeve skipped cheerfully over to the box she had been unpacking. "Now where is the fun in that?" she yelled over her shoulder as I made my way down the short, narrow hallway which led to the back of the apothecary.

Pushing open the heavy wooden door, I stepped inside the small, cosy room that held some of the more abnormal herbs and mixes the people of Pryhollow weren't as accustomed to. My mother's shop was mostly home to jars of tea to help people with stomach pains, herbs that aided in the healing process, and sticks of dried flowers and herbs that banished bad energy. However there were many witches that travelled near and far to the apothecary to purchase what they needed to make their potions and contribute to their spell casting. Even though most people in Pryhollow suspected witches lived in the town, having jars of snake oil, crows' eyes and fly wings in the shop weren't doing us any favours.

Looking around the dark room I spotted my mother by the bench that ran the length of the small room. I almost hadn't noticed her as the long black dress she wore blended perfectly with the dark cabinets. Watching her from the other side of the room I couldn't help but admire the way she moved with such ease and grace. Something that I never inherited. I had always been a clumsy child, tripping over my own feet and knocking things over. I had hoped that one day I might grow into the elegance that my mother possessed, but it never happened.

I watched as my mother's deft hands blended the herbs together in the stone mortar she always used for these types of recipes. Grinding them to a fine powder, she would mix them together to make the poultices we sold for things like rashes, bites, and other sinister ailments our customers came in for.

As an air witch, potion making shouldn't be something my mother was good at, but for some reason she seemed to have a knack for it. Her knowledge on all things potion exceeded any witch or warlock I knew, and she could create even the most complex of mixes without consulting our grimoire—the book which held all of our family's secrets, spells and potions recorded over the centuries. I couldn't do any magic without it. Seeing my mother mixing away reminded me of one of the lessons she'd held in this very room. It had been a bitterly cold day and the fire was crackling warmly in the fireplace. After coming home from school, we'd dived headfirst into my first Maleficia Magic lesson of the night. This one happened to be about grimoires and the power they held within their aged pages. While each witch and warlock family had their own grimoire which held general spells and potions, many families had their own magic section, dedicated to their family element. It wasn't uncommon for dark witches and warlocks to steal other grimoires to harness that power. Many years ago, a witch tried to do exactly this. She had slain families of witches and warlocks to gain their elemental secrets and then used that power to summon some of the worst demons known to our kind. They were called the Wraiths of Umbra. Summoned using dark magic, they obeyed their summoner without question and would perform any type of terrible desire the dark witch wanted. It led to a war that lasted years, and it had taken the power of the Great King of Ellesmere to bring an end to the terror. By decree of the Great King, the witch had been burnt at the stake. She was the first witch to burn in more than one hundred years. The story had terrified children everywhere. Myself included.

A small noise caught my attention and brought me out of my thoughts. Spinning around in a twirl of skirts, looking like a ballerina on pointe, my mother smiled as she saw me standing in the door frame.

"Oh Brae, I thought I heard you come in." Gliding over to me, she wrapped me up in a hug, her long skirts swishing around my ankles.

Pulling back, she turned her round, hazel eyes on me. They sparkled in the candlelight that lit most of the small room, but there was also a sadness that hadn't been there a moment ago.

"Is everything okay?" I asked quietly.

My mother chuckled lightly as she wiped away a tear that had escaped the corner of her eye.

"Of course, Brae." Her voice hitched on my name. "I just can't believe your ceremony day is here."

I gave her a small smile before shifting my gaze from her intense stare. Those knowing eyes had always been able to extract so many of my secrets. As a witch living in a superstitious town like Pryhollow, it hadn't been easy to grow up here. I had never been able to make many friends as most of the people my age were either too scared of me and my family or only wanted to be my friend to see if the superstitions were true. After a while, I'd become resigned to the fact that I could only truly rely on Maeve and my mother.

I obviously hadn't been quick enough in avoiding her scrutiny as she grabbed my chin gently and turned my face back to hers, fixing her eyes on mine. The green specks that spattered her hazel eyes shone bright in the candlelight.

"Something's bothering you, Brae. I can feel it." Her eyes searched mine lovingly, trying to find the source of what was on my mind.

It always astonished me how she could see into my very soul and know when something was wrong—sometimes before I even knew it myself. A mother's intuition.

"It's nothing. I'm just a little nervous about the ceremony." I could feel my stomach doing little flips as I thought about my looming induction.

"Oh honey," she said softly. "You have nothing to be nervous about."

She stroked my cheek and from the corner of my eye I could see her element rune peeking out from the palm of her hand. She must have seen me glance at it because she placed her palm in the air between us. The element rune for air magic stood out dark as night against the pink flesh of her hand. Taking up most of her palm, it was an outline of a triangle with a line cutting through the top third of the shape. To someone who wasn't a witch it simply looked like a tattoo, but unlike a normal tattoo that was simply drawn in ink, an element rune was melded to us. It becomes part of who we are. It felt so strange to me that, in just a short time, I too would have an element rune just like every other witch and warlock in our Coven. *Well, if one chooses me.* It was this flicker of doubt that must have shown on my face as my mother's eyebrows creased together in a frown.

"Braelyn, what is it that's truly worrying you so much about the ceremony?" Her voice was soft, but I could hear the concern behind her words.

Looking up from where her hand still hung in the air between us, I took a deep breath and let my fears come tumbling out like water from a faucet.

"What if an element doesn't choose me tonight? What if I never get an element rune!? What will happen to me? I will never be able to use magic the way you and Maeve do." My words came spurting out, brimming with my fear of not being good enough.

While I knew how to make healing potions and brew moon water, elemental magic was the most sacred of all magics and something I had dreamed of learning since I was young.

In all my reading leading up to tonight, I had come across countless retellings of witches and warlocks who simply never passed their induction and never received their element rune. These stories scared me more than I cared to admit. I couldn't bear the thought of not being able to wield my own element. My mother took my hand in hers and gave it a tight reassuring squeeze.

"Braelyn, please believe me when I say that you have absolutely nothing to be worried about. It has been a long time since a witch hasn't received her rune—back when witches and warlocks would marry humans to try to hide their magic." Giving my hand another firm squeeze she let it go and walked back to the bench where an abundance of herbs still lay scattered across the deep hardwood countertop. I followed and helped sort the different herbs into the jars labelled lavender, chamomile and rosemary. My mother's hands moved much quicker than mine, pouring and funnelling the herbs into their respective jars.

"How can you be sure though?" I asked. "What if I'm one of the few who are just not strong enough to wield any of the elements?" The herbs scattered over the bench as I nervously dropped one of the jars. Stopping what she was doing, my mother turned to me, her hands on her hips. Her eyes met mine in the dim light and a stern look settled on her beautiful face. I hadn't seen that expression since I was a child.

"Braelyn Grey, you are a stronger witch than you think. And you come from a line of some of the most talented witches of their times. Your father being one of them." She paused briefly and I could just make out the sadness in her eyes.

My father had died before I was born, and my mother didn't

speak of him. There were no photos of him at our house and, as a child, I used to dream up images of this handsome dark-haired man who had needed to leave us in order to save the world and adventure to far-off places. As the years went on, I tried asking my mother many times to tell me about him, but every time I mentioned him her eyes would turn distant. She would say that one day she would tell me about my father, but "now was not the time". It was never the time, so eventually I stopped asking altogether.

Helping her pick up the few jars that she had jam-packed so full of herbs they looked like they would burst, we placed them in one of the top cabinets and, glancing at the small grandfather clock, my mother startled.

"Braelyn, it's almost time for the Coven to start arriving, you need to go and get dressed." Closing the cabinet doors softly, she ran her hands over her dark hair, smoothing back the tiny hairs that had escaped her pristine bun. "I put your dress on your bed, now go and get changed while Maeve and I do the last few preparations." Placing a light kiss on my cheek, she walked out towards the front of the shop. I was left standing in the dim candlelit room, trying to collect my thoughts about the morsel of information she had shared about my unknown father.

I made my way up the rickety stairs which were hidden at the very back of the hallway and entered my room. Set at the top of the staircase directly in front of the entryway, it wasn't a very big space—fitting only my small bed and a bookshelf that ran the length of the wall opposite my bed frame.

The dress I had chosen for tonight's ceremony was laid out on my bed just as my mother had said. It was a Coven's tradition for the new witch or warlock to wear white for the night of their ceremony as it represented all that was good and pure. Slipping the dress over my head, the fabric felt soft and cool against my skin. Made of a light white material, it flowed and swished as I walked. Falling to just above my ankles, the beautiful white material hugged my body in all the right places, accentuating the curves at my waist and falling loosely over my hips. I fastened the two buttons at the back of the high neck, smoothing my hands to flatten the tiny creases I had made whilst dressing. Turning to face the long mirror that hung on the back of my bedroom door, I studied my reflection. Eyes like my mother's stared back at me, dull in the sun's dying light. Small lines creased my forehead as the anxiety of what awaited downstairs sent my stomach into a flurry. My dark hair tumbled past my shoulders in tangled waves. I tried running my fingers through the messy strands, but it was no use. My hair had a mind of its own. Taking a deep breath, I opened my bedroom door and began to make my way down the stairs when a strange noise flooded my ears. It sounded like a faint humming, almost like the thrumming of a bee's wings as it hovers over a flower. Closing my eyes, I tried to focus on the noise, but I couldn't pinpoint where it was coming from. Continuing to walk barefoot down the rest of the stairs, the noise grew almost deafening. Glancing down the length of the dark hallway, there was not a person in sight. Covering my ears, I grimaced as the noise grew so loud, I thought my eardrums would burst. Rushing towards the door that led to the small room where my ceremony would take place, I was so focused on trying to block out the noise that I hadn't seen Maeve walk out of the room. Running into her headfirst, I staggered back a little and gazed up at Maeve's confused face staring down at me. Her brows were furrowed, and her lips puckered.

"Whoa there, child. What's going on?" She held me at arm's length, stopping me from tumbling into the wall.

"Can you not hear that humming noise?"

Maeve gave me a strange look and placed a long, thin finger against her lips. Realising my hands were still over my ears I took them away, not noticing I had yelled my question at her. Looking up into Maeve's kind but concerned face, I realised the sound had stopped.

"Could you not hear that humming in the hallway?" I asked her, quieter this time.

Maeve continued to stare at me with a quizzical expression on her face. Shaking her head, she replied, "What are you talking about, pet?"

Blinking a few times to clear the confusion that clouded my head, I was astonished she had no idea what I was talking about. The noise had been so deafening I had barely been able to think, and my ears were still ringing even after it had stopped.

"That humming noise. It sounded like a million bees' wings beating at the same time." My eyebrows drew together in a small frown. "You honestly didn't hear anything?"

Maeve shook her head and her face continued to wrinkle in concern as she stared at me. "Braelyn, there has been no noise aside from the guests waiting for the ceremony to begin." She reached out and placed a wrinkled hand on my forehead. "Are you feeling okay? You look a bit flushed."

Leaning around Maeve, my eyes darted towards the gold oval mirror that was hanging just behind her, hidden behind her crazy mop of grey hair. My face was indeed glowing a warm red, and I felt hot and sweaty beneath my dress, despite the lightness of the fabric. Giving Maeve what I hoped was a reassuring smile, I reached up to squeeze her hand in mine.

"Yeah, sorry Maeve. I think I'm just still feeling a little nervous." Letting go of her hand I took a long breath in through my nose and released it after a few seconds. Feeling my body relax slightly, I pasted on my best excited smile.

"Should we go in?"

But before Maeve even had a chance to answer my question, I darted around her and stepped into the small room that was now buzzing with the voices of all the witches and warlocks in our Coven. It was time for the ceremony to begin.

T_{wo}

The small parlour at the back of my mother's apothecary felt even smaller with so many witches and warlocks crammed inside. While there were only eight guests standing at one end of the room, the small fire blazing in the hearth and all the extra bodies made the room feel uncomfortably warm. Wiping a small bead of sweat from my face as it made its slow descent down the side of my temple, I felt my stomach churn as I waited anxiously for the ceremony to begin. The blazing fire continued to warm my already hot skin as I stared out at the faces of the elders in our Coven—most of them no older than Maeve and my mother. Taking a few deep breaths, I tried to find my mother's face amongst the sea of witches and warlocks that littered the room. I spotted her over by our grandfather clock, quietly chatting to an elderly warlock who I had only seen a handful of times. The warlock's crystal blue eyes shone in the firelight as my mother laughed at something he said. Stroking his grey goatee, his piercing eyes met my own and he gestured in my direction with a quick nod of his head. Turning, my mother caught me watching her and gave me a brief smile. I returned it quickly. Sensing my nerves, she gave the old warlock a tiny bow and made her way through the throng of witches to stand beside me. Her long dark hair flowed like waves over her shoulders. She very rarely wore it out, but tonight was a special occasion.

"Are you ready, Brae?" Her words came out more as a statement than a question.

I nodded my head once, too nervous to speak. She gave me another reassuring smile, her eyes crinkling at the corners like they always did when she was happy and proud of something I had done.

"Okay, let's begin."

She faced the other witches and warlocks in the room, clearing her throat to capture everyone's attention. The room immediately fell silent. The only noise was my heavy, fast heartbeat that I swore everyone could hear.

As the head of our Coven, it was my mother's responsibility to run all our ceremonies and meetings. And tonight would be no different.

"Fellow witches and warlocks," she said. "Thank you for joining us tonight for another induction ceremony."

The group of witches bowed their heads in unison. A sign of respect for our kind. My eyes caught Maeve's in the firelight, and she winked at me as she hid a small smile, tucking a strand of grey hair behind her ear. Bowing my head in return I tried to stifle the small laugh that threatened to escape my lips.

"Braelyn Grey." My mother's voice echoed around the room, and my hands trembled in anticipation as I waited for her next instruction. "Please step into the pentacle."

On the floor before me was a large white star, drawn in the middle of a perfect circle. The witch's pentacle. Representing light magic and purity, it was a powerful symbol that was only ever used in the most difficult of spells. It offered protection to both the spell caster and the witch standing within the pentacle, warding them from any dark magic seeping in. As with all things magic, there was a light and dark side. Picking up my dress so that it wouldn't rub against any of the chalk, I stepped lightly into the middle of the five-pointed star and waited for my next instruction. My heart beat faster with each passing minute as I wondered what was coming. My mother walked around me, lighting the three white candles that were positioned evenly around the pentacle. As she lit the last one, her eyes locked with mine.

"Breathe," I heard her whisper.

Nodding once, I sucked in a shaky breath, trying to calm the nerves that made my hands tremble. Squeezing them into tight fists by my side, I turned back to the Coven as my mother's clear voice echoed around the room.

"Terra, Aqua, Ignis, Caeli, Spiritus."

It was an ancient language. The most sacred of languages spoken amongst our kind. I watched with bated breath as everyone in the room repeated the same five words after my mother. The words representing each element. At first nothing happened, and I listened to my heart thud loudly in my ears. My stomach flipped as the silence in the room threatened to crush me. *I'm a dud.* There was no magic flaring within me. All the books I'd read spoke of a feeling of awakening, as if their magic had come to life. Blossoming inside them like a flower in springtime. My body felt no different. As a wave of panic washed over me, threatening to send me to my knees, a small electric shock tingled in my fingers. The candles around the pentacle began to flicker violently until the flames eventually sputtered out, sending small wisps of smoke swirling in the air around me. I opened my clenched hands and felt the tingling sensation begin to flow through my arms and into my chest. My face grew hot, and I closed my eyes against the loud humming that vibrated through my skull. My head felt like it was going to explode. The inside of my skull burned, but my body felt as if it had been dipped into an icy river. Tiny pinpricks—like millions of ice shards—stabbed at my body, sending shivers over my arms and legs despite the warmth of the room. The pain and the noise were too much, and I squeezed my eyes shut, trying to will the pain to go away. Then, just as quickly as it had come, it all stopped. Opening my eyes, everyone's gaze was focused on me, watching and waiting with bated breath. For what, I didn't know. That's when a small witch—who I hadn't taken much notice of sitting at the back of the room—walked over to me. Her eyes were a milky white and they stared at me knowingly as if seeing into the depth of my soul. Her face had so many wrinkles they sagged her skin dramatically, but her face was kind. She held out a gnarled hand towards me, her milky eyes never leaving my hazel ones.

"Your hand, child." Her voice was raspy like a smoker's.

I tentatively stuck out my hand and she grasped it rather strongly in her own. It was at that moment I realised she was, in fact, the Wise Witch of our Coven. The witch who saw all. She was the one who would administer my rune, just like she had with everyone else in the Coven. Staring down at my palm, she covered it with her other wrinkled hand and uttered the words, "Ostende te." *Show yourself.*

There was no pain, but a dark mark immediately began to appear in the middle of my palm. The rune revealed itself slowly as the Wise Witch gazed at me quizzically. She smiled broadly, showing a gummy mouth, and spoke as if to herself, but I heard her every word.

"She will be our salvation."

My head reeled as I glanced down at the rune marking my skin. It was a perfect circle. The Wise Witch turned to face the rest of the Coven and spoke loudly. "The elements have chosen," she told everyone. "They bear upon the child Spiritus Magicae."

No one in the room made a sound. Glancing around at the faces before me, my heart picked up its pace. My chest tightened as I replayed the Wise Witch's words over in my head. *Spiritus Magicae. Spirit magic.* My eyes found Maeve's face and, even in the dim light, I could see she was ghostly pale, her mouth hanging open in surprise. Hushed murmurs began to flow through the room and my eyes widened as some of the whispers reached my ears.

"The most powerful—"

"She will be the one—"

I spun around trying to find my mother in the dimly lit room, hoping her caring gaze would help ease my worries. But as I spotted her in the crowd, I saw her swaying where she stood. She looked like she was going to faint. Rushing to her side, I took her face in my hands. She flinched at my touch. My heart sunk so low it felt like it was sitting in my stomach. My mother had never recoiled from me the way she just had, and I took a step back from her, feeling more alone than I ever had in my life.

"Mother," I muttered.

Blinking a few times, she cleared her throat before speaking to the rest of the Coven. "My fellow witches and warlocks, please welcome our newest member of the Coven. Braelyn Grey, spirit witch." My eyes widened as I heard my mother's words echo around the room. It was impossible. Spirit witches were powerful and all-knowing. I could barely remember how to make a potion without the use of our grimoire.

The room had gone deathly silent. The fire in the hearth had burned down, leaving only a few small logs in the bottom of the fireplace. A small crackle from the splintering timber was the only sound in the room. Slowly, the witches in front of me began to rouse from the shock my ceremony had cast over them. A few of them milled at the back of the room, continuing to speak in whispers and hushed tones all the while throwing wary glances in my direction. I scanned the crowd, desperately trying to find Maeve's familiar face, hoping she would be able to shed some light on the situation. She was nowhere to be seen. Turning back to my mother, I was pleased to see that some colour had returned to her face, but her eyes were veiled with worry as she continued to stare at me. I glanced behind me to make sure no one was near us before I spoke.

"Mother, are you okay?" My voice came out as barely a whisper.

Her knuckles were white as she clutched her dark skirt, but she gave me a small smile. "I'm fine Braelyn. Just... uh, just a little in shock. I never expected for you to be a spirit witch."

I stared back at her, a small twinge of annoyance flickering through me. Why was it so impossible for her to believe I could be a spirit witch? Did she not think I was good enough? As my heightened emotions flooded over me, my mother's worried eyes continued to analyse my face. Returning her stare, my fiery temper was slowly extinguished. She hadn't expected this and, honestly, neither had I.

Upon receiving their rune, most witches and warlocks were either chosen by Earth, Air, Fire, or Water. Spirit magic was one of the rarest and most powerful of all magic because, rather than being tied to just one of the elements, it allowed the wielder to use all of them. There had only ever been a small number of witches and warlocks throughout history who had been chosen by the spirit element, most of whom ended up practicing dark magic. I now understood why our Coven were looking at me like I was about to self-combust. Spirit magic was the least studied of all the elements. No one knew how or why only a few people were ever able to wield this type of magic. It was the unknown that scared them all.

My mother placed her hand on the side of my face, cupping my cheek gently as she ran her thumb over my cheekbone. She used to do this when I was a little girl to help me relax after nightmares had woken me throughout the night. Her skin was a little rough from the repetitive motion of using a mortar and pestle, but her touch soothed my erratic thoughts.

"Let me see the rest of the Coven out and then we can talk."

Leaving me standing in the small room on my own, I pressed myself up against the bench, suddenly realising how tired I felt. This whole evening had been so draining and I couldn't help but feel a small pang of worry in my stomach about what my newfound magic would mean for my future. For my family. Opening my hand slowly, I peered down at my palm. It was the first time since receiving my rune that I had the chance to look at it properly. The black ink stood out stark on the pink of my palm, just as my mother's did all these years later. I rubbed the dark circle with the pad of my thumb, expecting something to happen, but all I felt was a slight tingling in my right hand. My eyes lingered on the perfectly circular rune as my mind drifted to the comments uttered from the Coven. Lost in my thoughts for a time, I wondered what all of this meant, why it had been me the elements had chosen to instil this power.

A movement at the door caught my eye, and closing my hand again, I looked up to see my mother's worried face watching me from the door. She stood where I had mere moments ago, but it felt like years had passed since that moment. Wandering into the room, she warmed her hands by the dying fire before turning to me.

"Braelyn, there are a few things I need to tell you." Coming over to sit on one of the cushioned chairs that were positioned in front of the fire, she gestured for me to sit next to her. Pushing off from the bench, I made my way over to her, but I didn't sit, still too tense from tonight's events. Instead, I chose to stand in front of the fire, watching the flames sputter in the grate.

"Does this have something to do with my father?" I asked quietly, pointing down at the rune that lay hidden in my clenched fist.

I couldn't see my mother's reaction, but I heard her take a deep breath before she spoke.

"Braelyn, I know that I've not spoken to you about your father, but I think it's time you should know a few things about him." Her voice shook with every word.

Coming to sit next to her I leant forward, placing my hand over my mother's. My heart pounded in anticipation as I waited for her to continue. My mother's eyes glistened as she stared into the space between us, unseeing, focused on a long distant memory. I didn't say anything out of fear of startling her from her thoughts.

"Braelyn, your father was a remarkable man." She smiled to herself. "He was handsome, and kind, and he was one of the most talented warlocks I knew." As she looked up at me, a tear escaped her eye, rolling silently down her cheek. It left a faint trail on her skin that almost shimmered in the dim firelight.

"How did you meet?" I asked quietly.

"We lived in the same village. His family was much wealthier than mine, but your father didn't care. We were celebrating the Yule festival when he asked me to dance with him. I couldn't refuse his dashing smile." A flicker of joy played across my mother's face, and I knew in this moment she was back in her village with him. Swaying to an unknown song that only played in her memory.

"We danced and talked most of the night. Then, when it was time to say goodbye, he kissed my cheek, and I knew from that moment that I loved him." She was quiet for a few moments before she continued.

"We spent most of our days together and, at night, we would sneak out and meet by the edge of the forest to watch the stars. Time always passed so slowly when we were together. Sometimes it felt like time had stopped altogether, and it was just the two of us in the world." My mother's cheeks were flushed as she looked at me, her eyes dreamy. "One day you will know what I'm talking about."

I rubbed my face to hide my flushed cheeks from her. I hadn't even been kissed before so I couldn't imagine feeling a love like my mother and father had shared.

"So what happened to him?"

As much as I loved hearing her talk about my father, I desperately wanted to know what happened to him and why he was no longer a part of my life. From the sounds of it, he had clearly loved my mother fiercely, so if he hadn't fallen out of love with her... could it have been me? My stomach clenched at the thought of my father not being the hero I had always dreamt him to be.

"Not long after I found out I was pregnant with you, a rift between the kingdoms Royal Family broke out and a war was waged. Your father was concerned for our safety and told me to flee the village so no harm would come to us." Her lip quivered as she spoke. Wrapping her arms around herself she continued with her story. "Your father said he would meet me at your grandmother's house when it was safe for him to get away, but he never came. I knew as soon as I saw the king's army reach the village something terrible had happened, so your grandmother opened a portal, and I came here." She paused for a moment, her eyes filled with unshed tears.

"Where did you come from?" I asked quickly before she could continue. I stared into the smouldering embers in the hearth, unable to look at my mother anymore. I couldn't. Not right now.

"A place called Ellesmere. It's where our kind have lived for centuries and…" Her sentence trailed off as she shuffled closer to me. "Braelyn?" She tried to place her hand on my cheek, but I swatted it away quickly. Her face dropped, and I instantly felt ashamed for acting out so harshly, but I couldn't ignore the growing ball of annoyance that had begun to unfurl in my chest.

"How could you not tell me of my true home?" I breathed.

My eyes burned with unshed tears as I stared into the face of the one person who I thought I could trust. Clenching my hands in tight fists by my sides, I hoped this would help keep my growing temper at bay.

"Braelyn, I didn't keep this from you. I always wanted to tell you, but I wanted to wait until you were old enough to understand." She leant over to put a reassuring hand on my shoulder, but I pulled away.

Hurt flitted across her face once again and, as angry as I was, it pained me to know that I was the reason behind her sorrow. Still, I had never been so upset with her before.

"I have been asking for years about my father and where I came from, and all this time you knew and never said a word. No matter how many times I asked."

My face was burning. From anger or the heat of the room, I didn't know, but I needed some fresh air and time to myself. I needed time to come to terms with the fact that I was a spirit witch and my true home had never been Pryhollow, but instead was somewhere I hadn't known existed until mere seconds ago. Getting to my feet, I pushed past my mother to make my way to the door. Her skirts rustled on the stone floor as she hurried after me. Reaching for the door handle, she stepped in front of me, blocking me from going any farther.

"Please, Braelyn, don't shut me out. Talk to me." Her chest rose and fell quickly, and her eyes darted over my face pleading me to see reason, but I couldn't. All I wanted was to be as far from her as possible. To have time to process what she had told me before we spoke any further. I wanted her to feel some of the pain I was feeling.

"What, like you have done to me?" I said through gritted teeth.

My mother's face dropped, and I could tell that my words had hurt her. My heart ached a little. I regretted the words the moment they had come out of my mouth, but a small part of me was glad she was feeling my pain. That maybe now she would know how I had felt for all these years.

"I need some time to myself. Can I go now?"

She gave me a brief nod and, stepping past her into the dark hallway, I made my way towards the stairs and the solitude of my quiet bedroom. I wanted nothing more than to be alone with my thoughts. As my foot reached the bottom step, the same peculiar humming sound that I had heard earlier in the night flooded my ears. My heart fluttered in my chest as the tingling in my fingers started again. Pressing my hands together, a faint, glowing seam formed between my thumb and pointer finger. *What is happening to me?* I looked around to try and find the source of the sound. Standing with one foot on the stairs, I closed my eyes and tried to focus solely on what I could hear, trying to pinpoint where the noise was coming from. As I waited silently in the growing darkness, the noise grew louder. Opening my eyes, I turned and looked down the hallway. A faint sheen caught my eye and I squinted, trying to make out what it was that I saw. After only a few seconds a large shimmering oval began to take shape on the wall that separated the hallway from the small parlour where my ceremony had taken place. It sparkled like hundreds of tiny diamonds in sunlight, moving with the ease of flowing water. Taking a tentative step forward, I stretched out my hand, feeling as if something was pulling me forward. It was here that the humming noise was at its loudest. I pulled back from the shimmering space, my teeth worrying my bottom lip as I tried to rationalise what I was doing. But as I continued to gaze at the glittering oval, a thread tugged at my heart, inching me closer. Holding out my hand, I touched my fingertips to the swirling mass ebbing and flowing in front of me. I half expected it to be wet, but it was smooth and silky, like the touch of a flower petal. Curious, I slowly pushed my hand through the glimmering space. The moment my fingertips broke the surface, a gleaming, golden light erupted around me. The magic inside me tingled in my veins and I knew in that instant that this was a witch's portal. As I advanced through the golden light, the humming grew to a loud thrum, vibrating through my bones. My head pounded in rhythm with the noise as all my senses told me to stop and go back, but before I knew what was happening, everything went dark.

Three

Opening my eyes, my head pounded in time with the fast beating of my heart. There was no telling where in the world the portal had brought me to, but I wasn't anywhere near Pryhollow anymore.

I squinted against the gleaming sunlight beaming down on me. *Where the hell am I?* As my eyes started to adjust to the light, I surveyed my surroundings, trying to take in every detail. The portal had taken me to a small clearing surrounded by tall trees, their branches reaching so far into the sky I could barely see where the tops ended. Staring into the canopy, something to the right caught my eye. A large black crow landed gracefully on one of the long, spindly branches that encroached into the clearing. My breath hitched in my throat. To witches and warlocks, crows were symbolic omens. They brought good and bad news but one crow wasn't a good sign. A lonesome crow was the symbol of death.

All our history books said that when one of our kind fell ill beyond the Coven's cure, a crow would often be found sitting on the house or in a tree by the family's home. In many cases it meant they wouldn't be here much longer. *Was I dead? Is that what's happened to me?* Breathing rapidly, I searched the skies frantically for a another pair of silk black wings. Spinning so much my stomach began to churn, I spotted more crows sitting idly across the other side of the clearing, their beady little eyes watching me. Needing to regain my balance, I stood for a moment with my eyes closed. Finally feeling like I was no longer swaying, I opened my eyes and began to count the other crows. There were six. Seven including the first one I'd seen. They sat staring down at me. Their sleek feathers glistening in the sun splintering through the tree branches. *Well, seven is better than one,* but my superstitious mind still knew it left an ominous message. I tried to remember what it said in our grimoire, mentally sifting through the pages until I remembered the passage.

'The message to you I shall recite in verse. Seven crows conveyed is a mystery or a curse.'

I was already in an unknown place so that could very well be the mystery, but the gnawing feeling in my stomach made me think otherwise. *Could this have something to do with my spirit magic? Was that even a curse?* My head throbbed with the promise of a worsening headache and I closed my eyes, massaging my temples—hoping it would help ease the pain in my head. None of this made any sense and the more I tried to unravel everything the more my head pounded in protest. Taking a deep breath, I opened my eyes. I needed to find out where I was and how to get back to Pryhollow. The thought of home made my heart skip a beat. My mother would have no idea what had happened to me. *What if I never saw her again?* Anxiety began to build inside me and my hands grew clammy at the thought of being stuck forever in an unknown place. Tears welled in my eyes as I thought about my argument with my mother, and a few overflowed, running slowly down my cheek. What if I never got the chance to apologise for my rash behaviour? Taking a deep breath, I tried my best to push these thoughts to the back of my mind. I couldn't let them distract me. I needed to find out what this place was and why the portal had brought me here. Quickly brushing away the tears that had slipped down my cheeks, I looked around for a way out of the clearing.

I couldn't see any direct path through the trees and traipsing my way through a forest only to lose my way in the foliage was out of the question. The sun had started to fade and a cool breeze rustled through the trees, making the tall forest grass sway as if dancing to a silent song. The fine hairs on my arms stood on end as I realised night was fast approaching. Treading lightly as the soft grass tickled my bare feet, I walked along the edge of the tree line, peering through branches and past tree trunks in search of a pathway. But there was nothing. Only continuous lines of trees stretching beyond my line of sight. Walking around almost half of the clearing, my heart began to sink as I couldn't find a track leading out. The sky was darkening quickly and a small part of me worried I would never find a way out of this leafy prison. Turning, a small flicker of orange caught my eye. I squinted through the dense trees looming over me, trying to decipher what it was. It had to be a lantern of some sort. Surely it belonged to a house—whose phone I could use to call my mother and find a way back home. Smiling, I turned back to the crows who were still watching me from their perch high in the trees.

"I found a way out."

I didn't even let myself feel silly for speaking to them, happy that soon this nightmare would be over. The crows cawed at me softly and, in a flurry of wings, took off from their branches. I watched them until they were only shadows in the distance.

Making my way through the dense underbrush proved to be a difficult task. Sharp thistles scratched at my legs while twigs pulled at my hair, tangling themselves in the already messy curls. My bare feet ached as I stepped on crisp dried leaves and broken twigs, leaving the soles of my feet battered. Stopping just before the tree line ended, a small dirt path was now visible just over the heads of a few shrubs, and I found it led to a small cottage hidden amongst the forest. As I predicted, the glow I'd seen from the clearing was in fact a lantern. It hung by the cottage's door, casting a small pool of light on a tiny, shabby looking front porch. The house was modest, built from a dark wood that ran in slats horizontally around the entire house. A light was on in the front window, but from where I waited in the darkness, it was too hard to see if anyone was inside. Comfortably hidden by the shadows of the trees I took my time trying to decide if I should go and knock on the door. The sun had completely disappeared beyond the horizon, turning the night air cool. My teeth chattered loudly in the silence of the forest as my thin ceremony dress did little to keep out the chill. The cold eventually beat out my nerves and, with my arms shaking, I stepped through the shrubs out onto the dark dirt pathway. The small stones dug into my bare feet and I screwed up my nose, gritting my teeth against the sharp pain. Treading carefully, I made my way up to the porch and stood on the first narrow step. My heart raced as I stared at the heavy wooden door before me. I raised my hand to knock but, before my knuckles even touched the weathered wood, the door swung inwards. Startled, I took a tiny step back and lost my footing. Throwing my hands out behind me, I fell back onto the dirt path with a loud thud. I sat in a growing cloud of dust, too embarrassed by my clumsiness to meet the gaze of the person standing in front of me, but eventually curiosity got the better of me. Looking up from where I still lay sprawled on the ground, a tall woman stood framed in the wooden doorway. I couldn't see much of her face as she stood in front of the porch lamp, the orange glow illuminating her from behind, making her look almost spirit-like.

"Well, are you going to sit in the dirt all night or are you going to come in?" The woman's voice was stern and contained a hint of annoyance. She obviously didn't like being disturbed. Rising, I brushed my hands off on my dress—which was no longer the pristine white it had been—wincing as my grazed palms touched the soft fabric. My hands were stained and blood welled from the tiny open cuts that criss-crossed over the soft flesh of my palm.

The woman standing in front of me was not much taller than myself. Her dark grey hair was so curled that it stuck out at different angles and fell, untamed, around her shoulders, which were draped in an emerald robe. Her mouth was set in a firm, thin line and if I couldn't tell from her stern voice that she was annoyed, being able to see her face certainly confirmed my assumptions.

"Is there something wrong with you?" she asked tersely.

Looking me up and down she took in my appearance which clearly didn't make her any happier. "Come on, child, just get inside!"

She rushed me through the front door, and I stumbled over the threshold— too tired to really look where I was going—mumbling a brief apology.

Holding my arm in a vice-like grip, the woman led me over to a wing-backed armchair. It sat by a large hearth where a fire was blazing and crackling away in the grate. The grey-haired woman deposited me into the armchair and I immediately sunk into the soft cushions. As I watched the flames flicker, the weight of what happened back in the apothecary came crashing over me like waves beating down on the sand. Wrapping my arms around my middle, I let my feelings consume me. Hot tears rolled down my cheeks, soaking my face and, despite the blazing fire in front of me, I continued to shiver, feeling frozen down to my bones. After placing me down in the armchair, the woman had disappeared from my sight into another room towards the back of the small cottage. She returned shortly after, carrying a large woollen blanket and a change of clothes. She placed them on a small round table beside the armchair. As she knelt before me, I noticed she had a large basket tucked under her arm. As she placed it on the floor beside her, she stuck out her hands, and I saw the faded marks of an element rune etched into her skin. She was a witch. Again, she gestured for me to place my hands in hers. I was hesitant at first—not wanting her to see the circle rune on my right palm—but I could see her patience was wearing thin. I placed the my hands palm up in hers and she pulled them in to her chest. Her calloused hands were cool despite the warmth of the room, and I wondered if she'd spent her entire life working hard labour. Peering at my palms, she clicked her tongue in disapproval, placing both of my hands gently in one of her own while she searched through the basket next to her. If she had noticed my spirit rune, she never showed it. Glass clinked together and the distinct rustling of dried herbs reached my ears as she continued to rifle around in her basket. As I watched her dig her around in its depths, she eventually pulled out a small brown jar that was stoppered with a cork. With her free hand, she removed the lid, placing a few drops of bright red liquid on a fluffy white cotton ball.

"Now, this may hurt a little."

I winced at the harsh stinging from the solution. The scrapes burned, and I pulled my hands back, glaring at the woman.

"What is that?" My voice came out high-pitched and squeaky. "It feels like you just set my hands on fire."

Annoyed, the witch tugged my hand back towards her.

"It's just a simple extract of Witch Hazel and Calendula petals. Now stop being overdramatic, Braelyn, and let me finish cleaning your hand."

My eyes widened at her use of my name, but she said nothing further. Placing the cotton wool back on my cut palms, she cleaned away the blood and dirt in a gentle way that didn't match the tone of her voice. The cleansing extract still stung, but my mind was preoccupied. *How did this woman know my name?*

"Excuse me, but how do you know who I am?" Narrowing my eyes, I stared at the witch's wrinkled face, trying to remember if I had ever met her before. Nothing came to mind.

My heart felt like it was going to beat out of my chest, and the warmth of the fire sent hot flushes over my skin. The woman had finished her ministrations of my hands and was now packing away the leftover cotton balls she hadn't used. Closing her basket, she stood and turned her large eyes on me.

"What do you mean how do I know who you are? You look exactly like your mother when she was your age! It wasn't hard to figure out." She stood with her free hand on her hip, a small frown forming between her brows. "Braelyn, I'm Hazel, your grandmother." She paused for a second before she spoke again. "Did your mother not tell you of me?"

She raised a questioning eyebrow, and, not trusting myself to speak, I simply shook my head at her in reply. Tutting to herself she walked back into one of the rooms, disappearing out of sight. My mother had only mentioned my grandmother once and—as it had been in a fleeting comment referring to my father—I had never thought to ask more about her. Hazel returned from whichever room she had been in and sat in the matching armchair next to me.

"My mother never spoke to me about her family. Maybe you have the wrong person?" Glancing over at her, I saw her mouth quirk at the corner as if she wanted to smile but refused to give up her terse demeanour.

"Well I wouldn't say that I'm surprised. Nora has always been a secretive person, even when she was a child." Reaching up, she stroked something hanging around her neck. It looked like a pendant of some sort, and I couldn't help but wonder if it had once belonged to my mother.

"I must admit, however, that I'm a little surprised she didn't warn you about me before you came traipsing up my path." Her tone was clipped, and she was clearly annoyed by this slight, but I still didn't understand what she meant.

"I… I wasn't coming to see anyone," I stammered. "After my induction ceremony I heard a loud humming noise in our hallway, and I ended up here because of a witch's portal that turned up at my house." I couldn't stand the thought of sitting anymore. Standing up from my chair, my legs shook as I took a few steps towards the hearth.

"So, your mother didn't send you to me?" Her brow wrinkled as if in deep thought and there was a look in her crystal eyes that I couldn't decipher.

"No, she didn't send me here. I don't even know where I am or if you are who you say you are!" I threw my arms up in frustration.

Hazel gave me a hard stare. Her mouth was in such a thin line now it almost looked as if her lips were gone completely.

"Oh, by the elements. Braelyn, I have told you that I am your grandmother. Your mother, Nora, is my daughter. And this"—her hands gestured at the air around us—"is Ellesmere."

My brows shot up into my hairline as I stared at Hazel with

wide eyes, trying to take in her words. *I'm in Ellesmere.*

"I know what you said," I replied, "but how do I know you are telling the truth?" I quirked my eyebrows the same way she had done to me earlier.

Throwing her hands in the air— in a gesture so like my mother it was scary—she walked over to a small kitchen situated in a corner by the front door. She busied herself pulling teacups out of cupboards, then placed a large black kettle on the stove. Her movements were fluid as she made her way around the small space and, while I could see there were many similarities between my mother and Hazel, I needed more than just her word if I were to ask for her help. Gliding over to me, she placed a wooden serving tray on the small round table between the armchairs. In the middle of the board, Hazel had placed a short, round teapot intricately decorated with beautiful flowers. Two matching white teacups with the same floral pattern were placed on either side.

"What is this for?" I asked.

Varying types of herbs littered what remaining space was left on the tray and I felt proud that I recognised most of them from the apothecary, but there were a few which had been dried and chopped so finely by a practiced hand that I didn't recognise them.

"Well, clearly an honest word from an old woman means nothing to you, so this might put your mind at ease." Hazel placed all the herbs sitting on the tray into a large silver strainer and dipped it deeply into the steaming teapot.

Making her way to the hearth, she stuck a few dried leaves into the fire, pulling them out quickly after only a few seconds. She blew on the dying embers and fine tendrils of smoke began to flow from the ends of the burning leaves. She placed them into a small wooden bowl between us, the scent lingering in the air. Taking in a deep breath, I found myself instantly at ease. The leaves smouldering in the bowl smelt woodsy and musty and I leant in closer to get a better look.

"Is it sage?" I asked.

Hazel nodded her head once, not taking her eyes off the tea

still brewing between us.

"It helps cleanse the air and bring wisdom to the spell."

As the fruity scent of the tea began to mix with the smoky sage, Hazel picked up the teapot and poured us both a cup. The smell was overpowering. Picking up my cup, the yellow liquid sloshed around quietly, the smell of lemon making my nose tingle.

"What type of tea is this?" I asked, scrunching up my nose against the overpowering smell of citrus.

I had never liked the smell of dried fruits and my mother had always laughed, telling me that my soul was too sweet to handle such a sour smell.

"This is a memory tea. It will give you peace of mind that I am who I say I am, and we can move onto more pressing matters at hand."

Picking up her own teacup, Hazel held out her hand to me, her palm facing the cottage's worn ceiling. Her faded rune shimmered in the firelight.

"What will happen to me if I drink it?" I regretted asking instantly.

Hazel's lips thinned, her eyes hard and cold despite the blazing fire behind her.

"Oh, for heaven's sake, child. Nothing will happen to you. You will simply be able to see my memories of your mother so we can clear up all this nonsense." Thrusting her hand at me again, I placed my right hand on top of hers. Her grip was tight as our runes pressed together and I fidgeted uncomfortably at the pressure building in my chest.

"Now, once you have taken a sip of your tea, you will need to close your eyes and wait. It will take a few seconds for my memories to flow from me to you." Hazel raised her cup to her lips, and I followed her lead. Taking a large gulp of the tea it took all my might not to spit it back into the teacup. It tasted foul, like drinking lemon juice. I managed to swallow the disgusting liquid and closed my eyes as I had been told to. It didn't take long for the magic to work.

It was like a movie had begun playing behind my closed eyelids.

At first, I couldn't make out anything from the flashing images, but then they started to slow. A much younger version of Hazel stood before the small cottage we were currently sitting in, a smile lingering on her face as she stared down at a young woman who could have only been my mother. Her long dark hair was worn down and her hazel eyes shone golden in the sunlight as she gazed up at the cottage. She was standing with a tall dark-haired man I didn't recognise, and they were waving to Hazel who looked lovingly back at them, her eyes full of joy. Changing as quickly as they came, the images switched over to another set of memories. This time my mother was a little older, but she was with the same smiling dark-haired man from the previous memory. They were in what looked to be an old town square, which had been decorated beautifully with hanging lanterns that flickered and glowed. The square was filled with people dancing and enjoying some sort of celebration. My mother's face radiated happiness. Her cheeks were flushed and a smile lingered sweetly on her face as tiny snowflakes drifted on the air. I had only ever seen her this happy a handful of times throughout my life, and a lump formed in my throat as I watched her. Her hair was out, which she never did anymore, and it flowed over her shoulders as the man spun her around, laughing at her giggles. My heart skipped a beat as I remembered the information my mother had shared after my induction ceremony. The dark-haired man was my father. The memory skipped over, and I found myself sad that it had dissolved in front me. I could have stayed in that memory forever. Seeing my parents together and happy made me pine for all the family time I had missed when my father mysteriously died. The newest memory had me looking at my mother as I knew her today, only her stomach bulged with the signs of being with child. This must have been when she left with me, as the war had begun. She hugged Hazel tightly, tears streaming down her face as the women held each other in a loving embrace. I stared into my mother's glistening eyes and felt such a longing to reach out and hug her. To have her wrap her arms around me. But the memory was slowly fading, and everything went black.

"You can open your eyes now, child."

I complied and everything seemed so bright after having them closed for what felt like such a long time. I blinked a few times to refocus. Hazel still sat across from me, but her face no longer looked like a stranger's. After seeing even just a few of her memories of my mother, I couldn't help but feel more connected to her. She gave me a small smile that only tipped up one corner of her mouth.

"I'm sorry I didn't believe you." I tried to give her a reassuring smile, but my lip quivered and a small sob escaped my lips.

She placed her hand on top of mine, and my heart leaped nervously in my chest as I looked across at the grey-haired witch. A woman whose face now showed tiny variations of my mother's features. *I have a grandmother.* So much had changed in the last few hours that I didn't know whether to laugh or cry at this newfound knowledge running through my head.

"It's okay Braelyn," Hazel said soothingly. "I had hoped your mother would have shared something about me. It would have certainly made this whole thing a lot easier if she had." Giving my hand a small squeeze, she pushed herself out of the armchair and picked up the tray with the dirty teacups. I had so many questions I wanted to ask her, and I spun eagerly in the soft chair, following her movements.

"Why do you think she never told me about you or about this place?" I asked.

Hazel walked over to the kitchen and busied herself with emptying the teapot, placing the remaining herbs back into their specific bottles before she placed the dirty crockery into the sink. She wouldn't meet my gaze, and I wondered if all this talk about my mother made her sad that she hadn't seen her in seventeen years. I couldn't imagine not seeing my mother for that long. The thought of it made my heart sink.

"I'm not sure. Your mother had always been somewhat secretive as she grew up, but I'm sure she had her reasons for keeping this part of your life a secret from you." Her voice drifted off and I opened my mouth to ask another question, but before I could get it out Hazel interrupted my thoughts.

"I think that's enough questions for tonight. Why don't you go and clean yourself up and then I will show you to your room?" Without so much as a glance in my direction she pointed down the hallway to what I assumed was the bathroom, leaving me to my own devices.

After showering, I felt like a new person. I had scrubbed the dirt off my feet and washed away the dust coating my skin. After towelling myself dry, I felt a wave of exhaustion rush over me. Dressing in the floral cotton night shirt Hazel had lent me, I walked out into the living area and found her sitting in front of the slowly dying fire. She was staring into the flames, her expression hidden from me. As I approached, I noticed a large leather book was open in her lap. Long loopy letters had been written elegantly in the middle of the page, which was now old and worn. I craned my neck and tried to read what the words said, but as I took a small step a floorboard creaked beneath my feet, startling Hazel out of whatever trance she had been in. Slamming the large book closed, she looked up at me, a small frown pulling her eyebrows together.

"It's getting late. Come, I will show you to your room." Hazel rose, tucking the book under her arm to shield it from my lingering gaze. Three doors stood in a semi-circle at the end of the hall I followed her down. Hazel pushed the middle door open, revealing a small bedroom. It was lit by a single flickering candle, but it was enough to light the room. I could make out a small, steel bed frame over by the wall and a low dresser was placed underneath a window in front of me. The moon shone through the sheer curtains, illuminating a small portion of the white dresser which was cluttered with nick-nacks and covered in a thin layer of dust.

"This used to be your mother's room, so you may feel a little comfort staying in here for the time being."

A small smile danced across my lips as I looked at my mother's old belongings.

"Thank you," I whispered.

Hazel gave me a small, tight-lipped smile. "You're welcome child. I have also sent word to your mother, letting her know you are safe here. I hope that's okay. I thought it best we get word to her as quickly as possible, so I have sent it via air mail."

"Air mail?" I asked, my brow furrowed.

Hazel's smile disappeared. "Yes, child. I sent her a letter via raven. It will be the quickest way to get word to her that you are alright."

Clearing her throat, she said a soft goodnight and closed the door before I had the chance to ask another question. I looked around the small room, taking in every inch. There wasn't much in there aside from the furniture, but it made me feel like I was close to my mother and not an entire witch's portal away.

A faint musty smell wafted up from the bed covers as I pulled them back, but I was too tired to care. I sank into the mattress and allowed my tired body to relax into sleep.

Four

Waking the next morning to loud bangs coming from outside my room, I threw back the covers and yawned deeply as I sat on the edge of the springy bed. Walking over to the small dresser sitting underneath the large bedroom window, I picked up a small hand mirror and gave myself a quick once over. Dark semi-circles had formed under my eyes making me look tired—despite having slept soundly all night—and my hair was in a tangle of curls. I ran my fingers through my knotted locks, painfully trying to tame the nest of hair, but it was no use. I placed the mirror back down on the dresser, casting a quick glance out of the window, finally able to take in my surroundings a little better. The trees encompassing Hazel's small cottage were tall, wide oaks that ran as far as my eyes could see. The thick branches stretched high, their foliage covering the sky in a thick leafy blanket of oranges and reds. What little space there had been between the trees was taken up by large bushy shrubs covered in some sort of berry. Autumn had clearly begun in Ellesmere as the shrubs were a blazing orange and yellow, with small patches of green dotting the foliage—not yet consumed by Autumn's glorious colour. It was quite beautiful. More banging reached my ears from deep within the cottage's walls and I sighed softly. Turning away from my window, I gave the view one last glance before I made my way down the short hallway in search of Hazel. The sharp-tongued woman from last night was gone. In her place stood someone vastly different. Hazel's grey hair stood up at different angles and it seemed every cupboard in the small kitchen stood ajar. Pots and jars littered the countertop while others lay dirty and discarded in the small sink. Her night dress was covered in numerous stains in a variety of colours. As she noticed me watching, her cheeks flushed, clearly embarrassed by the show she was putting on.

"Are you okay?" I asked.

"Does it look like I'm okay, child?" Her voice came out sharp as a tack and I recoiled at the ferocity. Letting out a breathy sigh, she turned in my direction. "I'm sorry, Braelyn, I just have a lot to do before the Forest Festival. I would have prepared the herbs last night, but your surprise arrival made me forget about this little chore." Turning back to her task at hand, she continued shovelling dried herbs into jars.

I felt a little guilty that my showing up last night had caused Hazel to be so frantic this morning, but despite my hands itching to help her, the sharp ferocity of her earlier comment had me keeping my distance.

"What's a Forest Festival?" I asked, crinkling my nose as I tried to remember if my mother or Maeve had ever spoken of such a thing.

Hazel's green eyes locked with mine as she stared open-mouthed at my question. I suddenly felt very self-conscious of how little I knew of Ellesmere and its customs. Hazel shook her head almost disappointed I had even dared ask such a question.

"Go and get changed, child, and I will tell you on the way."

Hazel and I walked in silence along a gravel path leading into the Ironwood Village—where the Festival of the Forest would take place. Dirt crunched softly under my boots as I admired the dense forest stretching either side of the path. A light breeze ruffled the autumn leaves, caressing my face as I relished being outside in the open. Hazel walked silently next me, a large wicker basket cradled tightly in the curve of her arm.

"Will you tell me what the Festival of the Forest is now?" Glancing over at her, I expected to see her lips pursed, but she was so at ease out in the forest I almost thought I saw her lips twitch in a smile.

"It is part of the Autumn Equinox. The second Festival of the season where witches, warlocks and other magical beings get together to give thanks for the bounty life has offered us." She paused for the briefest of moments, giving me the chance to quickly spit out the question dancing on my tongue.

"What do you mean other magical beings? Are there others like us in Ellesmere?"

A flicker of frustration showed on Hazel's face—most likely at my lack of knowledge regarding this world—but it didn't last long.

"Yes, child, there are other magical beings residing in Ellesmere but"—she held up a finger towards me, stopping my questions from raining down upon her—"you will see for yourself shortly. Don't bombard me with questions. Just simply enjoy the view."

Letting out a frustrated breath, I used the opportunity to turn my attention to the forest buzzing with life around me. The view was perfect. Tiny birds flitted around the trees, darting this way and that as if playing games with each other. Bees hovered above beautiful white flowers—which smelt faintly of jasmine—as they carried pollen back to wherever their hive was hidden. It was incredibly peaceful and, for the first time since I arrived in Ellesmere, I felt at ease. My mind wasn't racing and the tightness in my chest had almost ceased to exist. Breathing in the crisp air, the faint scents of gardenia and pine trees tickled my nose. It was almost intoxicating. I threw a quick glance at Hazel and noticed she was watching me out of the corner of her eye.

"You seem very relaxed out here," she said, looking amused.

It was the first time I had seen her give me a true smile, one that made the wrinkles more pronounced at the corners of her eyes.

I grinned back at her. "The forest is so calming. I've never felt so at ease—I can almost hear it whispering to me through the breeze." My cheeks flushed with heat despite the coolness of the day. I felt a tinge of embarrassment thinking my admission might come across as strange, but Hazel continued to smile at me, nodding her head in agreement.

"I understand what you mean. I often hear the forest and its animals speak to me too. It's one of the truly amazing gifts of being an earth witch." She stopped walking and turned to face me. Taking my right hand, she turned it over so my palm faced her. The perfect round circle of my spirit rune was stark upon my flesh. Brushing her fingers over it gently, she looked up into my face.

"Braelyn, you must keep this a secret today, do you understand me?" Hazel's eyes flashed with concern, her lips pursing as she gazed at me. I ached to squeeze her hand, but I simply let my own rest in her palm. Hazel didn't seem like the type of witch who would fear anything. With her terse words and wisdom she didn't seem like someone you would ever want to meddle with, but the concern in her face made my heart beat anxiously in my chest. Seeing the terror in my face, her eyes softened slightly.

"I don't know what your mother told you on the night you received your rune, but spirit magic is very powerful and extremely rare." Glancing around to make sure we were alone, she continued. "The witches in this village have not heard of a spirit witch in many, many years and, if they discovered your power, I don't know what they'd do." Folding my hand into a fist so my element rune was no longer visible, she released me and touched my cheek lightly.

"No one has told me anything about my magic. All I've heard are whispers and even they don't make any sense." I gripped the fabric of my cotton dress playing with the material, hoping Hazel would be able to tell me something.

"Child, I wish I had all the answers you seek, but one thing I can say is that your showing up in Ellesmere when you did is no accident." Wrapping her wrinkled hands around my closed fist, she gave it a tight squeeze. "There are strange occurrences happening around the kingdom, Braelyn, and I believe certain people can't be trusted. Your arrival in Ellesmere only hours after your rune ceremony is part of something larger—I just don't know what it is yet."

I tried to decipher the strange expression Hazel was giving me, but it was no use. Like my mother, Hazel had a way of keeping her emotions a secret.

"I don't understand. Am I in danger here?"

I could see her trying to weigh up her answer, but she sighed before muttering, "I don't know."

A heavy weight dropped on my chest as I tried to deal with this new information. Hazel had resumed walking towards the village—leaving me standing on the narrow dirt path. I continued behind her, leaving a few steps between us, wanting to be alone with my thoughts. Hazel's voice continued to ring in my ears. *'I don't know.'* How could she not know if I was safe here or not? And if I wasn't, what exactly was I in danger from?

Five

Reaching the end of the dirt pathway, we came to a set of overarching trees opening into a large courtyard. It was paved with mismatched cobblestones and beautiful old buildings lined the outskirts of what could have only been the Ironwood Village. I instantly felt the presence of magic around me as my own power tingled my fingers in response. The square was bustling with witches and warlocks of varying ages, all using different types of elemental magic. I followed Hazel through the crowd, my eyes darting in every direction as I studied everything. Small tents had been set-up along one side of the village square, boasting all sorts of magical items. I watched in amazement as a tall witch with beautiful russet-brown skin conjured a small cloud in one of her hands. It floated mere inches off her upturned palm and, with a quick snap of her long fingers, magic lit the little grey cloud as if a tiny storm was brewing away inside. Smiling to myself, I watched her place the storm cloud in a large jar and hand it to a young warlock holding his mother's hand. The air witch waved them off as the child grinned at his new treasure.

We continued through the crowd, everyone greeting Hazel warmly as we passed. Many residents threw me odd looks before turning to their friend and whispering behind their hands. Hurrying so I could walk beside Hazel, I leaned in, whispering, "I think everyone is talking about me!" Peeking at the square, I realised most people had gone back to talking to their neighbours, but some still watched me with wary eyes—making me feel like an oddity. Hazel stopped in the middle of the square, placing her basket down on a rickety table standing beside an old witch selling fragrant candles.

"Of course they're talking about you," Hazel scoffed. "It's not often they see new faces around here." She stopped speaking and glanced around us before continuing, "which is why you need to be cautious."

She raised her grey brows, looking pointedly at me. Nodding, I started unpacking the jars from the basket, handing them to Hazel to place in long vertical lines on the table. As I passed her the last jar, I noticed she was setting them up in groups relating to use. Herbs like chamomile and lavender—which were often used for teas—sat on the left, while others such as vervain, rosemary, and thyme—used for potion making—were placed on the far right.

Hazel busied herself with perfecting the layout of her jars, giving me an opportunity to study my surroundings. I spied a few witches and warlocks who looked to be my age over by a large tent to the side of the village square. One of them appeared to be a water warlock—his hands conjuring a large ball of water from thin air—and I continued to watch in amazement as he lifted the ball high above his friends.

"Braelyn, why don't you go and enjoy the festival? You can meet me back here when it finishes."

Pulling my eyes from the warlock's magic, I found Hazel watching me, a small smile tugging at the corner of her mouth. I gave her a small grin and, without a second thought, made my way into the crowd.

Weaving my way through the growing pack of witches and warlocks, I couldn't help but feel amazed at the crowds. I had never seen this many witches and warlocks in one place before today. Soft, lilting music filled the air as I followed the bustling crowd, wandering between the different tables. An elderly warlock—with a beard so long it disappeared behind the table—yelled at passers-by about the quality of his cauldrons.

"Made of the finest dwarfish steel." He bellowed.

A middle-aged witch, who seemed intrigued by his speech, stopped by his table. "—will never break or split," I heard him explain to her as I continued past.

There were a few stalls holding smaller knick-knacks like tarot cards that could aid in the use of some potions or rune stones to help protect against bad spirits. Another witch sold dried herbs that smelled beautiful, wrapped in twine and ready to be used for cleansing magic. Continuing along the line of tables, one caught my eye. A rickety stand laden with old books stood in the shadows of a large oak tree at the edge of the village square. Wandering up to the piles of books, I was almost too scared to pick anything up, worried that even the slightest shift in weight would make the table collapse. Running my eyes over the large variety, I spotted a few old history books we had back home at the apothecary, but many of the others sitting upon the toppling piles I had never heard of before. My fingers itched to touch the leather covers and flick through the old, yellowed pages. Reaching out, I picked up a large tome so heavy I could barely hold it in two hands. Fumbling with the weight, I placed it back on the table just as a small book caught my attention. The cover was intricately designed with magnificent gold foiling pressed into the hard leather. Tiny golden leaf patterns twisted and wound into a picture of a large tree. There was no title on the cover, and as I reached to pick it up, I felt my magic tingle in my fingers.

The moment I touched the fragile pages, my fingers prickled with an overwhelming intensity. My vision blurred as tendrils of fog seeped into my mind. Magic thrummed in my veins, heat flooding my face as I squeezed my eyes shut to block out the pain. Something was terribly wrong. A scream sounded from behind me, and light flooded my eyes as they snapped open, trying to locate the source of the sound. As I took in the scene around me, the fiery heat soon ebbed from my face. The Ironwood Village was thrown into chaos as large creatures descended on the village square. My eyes bulged in terror as the people of Ellesmere screamed, fighting against the surge of crowds trying to escape whatever these terrifying beasts were. My heart raced as my mind turned to Hazel. I needed to find her. Pushing my fear into the depths of my belly, I ran from the book stand, still clutching the small book between clammy fingers. Sprinting towards Hazel's stand, I came up short, one of the creatures appearing before me. It was huge. Instead of flesh and bone, its entire body was formed of hundreds of gnarled tree branches. Each twisted and curled into four long limbs on either side of its small body. With each menacing movement the creature's body creaked and moaned, sending chills down my spine. A small sob escaped my lips as I stared at its face. A large ram skull perched atop its shoulders, its eyes like obsidian jewels. Staring into the dark eyes of the terrifying creature, my hands twitched by my sides, my magic reacting to my heightened fear. Screams echoed around me as a mix of townsfolk and creatures came together in a blur of magic and mayhem. Whirls of fire flashed menacingly, while water wielders tried to freeze the creatures in a prison of ice, but it was no use. No matter how hard the people of Ellesmere fought, the creatures still came in droves. Not daring to take my eyes off the one in front of me, I conjured a small flame in the palm of my hand, wanting to join the fight. The creature's mouth creaked as if laughing at my feeble attempt to protect myself, revealing teeth like long pointed needles that glistened in the firelight. It lifted a large hand—razor-sharp claws tipping the ends of its four long fingers. I swallowed the bile rising in my throat as fear threatened to consume me. Raising my hands, I tried throwing a flame towards the creature, hoping it would ignite like kindling. Instead, it merely burnt a dark patch into the creature's chest, barely causing it to stumble back. The creature let out an almighty growl, raising its taloned hand and arcing it down in one swift movement. The last thing I saw before the world went dark was blood dripping from its claws.

Six

My breaths came in ragged gasps. Blinking back the darkness tinging the edges of my vision, my stomach rolled as the overwhelming sensation to vomit surged up my throat. Swallowing hard, I turned my attention to the village square, terrified of the carnage I would find. Only … there was none. No bloodshed. No screams or terrifying creatures.

My brows pulled together. *What was going on?* Feeling the weight of something clutched between my fingers, I looked down, studying the pages of the small book I'd picked up from the table. Was it infused with magic?

"I believe that book belongs to me."

I jumped as the voice startled me from my thoughts. I had been so consumed with the book and what could have only been described as a vision, I hadn't noticed the tall, slender warlock standing behind the table. His black eyes scanned me as I held a hand to my rapidly beating heart.

"Sorry, sir, I didn't realise—" I trailed off as the mysterious stranger's dark eyes narrowed in my direction —the same colour as the creatures.

"What is your name? I don't recall having seen you in the Kingdom of Ellesmere before." His voice was smooth like silk and dripped with authority. I could hear Hazel's warning in the back of my mind, but as the silence wore on, his black eyes blazed with ravenous fury at having to wait for an answer. So, I decided to tell only half the truth.

"I, ah, only just got here. I'm visiting my grandmother for the Autumn Equinox. My name is Braelyn."

He didn't immediately reply but rather raised a thick eyebrow at my response. I waited, watching as his thin lips quirked up in half a smile. He was looking me up and down as if assessing my worth when his eyes settled about halfway down my body. For a small moment I thought he had gone back to browsing the table of books, but as he continued to stare I lowered my gaze, stomach plummeting. Bile rose in my throat as I realised my element rune was peeking out from beneath the book I held. The warlock let out a small bark of laughter as I pulled my hand back quickly.

"So, you are the one who is going to change the fate of Ellesmere." His lips curled as he gave me a menacing smile.

"I'm... I'm not going to do anything," I stammered out. My hands trembling like leaves in a warm breeze.

I turned to run, wanting to be as far away from the warlock as possible, but before I could escape, his long arm shot out towards me, grabbing my wrist in a tight grip.

"I know what you are!" he hissed at me.

With one last pull, I yanked free from his clutches, book still firmly grasped in my other hand. Spinning, I turned my back on the rickety table, putting as much distance between me and the warlock as possible. The memory of his dark eyes still burned my skin.

I managed to squeeze past a group of grumbling warlocks before I lost my footing on a loose cobblestone and stumbled into someone's back. Sticking my hand out to grab them, I felt a warm arm wrap around my waist, stopping me from pulling down whoever had the unfortunate luck of standing near me.

"Whoa, easy there, sweetheart. You wouldn't want to hurt yourself." The voice was deep, wavering slightly with unshed laughter.

I pulled myself free of my saviour's arm, cheeks blazing in

45

embarrassment at my clumsiness. Turning, a dark-haired warlock stared down at me, a small smirk pulling one side of his mouth. My breath hitched in my throat. I had never seen someone so handsome before. His skin was bronzed from time spent in the sun and his dark, curled hair fell just above his shoulders. His eyes were such a deep brown they almost appeared black from where I was standing. My heart raced a little in my chest as I tried not to stare.

"Are you sure you're okay? Did you hit your head on the way down?"

The warlock's dark brows crinkled into a small frown and I realised I still hadn't said anything since he caught me. As the crowd around us thinned, I cast a quick glance over to where I had come from—the small book still clasped tightly in one hand—but the warlock was gone. My eyes roamed the crowd as I frantically searched for the warlock, needing to know that I was far from him. *What had he meant that I would be the one to change Ellesmere's fate? Was this what Hazel had been talking about when she told me I was part of something important?* I needed to find her. Spinning to try and locate Hazel's tent, someone bumped into my back, pushing me into the dark-haired warlock who now looked at me with concern. His hands caught my waist, holding me steady, and again I felt my cheeks redden. Pressed up against his chest, I was conscious of how warm his hands felt through the soft cotton of my dress. Pulling away, I spun to chastise the rude person who had pushed me.

A tall man stood before me, but I quickly realised he wasn't a man at all. He towered over everyone around him, my face meeting his slim, uncovered chest. His silver skin shimmered and sparkled like the stars on a clear night. His hair matched the colour of his skin, and if that surprised me, it was nothing compared to what protruded from his scalp. Two long antlers twisted from his temples, extending up and over his head. A deep reddish brown, they were covered in a forest green moss, and despite my shock, my hand itched to reach out and touch him.

"Apologies, tiny witch, I did not see you there." His voice was cold like a winter's morning, sending a chill down my spine. *I wouldn't want to find myself on his bad side.* As he turned to pass through the crowd, I noticed the slight point to his long ears and, astonished, I spat out, "You're an elf!"

I remembered what Hazel had told me about seeing other magical creatures at the festival, but I had never expected them to be elves. I had read so many books on them as a child, but they always spoke of elves living in far lands and hidden forests. I never thought I would have seen one in my lifetime.

The silver elf turned back to me, a tired look on his beautiful face, as if the mere thought of conversing with me bored him immensely. I bit the side of my lip, worried I might have upset him with my outspoken thoughts, but he simply looked me up and down before wandering off, not even bothering to speak to me. I watched his silver-haired head moving fluidly through the crowd before turning back to the dark-haired warlock. He was still standing behind me, his arms folded across his chest and an amused look on his face.

"Thank you for your help," I murmured to him, embarrassed by my behaviour. He gave me a quick shrug.

"My pleasure. I'm always happy to help a damsel in distress." Winking, he stuck out his hand, and as I shook it, he told me his name was Julien. Again, I was surprised with how incredibly warm his hand felt compared to my own. It helped ease the chill still lingering from dealing with the elf.

"I'm Braelyn," I replied meekly.

The corner of his lip quirked up in a lopsided smile, and I felt my heartbeat quicken. I had never felt this frazzled around anyone before. Julian certainly had a curious effect on me.

"It's a pleasure to meet you," Julien replied.

A short distance away, someone called out to him, and Julien turned his head in the direction of the voice. The small group of witches and warlocks I had seen earlier stood by one of the small buildings on the corner of a narrow laneway. All of them seemed to be laughing and joking, except for a tall white-haired witch who scowled in our direction. Her gaze lingered on mine and Julien's clasped hands before it flickered up to my face, fire burning in her eyes. Julien's smile still lingered on his face as he turned back to me. If he had noticed the witch's scathing look, he didn't let it show.

"Would you like to join us?"

A part of me wanted to go with him—to talk more with Julien and find out why I felt such a connection to him—but a niggling feeling in my chest told me I had to find Hazel. I needed to speak to her about what had happened with the mysterious warlock and the vision.

I shook my head. "Thank you, but I should really be getting back. Besides, I don't think your friend wants me around. Maybe I'll see you soon?"

Amused, Julien watched me before his dark eyes flickered in the direction of the white-haired witch. "Oh, don't worry about Victoria. She's all bark and no bite, but I do hope to see you again."

Giving me a quick wave he carved a path through the crowd towards his friends. I watched him for a few seconds, seeing the tall witch rush over to him, throwing her long arms around his neck. Her gaze found mine and a look of what seemed to be triumph glistened in her icy eyes as her brows quirked up at me. Ignoring her, I made my way through the crowd back to Hazel's stall, which was now buzzing with life.

Hazel was speaking animatedly to a young warlock standing next her. His face was flushed a warm pink and he stood well above Hazel's small frame. Spotting me amongst her customers, Hazel beckoned me over with a quick gesture of her hand.

"Braelyn, I would like to introduce you to someone." She gestured to the warlock standing in front of me. "This is Theodore Edwards. I think you two would get along nicely." Giving me a short smile, she went back to her busy table before I even had the chance to talk to her. *Damn it.*

"It's a pleasure to meet you, Braelyn, Hazel has been telling me so much about you." A sprinkling of freckles covered Theodore's long nose, but it was the left-side of his face that caught my attention. A long pink scar ran from the top of his eye and down his cheek, finishing at the corner of his mouth. I wondered how someone so young had ended up with an injury that bad.

"It's nice to meet you, Theodore," I said. He blushed at my formality, making his freckles more prominent.

"Please, call me Theo. Only my mother calls me Theodore." He gave me a toothy smile, the scar on his face pulling his lip up in more of a grin. "If you like, I could show you around a little? Hazel told me you've never been to Ellesmere before."

Glancing at Hazel over my shoulder, I tried once more to catch her attention. I desperately wanted to talk to her, but she was deep in conversation with a small witch who seemed interested in buying a jar of herbs. I sighed, the conversation would clearly need to wait. Turning back to Theo, I tried to push the festival's earlier events to the back of my mind.

"That would be great."

We wandered through the bustling town square, and I couldn't help but notice everyone seemed to know everyone here. Theo waved and spoke brief pleasantries to many of the town's patrons as we continued weaving our way between groups of people.

We approached a small tent glowing a luminescent red inside. The smell of burnt sugar wafted up my nose as the biggest cauldron I had ever seen stood on the table in front of me. It seemed to take up most of the space inside the hot tent, and a tiny witch who was just visible over the cauldron's rim stirred whatever liquid was bubbling inside. Thick string ran across the length of the tent where bright red items dangled like Christmas lights, glistening in the fire burning beneath the cauldron. More bubbled away in the sweet-smelling syrup oozing and popping in the giant cauldron.

Theo turned to me, his cheeks rosy from standing so close to the warm stall. "Would you like one?"

Whatever the witch was cooking looked and smelled delicious, and my mouth watered as I wondered if it tasted as sweet as it smelled.

"Sure, but, um, what is it?"

Theo smacked his forehead. "Oh, sorry, I forgot you aren't from here." The little witch behind the cauldron eyed me warily as Theo continued. "It is called maleficis resina. It's a small round fruit that grows in the Ironwood and it's one of the most amazing things you will ever taste!"

I raised my eyebrow as Theo handed the witch a few silver coins before passing me one. Reaching out my right hand, Theo's eyes widened as my spirit rune flashed darkly in the twinkling lights.

"You're—you're a spirit witch," he stammered, his eyes glued on my circle rune.

My heart raced as I desperately tried to think of something to say, but there was no denying it. Theo had seen the dark circle on my palm as clear as day, but something deep in my belly told me I could trust him. He hadn't spoken the words maliciously like the dark-haired warlock by the bookstand, and I found myself taking a leap of faith and deciding to tell him the truth.

"I am, but please don't say anything to anyone. Hazel has asked me to keep it a secret."

Theo's mouth fell open as he gazed at me, awestruck. Shaking his head, his mouth quirked up in a friendly smile.

"It's okay, Brae. Your secret is safe with me. And in case you're wondering, I'm an earth warlock." Holding his palm up, an earth rune flashed at me—an upside-down triangle with a line drawn through the bottom.

It was the mirror image of my mother's air rune. The thought of her made a lump form in the back of my throat. I missed her desperately and wondered if she had received Hazel's letter yet. Shaking my head to clear my thoughts, I turned back to Theo who was watching me closely, his face soft and warm.

"Thank you for keeping my secret, Theo. Maybe you could teach me a little something about earth magic one day?" I smiled, trying to keep my voice light.

Theo's face turned downwards as he rubbed a large hand over

the back of his neck. "Yeah. Maybe." His voice was soft and held a touch of sadness that hadn't been there a moment before.

Turning my attention back to the maleficis resina, I was surprised to find it looked just like a candy apple, but as I bit into the thick red coating, I felt my tastebuds explode. It was unlike anything I had ever tasted. The sugary coating was crunchy and hints of rose tickled my tongue. The fruit inside was soft with a subtle taste of lavender and mint. It was so unusual, but the more I ate the better it tasted.

"This is delicious," I managed to choke out as the sweet syrup dripped over my hands.

Theo gave a small snort of laughter, and I smiled back, glad my earlier comment hadn't upset him. Theo was quickly growing on me. He was sweet, funny, and never seemed to run out of things to say. As we munched on the last of our maleficis resina, I noticed people had begun to gather in the centre of the town square.

"What's happening over there?" I asked, licking the last of the syrup from my sticky fingers.

Theo's face lit up.

"By the elements, the fire show is about to start and, if we don't get moving now, we won't see a thing."

Theo found us a good spot to see the show, and I listened to the excited murmurs erupting from the gathered witches and warlocks. From the whispers of those around me, it seemed the show had been the highlight of every Forest Festival for many years. Performed by the village's most talented fire wielders, it was apparently a wonder to behold. *What could be so amazing about fire magic?* I turned to Theo, wanting to ask him this question, but he was deep in conversation with a short warlock sitting next to him. His hair was a mousy brown that fell over his eyes every time he leaned closer to Theo, laughing at something he said. As I watched the two boys closely there was no mistaking the attraction that seemed to blossom between them. The boys golden eyes searched Theo's face with a warm loving glow, and I smiled to myself, recalling the same loving stare that had been in my mother's eyes as she looked upon my father in Hazel's memories. Not wanting to intrude on their moment, I turned my eyes away. While I waited for the show to start, I spotted a small group of witches and warlocks standing up in front of the growing crowd. There were around five or six of them, all varying in age. A small boy with greasy blonde hair and a cheeky smirk looked to be the youngest of the group, while a wild, fiery-haired witch with small wrinkles around her eyes looked to be the eldest. As I scanned the rest of their faces, I spotted Julien among the group.

"It's about to start," Theo whispered.

Music sounded loudly around us, peppering the air with beautiful, deep tones. I squeaked in surprise as my gaze fell on the band, causing Theo to raise a questioning brow. The silver-skinned elf from earlier was plucking the strings of what looked to be an overly large guitar. His companion swayed to the whimsical sounds as he ran long, elegant fingers over his piano keys. To my astonishment, the other elf was just as mesmerising as the silver one. His skin was a dark shade of blue, glittering with a spattering of golden flakes that almost looked the colour of the sun. His hair shimmered brightly compared to the other elf's silver hue and, like his friend, he also wore only trousers.

"Show-offs," Theo muttered to me. "They always seem to come to these festivals wearing as little as they possibly can." He shook his head, turning back to face the stage.

I wanted to ask him so many questions, like where the elves lived and what other magical creatures lived in Ellesmere, but they all died on my lips as Theo nudged me.

"Look," he whispered.

My breath hitched in my throat as the mysterious warlock I had encountered earlier walked onto the stage. A silence had settled over the crowd as the music died down to a low thrum.

"My fellow witches and warlocks, welcome to the Festival of the Forest." He spread his arms out wide and a few people near me whooped in cheery celebration. "Today we give thanks to the elements for the bounty the earth has offered to us." He beamed out at the sea of faces gazing up at him.

I turned to Theo, who was watching him with a small frown creasing his freckled brow.

"Who is that?" I whispered in his ear so he could hear me above the growing excitement.

"That is King Elias, the ruler of Ellesmere. He hasn't come to the Forest Festival in years. I wonder why he's here?"

I looked back to the stage where King Elias still stood, a heavy feeling settling in my stomach. None of this made sense. My encounter with the king and me arriving in Ellesmere when I did. One thing was for certain though: none of this could be coincidence. It had to mean something, and I was determined to find out.

The red-haired witch stepped into the centre of the small stage, staring out at the crowd. Her gaze was so intense I almost looked away, but my curiosity got the better of me, and I continued to stare back at her, my eyes locked onto her own. Theo's excitement seemed to build next to me and, like a stone being thrown into a river, it rippled through the rest of the crowd. Smiling, the red-haired witch stuck her hands out, conjuring a dancing flame in the palm of her hand.

I had to blink a few times to make sure it was real. My mouth dropped open in awe. I had never witnessed a fire witch using their magic before. The only elemental wielders in our Coven were water and air wielders and even seeing their magic first-hand was rare. Living in a town where everyone suspected you of sinister things, it was easier for us to act like humans.

This was one of the most beautiful magics I had ever seen. The flames flickered and danced as if she was holding a match against an open window, and as quickly as they came, the flame formed into the shape of a tiny red sprite. The small figure stood in her open palm, gliding in small circles. She opened her other hand and another small flame burst, turning itself into another flickering sprite made of the same fire magic. I watched her with rapt attention, not wanting to blink in case I missed something. The small figures danced and skipped in the middle of her palms, and as she slowly closed both hands, the fire began to sputter and both figures lay down and disappeared. The crowd whooped and cheered as the red-haired witch took a deep bow. My eyes followed her as she made her way back to the group and stopped in front of Julien. She gave him a high five as if to tag him in and sparks ignited between their hands like fireworks. *He was a fire warlock too.* The crowd cheered again. Everyone was on the edge of their seats, waiting to see what fire magic Julien would conjure. As he stepped onto the stage, he scanned the crowd as if looking for someone familiar, and his dark eyes locked with mine. I felt my heart race in my chest as a flicker of a smile lit his face.

"You." He pointed to me. "Come here." His voice was loud and direct.

Hoping he was pointing to someone else, I looked around expectantly. But he wasn't. Theo stared at me with wide eyes and I thought I saw something else flicker across his face. Wiping my sweaty palms on the sides of my dress, I stepped through the crowd until I stood in front of Julien. My heart felt as if it was going to explode through my chest. He gave me a lopsided smile before he spoke, but I didn't hear what he said. My hands shook slightly, and I bunched them into tight fists so he wouldn't see them tremble. *Was he going to set me on fire?* My mind reeled with the unknown, and my breath hitched as his warm hands spun me around so I was facing the crowd. Faces stared up at me as they waited expectantly for something amazing to happen.

"Don't be nervous," Julien whispered in my ear.

His breath tickled my neck and goosebumps formed along my arms. I could hear him whispering to himself, and I knew he was calling on his magic. As the crowd waited with bated breath, I focused on a point above everyone's heads, trying to rein in my nerves. Then fire erupted around me.

Seven

The bright, flickering flames enveloped me in a warm blanket of orange light. Expecting to feel my body singed by the hot embers I stumbled backward, but the fire seemed to move with me. My heart raced as the fire blazed in a continuous swirl around me. The heat should have been unbearable and sweat should have been dripping down my face, but it was oddly comforting—like I was back in Hazel's cottage sitting in front of her hearth. My heart slowed, and a thrumming in my veins made my skin tingle like pins and needles. Without even thinking about what I was doing, I reached out to the swirling flames. My fingertips were enveloped in the warmth of the fire, and my hand instantly felt as if it had been submerged into hot water, but my skin didn't burn. I moved my hand around in the flame and watched as it flickered with my every movement as if reacting to a breeze. The crowd in front of me watched in amazement at Julien's magic. Bringing his arms out wide, the flickering flames moved with the utmost ease as he formed a large dome around the two of us. Spinning around in amazement, my eyes locked with his. The flames flickered in their dark depths as he gave me a quick wink. He clapped his palms together once and, in an instant, the dome of fire burst like a firework against the darkening sky. Tiny embers floated down around me like glowing fireflies. The crowd erupted in raucous applause as Julien stood at my side. His eyes swept over me quickly as the glowing embers clung to my skin.

"I wouldn't have picked you to be a fire witch," he said, raising a dark brow in my direction.

"What makes you think I'm a fire witch? I haven't used any magic?"

Julien chuckled, his eyes creasing in the corners. "Well, any other elemental witch wouldn't have been able to stand that type of heat, but you seemed almost drawn to it."

I remembered the way my skin tingled when I had reached into the flames, the way my body seemed to welcome the searing heat rather than recoil against it. No wonder Julien thought I was a fire witch, but it seemed the perfect way to shield my spirit magic from prying eyes.

I smiled back, mimicking his raised brow. "And what type of witch would you have expected me to be?"

Julien shrugged his shoulders nonchalantly, a grin tugging one side of his mouth. "I don't know, but all I can say is you are full of surprises." He gave me another wink and walked back to his companions. I snorted to myself. *You have no idea!*

Still smiling, I took my seat by Theo's side, who was staring at me with an odd look on his face. "Is everything okay?" I asked.

Theo's eyes flashed to Julien, a look of loathing replacing the usual kindness. This seemed so out of character for Theo—who from the moment I'd met him radiated happiness—and I wondered what it was about Julien that made him feel such hatred towards the fire warlock.

"Yeah, I'm fine it's just… I noticed Julien Thorne talking to you after the performance and wondered how you knew him?" The look of loathing had vanished, and his attention was now on his hands, as if he couldn't bear to look at me.

"I don't really know him at all," I replied honestly. "He just spared me some embarrassment earlier today and we spoke a little. Why?"

I watched him carefully, waiting for him to tell me what was on his mind. It didn't take long.

"It's nothing to worry about, Braelyn, just promise me that if you do come across Julien Thorne again you'll be careful." His hand traced the long pink scar on his freckled cheek. It was such a quick movement I almost thought I'd imagined it, but I couldn't mistake the sadness filling his face.

"Theo, did something happen between you and Julien?" I leant forward, giving his hand a squeeze. He gave me a tight-lipped smile and gently patted my hand.

"It was a long time ago and I don't want to burden you with my sombre story." Still clutching my hand, he pulled me to my feet. "Come on, let's go and enjoy the rest of the festival." He made his way towards where the Elvish band had been playing earlier in the night. Hurrying after him, I couldn't help but speculate over our conversation. What had happened between him and Julien that made Theo feel the way he did? I remembered what Hazel told me this morning. *People can't be trusted.* Could it be that Julien was part of the reason Hazel told me to be cautious?

After my conversation with Theo, I thought it might be the end of his jovial mood, but he seemed to regain his happy composure quickly. We spent the last few hours of the Forest Festival dancing to the Elvish music rolling around the large town square. I hadn't felt this light since arriving in Ellesmere and Theo's warm, happy nature seemed to rub off on me, leaving me giddy with happiness.

After hours of dancing, Theo stopped and glanced at his small wristwatch, his eyes wide. It was almost time to meet Hazel back at her tent and I couldn't help but feel a tiny bit disappointed that the night was almost over.

We walked back through the thinning crowd in a dreamy silence, but something ate away at me. Since our conversation, I hadn't been able to stop thinking about what Theo had said about Julien.

"Who is Julien Thorne?" I asked quickly, before my nerves got the better of me.

Theo's blue eyes shone in the dim lights hanging throughout the trees, a thin line creasing his forehead. He had obviously been concerned about whatever relationship I had with Julien—if you could even call it that—and I needed to know more about him. Theo glanced over his shoulder to where the fire performance had taken place earlier in the night, but it was empty now.

He let out a long breath. "The Thorne family has somewhat of a bad reputation—not just in the Ironwood Village, but throughout Ellesmere. Anyone who becomes involved with the family always ends up worse off for it."

I was starting to get the feeling that Theo may have had more experience with the Thorne family than he was letting on. Theo was my only friend in this new world, and I didn't want to upset him, but I couldn't help feeling curious about Julien and what had created his family's terrible reputation.

"I don't understand. What's made them so bad?"

Theo rubbed a hand over the back of his neck. "Look, I know we haven't known each other long Braelyn, but you seem like a nice person and I would feel awful if I didn't say anything and you ended up hurt." His voice was gentle. Caring.

My heart flitted like tiny bird's wings in my chest at the thought of having a friend who liked me for who I was—not someone who only wanted to befriend me to find out if the rumours were true.

"You're a good friend, Theo."

He beamed at me, and my heart lifted. "And just so you know, I won't tell anyone about your—" He didn't finish his sentence but simply pointed at my right-hand where my spirit rune was. Tears prickled behind my eyes as I tried to hold back the overwhelming feeling of happiness that flooded through me.

"Thank you," I said simply.

Hazel had almost finished packing up her belongings when someone shoved past me. Jolting forward, I half turned to see Julien's blonde-haired friend, Victoria. A cruel smirk disfigured her pretty face as she looked me up and down, laughing with another witch.

"Oh, sorry, I didn't see anyone standing there, qui decepitor." She spat her words at me, sounding more like a snake than a witch. Her use of the ancient word for deceiver caught me off guard and I frowned in her direction.

When I was a child, my mother would tell me stories of the name witches and warlocks gave to an outsider who came through the villages. The qui decepitor would arrive as darkness settled over the village. When the shadows were long, their tendrils stretching into every nook and cranny, they would cast dark spells over the sleeping villagers, tricking them into divulging the whereabouts of their grimoires and other treasured magical items. Once they had filled their pockets, the qui decepitor would vanish, leaving the villagers wondering what had happened to their most prized possessions.

Regaining my composure, I looked at Victoria, a smirk curving the corner of my mouth. I might not have had much experience in dealing with school drama, but my mother had always taught me to stand up for myself and those I loved, so I wasn't going to let this horrible witch think she had something over me.

"Oh, how sweet, you still believe in bedtime stories. I'm certain you did see me here, but don't worry, I'll make sure you don't mistake me next time."

My words came out calmer than I expected.

Taking a few steps back, her eyes grew wide as the shock of my response showed on her pretty face, but it was only for a brief second before she regained her cruel composure. She barked a harsh laugh.

"Just remember, decepitor, outsiders aren't welcome in the Ironwood Village, so you should watch your back from now on. And stay away from Julien! He's mine." Turning her back on me, she disappeared down one of the narrow streets, sniggering and whispering with her friend.

My first day in Ellesmere, and I'd already made an enemy.

It was late when we arrived at the cottage and, after placing her basket down, Hazel went straight to the kitchen, busying herself with putting a pot of tea on the stove. The cottage was cold and a small shiver raised bumps over my skin. Bending down by the hearth, I piled a few logs into the fireplace, feeling the night's cool air seep down the chimney. Placing the last log into position, a thought entered my mind. *Could I conjure fire?* I hadn't tried using any magic since receiving my spirit rune and the events with Julien's magic tonight had my fingers tingling with excitement at the thought of testing out my strength. Closing my eyes, I took a deep breath in through my nose, letting it out slowly I opened my eyes and pictured a flickering flame in my hand. Feeling the magic tingle in my fingertips, a warmth washed over my palm as I brought my thumb and middle finger together, a spark igniting between them. Clicking my fingers together, a flame sparked to life, and I beamed as the fire flickered brightly along my fingers. Leaning towards the hearth, I blew on the flames and they unfurled like a bird opening its wings to take flight. It caught the dry wood and lit the small fireplace in a crackling blaze. Closing my hand, the flames snuffed out, leaving nothing but a small plume of smoke.

"Clever trick, child."

I jumped, startled by Hazel's voice. She watched me from her usual armchair, a cup of tea held up to her thin lips. I hadn't heard her come in.

"You show great strength already." She took a sip of her tea, placing it back down on the porcelain saucer with a small clink. Taking a seat on the other armchair, I picked up my own cup and drank deeply. I had been waiting for this moment all night—to be able to talk to Hazel about King Elias's words—but now that the moment was here, I didn't know if I was ready to find out the answers.

"What's bothering you, child?"

Hazel watched me closely. Her eyes shone like emeralds in the firelight, and they seemed to pull my questions and secrets out of me before I even had the chance to ask.

"I had the pleasure of meeting King Elias today. He was looking for this book." I pulled out the small leather-bound notebook and placed it on the tea tray. Hazel's eyes widened as she picked it up, running a thumb over the golden detailing.

"Where did you get this, Braelyn?" Her voice was no more than a whisper over the crackling of the fire.

"I found it at one of the stalls at the Forest Festival tonight. When I touched it I seemed to have some sort of vision."

Hazel's eyes went wide, burning brightly in the firelight. "What do you mean you had a vision?"

I gave her a small shrug. "As soon as I picked up the book and touched the pages I saw these creatures swarm the village. They attacked everyone, including me. That's when the vision ended, when the creature attacked me. King Elias seemed quite possessive of it after this. He mentioned something about me being the saviour of Ellesmere."

Hazel looked away from me, her lips pressed into a thin line as she considered my words. "This book belonged to a very cunning and clever Wise Witch who died in the royal war many years ago."

I thought of the Wise Witch who had given me my spirit rune. She was one of the oldest witches of our Coven and was gifted with the magic of old. A magic that was so consuming, many who'd tried it had turned to dark magics like necromancy to satiate their hunger for power. Only a few had the strength to resist the pull of darkness.

"Why would he want a Wise Witch's book?" I narrowed my eyes at the small tome, confused as to what King Elias could possibly want with it.

Hazel let out a long breath. "Because of the message it contains, child." She opened the book and flipped through the pages until landing on the one she wanted. Handing it back to me, I peered down at the yellowed pages.

"The Prophecy," I read aloud. The following text was written in the old tongue. A language spoken long ago that very few witches and warlocks could now read. I looked up into Hazel's face. "What does it say?"

"I don't read the old language, but I know of what it speaks. Just before the royal war broke out, the Wise Witch Althea—whose book you hold in your hands—came to me rambling about a prophecy she had foreseen of a young witch who would be the salvation of Ellesmere." Hazel stopped for a moment, staring into the glowing embers of the dying fire and taking a long sip of her tea before she continued. "This child would be born during the Spring Equinox and was destined to unite the kingdom by overthrowing the king."

I clutched the book tightly as I stared at Hazel with wide eyes. "And you think this is about me?" I asked.

Hazel looked into my face and let out a long breath. "The day you were born, Althea came to me again. She told me more of the prophecy had been revealed to her. That the child was born of royal blood and would be the only one strong enough to challenge King Elias."

My eyes widened at the mention of royal blood.

Hazel continued. "Your father, Braelyn, was the prince of Ellesmere. The true king—that is, until his brother Elias stole it from him out of greed."

I couldn't believe what Hazel was telling me. My heart pounded heavily in my chest and I stared down at the small book, trying to get my head around the words Hazel was telling me. *How could I have royal blood?*

I shook my head. "No, my mother told me my father came from a wealthy family," I retorted. "Not that he was a prince!"

Bending down, Hazel pulled an old photograph from between the pages of a book hidden beneath her armchair. As she handed it over my mother's face stared back at me. Her long dark hair flowed over her shoulders like dark satin. She stood smiling with the man who I recognised from Hazel's memory tea. He stood tall and proud in a dark red tunic which was buttoned up to his throat. As my eyes roamed the photograph, drinking in all the details, I found what I was looking for. My father's hand clutched a gilded crown. My breath caught in my throat as I stared into a face that looked so like my own. Growing up, I had heard so often how much I looked like my mother, but no one had known my father or what he had looked like. We shared the same brown, unruly hair, full pink lips and button nose. The only difference between us was our eyes. Where mine were hazel, my fathers were grey. The colour of a stormy sea. I stared at the photograph for some time, tears threatening to spill from the corners of my eyes.

"How could my mother not tell me this?" I asked.

"Well, I suspect, like many have done since you were born, she was trying to protect you, child."

Hazel's voice was soft, but her response only made my blood boil. I threw myself out of the armchair, Althea's small book flying across the room. My hands tingled all over as my magic erupted in my veins in response to my anger. My sadness. Tiny blue sparks darted like fireflies from my fingers and Hazel's eyes widened in surprise.

"I don't get how any of this is going to protect me," I said, voice rising a few octaves. "My mother knew she would need to tell me eventually, so why not tell me sooner so I would know what to do!?"

The tears I had tried so hard to keep at bay begun to flow hot and angry down my cheeks. I hastily brushed them away, frustrated for letting myself get so upset. Hazel had gotten to her feet and now stood in front of me, her hands clasped firmly on the tops of my arms.

"I know you might be angry, but your mother's sole focus has always been to keep you safe. Now that King Elias knows you're here, you need to learn how to use your magic so you can protect yourself." Releasing her hold on my arms she gently brushed a tear from cheek. "So, are you ready to learn how to be a spirit witch?"

Despite my heart pounding in my chest I lifted my chin, looking her square in the eye. "I'm ready."

Hazel nod her head once. "Good. Because I believe the vision you had, Braelyn, is only a glimpse of what will happen to Ellesmere should you fail."

Eight

I slept in late and woke to the sun streaming through the small slits in the curtain. Lying cocooned in the warm blankets, my eyes followed the dust motes as they shifted in the breeze, and I watched them float in the autumn light as my mind went over the events of last night. My first attempt at using fire magic had felt exhilarating. My hands still tingled slightly as I remembered the way the flames had danced on my fingertips. If I was ever going to be strong enough to beat King Elias, I needed to know more about my magic.

As I threw the blankets aside, the movement stirred the dust motes, making them dance even higher. I shivered as the cool air touched my warmed skin. Picking up the old dressing gown Hazel had left by the side of the bed, I padded down the hallway and noticed Hazel's bedroom door was open—her bed already made. Walking into the kitchen, everything was exactly as it had been last night. There wasn't an item out of place. Shrugging, I made my way to the fireplace, stacking a few logs on to light a fire when a loud bang from outside the cottage startled me. My hands darted to the fire poker hanging on the wall and I tiptoed to the small square window overlooking the back of the cottage. A low fog had rolled in through the night, clinging to the forest floor. Small patches of sunlight managed to break through the dense cloud, creating an eerie scene. My eyes roamed the back of the cottage, searching for whatever had made the banging sound. Spotting

Hazel out amongst the fog, I breathed a sigh of relief. The sound had come from a broken pot. Placing the fire poker against the wall, I unlatched the back door and stepped out into the cool morning, my breath creating small wisps of fog in the air. A short stone path snaked down from the cottage, leading to a small greenhouse which was nestled amongst a copse of pine trees. The windows were fogged over, but upon closer inspection, I realised the glass was simply coated in a layer of grime and dust. The door was propped open with a large grey rock and, peeking inside, I found Hazel busy cleaning up the remnants of a broken terracotta pot. She looked so at ease as her hands fluttered over various plants and fungi as she sorted them into piles.

"Good morning, child. Care to join me?" Hazel's voice came out calm and dreamy. Her light and airy demeanour was nothing like the stern witch I had come to know her to be, but it was a welcome change.

Stepping into the greenhouse, I held my hands tight by my sides, not wanting to knock over one of the many pots that scattered the tiny space. For such a small greenhouse, I was amazed at just how many plants Hazel had squeezed in there. Two long wooden benchtops lined either side of the greenhouse with a variety of plants covering almost every inch of free space. Some stood tall in large, bright orange pots, while others had some growing to do in order to catch up to their neighbours. Tiered shelving lined the back wall, holding even more plants as well as a variety of gardening tools still smeared with soil. The smell of freshly cut grass tickled my nose as I breathed in the heady scent. My hands itched to touch every plant within my reach. Approaching one of the long benches, I watched as Hazel pulled a small seedling out of a tiny, teacup-sized pot. The plant came out with one small tug and the dirt that hadn't been clinging to the long roots sprinkled the bench like tiny brown raindrops, covering the counter in a light layer of soil. Hazel dusted off a little more of the dirt and pulled a larger pot towards her. As she placed the plant inside, I heard her utter a word unfamiliar to my ears. Watching the little seedling carefully, I waited for something to happen, but a small movement to my left caught my eye, making me stumble back in surprise. A stream of what appeared to be soil floated through the air as if it was a piece of string being pulled from a ball of wool. My mouth hung open in surprise as the line of soil trailed in one single movement over to the pot with the tiny plant. As the swirling stream of dirt hovered over the seedling's bright green leaves, it formed itself into a ball— no bigger than the size of an apple. Hazel's left hand was curled into a small fist, and as she brought it down towards the bench, the dirt mimicked her movements, lowering itself towards the pot and settling gently over the plant's exposed roots, blanketing it warmly. The seedling appeared to shudder in contentment. If it had a face, I could only imagine it would be smiling happily. With a flick of her hand, one of the small shovels floated over, landing in Hazel's outstretched palm. Pulling a bag of what smelled like manure over, she scooped a mound of the stinking soil out of the bag and sprinkled a small spattering on top of the dirt in the pot. The plant gave another happy shudder before it stopped moving altogether. Having completed her task, Hazel turned to me with a smile. My mouth hung open in amazement as I stepped closer to the bench, staring at the seedling in utter wonderment. Hazel chuckled, startling me from my daze.

"I take it you've not been privy to watching an earth wielder use their magic?" Her voice was light and teasing.

Closing my mouth, I ran my tongue over my dry lips. "I, ah, no. I haven't."

Growing up, my mother had explained most earth witches preferred to live in open spaces with plenty of greenery. So, living in a town with only one park and not much space for people to have a garden, most of the witches and warlocks in our Coven were either air or water wielders. There was a time when we had a few fire wielders in our town, but they never stuck around for long.

Hazel had busied herself with other plants, so I wandered over to where the little seedling still sat in its pot. Its leaves were plump at the top and came to a curved point at the end. Rubbing the leaves between my fingers, the smell of mint wafted up to me and I smiled. It was one of my favourite herbs, the fresh scent reminding of me of summer days spent underneath the sun. The little leaf shuddered between my fingers, startling me out of my daydream. I could *feel* its happiness radiating out from the stem and through my fingers. Letting go, I took a tiny step back, bumping into Hazel, who I hadn't realised was standing right behind me.

"It likes you," she said matter-of-factly, as if knowing a plant's feelings was as normal as breathing.

Pressing my back against the bench, I tilted my head slightly, confusion pulling my brows together. "I don't understand?"

"Earth wielders are bound to the earth. All organic matter grows and dies there. So, when an earth wielder uses their magic and connects with these things, we can almost feel the life force running through them. Or, in some cases, when things are dying." Pausing for a moment, she walked to the back of the greenhouse and picked up a medium-sized plant that looked as if it had shrivelled and died in a heat wave. Setting it between us, she continued. "Place your hand on the leaves of this plant."

Eying her suspiciously, I took hold of the long thin leaves and instantly felt the difference. The plant moved rigid and slow. It was nothing like the little seedling swaying happily behind me. Pulling my hand away quickly, my heart ached at the sadness rippling through the plant's leaves. My voice came out no more than a whisper. "It's dying!"

Hazel nodded her head once in acknowledgement and, in her hooded eyes, I saw the same feelings reflected at me.

"But the incredible thing about being an earth wielder is this."

With a touch as soft as a feather, Hazel placed her hand on the top soil and closed her eyes. For a few seconds nothing happened. Then, to my amazement, the wilting yellowed leaves that had once occupied the pot were now changing to a beautiful forest green. Instantly, the leaves straightened and swayed as if a breeze had come through the open door. I couldn't believe my eyes. Reaching out a tentative hand, I placed it on Hazel's and instantly felt her magic pulse through me. A smile spread across my face. *This was incredible.* Pulling my hand away, I went to touch the leaves of the plant again, wanting to feel the happiness and life that undoubtedly would be present, but the sight of Hazel's hand made my heart sink—wiping the excited smile from my face. The pale and wrinkled skin of Hazel's hand was covered in thin green lines. They twisted and swirled like green veins on the top of her hand, curving to morph into her palm. I took her hand in my own and watched as the green veins continued to spread like tiny rivers up the top of her wrist. I locked eyes with Hazel, not realising she had been watching me the entire time.

She took in my shocked expression. "I take it you have never witnessed this before?"

Shaking my head, I released Hazel's hand, taking a moment to gather my thoughts.

"What is this?" I asked quietly.

Hazel looked down at her hand as if trying to put into words what she was seeing. "You would know from your earlier lessons with your mother that, as witches, we draw our magic from the element we associate with." Hazel looked up at me expectantly and I nodded my understanding. "Well, that magic has a price, Braelyn, and it draws on our soul when we need to use it. This is the consequence of using our magic." She held up her hand that was now criss-crossed with hundreds of tiny green lines.

I flinched at the sight. "Then why do we use magic if it harms us?"

"That's like asking why a cow produces milk when they don't benefit from it. It is who we are and what we do, child. Magic has consequences, but there are ways to remedy the use of our magic."

"How come my hand doesn't have the lines like yours? And why doesn't this happen when we use other types of magic like botany and potion making?" I asked, studying my own hand's rosy complexion.

"Spirit wielders differ because they are stronger with their magic and can resist the pull on their soul a little more than the rest of us. As for other magics, like potion-making, they don't pull on our energies like elemental magic does. They draw on the energies within the ingredient so that's why there are no consequences." Hazel's expression darkened slightly as her mouth turned down in a small frown.

"So regardless of how much spirit magic I use, I will never have this happen?" I pursed my lips, slightly relieved I might not have to endure what Hazel was.

"Not exactly, even spirit wielders have their limits and require remedies."

Opening my lips to ask another question, Hazel held up a long thin finger in silence.

"Speaking of remedies," she interrupted, "I need you to go into town and fetch a few things from the apothecary to make a healing elixir. This will be your first lesson for the day." Turning on her heel, Hazel walked out the small doorway of the greenhouse and back along the narrow path towards the cottage. Always a step behind, I raced after her, my heart beating an excited rhythm in my chest at the prospect of learning more magic.

I walked along the winding narrow path that led into town with Hazel's list of ingredients tucked inside my jacket pocket. The trees rustled in the cool breeze as my mind sifted through the events of the morning. It had been incredible watching Hazel use her magic and my stomach fluttered excitedly to have her teach me how to use my own, but I would be lying to myself if the idea of such a sacrifice didn't scare me. The memory of Hazel's hand sent a shiver down my spine despite the warmth of my coat.

Taking out the square piece of paper Hazel had given me, I unfolded it to scan the items requested. The list was only short and scrawled in an elegant script, reminding me of the beautiful letters my mother used to write. My heart ached at the thought of her and how the last thing we had done when we were together was argue. Allowing myself to feel the pain that had been bottled inside me, a spark flittered along my fingertips. My magic reacting to my emotions. I desperately wanted to be back in our apothecary, drinking tea while she taught me how to brew potions. But instead I was in this strange yet wonderful place and, while I knew it was all for a reason, my mind conjured the selfish thought of *why me?*

Too busy with my own thoughts, I didn't notice the archway of trees leading into the village until they loomed above me. The small shopfront was just across the square. It was slightly set back from the other shops and blended perfectly into the shadows with its dark wooden door and dim windows. If I hadn't just seen someone walk through the door, I would have walked right past it. As I reached the entry, a cool breeze rustled the leaves of the nearby trees, making me shiver. Wrapping my arms around myself, the list Hazel had given me flew from my grasp in a flurry of dried leaves and dust. It fluttered along the cobblestones, and, cursing under my breath, I ran after it. Hazel would not be impressed if I came back with only half of what I needed to make the healing elixir. Pushing my hair out my face as I ran, the wind began to die down, depositing my list between the weaving branches of hanging ivy covering most of the buildings in the village. Reaching out to pry it from the plants, a pale hand darted out in front of me, plucking the paper before I had the chance. I didn't need to look at the person to know who it would be and, letting out a frustrated sigh, I met Victoria's light blue eyes with my own.

A sneer appeared on her face. Hazel's list was suspended above her palm as her fingers beckoned the wind holding it aloft. She was an air witch.

"Well, well, well, back here again, are we?" she crooned.

The dark-haired witch who had been with Victoria at the Forest Festival stood behind her, sniggering at the comment her friend had made. She wasn't as tall as Victoria, but from the cruel grin on her face, I assumed she was just as mean.

"Of course I'm here Victoria. I live in the village. What, did you expect me to stay away just because of your little comment at the Forest Festival?" I raised a questioning eyebrow in her direction.

From the look of fury in her icy eyes, she clearly hadn't gotten the response she was looking for. I smiled in amusement at the anger it caused her. I wouldn't let her beat me, no matter how frightening she seemed. Bringing herself up to her full height, Victoria leered at me, her face mere inches from my own.

"I will find out who you are, qui decepitor, and when I do you will regret the day you ever came to Ellesmere."

Crumpling the paper, she threw Hazel's list to the ground before turning on her heel and stomping off in the other direction. Picking up the crumpled paper, I stuffed it back in my coat pocket, my hands trembling ever so slightly. Despite Julien's earlier comments about Victoria being harmless, I would need to watch my back.

Stepping into the apothecary a bell chimed above me.

"I'll be there in a second," someone yelled from the back of the store.

Pulling the now crumpled list from my pocket, I glanced around the tiny shop and couldn't help but notice the apothecary was nothing like my mother's. It was dark and dimly lit by a small fire burning fiercely in the corner, making the room feel uncomfortably warm. Taking off my coat to expel some of the heat, I placed it on a rickety coat rack by the door and made my way over to a set of large shelves standing at the very back of the old shop. Hundreds of square jars lined each shelf, their yellowed labels peeling away, making it difficult to read what was in each of the bottles. There seemed to be no order to them—unlike at my mother's shop, which had all its shelves arranged in alphabetical order. I picked up a small jar, unable to decipher the text. Squinting closely, I tried to read the label when a touch on my shoulder startled me—almost making me drop the bottle. A voice sounded from behind me as I tried to calm my racing heart.

"Sorry, I didn't mean to startle you. It's Braelyn, right?"

The voice was deep, smooth, and sounded more familiar than

I cared to admit. Turning around, I was met with Julien's face—the fire warlock from the Forest Festival last night. The very one Victoria had told me to stay away from and Theo asked me to be careful of.

"It's okay. I just wasn't expecting someone to creep up on me."

My voice came out a little softer than I had wanted it to. Julien's dark eyes watched me carefully, his mouth pulling up at the corner in a small smirk. Reaching out a large hand, he plucked a dried leaf from my mussed hair, tossing it into the crackling flames of the fire behind me. Heat flushed in my cheeks as I stared back into Julien's face.

"Again, I apologise if I startled you, but you looked as if you needed some help." This came out as a statement rather than a question and it made my fingers twitch in agitation. Not that Julien would know I'd been raised in an apothecary. But my mind still couldn't accept the fact he'd assumed I needed his help.

"You were wrong. I don't need any help." Sticking my chin out defiantly, I turned back to the shelves, but rather than leaving me to my own devices, Julien stayed where he was, watching my every move. I pried at the lid of the bottle I was holding, hoping to smell the substance inside. With the labels being so faded and unreadable, this was the only way I would discover the contents, but the cap was on so tight, even applying all my strength wouldn't budge the lid. Feeling foolish and irritated that Julien was still behind me, I spun around in a flurry, almost knocking into the shelves which looked as if a gust of wind would blow them over. Julian caught me by the elbow, his touch hot on my already warmed skin. I tried to pull my arm from his grip, feeling my stomach flutter, but his hand lingered lightly.

"I told you I don't need your help."

My voice came out in a squeak as my cheeks flushed deeper at both the heat in the room and the fact Julien's hand was still resting on my arm.

He raised a dark eyebrow at me. "It seems to me that you do, considering you were trying to open a jar of arsenic which would have caused you severe pain if you had managed to get the jar open."

The heat in my cheeks disappeared as the colour drained from my face. Seeing that my expression betrayed my know-it-all demeanour, his face softened, and a small smile played across his face.

"Please let me help you. What is it that you need?"

Breathing out a reluctant sigh, I handed over the list Hazel had given me, watching as he glanced down the ingredients, nodding.

"No problem, we have all this. Follow me." Making his way towards the shelves on the left-hand side of the shop, Julien busied himself with looking through different bottles to find what Hazel was after.

"You certainly seem to know your way around," I said.

I studied him closely as he pulled bottles from the shelves without even looking. He seemed so at ease here.

He chuckled softly. "Well, I basically grew up in this place, so I can probably tell you where everything is with my eyes closed."

After only a few minutes Julien had managed to find me all the ingredients on Hazel's list. As much as needing his help to find the ingredients annoyed me, I was thankful for it. I could have been in the apothecary for hours and still never would have looked in the places he had found them.

"Does your family run this place?" I asked, gazing around the small shop.

Despite the haphazard way the apothecary was stocked, it was a quaint little store with a homely feel. The fire continued crackling in the grate, illuminating the room with a warm glow. A bunch of old books sat stacked on one of the old rickety tables, and my fingers brushed over the dusty covers. I smiled at the musky smell that reminded me so much of our bookshelves at home.

"Yeah, they used to, but now… it's just me." His voice sounded distant as he turned away and I wondered if it had something to do with the bad reputation clinging to his family's name.

Walking me over to a small table at the front of the shop, he busied himself with writing down the ingredients in a small book. He placed the three jars in a brown paper bag and passed them to me, his hand brushing mine softly and sending goosebumps over my skin. Handing him the few silver coins Hazel had given me, he threw them in a small square tin and came around to stand on the other side of the table. His eyes met mine and I felt a flush rise on my neck.

"You're not from around here are you, Braelyn?" He raised an eyebrow in my direction. His lips quirked in a playful manner.

I chuckled lightly. "What tipped you off?"

"One, I haven't seen you around here before last night, and two, a friend of mine doesn't seem to like you very much. She seems to think you are a qui decepitor." He chuckled deeply, making his dark hair shake slightly with the movement. "Was that a good enough answer for you?" He raised a questioning eyebrow at me again.

"I guess some of your assumptions are right," I replied, thinking back to Victoria's comments from last night.

He shook his head as if amused by my response. "I don't think you're here to deceive anyone."

Julien's small admission surprised me, and I couldn't help but feel a small tinge of happiness pull at my heart. Whatever reason Victoria hated me for, it hadn't rubbed off on him.

I wanted to thank him for not believing Victoria's rumour, but something outside had caught his attention. Following Julien's gaze, I squinted through the apothecary's grimy windows and saw a group of men dragging a long wooden cart behind them as they walked around the town square. Julien stepped back behind the counter, quickly grabbing a large paper bag that was almost overflowing with what appeared to be jars and other items from the apothecary. Opening the door, he beckoned for me to follow him. The little bell chimed happily as we walked out into the cool autumn morning.

Nine

Four men walked around the cobblestoned square, their chests puffed out, heads held high in a show of importance. Clad in silver armour, they made a menacing entourage. I stood behind Julien, watching the burly men make their way around the square—going into each shop and coming out with bags or baskets full of different items. Most witches and warlocks in town looked afraid of the armoured men, but there were some like Julien, whose hatred you could almost feel radiating off them.

"Who are they?" I whispered as they continued around the square, ducking into each shop for mere seconds as they passed.

"They are King Elias's guards," Julien whispered back. "They are here to collect stock for the kingdom. They come to each village once a month and take more than what they need for the castle and the king." His eyes narrowed towards the four approaching men.

"Why doesn't anyone stand up to the king? Or the guards, for that matter?"

Julien made a small noise in the back of his throat, as if the words I had uttered were ridiculous.

"There is no standing against King Elias, Braelyn. To do so would be treason. He would have you thrown in his dungeons to rot or worse." Julien's eyes darted to where two of the men were throwing bags of goods into the back of the wooden cart.

"What could be worse than—"

I never got to finish my question. Julien held a large finger to his lips, silencing me.

One of the men had stopped in front of a small shopfront two buildings up from Julien's apothecary. A small, curly-haired witch stood out the front looking more than terrified. Her small hands were wound in her pale apron and her eyes shone brightly in the autumn light as she trembled. She looked like she was going to cry. The tallest guard entered the shop only to step back out a split second later. He was followed by a tall brown-haired boy who I recognised as Theo's friend from the Forest Festival. The boy now sported a growing black eye, which I was sure had to be a result of an altercation with the armoured man. I watched closely as the tall guard bent down and whispered something in the girl's ear. Her whole body trembled as her lips moved in a soft reply. Whatever she had said didn't go over well with the armoured man, because in the next instant he grabbed the girl by the hair, flinging her to the ground. My feet moved across the cobblestones before my mind could even process what was happening. Dropping my bag, I ran over to the girl who was lying in a ball on the stones, trying to make herself as small as she could.

"What do you think you are doing?" I yelled at the guard, who now seemed a hell of a lot taller than I originally thought.

He loomed over me like a raging bear ready to attack its prey. A bushy blond beard covered most of his face, but it couldn't conceal the hatred his light eyes pierced me with.

"What did you say, girl?"

The man's voice was a cold and sinister whisper, sending a chill down my spine. The small curly-haired girl now stood hidden behind me. I was surprised she was able to stand with the force the soldier had used against her. Fear boiled inside me, but I didn't want to give this monster the satisfaction of knowing, deep down, my stomach felt as if it was filled with rocks. So, I shoved my nerves down deep in my belly before I replied.

"Who do you think you are picking on a small and innocent girl like that? Does it make you feel tough to pick on someone smaller than you?" My words came out calm and strong, but my heart raced, and I wondered if he could hear it beneath my chest.

The burly guard growled low, my words obviously striking a nerve. He lifted his large, bear-like hand, and my heart hammered in my chest as I waited for the strike to fall, but then my attention turned to the red tinge of his palm. No. He wasn't going to hit me, he planned to use fire magic against me. The fear I had shoved away only seconds before now bubbled to the surface, making the fire warlock grin in satisfaction. As the flame in his hand ignited, I readied myself to react as quickly as possible with my own magic, but before I even lifted a hand Julien was in front of me—catching the man's hand between his own. Eyeing the other three soldiers, they made to step forward, but the blond-haired guard waved them back. They stood their ground, their hands not on swords as I had expected, but held out in front of them as if readying to fist fight. This wasn't the case though, as fire flickered on the hands of a dark guard, a second, shorter man rubbed icy hands together. Focusing my energy on my own magic in case one of the guards made a move, my brows pulled together in concentration. Nothing happened. I didn't feel any tingling in my fingers like the first time my magic had made itself present, there was just... nothing. The air between Julien and the man in front of us felt tense, like you could cut it with a knife.

"What do you think you're doin' Julien? Gettin' between a king's guard and a disobedient witch?" the soldier spat.

I couldn't see Julien's face, but his shoulders were stiff, and his hands were now in tight fists by his side. The soldier extinguished his flame.

"She's done nothing wrong, Blight!" Julien replied with an air of calm. "Just finish your job and go back to whatever hole you crawled out from."

Blight's nostrils flared. He bared his teeth before growling low in his throat, sounding more like an animal than a warlock. Fire flickered within his blue eyes and my heart raced in my chest. If there was going to be a battle between these two, I didn't want to be standing too close. Blight raised his hands, flames bursting to life. My eyes widened in fear and wonderment at the magic rippling in the air, and I took a tiny step back, but Julien stood his ground.

"Come on, Blight." Julian said. "I'm sure the king won't be happy to hear you started a fight against me." He snickered and pronounced 'me' as if he meant something to the king. My hands shook by my sides and I clenched them into small fists to stop them from trembling. Who was Julien Thorne and what relationship did he have with the king to make these men question their actions against him? Feeling a little nervous, I took another small step back.

"It's not 'er that's the problem!" He thrust his giant shaggy head in my direction before pointing at the timid girl behind me and the brown-haired boy who now stood near her.

"It's 'er and 'im! They ain't got what we need for the king and what do you think is gunna to happen if I go back one bag short, 'eh?" Blight crossed his arms over his large, broad chest and stood his ground. "I'm not leavin' one bag short!" His hands still blazed with red hot flame as he stared down at Julien with a steely gaze.

"I'll give you an extra bag from the apothecary. Just leave them alone," Julien replied.

Blight looked down at him with an unreadable expression. Not knowing what this man was capable of, I readied myself for a fight in case he managed to knock Julien out of the way. But he didn't. He simply unfolded his arms, palms now free of fire.

"Fine. 'Ave it your way Julien, but don't think I'm gunna forget what 'appened 'ere!" With a nod toward the other three soldiers, they sauntered over to the apothecary, taking what they needed. Before they left, they picked up the bag Julien had brought out and threw it on top of the other items they had collected.

"See you in a month," Blight yelled at everyone before turning on his heel and following the now overflowing cart out of the village.

Julien didn't drop his defensive stance until Blight and the other armoured warlocks had left the town square. Turning to face me, his shoulders relaxed as a strange expression played across his dark features.

"Are you okay?" he asked.

I nodded my head once as the girl who still hid behind me stepped out and took my hand in hers.

"Thank you," she said softly.

Her large blue eyes glowed as a few tears trickled down her face. She looked only a few years younger than me.

"It's okay," I said quietly. "You're safe now."

I gave the girl's hand a tight, reassuring squeeze, and a beautiful smile spread across her tear-stained face. The brown-haired boy came up to Julien a moment later and grasped his hand.

"Thank you to both of you." He gave a small smile to Julien who returned it warmly.

"It's okay, Grey. Tell your mother not to worry, but make sure she has something ready for them when they return next month."

Grey nodded his head and gestured to the curly-haired girl.

"Come on Gillie, let's go make sure mother is okay."

Squeezing my hand once more, she ran back to her mother's shop—which appeared to be a fabric store—her brother not far behind her.

"Will they be okay?" I asked, not knowing if I truly wanted to know the answer. Julien's face was unreadable.

"As long as they have something for the king next month, they will be fine."

He touched the side of my face, his thumb stroking down my cheek softly. Our eyes locked and my heart quickened as if a million butterfly wings fluttered in my chest. My mind whirled as I tried to make sense of where these feelings were coming from. Nothing like this had ever happened to me in Pryhollow. Tearing my gaze away from him, I pulled his hand from my cheek, our fingers intertwining for the briefest moment before Julien's hand quickly dropped to his side.

"Yes, I'm okay. Thank you for stepping in, but I really should be getting back now." Walking back to the front of the apothecary, I picked up my discarded bag, leaving Julien behind me. Weaving through the groups of people who milled around the square I stepped back through the arching trees into the serenity of the forest. Walking the familiar path back to Hazel's cottage, I knew that wouldn't be the last time I'd see Julien.

I found Hazel pacing back and forth across the small living room when I arrived, her face pinched in a frown.

"By the elements, what took you so bloody long, child?" Hazel yelled.

She snatched the paper bag from me and dug through it, pulling out the jars and placing them on the counter. Kicking off my dirty boots, I stood by the fireplace, warming my frozen skin in front of the crackling fire. My mind was still humming from my morning in town.

"I'm sorry, Hazel. I didn't mean to take so long, but there was a commotion in the village with some of King Elias's men." My voice was soft and earnest, but Hazel's eyes were wide.

"Hazel, are you okay? Is it your hand?" Her hand still pulsed with green veins, but it didn't seem to be paining her. Taking a seat in her armchair, she gripped the chair with white knuckles. She seemed to be regaining her composure, blinking a few times as if to clear a fog clouding her mind.

"Yes, yes, I'm fine. Just worried you had gotten yourself lost in the forest somewhere. Did any of the soldiers ask you who you were?"

I shook my head. "They were more interested in trying to hurt Gillie than asking who I was. I'm pretty sure one of them punched Grey in the face."

Hazel shook her head. "Those guards are swines. Always picking fights with those weaker than themselves. You didn't use magic in front of them, did you?" Again I shook my head. "That's good child. The last thing we need is King Elias learning you know how to use your magic. We need him to think you don't know what you're doing. It will buy us some time."

Releasing a long sigh, I explained what had happened with

Blight, the way the guards had treated Gillie and how they had reacted when Julien stepped in.

"I did try to use my magic at one point, but nothing happened. It was the strangest feeling, I felt nothing." I searched Hazel's face, hoping to find an expression to put my mind at ease, but her face was blank. So, I asked the question that had plagued my mind since my magic had suddenly disappeared. "Is there something wrong with me?" I asked quietly.

Hazel turned her emerald eyes to me, her face softening. "No, child, there is nothing wrong with you. King Elias's guards wear armour forged by the dwarves in the mountains of the Ironwood. The iron stops anyone from using magic against them. As you can imagine, there are many witches and warlocks all over Ellesmere who despise the king for what he did in the war, so he protects his followers."

My mother had told me briefly of the war that had broken out in Ellesmere, but I had no idea what King Elias had done in order to start the rift between the king's followers and everyone else who lived in Ellesmere.

"What did he to do?"

Restlessly, I shifted back and forth, waiting for Hazel to tell me about my family history. After a few moments she sighed deeply, "You must know, Braelyn, that Ellesmere wasn't always like this—where people feared the king and his followers. Many years ago Ellesmere was peaceful and there were no divides between witches, warlocks, elves, and dwarves. We lived in perfect harmony."

Hazel leant back in her armchair, her wrinkled hands resting lightly in her lap. It seemed as if she was reminiscing on those happier times, and I waited for her to continue, hands trembling in anticipation.

"Your father and Elias were inseparable when they were younger. They were doted on by all in the kingdom, but as they matured into young warlocks, many started to notice a darkness to Elias that wasn't noticeable in your father. Despite the rumours, your father was always loyal to his brother, never swaying from the belief those rumours were simply jealous whispers." Pausing briefly, Hazel ran her long fingers over her damaged hand. It looked dreadfully painful, but it didn't seem to be hurting her.

"So what happened in the end?" I asked.

"Well, as the oldest of the king's sons, Elias had believed it was his right to rule Ellesmere, but your grandfather believed the title was earnt, not given. When the time came, the title was passed to your father instead of Elias, who became enraged. In the end, the dark magic inside Elias won out and he killed the king and queen before unleashing his power on your father and the rest of the kingdom."

A tear slipped down my cheek. No wonder my mother had such a hard time speaking of my father. He had been murdered in cold blood by his own brother. Anger washed over me as my muscles tensed, my hands clenching by my sides. *How could a person do such a thing? To someone who loved them and showed them kindness when others hadn't?*

"Elias's thirst for power was more important to him than even his own family and, as the war raged on, he eradicated every witch and warlock with the power to challenge him." Hazel paused for a moment, studying my face, waiting for me to make the connection.

"Those with spirit magic."

She nodded her head once. "That's right, child. His most loyal followers were sent out to find every single witch and warlock who had the ability to use spirit magic. Many tried to flee Ellesmere, but he eventually tracked them down. They were taken to Ellesmere Castle and haven't been seen since."

When the king's men arrived in the village today, it had been obvious the people were not allies of King Elias, but it made me wonder where the rest of his followers resided.

Chewing my lip, I asked, "Do any of King Elias' followers live in the village?"

Hazel shook her head. "Not anymore. A few stuck around after the war to encourage others to follow the new king, but after so many failed attempts they moved on to the castle village where all of King Elias's followers stay."

"What about the elves and the dwarves? Are they loyal to him?"

"They are now loyal only to their own kind. They have very little to do with witches and warlocks anymore, as they see what King Elias did as a representation of all of us."

I opened my mouth to ask Hazel another question, but she held up a long, pointed finger. The green lines appearing were almost fluorescent in the warm firelight.

"No more questions for now, child. I know you have many of them and I will answer them all in good time, but first let me show you how to brew this healing elixir."

My mind had been so distracted with the events at the apothecary and learning more about Elias that I had almost forgotten about Hazel's ailing hand. She stepped past me and pulled down a small black cauldron that had been hanging on the bricks beside the hearth. Placing it before me, along with a worn leather-bound book, she made her way over to the small kitchen, busying herself with the ingredients needed. The book's thick spine cracked as my fingers skimmed through the yellowed pages. Stains smudged the corners and, as I turned to the cover, my breath hitched in my throat. *Redferne Family Grimoire*. Goosebumps prickled my skin as I gazed down at Hazel's grimoire—the book my mother and grandmother had learned from. Our Grimoires were passed down from generation to generation and held the family's spells and learnings from centuries ago. Placing my hand over the worn leather cover, my fingertips tingled with the magic I knew lay within its pages. Flicking to the list of spells at the front of the book, I found the one for the healing elixir and turned to the correct page. The book had been heavily handled and the parchment on some pages was torn, but the ink stood out stark and easy to read. Not like the faded labels in Julien's apothecary. Looking down the list of ingredients, I scanned the steps, trying to memorise the way to make the elixir. Hazel had come back over to the fireplace, a tray full of herbs clutched between her wrinkled hands. Placing the tray on the small table, she went back to sit in her armchair.

"Well, on with it, child," she snapped, pointing to the page between us.

"Aren't you going to help me?" I asked.

She shook her head, leaning back in her chair and watching me intently. Taking the cauldron to the small fire now burning low in the grate, I tipped a small amount of moon water into the depths of the cauldron.

Moon water had always been my favourite thing to brew. It wasn't a difficult potion to make, but I would get so excited watching Maeve summon her water magic to use for the brew. We would place the water on the windowsill in full view of the moon, letting its power infuse with the water. In the morning, it would be ready to be bottled and used for cleansing potions.

I grabbed the mortar and pestle Hazel had placed on the tray and took a pinch of pink salt, a teaspoon of dried ginger, a teaspoon of coltsfoot, and a pinch of apple blossom—placing them all in the small concrete dish. I ground the ingredients together with the pestle as Hazel watched my every move. I tipped the ground herbs into the bubbling moon water, where they floated before sinking slowly to the bottom. As the grimoire advised, I stirred every so often and, after a few minutes of watching the herbs steep, Hazel handed me a strip of cloth to wrap around the cauldron's handle. Carefully, I placed the cauldron on the stones in front of the fire and ladled a spoonful of the elixir into the small glass vile Hazel had brought over from the kitchen. Stoppering it and handing the vial to Hazel, she inspected it carefully.

"Well," she said. "I have to commend your mother. She taught you well."

It was the nicest thing Hazel had said to me since arriving in Ellesmere and my chest filled with pride. She handed me back the vial.

"Now, you will need to place three drops of the elixir on to my hand equal distances apart."

Her tone was back to its usual bossy self and, taking a seat in front of her, I picked up her hand and did as she had told me, but nothing happened. Hazel's hand was still riddled with green. At first, I thought something had gone wrong during the brewing process, but after a few anxiety filled seconds, my eyes grew wide at what happened before me. The dark green veins covering Hazel's hand were now receding, like waves being swept back out to sea. I watched in awe as the green tinge disappeared, leaving Hazel's pink wrinkled hand in its place.

"Good work child," she said, patting me once on the head. "Now get this mess cleaned up and then meet me outside the front of the cottage."

Ten

I hurried around the small kitchen, cleaning as quickly as my hands could move. I was eager to learn more and my brain thrummed at the promise of taking in more knowledge. After placing the last bottle in the cupboard, I ran to the front door of the cottage and stepped out into the afternoon sun. The temperature had grown a little cooler since this morning, but my whole body felt warm and thrummed with excitement. Hazel stood by the edge of the path leading into the Ironwood Village, her hands clasped behind her back as she stared into the sea of trees stretching in every direction. Stepping down onto the rocky pathway, small stones crunched loudly beneath my boots, causing Hazel to turn and face me. A lovely, dreamy look lit her face, making her look years younger. The forest seemed to have this effect on her and I liked seeing her so carefree, but it didn't last long. She jumped right into our lesson.

"Usually the parent with the same elemental magic as you would teach you how to wield your magic, but being a spirit witch, we are going to need some help from a few others," she explained.

My brows knitted together. "But I thought you said no one could know about my spirit magic?"

Hazel's eyes crinkled as a smile touched her usually thin lips. "I know what I said, but there are a few witches and warlocks who I trust enough to help us." Nodding once, she continued, "Now, to be able to use your magic you need to first call on your element.

Do you know how to do this?"

I had only ever seen my mother and Maeve do this a handful of times and usually it consisted of them uttering a few quiet words. They would then have full use of their magic, but unsure just how to do that, I stayed quiet and shook my head.

"Stick out your hand." Hazel stretched her palm towards the sky, her earth rune dark against her skin.

Mimicking her movement, I stared down at the circular rune covering most of my palm. My stomach fluttered and rolled in anticipation as I waited for Hazel's next instruction.

"To call the magic, we need to speak the old language. Do you know the word for spirit?" She looked at me expectantly and a smile played across my lips.

"Spiritus." I spoke the word into the air between us.

The tingling sensation started at the tips of my fingers and spread all the way up my arms. My heart fluttered in my chest as magic flooded my veins. I let out a shuddering breath.

Hazel placed her hand on my shoulder. "It's okay Braelyn," she said soothingly. "You need to feel the magic inside. You need to become one with it and let it mesh to your very being."

Hazel's words helped ease my anxious feelings and closing my eyes I let myself embrace the magic. Relaxing my muscles, I let it surge through me. Heat rushed over my skin as my fire magic ignited and my mind began to fog as I felt air magic brew like a growing storm behind my closed eyes. As I listened to the breeze whisper through the trees, the sweet scents of lavender, jasmine and honeysuckle tickled my nose as my senses heightened in response to my earth magic. Lastly, I felt the cold snap of ice trickle down my spine like a melting waterfall as my water magic rushed to the surface. It was a lot to take in, but as each of the elements began to entangle one another like vines wrapping around my heart, the tingling eased from my fingers and my breathing returned to a steady rhythm. It was a strange sensation. I felt lighter, as if I had been lifted off the ground, but my mind felt more connected to what was around me. As I opened my eyes, I found Hazel's green orbs watching with such intensity I took a step backwards. The muscles in her face relaxed as she saw I was okay.

"So what happens now?" I asked eagerly.

"As a spirit witch, you can call on all the elements, but as I can only use magic connected to the earth, we will simply focus on that for now. In order to do this you need to empty your mind and focus on what you're asking your magic to do."

She looked at me expectantly, as if waiting for me to summon my magic with a quick snap of my fingers. Unfortunately, trying to empty my mind seemed to be a lot harder than just simply switching off my thoughts. Closing my eyes once again, I tried to block out the world around me, but it didn't work. Birds chirped happily in the trees above us, and the leaves rustling in the slight breeze distracted me. Frustrated, I fisted my hands and threw open my eyes.

"This is hopeless," I spat out. "How can someone truly clear their mind? Especially out here where there is so much noise." I huffed out a sigh like a petulant child.

"This is not something you just learn overnight, child. It takes years of practice to be one with your magic, but you will get there."

"It just seems impossible." My whining sounded childish, even to my own ears.

"Nothing is impossible. Rather than trying to rid your mind of every thought and sound, you just need to focus on the action you want to do." Hands held behind her back, Hazel continued, "Try lifting that leaf on the ground by your shoe."

Spotting the leaf Hazel was speaking about, I closed my eyes, readying myself to ease into a more meditative state.

"No, Braelyn, keep your eyes open. You need to focus, and you can't do this with your eyes closed. Magic requires all five senses." Hazel backed away a few steps to give me space.

I focused my eyes on the leaf and took a deep breath, letting the cool air fill my lungs before releasing it slowly. A white puff of warm air materialised before me. Watching the brown leaf, I emptied my mind and slowly lifted my hand. Lazily, the leaf moved as if attached to an invisible string. It rose from the damp grass, hanging a few inches off the ground. From the corner of my eye I could see Hazel nodding her head in approval, and a smile spread across my face. Lifting my hand a little higher, the leaf seemed to obey as if it had been tethered to my fingers. Feeling as though I was one with my magic, I continued to practice moving the little leaf in different directions when a sound from one of the bushes startled me, breaking my concentration. The little leaf fell to the grass as if nothing had touched it. The bushes rustled once more as a tiny rabbit hopped out from between the leaves. Its tiny nose twitched as it sniffed the air before darting across the path and back into the shadows of the forest. I let out a long sigh.

"This is harder than you make it look." Rubbing my eyes gently, a wave of exhaustion washed over me. While my hands were free of the vein-like marks Hazel had received, my mind felt weak, my limbs heavy with exhaustion.

Hazel chuckled softly. "I have had many years of practice, but you will get there. You are much stronger than you know and, the more you use your magic, the stronger you will become." Patting me softly on the shoulder, she made her way towards the cottage. "Come, let's get some rest. You will have a busy few days ahead of you." She stepped inside, leaving me standing in the middle of her leafy garden, grinning from ear to ear at the prospect of using more magic.

Eleven

T he next few days passed in somewhat of a blur. Hazel had me practicing my earth magic from the moment I stepped out of bed, still bleary-eyed and barely able to function, right up until the sun dipped behind the trees. With each passing day she would have me try something different and, as each day rolled into the next, I found myself getting stronger. Not knowing much about training me in the other elements, Hazel told me she was bringing in a few other witches and warlocks to help me. And after days of only being able to conjure my earth magic, I was eager for the chance to test out the other elements.

Stepping into the front garden of Hazel's cottage, my hands tingled in anticipation at today's lesson. The day was crisp, but the sun's golden rays warmed my skin. Getting halfway across the grass, I spotted a familiar figure by the treeline. Theo leant against one of the great oak trees, grinning at me like a Cheshire cat. His sandy blond hair was tousled as though he had just rolled out of bed, but he looked neat in crisp brown pants and a sweater that was a little too short for his long arms. Grey was next to him, dressed beautifully in a dark blue trench coat, his hands shoved into the pockets as he gave me a shy smile. His eye was still a little swollen from his altercation with Elias's men. I had only spoken to him once and it had been in the heat of an argument with some of the king's guards, but he seemed like a sweet warlock. I beamed broadly at them as I reached the treeline.

"Braelyn, this is Grey Bishop. He is a very talented water warlock and I thought he would be the best person to teach you how to use your water magic. You'll need his help to be strong enough when you come up against the king."

My eyes widened at Hazel mentioning the prophecy in front of Theo and Grey. I had expected her to want to keep it quiet, the same way she had told me to keep my spirit magic a secret.

"I... ah... didn't realise we were telling people about the prophecy," I spluttered, fiddling with the buttons on my coat.

"Only those I know to be trustworthy have been told about the prophecy, child. I thought it best to explain what the stakes were so they can help as best as they can."

I nodded, agreeing with her reasoning, but deep down my stomach fluttered nervously under the weight of my destiny, and the consequences should I fail.

"It's nice to officially meet you Braelyn. Thank you again for the kindness you showed my sister the other day in the village. She hasn't stopped talking about you."

Grey's light voice broke through my nervous thoughts as I remembered my encounter with the sweet, dark-haired girl who had come face-to-face with Blight's fiery temper.

"It's nice to meet you too—officially, that is. I'm glad to hear Gillie's okay."

Grey gave me a small smile before Hazel's voice broke the short silence.

"Oh yes, those horrid men need to learn some proper manners," she tsked, turning her cool green gaze to me. "So, shall we begin child?"

Hazel's praise about Grey being an extremely talented water warlock was an understatement. He was able to conjure water in ways that would put Maeve's tricks to shame. I watched in utter amazement as he conjured a sphere of water out of thin air. Turning it in his hands, the orb began to twist and shudder as it separated into tiny icicles, pointed and razor-sharp like hundreds of needles.

Clenching his hand into a small fist, the ice suspended in mid-air as if hundreds of frozen arrows were knocked in invisible bows. Opening his hand wide, the icicles shot through the air, embedding themselves in the trunks of a few trees just beyond Hazel's garden. I sucked in a quick breath as my eyes darted to Theo. His eyes were wide and gleaming as he stared at Grey with a look of wonderment and admiration. Not only was Grey's power impressive, but he was a good teacher too. By the end of my lesson, I was able to conjure a ball of water and turn it to ice with just the flick of my hand.

As both my mother and father's elements were air, conjuring this element seemed to come naturally without any help. It was as easy as breathing for me. The breeze answered my power as I conjured a gust of wind through the garden, throwing a dusting of leaves to the ground. Summoning a mist so thick it clouded the garden in a thick fog, I manipulated it in such a way that once it surrounded Theo, he was blind to anything in front of him. But, despite my strengths, I had weaknesses too, and the element I struggled with the most was fire. It frustrated me more than I cared to admit. Not being able to summon more than a flickering flame, my frustration showed as my lips pinched together, and my muscles tensed. Hazel tried to reassure me fire magic was the hardest to learn, but it did little to settle my growing impatience at not being able to wield it like the others.

On my fifth day in Ellesmere, I descended the few stairs leading into the front garden and found Theo and Grey waiting for me. Their heads bent together as they whispered. Theo laughed heartily as Grey turned away, a smile on his face. He gave me a wave as I reached them. His black eye was healing slowly, and the once purple bruise was now a shade of yellowy-green.

"Have you seen Hazel? She wasn't inside when I woke."

Looking around the small garden, I frowned, wondering where she might be. She was usually already outside when I came down the front steps.

"It's okay, child. I'm here." Hazel stepped off the path leading out of the forest with a woman with flaming red hair, and I immediately recognised her as one of the performers from the Forest Festival.

"Braelyn, this is Verena. She is a very skilled fire witch and I think she will be most helpful for your fire magic."

Verena held out her hand as she approached. Grasping it tightly in my own, I felt her warm grasp wrap tight around my fingers.

"It's a pleasure to meet you, Braelyn."

Her voice was sweet, but it held a sharp edge that made her sound like a witch you wouldn't want to mess with. She was also incredibly beautiful. Her eyes were such a light hazel, they almost glowed golden in the morning sun. Her fiery hair had been pulled into a messy bun which sat high on her head, and the tight shirt and trousers she wore accentuated her curves beautifully.

"So," she said with a smile, bringing me back to the present. "Shall we begin?"

Taking up a spot on the grass before me, Verena turned the full strength of her golden gaze on me, watching closely as I tried without success to conjure more than just a few fingertips of flame.

"It's a good start, Braelyn, but fire magic is different to the other elements. Earth, air and water are all light magics. Fire is a darker sort of magic. As it's more powerful, it requires a greater strength to wield it."

Clicking her fingers together, her fire ignited and, with a flick of her hand, the flames shot into the air, a glowing ball of flickering red and orange. I stared open-mouthed as she conjured another ball of fire in her other hand and watched with rapt attention as she joined the two together.

"It's also a harder element to control and takes immense concentration in order to keep the flames at bay. Fire spreads, wanting nothing more than to be unleashed, but with time controlling it will be like second nature to you."

Clapping her hands together, the large flaming ball

disappeared into a shower of ash and sparks, leaving only a few singed blades of grass as evidence it had ever existed.

"Now you try."

Flames flickered to life in my palm, dancing in the light breeze as I pictured Verena's flaming ball, trying to create one of my own. The light in my palm grew brighter as the flames began to lick at the rest of my hand. Focusing on turning my wrist the way Verena had done, I mimicked her movement exactly, but nothing happened. I tried again. Nothing. My nostrils flared as my lips pressed together in a hard line, a rush of anger surging inside me at not being able to master my fire magic. The flame flickering in my hand flashed menacingly before it suddenly split in two, as if reacting to the anger inside my chest. Stumbling back, my eyes grew wide as the flames continued to grow, now looking like two flaming swords. The magic coursing through my veins was overwhelming, and I gritted my teeth against the weight of it. Out of the corner of my eye I could see Grey conjuring an orb of water between both of his hands. It floated in the air for a fraction of a second before he directed it towards my blazing hands. The water soared in an arc through the air, dowsing the flames in a streaming spout of water, but instead of putting out the fire it merely turned it to a fine mist—no match for the fiery tendrils blazing from my hands.

"She's too powerful," I heard him yell to Verena.

Taking a deep breath, I threw all my strength into containing the blaze before me, conscious of the forest around me. Bringing my arms down in a long sweeping motion, I clenched my fists together, imagining the flames turning to ash. As my hands cut through the air in a slicing motion, the fire sputtered, turning to tiny candle flames along my fingertips. Feeling my knees go weak and give out underneath me, Theo rushed to my side, catching me before I managed to hit the ground. His long arms snaked around my waist protectively as he held me steady.

"Brae, are you alright?" His voice was soft in my ear.

Too tired to answer, I simply nodded. My hands trembled as Theo released me from his hold.

"It's okay Braelyn," Verena said. "With time you will control your fire magic. You will reach a stage where you barely have to think about conjuring it." With a quick squeeze of my arm, she spun away from me and went to stand back by Hazel's side. "Now let's go again," she said with a wickedly beautiful smile.

We spent the rest of the day in a frenzy of fire. Verena yelled encouraging instructions as I tried desperately to conjure more than a few weak flames but, as the day wore on, I found myself growing more agitated with each failed attempt. By early evening everyone was exhausted. Theo and Grey lounged under a nearby oak tree, their heads resting close together against the dark wood. Hazel had taken a seat on a rickety wooden bench which was nestled amongst the berry bushes in the garden. She watched me cautiously as Verena and I battled through our long training session. In the many hours since nearly setting the forest on fire, I had only just managed to conjure a flame the size of an apple, and even that put a huge strain on my strength. Holding the flame in front of me, I let it blaze as I doubled over, placing my hands on my knees.

"I... I don't know if I can do this," I breathed, finally able to find my voice.

Hazel lifted herself from the wooden seat and came over to stand by my side, laying a soft hand on my shoulder. "What are you talking about child?"

My face blazed hotly as everyone stared at me. "This," I shouted, throwing my arms out wide and gesturing around me. "I almost set the forest on fire earlier today. I can't for the life of me conjure more than a flicker of a flame. There is no way I will ever be ready to go up against King Elias." I wiped a shaky hand over my face and, turning towards a small dirt pathway, stomped away from the cottage and all the stunned faces.

"Where are you going?" Hazel called out after me.

"I just need some time by myself," I shot back, not bothering to turn around.

The trees enveloped me in a leafy embrace, shielding me from everyone's watchful gaze. My heart slowed as the forest's earthy magic eased the anger inside me. As I sifted through all the information I had been given over the last few days, my heart sank. How was I going to deal with it all? An owl hooted somewhere in the canopy, startling me out of my thoughts. Walking through the dim light filtering through the treetops, I came upon a small clearing. It seemed to divide the lush, leafy forest surrounding Hazel's cottage with the beginning of a denser, darker one. Even in the dull light of the setting sun, I could barely see through the thick tangles of thorns and vines. A shudder ran over me as I stared—unable to look away—from the darkness oozing from the strange forest. Blinking a few times to clear the fog clouding my mind, I took a tentative seat on a fallen tree log, making sure my back was facing the tangle of trees. I pulled my legs to my chest and rested my forehead on my knees. My head felt like it was going to explode. My vision and the prophecy weighed heavily on my mind, and I had no idea how they expected someone like me—a witch who could barely wield her spirit magic—to be able to overthrow a king who had murdered his entire family to claim the throne. Suddenly feeling sick to my stomach, I lifted my head and gulped in a lungful of cool air. In such a short period of time my life had changed so much. The elements had gifted me the power to wield spirit magic and, while this power scared me, I knew it was for a reason. Whether I liked it or not, royal blood flowed through my veins, and I would be lying to myself if a tiny part of me wasn't intrigued by the throne. To have the strength to unite the people of Ellesmere once again and bring peace to a place I was quickly growing fond of. Whoever had conjured the portal to bring me here must have known about the prophecy and my lineage. Could fulfilling the prophecy and defeating King Elias be my ticket home? There had still been no response from the raven Hazel had sent my mother and a small part of me worried the message might not have arrived.

Wiping the sweat from my forehead, I closed my eyes and tried to still my racing mind, but the sharp crack of a fallen branch pulled my attention. My eyes shot open. Spinning around, I searched the growing darkness to find the source of the noise, but the forest had slipped back into an eerie silence. As I squinted into the darkness a shadowy figure slipped between the twisted branches and someone I did not expect to see this far into the forest came into view. A break in the dense crop of trees before me revealed Julien's large, shadowed form. He was dressed in a long, black woollen coat that flowed to just below his knees. Chunky black boots had been laced around his feet and a large satchel was looped across his chest. He looked as if he was trying to shove something into the opening of his bag and I squinted into the shadows, trying to catch a glimpse of what it was, but his satchel was partially hidden by his coat and shielded whatever it was from my line of sight.

"Julien," I called out. My voice echoed loudly around the clearing.

If I had been stunned to see him here, he was even more shocked to see me sitting before him. His eyes widened, dark circles shadowing them in the grey light. He held something purple and luminescent in his gloved hands as he continued to shove the object into his bag. As he took a seat next to me, his body warmth washed over my chilled skin, as if I had just taken a seat in the morning sun. My entire body urged me to move closer, but I stayed where I was, my skin rising in goosebumps.

"Sorry if I startled you," he said apologetically. "I wasn't expecting to see anyone else out here at this time of night."

He had dropped his bag at his feet and a strange smell wafted from the opening. Wrinkling my nose against the foul smell, a cough escaped my mouth as the decaying scent settled in the back of my nose.

"What are you doing out here?" I asked. "And what is that terrible smell?"

He laughed and ran a hand through his dark hair, causing it to stand up at all different angles. "Yeah, sorry about that, it's actually why I'm out here after dark. I've been foraging for mushrooms."

Tilting my head in confusion, a wide smile spread across his face, making his eyes wrinkle at the sides.

"I needed to get more for the apothecary."

As he rustled around in his bag, he pulled out the mushroom causing the terrible stench. It was unlike any fungi I had ever seen. The stem was so pale it was almost translucent and, instead of the brown or red of common mushroom caps, this one shone a magnificent blue. How could something so beautiful have such a terrible stench? Reaching out a tentative hand, I made to take the mushroom from Julien's hand, but he snatched it back quickly before my fingers were able to touch it.

"You don't want to be doing that without gloves," he said.

I stared at the thick, black leather gloves covering his hands, withdrawing my own.

"So why can't you look for these during the day?" I asked, still curious as to what this strange mushroom was used for. Assisting my mother at her apothecary, I had watched her prepare so many different potions over the years and none of them had ever required luminescent fungi.

Julien placed the mushroom back in his satchel. "They only come out at night when the moon is full."

Looking up at the starlit sky, the moon shone brightly above us.

"So what is it used for?"

Julien raised his eyebrow at me. "You ask a lot of questions, don't you?"

I shrugged a shoulder in response and he simply shook his head.

"It's only used for one potion, and it's not brewed commonly, but as the only apothecary in the Ironwood Village, I need to make sure we always have some available."

His gaze was focused on something across the other side of the clearing and for the next few seconds he avoided my gaze. As the silence wore on, my mind's eye flipped through my mother's grimoire, trying to figure out what potion this mushroom was used in, but again nothing came to mind. I was eager to know more about it, but before I was able to get my question out, Julien spoke.

"So, ah, what are you doing out here by yourself? Night-time isn't really the greatest hour to be out near the Ironwood alone."

Julien's gaze lingered on the dark trees before turning his gaze back to me, waiting for a response. I shivered at the tendrils of a cool breeze that had picked up and tickled the hairs on the back of my neck. Seeing my shiver, Julien pulled off his woollen coat, throwing it around my shoulders. It felt like I had been dunked into a steaming hot bath, his coat instantly warming my chilled skin. I pulled the woollen jacket tight around me, thankful for the heat it brought. Feeling a flush creep into my cheeks at his kind and gentlemanly gesture, I was thankful for the shadows hiding my embarrassment. Managing to mumble out a thanks to him, he waved a hand at me as if brushing it away.

"Soooo… are you going to tell me why you're out here?"

In what light there was from the full moon, I could see his eyebrow was raised in question again.

"It's nothing. I just had an argument with Hazel and needed some space."

Twisting a stray piece of cotton that had come away from the sleeve of Julien's coat, I didn't elaborate further. I didn't trust myself to be able to stop once the words started flowing as, for whatever reason, I found Julien an easy person to talk too. I wished I was able to talk to him about the prophecy, to let go of all the fear and anger and ask him what it was I needed to do. Could I trust him? The way he had spoken to Blight about the king made me feel like he might be closer to King Elias than he wanted me to know. On the other hand, as we sat there quietly, something Theo said at the Forest Festival rang in my mind. He told me Julien's family had a bad reputation around the village, but Julien didn't seem like a bad person. And from what I had found out over the last few days, it seemed like part of my family's reputation was even worse than Julien's. My intuition told me he was a good person, but I still couldn't deny the comments others had made about him. Maybe by divulging just a little to him I would be able to figure out his true nature.

"Have you ever felt like you were this particular person for your entire life, but then found out everyone else wanted you to be something different?"

The words came out of my mouth in what sounded like a single, mashed-up question, but understanding lightened Julien's dark eyes. An overwhelming sensation to be wrapped in Julien's arms washed over me. To be held in a tight embrace as if nothing could hurt me. I had always been someone who never needed to be surrounded by people, happy in my own company, but since finding out about the prophecy I had never felt so alone. Julien considered my question before he responded, his brows furrowed in thought.

"Yes. My family always expected so much from me. They wanted me to be someone I wasn't, and I have probably turned out to be their biggest disappointment."

His voice sounded sad, but there was also a small amount of bitterness tinging his words. He clearly wanted nothing to do with his family or what they stood for, so it made me wonder how true Theo's story was and how much had been spread by malicious rumours.

"So what does your family want you to be, Braelyn? I can't imagine Hazel pressuring you to be anything other than what you are?"

His voice had resumed its light and teasing tone and my heart fluttered a little in my chest. Breathing in the cool night air to steady my racing pulse, I chose my words carefully, so as not to give too much away. As much as my heart told me that many people's perceptions about Julien were not entirely true, my head told me I needed to tread carefully with this new information.

"Hazel recently told me something important about my family. She also said I would need to face this new truth with courage and strength because people are relying on me to fix this problem."

Saying these words aloud—no matter how carefully thought out they were—made me feel like a heavy weight had been lifted off my shoulders. Admitting this truth not only to Julien but myself didn't seem dreadful, but I knew the reality of the situation. It was dire, and without me Ellesmere's fate would be imperilled. My mind flashed to the monsters from my vision, sending a cold shiver down my spine—despite Julien's warm coat. I couldn't let that happen. Rubbing my thumb over my spirit rune, I found Julien's handsome face watching me closely.

Sighing, I continued. "So I came out here to try and work through this newfound information, away from the intense gaze of my grandmother. And I think I know what I need to do."

A smirk pulled up the corner of his mouth, a small dimple forming on his cheek. "So you thought a good place to process would be at the edge of the Ironwood?"

His tone was amused, though teasing. It was pitch black now as the moon hid behind some clouds and, despite not wanting to acknowledge Julien's words, he did have a very valid point.

"Well it seemed like a good idea at the time." I retorted. A small smile tugging at my lips.

Julien laughed softly and shook his head. "Your willingness to throw yourself into danger astounds me, Braelyn. Whatever you need to work through, I'm sure you will work it out because you might just be one of the bravest witches I know."

My eyes widened at his comment, and I waited for him to laugh and come up with a quip that showed me he was joking, but he stayed silent. His eyes were full of wonder and I felt lighter than I had in days. I couldn't quite believe that Julien Thorne—the person everyone in the Ironwood Village seemed to be wary of—was the one to help me.

A noise to the right of me made me jump, startling me out of my thoughts. Julien was on his feet in an instant, a flame blossoming from the palm of his left hand, ready to use it against an oncoming attacker. But as my eyes adjusted to the darkness, I realised with a sinking heart it wasn't an enemy at all. Though, with the look of rage appearing on the face of the person standing before us, Julien might not say the same.

Twelve

Hazel stood by the small crop of trees bordering the clearing and her cottage, her face contorted with rage in the glowing light of a lantern. I had never seen her quite this angry. Her nostrils were flared and her small hand clutched the lantern so tightly the metal squealed in protest. Julien lowered his hands and the flames flickered out without a second thought. Hazel continued to glare between Julien and me as if she was weighing up which one she was going to devour first. I saved her the hassle and stood up, handing Julien his coat back with a mouthed "Thank you". He didn't reply, but simply nodded once. I didn't blame him for not wanting to speak. Hazel's eyes were still narrowed in Julien's direction as I opened my mouth to apologise, but she simply held her finger up in warning. My mouth hung open, and I didn't dare antagonise her any more than I already had tonight. Turning, Hazel stormed back through the trees towards her cottage without a word. Glancing back at Julien, he gave me a playful wink and, smiling to myself, I followed in Hazel's stead. We walked through the woods in utter silence. Not even the sound of nocturnal animals could be heard as we followed the path back to Hazel's garden. It made the night feel eerie, dead, and I shivered against the cold chill of both the darkness and Hazel's anger. The walk back to the cottage felt longer than any I had ever done. Anger still radiated off Hazel in waves as her shoulders remained tense, and her hand was white from gripping the lantern tightly. We finally reached the door of the cottage and I was eager to get in and warm my frozen body by the fire. My teeth chattered audibly as Hazel huffed loudly in my direction, probably at my stupidity at not taking a coat with me. As I stepped over the threshold, the warmth of the fire enveloped me. Feeling like I had been wrapped in a large warm blanket, I smiled at the instant comfort, but my happiness was short-lived as Hazel launched into a tirade over my actions.

"Are you stupid, child? What were you thinking wandering off into the woods like that? Especially after everything I have told you. Do you understand how much danger you put yourself in by gallivanting off by yourself? And to go to the Ironwood of all places." Hazel's eyes bore into me, her hands on her hips, waiting for a response.

"I'm sorry," I replied. "I just needed some time to think. And I didn't mean to go to the Ironwood. I just sort of ended up there."

Speaking the words aloud spurred something in the back of my mind. I wasn't sure how I ended up at the edge of the Ironwood in the first place. It seemed like my mind had instinctively led me there on its own.

"Well, even if you didn't intend to end up at the Ironwood, it was foolish. The woods aren't safe after dark if you don't know your way around them." Shaking her head, Hazel took a deep breath. "And what were you doing with the Thorne boy?" she said, raising a thin grey brow at me.

Annoyance flickered inside me at her tone. Hazel obviously had the same opinions about Julien that the rest of the village did. I wanted to tell her about the way he had made me feel better about this whole situation, but the image of her wrathful face back in the clearing stopped me. My body ached with exhaustion, and I didn't think I could handle another fiery battle with Hazel right now.

"Julien was already there when I ended up in the clearing. He just kept me company and we talked for a while."

Hazel's eyes narrowed at me, and I sighed.

"I didn't tell him about the prophecy." The words came out calmer than I expected. "I don't understand why you all think so badly of him?"

Hazel let out an exasperated sigh. "His family has a bad reputation, Braelyn."

"Yeah, so everyone keeps telling me, but that doesn't mean he is a bad person, Hazel." Folding my arms across my chest, Hazel's emerald eyes narrowed in my direction.

"The Thorne family are known to be the king's followers. Both of Julien's parents sided with him when the war broke out and many don't trust Julien because of this."

I shook my head. "Just because someone comes from a bad family doesn't make them a bad person."

"No it doesn't, child, but it does leave horrible reminders for those who suffered from the terrors the king's followers unleashed." Hazel rubbed a wrinkled hand over her face, stifling a yawn. "I think that's enough excitement for one day. Clean yourself off and get to bed. We need to be up early tomorrow."

She latched the chain lock on the front door and waved goodnight to me as she made her way to her bedroom. I heard the door click shut and let out a long breath. Somehow I had known deep inside that Julien's family had been involved with the king but, instead of feeling terror towards him, my heart ached in sympathy. I knew how it felt to be associated with someone who did terrible things that you didn't agree with, and maybe that's what connected me so closely with Julien. Rubbing at my tired, sore eyes, a large yawn escaped my mouth. Making my way to my mother's old bedroom, too tired to wash away the dirt and dust clinging to my skin from my hours of training, I lay down on top of the covers. As I closed my eyes and welcomed the darkness, my muscles slowly relaxed and sleep settled over me. The last thing that flashed through my mind was the tall trees of the Ironwood and a pair of crimson eyes looking back at me from the dark.

I woke the next morning to Hazel nudging me, and I blinked a few times, trying to shake the sleepiness from my eyes. Hazel had opened the curtains to my window and left a dress on the end of my bed. It must have been early morning as the sun hadn't yet risen and moonlight still flooded the small room with silvery light. As I glanced at the dress Hazel had left me, I sucked in a breath. I had never seen anything so pretty. The fabric was soft and creamy, and all over the dress were tiny sprigs of embroidered lavender. Someone had taken extreme care to make such a beautiful piece. Once dressed, I pulled a comb through my tangled mess of hair and watched as my usual waves pulled straight through the comb's teeth before bouncing back into place. Bits stuck out here and there, but it was the best it was ever going to get. Opening the bedroom window to check the temperature outside, a cool breeze blew onto my face, sending goosebumps over my arms. Rifling through the dresser, I found a knitted jumper almost the same colour as the fabric of the dress and tucked it under my arm. Coming into the living area where Hazel was waiting for me with her back turned, I cleared my throat to let her know I was ready. Catching a glimpse of me as she turned towards the door, she stopped and looked me up and down, as if assessing whether I looked presentable enough. But instead of a terse comment or chastising, she surprised me.

"You look just like Nora did when she was your age." Her voice sounded mystical and reminiscent, and I felt bad for thinking she was going to say something mean.

Hazel had tried to make me feel comfortable and safe, and my stomach clenched at how horrible I had acted towards her last night. It seemed hot-headedness ran in the family. Giving her a small smile, we left the cottage to make our way into the village for the last day of the Autumn Equinox and the Mabon Festival. Hazel had told me the Mabon Festival was the last celebration of autumn and was one of the biggest festivals of the year, aside from Yule season. She also told me the Mabon festivities lasted from sunrise to sunset, and everyone ate and danced merrily until well into the night. It was apparently a very magical time.

We arrived at the village just a few minutes after leaving the cottage and Hazel hadn't been exaggerating. The entire village had been transformed into what could only be described as a fairy land. Small twinkling lights covered every building in the town square, glittering like hundreds of fireflies between the shops and houses. The large well in the middle of the square had been decorated with vines of ivy that wrapped and fell around the stones like a large crown. As we crossed the square, I spotted Theo standing with a woman who must be his mother. She was a pretty witch with the same spattering of freckles Theo possessed. Their hair was a matching shade of dirty blonde and she had it tucked behind her ears which stuck out from her face. The shop they stood before had been decorated in the spirit of Mabon. Candles and pumpkins littered the small window and small ornaments made from broken sticks and twine hung from the small doorway. I hadn't seen or spoken to Theo since yesterday afternoon and I worried about how he would react towards me. I'd never had the chance to apologise for storming off like a bad-tempered child last night. My stomach did small flips as nerves bubbled up inside me, but when we came to stop in front of the sweet-smelling shop I was relieved to see Theo's happy, lopsided smile beaming down at me.

"Happy Mabon," Theo chimed.

His usual jeans and sweater had been replaced with more formal attire. Dressed in brown suede pants and a white button up shirt—that appeared as if someone had placed a dirty handprint right at the bottom—he cut quite the dashing figure.

"And happy Mabon to you too," I replied, trying not to laugh. "You know someone's dirtied your shirt?"

Theo glanced down, looking more than annoyed. Spinning around, three curly-haired little girls giggled as Theo's cheeks blazed a dark crimson. His siblings seemed to have found a pile of dirt that littered the bottom of the shop's window and had begun placing filthy handprints on whatever was closest to them. Poor Theo happened to be one of those things. Telling the three of them off, they simply stuck their tongue out and continued their game. I grinned as he turned around and muttered something unintelligible before pulling me towards the middle of the square, away from his younger sisters. We walked in silence to the fountain where we had sat for the Forest Festival, but instead of allowing a place to sit, hundreds of candles flickered in the early morning breeze. All were differing sizes and created a warm hue that made the stone fountain seem so much more dark and eerie than it normally was.

"I'm sorry about what happened last night, Theo. I wanted to apologise when Hazel brought me back to the cottage, but you weren't there." I picked at a loose thread on my cream sweater, thankful I had thrown it on over my dress. The early morning was still crisp. I didn't have the courage to look at Theo as I waited for his reply, too frightened about what I might find in his expression. I didn't think my heart could take losing his friendship. Feeling a soft touch on my shoulder, I looked up to find Theo's sea-blue eyes gazing down at me. I gave him a small smile which he returned, and I instantly felt relief flood through me. He wasn't mad.

"You don't need to apologise to me, Brae. You were upset." Pausing, he gave my shoulder a tight squeeze. "Just know that you are one of the bravest and most courageous witches I know. Whatever this prophecy throws at you, King Elias doesn't stand a chance."

My heart lifted as I felt the sting of tears behind my eyes. Throwing my arms around Theo's torso, I wrapped him in a tight hug, not knowing what I'd done to deserve his friendship. My cheek rested on his bony chest as his low chuckle reverberated through me. After my tearful apology, we took a seat on some small wooden boxes that had been scattered around the cobblestoned square as makeshift seats. A low thrumming sounded from somewhere behind me. The noise was soft and airy, like the strings of a harp. From the beautiful notes dancing in the air, I guessed the musicians were elves. Only they could make music feel like a picture was being painted before you. Observing my surroundings, I found my assumptions were correct. Three beautiful elves stood in a corner of the village, not far from Julien's apothecary. Their eyes were closed against the growing morning light as they swayed to the flow of the music. The tallest of the three stood at the front of the group, his long fingers brushing the strings of a large gold harp that seemed to match the colour of his hair, which flowed long and string-like over his shoulders. His skin was tinged a funny shade of green, and as my eyes lingered on his face, I came to realise he was covered in forest moss. It ran down one side of his face and cascaded onto his broad bare chest. *Did any of these elves wear shirts?* Unlike the golden-haired elf, the other two were shorter in stature, but still towered over the many passing witches and warlocks. They looked so similar I thought they might have been twins. Their dark hair fell in waves around their faces, and both wore tunics of sheer white fabric that showed the faintest pattern of orange leaves tattooing their dark skin. They were all so beautiful and, together, they were mesmerising. Wondering if the elf I had run into at the Forest Festival would be here again, I surveyed my surroundings and, sure enough, caught the silver elf staring in my direction. His eyes locked with mine as a chill ran down my spine. Shivering, I pulled my gaze away, turning to Theo.

"Who's that elf over there by the musicians?" I asked, keeping my voice light and curious.

Theo followed my line of sight and frowned. "Oh, that's Balor. He is the prince of the Ironwood Elves."

It made sense now. He had the air of a snobby prince who thought everyone else was beneath him. I thought his dislike towards me was because I was a witch, but seeing him briefly amongst the other elves of the Ironwood, he seemed to look down his nose at them as well.

"Is he dangerous?" I asked quietly. While there weren't many people near us, I didn't want anyone to overhear and inform Balor. I didn't need another reason for him not to like me.

Theo thought for a second before he replied. "I don't think so. His father, King Draven, was known to be a great warrior and hunter but, since the royal war with King Elias, the elves have kept their distance. We only see them at celebrations like this one, where they can perform, drink our mead and get supplies." He cocked an eyebrow at me questioningly. "Why, has he said something to you?"

I shook my head. "No, nothing. I just get the feeling he doesn't like me."

Theo shrugged nonchalantly. "I wouldn't take it personally, Brae. Not many of the high elves like witches and warlocks much."

"Then why do they come here? If they dislike us that much?"

"For the fun," Theo said.

I threw a quick look towards Balor and the other elves. The prince glowered at his surroundings but the other elves seemed to be having a joyous time. Giving Theo a reassuring smile, I changed the subject to something a little more light-hearted, pushing my thoughts of Balor aside.

"Why do we need to be up so early for Mabon?" I asked, covering my mouth to stifle a long yawn.

"It's tradition to watch the sun rise on the last day of the Autumn Equinox. It's almost like a thank you to the sun for blessing the bounty the elements have bestowed upon us throughout autumn." Theo shrugged his shoulders as if he thought it was ridiculous.

"You don't believe the elements gift us our magic and give us all this?" I waved my arm around the magical village still glittering like a million stars against the night sky.

My mother had told me the elements were what made us who we are and that we should always give thanks to them when the time presented itself. There would be many times as a child I would find my mother in the back room at the apothecary, giving her thanks at the small alter we had set up. It was nothing special, just a small wooden desk so old the brown paint would peel and chip anytime someone placed a hand upon it. A bowl of water would be laid out on the table, surrounded by dried leaves and sprigs of flowers suited to each season. A white candle would always be burning, and the tiny flame would flicker and ripple in the reflection of the water. Incense represented air and burnt continuously, spreading its misty tendrils into every corner of the apothecary.

Smiling at the memory, I waited for Theo to answer me.

"It's not that I don't believe it exactly, it's just…" Theo rubbed the back of his neck, cheeks reddening. "I'm not very good with my magic and, the more I practice, the worse I seem to get. Sometimes I think only part of my rune was administered." His face was resigned, almost bitter. "I just don't want to give thanks to the elements for gifting me faulty magic." Theo turned away, but I couldn't mistake the sadness in his voice.

Thinking about the last few days practicing with my own magic, it only just occurred to me that I had never seen Theo use his earth magic at all. Everyone else had been happy to show me tricks and teach me all they had learnt, but Theo had always stayed quiet. I had thought it was because Hazel, being an earth witch herself, had taken charge of training me in that element, but I'd never expected him not to know how to wield his magic. I placed a hand on his shoulder and squeezed, and Theo turned his eyes towards me. His bright eyes were rimmed red as he gave me a gentle smile.

"Come on," I said, jumping up from the little wooden box. I reached for his hand and pulled Theo to his feet. My small hand fit perfectly in his large one. "Enough talk of magic and training, let's just enjoy the festival together."

Theo's eyes crinkled at the sides as he gave me one of his usual toothy grins. "Sounds like fun."

The Mabon Festival activities carried on throughout the day and into the early evening. Music streamed continuously, keeping the atmosphere light and happy. Witches, warlocks and elves alike mingled together and, while the uneasiness I had felt at the beginning of the festival was still there, my spirits had lifted as I sat with Theo under a large tree just to the side of the village square.

I had never been to such an extravagant event. Food was laid out on long tables arranged around the candlelit fountain, and everyone talked and laughed as they ate the delicious food that had been brought by everyone in the Ironwood Village. The tables were strewn with roasted pumpkins smelling of cinnamon and the bread was still warm, as if it had been pulled from the oven and put directly onto the tables to cool. Baked apples were dotted throughout the table, and I watched as Theo's younger siblings dipped them in melted caramel, sticky syrup running down their little arms as they danced around. Theo handed me a silver cup filled with steaming liquid which smelt strongly like apple pie, and I took a tentative sip, not knowing what was inside. My insides warmed instantly. The hot cider was an explosion of flavours. The flavours of apple, cinnamon and honey danced on my tongue, making me feel as if a fire had been lit inside my chest. I closed my eyes as the warmth washed through me and the elvish music called with beckoning fingers. I gave Theo a warm smile as I opened my eyes, pulling him towards the music. Despite his best efforts to escape my grasp, in the end he gave up trying to shake me off and joined me as we lost ourselves to the music.

We managed to dance through two extremely long acoustic songs and, by the time we finished, I could feel the cider sitting heavy in my stomach. The music made me feel light as a feather floating in the autumn breeze. We laughed together as we stepped underneath the low hanging trees, fairy lights still twinkling elegantly amongst the leaves. I noticed everyone's attention had been pulled away from the food-laden tables, faces turned to the street opposite the woods. People whispered, craning their heads to see.

"What's everyone looking at?" I asked Theo quietly, taking another sip of cooling cider.

He shrugged his shoulders while making his way over to the fountain. A flurry of noise above caught my attention and, glancing up to the night sky, a murder of crows descended, coming to rest on the brown wooden roof of one of the buildings. Eleven. My breath hitched in my throat. *Eleven crows you are surprised to see, your secrets shall be revealed to thee.* I pushed aside some of the flickering candles still burning brightly on the fountain's edge. My heart pounded in my chest as I stood on the edge of the fountain and finally had a bird's eye view of what everyone was looking at. A dark silhouette, half hidden in shadow, stood at the edge of the square. At first, I thought it was just a trick of my eyes, but as the shadowy figure moved into the light, I realised it wasn't a shadow at all. Pulling back a black feathered hood, a tall witch stood in a pool of lamplight at the edge of the village, scanning the group of people gathered before her. Bloodless skin was pulled tight across the bones in her face, and from where I was standing, she looked deathly ill. Her large, obsidian eyes stood out stark against her face like two menacing black orbs. Her cloak swayed around her feet as she made her way through the parting crowd, stopping just before the fountain's edge. A fiery-haired warlock who looked to be no older than my mother was the first to break the numbing silence.

"Who are you?" The warlock's voice came out strong, echoing around the gathering of people.

Tiny whispers still rippled around the group, but the square was so quiet you could have heard a pin drop.

"My name is Morrigan, and I come on behalf of King Elias." Her words rang out around the square.

At the mention of the king's name, hushed whispers spread through the crowd, setting tensions high. I threw a quick glance towards Theo, whose face had paled.

"Why are you here, Morrigan?" said a grey-haired witch who I recalled seeing at the Forest Festival but, unlike the warlock, her voice wavered.

Looking around the crowd of witches, warlocks and elves, I could see the same expressions reflected at me. Everyone was frightened and on edge. Eyes bulged and chins trembled in fear. The crows' ominous message rang in the back of my mind all the while.

"I have come to deliver a message to the spirit witch." Her words were as cold as ice and pierced my heart like a shard of glass.

She was here for *me*. The king had finally decided to challenge me. A chorus of voices erupted around the crowd of witches, warlocks, and elves, all of them exclaiming there were no spirit witches around and there hadn't been for many years. Theo stiffened beside me and I searched for Hazel's familiar face, but she was lost in the sea of people now scrambling to find their friends or family members. No doubt to talk about the unknown spirit witch who was standing only metres away from them.

"There's no spirit witch in this village," I heard a young witch yell out to Morrigan as more witches and warlocks plucked up the courage to shout the same thing.

The elves had begun to gather in a small group near the musicians. They spoke in hushed tones and threw wary glances around the crowd, as if trying to sense where the spirit witch was located.

"Silence," yelled Morrigan.

Her voice boomed like thunder, and she was growing more impatient with every shout. Her anger flashed like grey clouds before a storm.

"You're all fools," she spat. "A spirit witch stands among you and you don't even know the power she possesses." Morrigan focused her dark eyes directly on my face.

Hands trembling by my sides, my breath came in quick bursts, heart thudding loudly in my ears. Theo and I still stood on the edge of the well, clearly visible to every witch, warlock, and elf in the village. Theo took my hand and squeezed tightly. A sea of blank faces looked up at me. Half of them had never seen me before now.

Swallowing, I took a shaky breath. "How is it you know who I am?" My voice wavering slightly at the end.

Morrigan let out a high-pitched cackle, sounding more like the crows still sitting above us. "You would do better to hide your rune, girl. The king spied it the first time he saw you."

Whispers spread through the crowd like a growing song played on the elves' harps. The buzz grew louder as all eyes turned to me. I fidgeted where I stood, suddenly feeling extremely exposed upon the fountain's edge, remembering the day at the Forest Festival when I had encountered the warlock by the book tent.

Pointing a long, gnarled finger in my direction, Morrigan's voice echoed loudly. "Braelyn Gray, King Elias wishes to meet the next heir to his throne. He will be expecting you to come to his castle in three days." Morrigan held up three fingers. Her nails were long and sharpened like knives. I shuddered to think what harm she could bring with them. I swallowed hard before replying.

"And what if I refuse?" I asked, my voice loud in the silence.

A few quiet gasps reached my ears from the witches and warlocks closest to me. My guess was that King Elias's invitations didn't often get refused. Morrigan's lips parted, her cruel laugh filling the air.

"Well, let's just say that if you don't come, someone you love will pay the price for your foolishness." A large toothy grin filled her mouth and twisted her features as she clicked her fingers—a dark cloud rippling into focus. At first, I couldn't make out the picture materialising in front of me, but as the smoke stilled, I saw my worst nightmare. My breath caught in my throat and my legs shook, threatening to give out from beneath me. In the glistening orb balanced on Morrigan's hand like a crystal ball, was my mother. She was sitting in a dark and dingy room which, from the look of the bars in front of her, could have only been a dungeon cell. My hands began to shake as I quickly pulled away from Theo's grip. My palms tingled and I felt the spark of magic before I saw it. A small fork of lightning shot from my fingertips, making the flames on the candles before me spark and spit fire. A few witches standing near Morrigan jumped aside—frightened looks on their faces—but Morrigan simply remained where she stood, a gleam in her beady black eyes. Feeling Theo's hand rest on my shoulder, I tried to rein in my anger before my magic spiralled out of control.

"Tell King Elias I'll be seeing him soon," I ground out between my teeth.

My hands still shook with rage, but I had managed to restrain my magic—despite the tingling still rippling through my palms. Morrigan clicked her fingers and the orb vanished into thin air. Smiling wickedly, Morrigan flicked her hood back over her shimmering dark hair and made to leave the way she had come, but something made her pause. Turning back to me, her black eyes met mine.

"Make sure you're on time, Braelyn Grey; the king doesn't like to be kept waiting." Smirking, she turned on her heel and glided out of the village like smoke on a breeze, leaving everyone's gaze focused directly on me.

Thirteen

The weight of every witch, warlock, and elf's stare crushed me like rocks. No matter how many deep breaths I tried to take, I simply couldn't catch my breath. Placing a sturdy hand on my elbow, Theo carefully pulled me down from the fountain, trying to shield me from the prying eyes of anyone standing close by. My stomach churned and my ears rang. It felt like a loud blast had gone off beside me. I could hear the hum of chatter, but my mind couldn't comprehend a word coming out of their mouths. Theo dragged me along behind him, his hand strong and familiar on my elbow like an anchor keeping me from drifting away. As we reached the small bakery we stood at earlier, Theo pushed on the wooden door, pulling me inside the dark shop. Placing me on a soft bench by the window, he disappeared into the dark store. My mind reeled. King Elias had taken my mother prisoner to use as leverage. After all these years of hiding, he had finally found her only days after I had come to Ellesmere. None of it made sense. How had he managed to find her? I swiped at the tears beginning to tumble down my cheeks and took another deep breath, trying to calm my racing heart. Theo came back with a glass of water, handing it to me as he sat down and gently took my free hand in his own.

"Are you okay?" he asked quietly, concern lacing his tone. I looked up into his blue eyes, lip trembling ever so slightly. He squeezed my hand as the tears continued to fall.

"I don't understand how he found her Theo. After all this time, why now?" My voice hitched on the last word. It made no sense to me. Only a handful of people in the village knew who I really was, and I knew deep in my heart none of them would have betrayed me to the king. The image of my mother sitting on the cold concrete floor made me shiver as Theo replied.

"I don't know either Brae, but…" Theo's voice trailed off as something appeared to dawn on him, a crease forming between his bushy brows.

"What is it?" I asked, leaning toward him.

"It's just, I think I know how King Elias was able to find your mother, Brae." He rested his hand on his chin, brows still pinched in thought. "I remember reading in one of our history books that, occasionally, the magic of old can be used to trace the whereabouts of witches and warlocks. It's like the magic sends out a beacon to anyone who is searching."

"But it makes no sense Theo. I never used any of my magic at the apothecary."

Theo shook his head. "That doesn't matter, Brae. If King Elias knew about the prophecy, he could have been searching for a spirit witch long before you received your element rune. Once they administered it, your magic would have led him right to you."

I stared wide-eyed at my friend, fresh tears threatening to overflow. "But why would he take my mother? Why wouldn't he just come after me?"

"I don't know, Brae, but I promise we will find out." He gave me a small smile and pulled me into a hug that made me relax into his embrace.

Over Theo's shoulder, I could see Julien walking in our direction. His eyes found mine through the window and his expression looked like it had been carved from stone. Pulling away from Theo, I stood from the bench and went out into the bustling street to meet him. Julien closed the distance between us in a few long strides. He stood so close to me I could see the small flecks of amber in his deep brown eyes.

"Are you okay?" Julien's voice echoed concern as his hand flew to my cheek.

It smelt of burnt wood and smoke, and I leaned into the calloused palm. His thumb traced my cheek bone, the rough skin of his fingers tickling my skin. Theo stared through the bakery window at us with a strange look on his face. Gently, I pulled Julien's hand away, not wanting Theo to suspect anything was happening between us. While I couldn't deny my feelings for Julien had grown, I didn't need everyone else knowing how I felt about him. The time would come when I would need to tell Theo my feelings but, for now, the only thing that mattered was finding my mother.

"I'm fine. It's just... I have to find her, Julien. She is in this mess because of me." I bit the side of my lip to stop it from trembling.

"It's okay, Braelyn. We will find her. That's why I came to find you. I know a way to get to your mother quickly, but it's a dangerous journey."

I shook my head. "I don't care, just tell me how."

Julien chuckled, his shaggy brown curls bouncing slightly. "Always willing to put yourself in the middle of harm's way. You certainly are a thrill seeker, Braelyn Grey." My heart fluttered as he said my name. "I'll meet you at the edge of the Ironwood later tonight—in the clearing where we spoke the other night. Don't worry, sweetheart, we will find your mother." With one last smile, Julien released my hand and disappeared into the crowd.

I ran my hands over my face. A headache had begun to form, and I rubbed at my temples, willing it to disappear. Hearing the heavy wooden door groan behind me, I pulled my head up.

"What did Julien Thorne want?" Theo's voice was low, and I could hear the concern lacing his words. I knew he had his reservations about Julien, but we needed his help. I just hoped Theo would eventually understand.

"He said he knows a quick way to find my mother." I shrugged, hoping it would be enough for Theo to drop talk of Julien.

Heavy footsteps made me glance up and, as the small group of witches in front of us parted, I saw Hazel hurrying towards us. Her long skirts were gathered in her hands, her brows knitted together. My heart lifted in my chest as I closed the distance between us. As she threw her arms around me, I almost sank to the ground in utter exhaustion. I sobbed into Hazel's chest as she brushed my hair back from my face, making shushing sounds in my ear. Hot tears swept down my face but, slowly, my chest eased, my breathing returning to normal. Hazel held me at arm's length, looking into my face as if assessing me like one would a crystal ball.

"Where have you been?" I blurted out.

I had searched the crowd for her face after Morrigan left the village, but I hadn't been able to spot her anywhere. Now was the first time I was seeing her since we arrived at the Mabon Festival many hours earlier.

"I'm sorry, child. After Morrigan left, the elders of the village accosted me. They want to speak with you, and I have been rushing around for the last few minutes searching for you." Her cheeks were flushed and beads of sweat dotted her hairline. I felt terrible for causing her stress, but the mention of the elders had caught my attention, making me feel queasy.

"What do they want to see me for?" I asked.

I knew it was a stupid question the moment it shot from my mouth, but Hazel only took my hand in hers, dragging me towards the street Morrigan had come through.

"The elders resolve matters of importance. It's customary to make sure order is upheld throughout the village by the witches and warlocks who live here."

We rounded a corner just a few metres away from the main square, and a large stone building loomed in front of us. The exterior was much like every other building in the village, but the high, pointed roof and large wooden door made it stand out from the rest. As we approached the front steps, voices rose from the depths of the building.

"What is this?" I asked, keeping my voice low.

Hazel slowed as we ascended the stone stairs and pushed

through the crowd of witches and warlocks who stood inside—they had obviously made their way here after Morrigan left. As we neared the front of the large room, she turned to me.

"This is the meeting hall where the elders discuss town affairs. They will want to speak with you about Morrigan and your mother." She looked me up and down, assessing my appearance. Wiping my clammy hands on the front of my dress, I instantly felt self-conscious and wary of the elders I was about to meet. Smiling down at me, Hazel pushed a stray curl behind my ear.

"You will be fine, child. Just speak when you are spoken to. Everything will be alright."

Hazel pushed me towards the front of the room and took her place at the front of the crowd. As the line of people parted for me, a long table came into view, where four people sat and stared down at me—expressions of interest and concern written across their faces.

The elders appeared to be around the same age as Hazel and looked to be wise beyond their years. Upon a large dais sat two witches and two warlocks, who peered down at me. The witch who sat in one of the centre seats raised a hand to the gathering of people behind me and a hush fell over the room. My heart beat so loudly I was sure everyone could hear.

"Braelyn Grey, do you know why you have been brought before us?" The witch's voice echoed around the quiet hall. Her long dark hair was streaked with grey and it fell in front of her as she leant on the wooden table. Not trusting my voice to stay strong, I nodded my head once and waited for her to speak again.

"Good." Her voice was sharp and crisp, but not nasty. She got straight to the point. "Fellow witches and warlocks of the Ironwood Village, we are faced with a very rare problem."

A wave of whispers began to spread through the people behind me. I glanced around quickly, looking for comfort in the familiarity of Hazel's face. When I caught her eye, I also spotted Theo standing amongst an array of aging warlocks. He gave me a reassuring nod and the tension in my muscles eased slightly. I faced the elders once again, and the warlock seated on one end of the table raised his hand for silence.

"Braelyn Grey, does Morrigan speak the truth? Are you a witch of Spiritus Magicae?" His voice was deep and smooth.

I took a deep breath. "Yes, it is true. I do have the ability to use spirit magic."

The crowd behind me erupted in conversation. So many voices echoed around the once silent room that my head began to throb at the sound. Pressing a hand to my temple, I massaged the spot where the pain blossomed, hoping the noise would stop.

"Silence!" yelled the first witch.

Her voice boomed around the hall and everyone immediately fell silent. She inclined her head to her colleague for him to continue his questioning.

"And is it true that your mother is Nora Grey, the woman who Morrigan showed in the orb?"

I nodded again, not wanting to speak out of fear of crying. I kept my eyes focused on the four elders in front of me, trying to blink back the tears.

"And do you know how to wield your spirit magic?"

The four elders watched me carefully as I thought about my answer. While my sessions at the cottage were a success and most of my magic seemed to come naturally, the memory of losing control of my fire magic still burned inside me. I didn't know how to fully wield my magic, but the elders didn't need to know.

"I have been practising my magic and feel I can wield it well enough." My voice came out louder than I expected.

Opening my mouth to try and explain what little training I had done, the second witch—who appeared to be the eldest of the four—got to her feet and placed a shaking hand on the warlock next to her, steadying herself.

"I know you are not telling the truth, young spirit witch" Her voice was raspy, like she hadn't used it in a long time. "Braelyn Grey, I have been around a long time and know when I am being lied to." She looked between the other elders, who all dipped their head lightly as if agreeing to some unspoken decision. "As you have not had enough physical training, it would not be safe or wise for you to meet with King Elias."

The crowd murmured behind me, but I could barely hear them over the ringing in my ears. My mouth hung open in astonishment as I stood in front of the elders, dumbfounded by their decision.

"But what about my mother? She is being held captive by the king and, if I don't show up, he will hurt her!" *Or worse,* I thought. My eyes darted to each of the elders, searching their face for sympathy or support, but there was nothing. The witch who had spoken—clearly the eldest of the four—continued.

"Miss Grey, while it is tragic news about your mother, we cannot risk the safety of the only known spirit witch for the safety of an air witch who abandoned her fellow witches and warlocks over a decade ago." Her words were not unkind, but they were spoken with a finality I assumed was meant to put me in my place.

As the witches and warlocks in the room began to voice their agreement with the elderly witch, anger boiled up inside of me. My hands clenched into fists at my sides as the magic in my veins coursed to life. But before the faintest sign of magic appeared, I felt a soft touch on my arm. Theo had come to stand beside me. Looking into his freckled face, I could see the unspoken warning flickering behind his light eyes. As the room began to simmer into silence, I took a deep breath, trying to ease my temper before gazing back to the four elders.

"I'm sorry, but that can't be your decision. My mother is in trouble, and I need to ensure her safety, which is what she was doing for me when she left all those years ago."

The four elders of the Ironwood Village conferred in hushed tones. A few moments later their piercing gaze turned back to me. Bouncing between each foot eagerly, I waited for their response. As the elderly witch stood again before me, I felt my heart pick up its rhythm. My hands were slick with sweat.

"We're sorry, Miss Grey, we understand your need to find your mother but our decision still stands. You are too valuable to lose."

As the eldest witch spoke her last words, my head began to spin. Theo stiffened beside me as all hell broke out in the hall, but I barely heard a word. Swaying on the spot, my eyes unable to focus on anything, I saw a blurred figure rushing towards me and, before I knew it, everything went black.

Fourteen

My eyes fluttered open, and a wave of dizziness washed over me. Slowly sitting up, I searched my surroundings, realising I was no longer in the Ironwood Village. My head still felt foggy, but the last thing I could remember before everything went dark was being in the meeting hall. As my vision refocused, it dawned on me that I was back in Hazel's cottage. The bedroom door stood slightly ajar and the sounds of hushed voices floated up the hallway. I heard the distinct crispness of Hazel's voice, but the others were too hushed to distinguish.

My head throbbed and I rubbed my eyes to remove the heavy feeling threatening to pull my lids closed again. Through the slit in the curtains, the darkened sky offered no hints as to what time of day it was, but a quick glance at the small clock on the dresser told me it was quite late in the evening. I was still wearing my cream sweater and lavender print dress, but my leather boots had been removed and were placed at the end of my bed. Swinging my legs over the side, I rose carefully. My mind ran through the last thing the elders had said to me back at the village hall and a faint aching bloomed in my chest. They refused to help my mother, but I wouldn't let her rot away in the dungeons of King Elias's castle. Julien knew a way to get to the castle in time. He'd told me he would meet me at the edge of the Ironwood after Mabon, but how long had I been asleep for?

Creeping down the hall, I found Theo sitting at Hazel's

kitchen bench, his head bent over a steaming cup of tea. Upon seeing me, he rushed over in a flurry of long arms. Wrapping me in a tight embrace, he gave me a bear hug before letting me go and holding me at arms-length.

"Are you okay, Brae? I've been so worried."

"I'm okay," I replied. Placing my hand on Theo's arm, I gave it a reassuring squeeze.

Hazel was sitting in her armchair in front of the fire. She hadn't seemed to notice me until I walked to the edge of her chair, her eyes glazed and distant. She grasped a small teacup between her bony fingers, holding it close to her chest. Her green eyes were unfocused as she stared into the flickering fire, so I pressed my hand to her shoulder, startling her from her thoughts. The tea in her cup sloshed onto the saucer as she jumped. Apologising, she brushed it away with a quick flick of her hand. She placed the cup on the small table and, to my surprise, pulled me into a warm embrace. I felt my body relax. The tension of the evening's events were squeezed out of me like lemon in a juicer.

"Are you okay, child?" she whispered. Her voice soft and full of emotion and, as she pulled back, her eyes locked on my face.

I shrugged a shoulder. "I need to find her, Hazel. I can't stand by and just leave her in that awful place." My voice was firm as I stared down at my hands, clenching them into fists. I knew what I needed to do. The anger I expected to see in Hazel's face wasn't there. Instead sadness rimmed her eyes.

"I know, child, and I'm not going to stop you." Hazel grasped my hand in hers. "You have the same bravery that your father had. He would be proud of you."

A tear fell down my cheek and I brushed it away, giving Hazel a warm smile.

Theo had come to sit on the second armchair by Hazel's side. His gaze was turned away from us as he stared into the fire, his brows pulled together.

"I'm going to leave you two to discuss some things," Hazel said. "I'll be down the hall when you're ready, Braelyn."

Hazel left on quiet feet. Slumping into her armchair, I felt the soft cushions wrap around my tired body and I sighed softly.

"I'm leaving for Ellesmere Castle tonight."

I waited for Theo to say something, but he simply sat in front of the fire, just staring into the flames. Thinking he may not have heard me, I tried telling him again, and this time he blinked in my direction.

"I heard you the first time, Brae, but I just don't..." His voice trailed off as he paced slowly around the small living area, carving a path through Hazel's large rug. I watched him for a few seconds as he chewed at his nails before turning to face me. "The elders said you can't go!"

Now it was my turn to look surprised. I stared at him as if he had just slapped me. I knew Theo didn't like breaking rules or doing anything reckless, but I thought he would understand this situation was different.

"I know that's what they said, but I'm not going to leave my mother to rot in some dungeon. I'm going after her, with or without you." Feeling flustered, my annoyance at Theo rose inside me. If it was Theo's mother or siblings that were in trouble, I would not have questioned him and instead followed him to wherever he needed to go.

"Brae, you don't understand. The elders are the ones who uphold the law in the village. If you go to Ellesmere Castle against their wishes, there will be serious consequences." I could hear the panic in Theo's voice and knew I would be putting both of us at risk by leaving, but my mind was already made up. No amount of trouble was going to stop me from finding my mother. Besides, Julien said he knew the way.

"I have to do this, Theo. She's my mother. I can't lose her." The thought of anything happening to my mother made my stomach churn. Sighing deeply, Theo ran a giant hand over his face.

"Well, if you're going to throw yourself into unknown dangers, I can't let you do it alone." He smiled at me nervously, the motion not quite touching his eyes. Standing, I pulled him to me, wrapping

Kirsty Inic

my arms around his lanky frame.

"Thank you," I whispered.

"Don't thank me yet, Brae. We have to make it through the Ironwood first."

Fifteen

After agreeing to meet me at the edge of the Ironwood in one hour, Theo went home to grab some supplies. Making use of the alone time, I took a long shower, letting the steaming water ease some of the tension from my shoulders. Changing into a pair of dark trousers I found stuffed into the dresser, I threw a soft, honey-coloured jumper over the top of a white blouse that was a little tighter than I normally wore. Stuffing my feet into my leather boots and walking out into the kitchen, I noticed Hazel was standing by the bench with a small, wrapped parcel in her hands.

"Hazel, I…" But she didn't let me finish. Holding up one slender finger—this seemed to be our thing when I tried to say something she didn't want to hear—she silenced me.

"I don't want you to tell me anything, child, I believe it will be safer for you if I don't know what you have planned. If the elders come looking for you, I will be able to swear on the elements that I don't know your plans." Clearing her throat, she pushed the wrapped package into my arms.

"What's this?" I asked, turning the package over in my hands.

"Well, if you open it, you will find out." The clipped tone to Hazel's voice was back, making me smile at the familiar sound.

The small, square package was wrapped in a soft linen cloth, and as I unfolded the materiel, I found a small, brown leather satchel inside. It was beautifully crafted. The leather was slightly worn in places and soft from use, but I could tell someone had once loved this dearly.

"It's beautiful," I said. "Is it yours?"

Hazel chuckled and the notion lifted my spirits a little. After our evening at the Mabon Festival, it was a welcome sound.

"No child, it's not mine. It was your mother's. Your father made it for her as a gift when they first met." Her lips turned downward in a sad smile and her eyes grew distant as she was lost to a memory.

"It's gorgeous," I whispered. "Why did he make it for her?"

"Your mother loved being out in the forest as a child. She was always foraging for mushrooms and herbs. I always thought the elements had chosen wrong when she was gifted with air magic. She would never take a basket with her and often came home with her dress pockets stuffed full of plants and fungi." Hazel chuckled to herself.

The thought of my mother out in the forest, carefree and covered in dirt, remained a mystery to me. It was a side of her I had never seen and a part of me wondered if Hazel's story might have been why she'd never told me. It reminded her of my father.

"Your father was always thoughtful. He figured she would finally have somewhere to stuff her treasures and stop making me so mad at how dirty she would get."

I ran my fingers over the soft leather, feeling two small letters that had been pressed into the front of the bag. N.R. My mother's initials.

"Your father was a truly remarkable man, Braelyn. He was a talented air warlock, but he also had a knack for making things."

Hazel pulled out a miniature wooden object from her pocket. She placed it on top of the leather satchel, and I gazed at it, not really knowing what it was. At first glance it looked like a rabbit, but on closer inspection it had antlers just behind its ears. I tilted my head, trying to figure out what animal it could be.

"It's called a jackalope," Hazel explained as she sensed my confusion. "They are similar to rabbits, but not as friendly." She screwed her nose up a little as she said it.

Running my thumb over the smooth wood, I looked up at Hazel—who was watching me intently. My brows pulled together in a frown, still not understanding the meaning behind the toy. The small wood carving was beautiful—so intricately carved I could see every tiny detail.

"While a jackalope might be dangerous to some, they are fiercely loyal to those they love and offer protection to those who need it. They are rare creatures, and to see one is a great omen. They are often given for luck and protection."

Rounding the bench to stand before me, Hazel placed a warm hand on my cheek. The wet, musty smell of soil wafting up my noise.

"I have been wanting to give you that since you arrived, but it never seemed like the right time."

"What made you decide to give it to me now?" I asked.

Hazel's mouth twitched slightly at the corners, as if she was trying to hold back a laugh.

"Oh, just an old women's intuition that her granddaughter may need a good omen over the next few days."

Leaving the cottage just before midnight, I walked through the front garden, shooting a quick look behind me at the small wooden building that had become my home over the last week. I didn't know when I might see Hazel or the cottage again and my heart yearned to go back, but I couldn't abandon my mother. Taking a deep breath, I continued through the dark woods that would spit me out at the edge of the Ironwood.

The forest was bathed in darkness—even the dim light of the waxing moon did little to guide me through the trees. I thought of conjuring a small flame to help light the way, but I couldn't risk losing control of my fire magic. Keeping to the narrow footpath as best I could, the crunch of dried leaves and sticks under my boots were the only sounds in the eerie silence. Despite the darkness, I felt a calming sensation being out in the forest. The sounds of night animals rustled around me, and I focused on the path that lay before me.

A small lantern sat on the grass by the fallen tree Julien and I had sat on a few nights ago. I wasn't sure which of the boys had arrived to the clearing first, but upon closer inspection I saw it was Julien. He stood in the shadow of the dim yellow light, staring into the thicket of trees bordering the Ironwood. What little space that could be seen between the trees was near impossible to see in the darkness. Despite the late hour, the lack of light in this part of the woods felt different. Darkness seeped into every space between the trees, clinging to every living thing in sight. A small shiver ran down my spine as my eyes adjusted to the dense woods, a movement in the shadows catching my eye. I continued to stare into the trees, squinting as I tried to make out what lingered in the shadows. It looked to be the shape of a person, but its stance was much larger. It wavered slightly as if gesturing towards me, and I suddenly felt a strong urge to take a step forward onto the path. It was like someone was calling my name, beckoning me closer. I went to step forward when Julien's voice tugged at my mind.

"Braelyn."

Blinking a few times to clear the fog in my head, I turned around to find Julien frowning at me.

"Are you okay?" His voice echoed the concern reflected on his face.

Whatever magic had pulled me towards the Ironwood was now gone—along with the large shadow—but I couldn't shake the eerie feeling.

"Did you feel anything when you were looking into the trees?" I asked.

Julien shook his head firmly. "No. Nothing but trees and darkness."

Despite the calm tone, his response rested heavily on my chest. While I'd heard the whispered stories of the Ironwood in the small amount of time I had spent in the village, something else tugged at me. There was something *wrong* with these woods and I had a feeling the twisted, gnarled tree branches were only the beginning.

The snapping of a twig caught my attention and, spinning around to the entrance of the clearing, I found Theo stumbling along the path with a heavy backpack strung over his shoulders.

"Sorry, sorry, I know I'm late but…" His sentence trailed off as he spotted Julien standing next to me.

My stomach twisted into tight knots as I waited for his reaction.

"What is he doing here?" Theo shot at me.

I recoiled slightly at the severity of his words but, before I could reply, Julien beat me to it.

"Braelyn asked me to come along."

If Theo had been hurt by Julien's words, he didn't show it.

"We don't need you to come with us, Julien." Theo's tone was harsh, but Julien simply turned to him, a smirk plastered on his face.

"Oh really? Have you ever stepped foot into the Ironwood? Do you even know what path to take?" Julien waited for Theo's reply, but it never came. I could see he was defeated, that what Julien said was true. He knew the Ironwood and had ventured there many times. As much as it pained me to see Theo so hurt, we needed his help.

"He has a map with the safest and quickest way to get to the castle, Theo. I've already wasted too much time. We need Julien to come with us." I shot him a look of apology, hoping he would understand. "Please."

Theo gave a long sigh, but the sadness in his eyes remained. "Okay, Julien. Lead the way."

Julien's triumphant smile was his only response.

Theo hadn't spoken to me since we'd stepped into the dark treeline of the Ironwood. Julien had led us into the woods with only the dim light of the lantern lighting the way through the dark trees. I was curious to know why he didn't just conjure a flame and asked him as much when I caught up with him.

"The Ironwood reacts strangely to magic, Braelyn. It's best we refrain from using it unless absolutely necessary." His spoke softly, but with an edge that suggested the conversation was over, so we sank into unnatural silence.

The tension between Julien and Theo seemed to be growing and it made the air feel even heavier between the thick-set trees. I wanted to break the awkward silence between us, but it never seemed like the right time. Julien walked ahead of me, his nose buried in the worn map he carried and Theo's heavy footsteps sounded behind me on the stone pathway. Walking in a single line made it hard to start a conversation with either of them so, instead, I took in my surroundings, trying to commit every detail to memory. The Ironwood was nothing like the forest near Hazel's cottage. There the oak trees stood tall and broad, the sun's rays shining easily through the canopy, lightening the woods with a beautiful golden glow. Here the trees were small and twisted, huddled so closely the lantern light barely showed us what lay beyond their mangled trunks. The tiniest scurry of a forest animal echoed around the silent woods—leaving me guessing as to which direction it had come from—but it sent the strange feeling of magic running over my skin. The usual light tingling of magic in my fingers had been replaced with a feeling like static. Where before my magic ebbed and flowed in my veins like a smooth, running river, it now felt jagged and angry as if a dark storm brewed within me.

Sticking to the small path proved to be more difficult than I had anticipated and, even though he seemed to bring trouble with him wherever he went, I was glad Julien was with us. The path snaked through the gnarled trees, twisting and turning so often my head started to spin. Tree roots stuck out of the ground at every angle, threatening to trip us every chance they got, but Julien managed to spot most of them—calling out to us before we caught our feet in their tangled grip. Trying to avoid a rather large tree root that protruded from the moss-covered ground, I lost my balance. As I fell, Theo's steady hands caught the tops of my arms before I could hit the ground. Muttering embarrassed thanks, I tried to strike up a conversation with him. I felt terrible for upsetting him earlier and wanted to apologise, but I also wanted him to understand that, without Julien, we would have been lost the second we entered the Ironwood. While the path seemed easy enough to follow at the beginning of the woods, the farther we ventured, the more the dim light and surrounding trees made everything look identical. It would have been too easy for us to get turned in a circle without the use of Julien's map. Theo set me upright again and continued behind Julien without a second glance. Sighing in frustration, I picked up my pace to a slow jog to catch up with them both, the small leather satchel bouncing at my side.

Julien stuck out his arm abruptly, stopping me from walking any further. Feeling the air rush out of my chest with a whoomph, I moved to stand by Julien's right shoulder. It was the closest I had been to him since our conversation at the Mabon Festival, which now felt like a distant memory. The scent of burnt wood lingered on his jacket and my heart picked up its pace as I breathed in the heady smell. My fingers itched to reach out and feel the warmth of his hand in mine to ease the chill in my bones.

"What's the problem?" Theo asked. His voice dripped with agitation.

Julien held up a finger to silence him and Theo scoffed in annoyance. Squinting, I tried to see what had caught his eye, but there was nothing but a sea of darkness stretching silent and deadly before us. Standing on the tips of my toes, I leant in close to Julien's ear.

What is it?" I whispered.

Julien didn't say a word, but he held his hand out palm up to the night sky. A small flame blossomed, casting an orangey-red glow in front of us. With the flame and the lantern light, it made it easier to see what Julien was staring at. What I saw made my eyes go wide.

Standing a few metres ahead of us was a small creature no taller than my knees. It was covered in a grimy brown fur and its arms and legs looked almost too long for its stumpy body. Watching with rapt attention, it dug around in the underbrush as if looking for something it had lost. The creature was so intent on foraging and throwing around the mouldy damp leaves that it didn't seem to realise we were there. As we waited for the creature to move off into the trees, a noise from behind me caught its attention. I started at the sound and spun around quickly. Theo's large bag had knocked into a branch on one of the trees, but it wasn't the noise that had me covering my mouth with a shaky hand. Two of the brown-furred creatures sat perched on top of the branch, looking like cats ready to pounce on a mouse. Their greedy yellow eyes were glued to Theo's bag, which clinked noisily in the eerie silence. Taking a tentative step forward I held out my hand to Theo, my eyes urging him to take it. Sensing my panic he spun around, startling the creatures from their branch. With a high-pitched screech they lunged at Theo's bag, sharp claws tearing at the fabric, trying to get inside. As I tried to dispel the odd-looking creatures, I found Julien already there, his flaming hands held high. Not accustomed to the glowing brightness, one of the creatures hissed ferociously before they all skittered off in a flurry of dead leaves and cracking branches. Closing my eyes, I wiped a shaking hand over my forehead, drying the sweat beading my hairline.

"Watch what you're doing next time," Julien breathed out angrily before he spun around, lighting the path ahead.

Theo gave me an apologetic look and I spun back around. The first creature had now stopped its foraging, large yellow eyes watching us intently. I didn't know what to do. My instincts told me to turn in the opposite direction, but we needed to get past. As if Julien had heard my thoughts, he took a silent step towards the creature, his flames still held aloft. With a movement so quick I barely saw it, the creature ran off into the darkness.

"What was that?" I asked.

"It was a gremlin," Julien replied stiffly.

135

His expression was stern and the flame in his hand sputtered before he extinguished it by closing his palm.

"Are they bad?" I asked hesitantly, not really sure I wanted to know the answer.

The Ironwood seemed to fill with animal noises coming deep within the forest and, despite Julien's assumptions of my braveness, the long needle-like claws of the gremlins scared me. Julien shook his head, but it was Theo's voice that replied from behind me.

"No, they aren't bad, but they are mischievous creatures who love nothing more than to cause havoc for unsuspecting travellers."

I stared at Theo, my eyes going wide, not knowing whether to laugh or cry at the fact that a small, possum-like creature could be so devious as to plot against witches and warlocks venturing into the Ironwood. It was like a fairy tale, though, and seeing the glint of Julien's fire on its sharp, needle-like teeth made me feel a little weak at the knees.

"Come on, we need to get moving, there is a small alcove in the trees up ahead where we can camp for the night. If we keep the lantern lit, it should ward off the gremlins until the sun rises." Julien's hard voice pulled me out of my thoughts and I followed him farther into the Ironwood where I could only imagine what other creatures waited for us.

Sixteen

We stumbled into the small alcove of trees a little while later. The spot gave us a clear view of the path through the foliage while also protecting us from the cool wind that had picked up. The promise of early morning loomed over us. Julien had gone to collect wood to build a fire and I thought it the perfect time to broach the subject of Julien with Theo. He was sitting on the moss-covered ground not far from the edge of the path, rifling through his bag, looking for something. I crossed my legs as I sat next to him, and Theo gave me a rueful smile.

"I'm sorry."

It came out of both our mouths before either of us could stop ourselves. A smile broke across my face and we both laughed quietly together.

"I'm sorry for not asking you about Julien coming along. It just seemed like the best way to get to my mother as quickly as possible." I played with a small leaf on the ground. "I didn't mean to upset you." My hands continued to toy with the crumpled leaf until I felt Theo's hand on top of mine. I gave him a warm smile. He returned the expression, but his shoulders were slumped and there was a sadness lining his eyes.

"You don't need to apologise, Brae. I shouldn't have acted the way I did. This isn't about me, it's about finding your mother. And if Julien's the best way of finding her, I'm with you all the way." He gave my hand a light squeeze.

My heart swelled at Theo's words. His kindness had been something I had admired and loved about him from the moment we met, but this was something else. To put aside his animosity about Julien in order to help me was something I would never be able to repay him for, but would spend the rest of my days trying. I placed my other hand lightly on his freckled one, trying to convey all my thanks in this one gesture.

"I don't know what I did to deserve your friendship, Theo, but I'm glad you're here."

Theo beamed brightly at me, his ocean blue eyes crinkling at the sides. He gave me a playful nudge before going back to his bag where he continued to rifle through its contents. A small crease had formed between his eyes, which deepened the longer he looked through the bag. He had emptied most of the contents onto the ground and I spied a few different jars—yellowed labels stuck tightly to the small glass vials. Picking one up, I read the messy writing scrawled on the front. *Sanitatem.* A healing poultice. A few other jars had also been labelled with the same messy handwriting. Spotting the healing elixir I had used to mend Hazel's hand as well as a jar full of moon water, I smiled to myself and felt a swell of emotion looking at the necessities Theo had packed. He had thought of everything. Pulling the jars together into a small pile so I could pack them back into Theo's backpack, I went to hand them back to him, but the look on Theo's face made me pause.

"What's wrong?" I asked, my voice tinged with concern.

Theo's face had gone grey and he looked ready to vomit on the scattered leaves at our feet. Discarding the jars onto the mossy ground, I placed both my hands on either side of his face, forcing him to meet my gaze.

"Theo, talk to me." My voice was strong and steady, acting like a beacon to bring him out of his thoughts. Blinking a few times, his eyes cleared, and a frightened look appeared on his face.

"The grimoire I brought with me... it's gone."

Staring in disbelief, I tried to process his words. Family grimoires were some of the most precious magical objects to witches and warlocks alike, and they were to be protected at all costs. I didn't know why Theo thought it a good idea to bring one along with him, but I could see my panic reflected in his face. His shoulders were tense, his chest heaving as his breath quickened. Standing up, I began to pace in front of him. He watched me with a blank look on his face.

"Why did you bring a grimoire, Theo? You know they aren't to be taken from the household." I rubbed a hand over my face, letting an exasperated sigh escape my lips.

"I'm sorry, Brae, but I told you I'm not very good with magic and I needed to bring it with me if I was going to be any help to you."

I stopped my pacing and turned to Theo, a retort ready on my lips, but he sat on the mossy ground with his head held in his hands. It was a pitiful sight and, as stupid as his decision was to bring it along, I knew lecturing him would do us no good. We needed to find it before it got into the wrong hands because, if it did, Theo would have more than just the repercussions of his family to worry about.

In all my pacing, I hadn't noticed Julien step back into the small space we were occupying. He held a large pile of rough sticks in his hands and looked between Theo and me with a curious glint in his eye.

"What's with all the pacing? Did I walk in on something I shouldn't have?" He quirked an eyebrow and, out of the corner of my eye, I saw Theo's cheeks turn a deep shade of crimson.

"No." I gave a short sigh. "Theo seems to have misplaced something he brought along with him and we need to find it." I didn't want to tell Julien it was a grimoire. Theo already felt terrible about losing it and he certainly didn't need Julien's scorn.

Dropping the sticks, he began to build up a small fire made from some of the smaller twigs and dried grass he must have found deeper in the Ironwood. I didn't know how Julien had managed to find something dry as most of the ground in this place was damp with dew—the trees too dense for the sun's tendrils to reach the ground. Placing the dried grass on the top of the sticks, he held his hand over the top and, with a click of his fingers, a small spark ignited. The ember sputtered to life and a small flame spread over the dried twigs, erupting into a fire. I wanted nothing more than to warm myself in front of it and perhaps see if Julien would teach me something about fire magic, but now was not the time. We needed to find the missing grimoire.

Julien looked at Theo. "What is it that you have somehow lost in the mere hours we have been gone?"

I was right in not telling Julien exactly what Theo had lost because the ice in his voice chilled me to the bone. I didn't know how he could go from joking to serious so quickly, but it was terrifying to watch.

Taking a protective step in front of Theo to shield him from Julien's icy stare, I simply replied, "It's just something important. Trust me when I say we really need to find it."

As if saying the words out loud had summoned something to us, a flash of brown fur caught my eye behind Julien's broad shoulders. A small gremlin sat in the fork of one of the large trees lining the alcove, holding the grimoire in its clawed little hand. Theo scrambled to his feet, staring open-mouthed at the mischievous creature that appeared to have a smirk on its hideous little face. Catching the looks on our faces, Julien spun around and the gremlin jumped to the next tree with the ease of a creature who spent most of its life amongst the trees.

"Come on," I said. "We need to follow it before it gets too far ahead."

"Braelyn wait…"

I heard Julien's voice but took no notice. My mind was already focused on catching the gremlin and getting Theo's grimoire back. Running to where I had left my satchel, I snatched it up by the long strap and threw it over my head, chasing the gremlin through the trees. It wasn't a fast creature, but the fact it could jump from tree to tree with ease made it harder for me to keep up. I could hear Julien and Theo barrelling through the tangle of undergrowth behind me, but I kept my eyes focused on the little creature.

"Slow down, Braelyn!" Julien called from somewhere behind me, but I couldn't stop. Not when I was so close to the gremlin.

As I climbed over tree roots and darted between the dense trees, slim leafless branches grabbed at my face, nicking my cheeks and leaving stinging cuts which burned as the cool air hit my face. The gremlin was quick and, despite its tight grasp on the grimoire, it never slowed. I weaved my way through the maze of trees and bushes, listening behind me for Julien and Theo. They were only a few metres away so I kept pushing on. The creature had taken us so deep into the Ironwood, I could barely see the starry sky through the twisting canopy of trees. My lungs burned from the exertion and, beginning to slow my pace, I was relieved when the gremlin came to a sudden stop to sit on the branch of one of the largest trees I had ever seen. The roots twisted and curled towards the canopy, melding into one large, gnarled trunk. As I approached, I could see a giant gaping hole had formed where the rest of the trunk should have been. It was almost like the tree had grown around something no longer inhabiting the space, leaving a peep hole that allowed me to see to the other side of the Ironwood. As my eyes lingered on the gigantic tree, the same unusual feeling I'd felt at the edge of the Ironwood spread over me. Magic beckoned from the other side of the gaping hole, as if the giant tree was urging me closer to see if I would take the step and disappear into its prison of twisting branches. I was aware of the gremlin watching me as I tentatively approached. Its yellow eyes flickered like two pools of gold. I felt a pulse spread through my body, almost like an electric shock—as if my magic was being pulled by the power of the tree. Tendrils of magic caressed my skin, pulling me forward. Feeling the tingle in my palms, my fingers twitched in anticipation of the promise to use my magic. Slowly, the leaves littering the ground began to rise, floating in the air like falling rain. It felt almost effortless using my magic here, not at all like the hard and concentrated magic I felt when Hazel was teaching me back at the cottage. My heart beat a fast rhythm in my chest and a smile spread across my face.

Watching the leaves spin and glide around me, I spotted a long, thin vine wrapped around the trunk of a smaller tree. As I reached out my hand, I felt my magic thrum lightly in my veins. I imagined pulling the vine towards me and, slowly, it unwound itself from the dark trunk, snaking its way through the dead leaves towards my feet. I had never felt so much power while using my magic before. It felt *incredible,* and I longed to test my strength.

Surveying my surroundings to find more ways to test my magic, I noticed the gremlin was watching me, its large eyes appearing as if they had grown even bigger in size.

"*Stop,*" it pleaded. "*This is not a good place for you to use magic.*"

I gawked at the creature in front of me. It had moved its mouth, but the voice I'd heard had only sounded in my head. Startled, I dropped my hands to my sides, the leaves slumping once again on the damp ground. The vine that had wrapped loosely around my arm fell lifeless at my feet. I opened and closed my mouth, not knowing what was happening, staring wide-eyed at the creature as I tried to find my voice.

"Did you just—just speak to me?" I sputtered, not recognising my own voice. The gremlin simply stared at me, but I heard the small croaky voice again.

"*You be a spirit witch.*" It crawled down the branch it had perched on, Theo's grimoire still grasped tightly in its grimy clawed hand. "*You can speak to magical creatures, like Grugo.*" It pointed a little spindly finger at its chest.

"How do you know I'm a spirit witch?" I asked.

I felt somewhat foolish speaking to a creature who normally would not even know what I was saying, but Grugo was unfazed and simply shrugged back at me.

"*It hard to explain, but Grugo and other gremlins can sense magic. It be part of gremlin nature. That how I know this be magic witch book.*" It held up the grimoire and stared at the cover with eyes full of wonderment. The creature seemed lost in a trance simply by gazing at the grimoire, but it placed the book by its feet. Grugo's eyes returned to my face.

"So how is it that I can understand what you're saying?" I looked expectantly at the little creature, hoping it could tell me why, but again Grugo simply shrugged his bony little shoulders at me.

I breathed out a long sigh. "So you stole the grimoire because you can sense its magic? What would you do with a witch's book? Can you read it?"

Grugo hung his head in what looked like shame. My heart gave a tiny lurch for the small creature.

"Yes, Grugo is sorry, but I cannot help it. Magic calls to us and this witch's book make Grugo best magic finder in all of Gremlin Grove."

"What is Gremlin Grove?" I asked, keeping a wary eye on the creature, edging a little closer with each tentative step.

"It is where Grugo and other gremlins live." He pointed to the canopy of the Ironwood, past the giant otherworldly tree whose magic still reached out to me like an enticing hand. *"It up high in the trees where all the best mushrooms grow, far away from sneaky dwarf eyes."* Grugo's large yellow eyes narrowed at the mention of dwarves, and I wondered why he was so sceptical of them.

"Do you not like the dwarves?" I asked, curious to see what his answer would be.

Grugo shook his head as he scrunched up his tiny rat-like nose. *"No, they come in the darkness and steal the magic treasures we find. They take them back to their mountains and use them to make magic sharpies that sting and cut."*

I was yet to see the dwarves of the Ironwood Mountains since arriving in Ellesmere, but Theo had told me a little about them at the Mabon Festival. Preferring the secluded life under their hills, they were hardly seen, but made some of the greatest weapons forged with steel and iron. I wasn't surprised to hear the dwarves would steal the magic treasures they found. Witch and warlock relics were prized possessions to anyone able to get a hold of them.

"It's okay," I said. "I'm not going to take anything, but I am asking you to give the book back." I reached my hand out towards the grimoire, meaning to take it from the gremlin the first chance I got, but Grugo hesitated, pulling it towards himself. His greedy little hands clutched at the book as if it was a lifeline. I decided to take a different stance. Kneeling in front of him so I was almost the same height, I realised Grugo wasn't as small as I'd originally thought. His hands were about the same size as my own, but his long claws made them look even bigger. Placing my hand out to him, my palm in the air, it hung in the space between us as his large eyes watched me carefully.

"Please, Grugo, you don't know how much trouble that little book can cause in the wrong hands. I need it back." My voice was pleading and soft.

I didn't know if it was my pleading or something else, but it only took a few seconds before he placed the grimoire in my outstretched hand. Breathing a sigh of relief, I held the book to my chest. Grugo had receded a few steps, as if handing the grimoire back to me had broken some trance he had been in. Despite our short conversation, he looked almost scared of me. He hopped into a higher branch, sitting like a cat perched on a garden wall. As I opened my mouth to thank him, a small sound behind me startled him and he skittered off into the trees without a backward glance at me or the grimoire.

Turning around, I saw Julien and Theo standing in the shadows cast by the twisted trees. *How much had they seen?* Whatever it was they had witnessed, I wasn't ready to speak openly about it. Walking towards them slowly, my footsteps fell silent on the damp ground. Nearing their hiding spot, I gave them both a reassuring smile, but they looked at me with identical, unreadable expressions on their faces.

"Brae, were you just—"

I didn't let Theo finish his sentence. I wasn't ready to speak about how being a spirit witch somehow made me capable to talk to other magical creatures. I needed time to wrap my head around this new gift before I could explain it to anyone else, but more than that I wanted some time to find out what it was about this tree that made me feel so powerful. I stuck the grimoire in front of me, hoping this would distract Theo from his question. A relieved smile lightened his face.

"You got it," he breathed out quietly. I gave him a small shrug and he chuckled lightly. "You are just full of surprises, Brae."

Theo placed the grimoire in his backpack, burying it under everything he carried and covering it with a sweater. It seemed he wasn't going to make the same mistake as last time.

Since I spotted them, Julien hadn't said a word, instead watching me carefully with his dark gaze.

"You can say that again," he said sarcastically under his breath.

I don't think he expected anyone to hear him, but his mumbled voice had reached my ears. Annoyance flared up inside me like a volcano ready to erupt. I stomped over to him, pointing a finger at his large chest.

"Hey, if it wasn't for me, Theo would have never gotten his family grimoire back." It slipped out of my mouth before I realised what I'd said.

Julien's face looked as if it had turned to stone. His eyes were wide as they darted between Theo and me.

"You brought a grimoire with you?" he spat out between gritted teeth.

Theo shuffled his feet in the damp leaves and tried to look anywhere but at Julien's deathly stare. My patience towards him and the way he kept treating Theo was growing thin, and I could feel my magic reacting to my heated temper. My fingers tingled menacingly by my sides.

"It doesn't matter anymore," I spat back at him. "I got the grimoire back so we can go now."

Julien hesitated and then laughed. But it wasn't the light, playful chuckle I'd heard in the apothecary; it was dark, empty, and it made me recoil back from him. He shook his head, raking a large hand through his already tousled hair.

"We can't just go back, Braelyn. Your wild gremlin chase led us too far into the Ironwood and I have no idea where the hell we are." His dark eyes bore into me with such intense frustration I had to look away. Anger still bubbled away inside me, but Julien's gaze was enough to keep my heated comments from bubbling over.

"But you have a map—just find out where we are, and we can make our way back to the path."

Julien's dark laugh echoed around us as he held the map out in front of him.

"Then tell me, Braelyn, where exactly do you think we are?"

His words were like knives, steely and sharp as they cut into me. He had never used this tone before, and I finally began to understand why so many people thought him to be dangerous. Looking over the crumpled paper, I tried to locate the crop of trees we had been sitting in. When I finally found it, I tried to map my way through the trees the gremlin had led me through, but it was no use. From that point on there was nothing but blank space. It was unchartered territory, and I had led us right into it without a second thought. My anger began to dissipate as the realisation of what I had done overwhelmed me.

"I'm sorry," I said quietly.

My voice felt shaky with emotion, and I couldn't look at Julien's face, not knowing if I could stand the anger flickering in his eyes. He had tried to stop me, but I'd rushed off, too eager to fix the problem. Now I was the reason we were lost in the middle of the most dangerous wood in Ellesmere.

Looking up through my lashes, I watched Julien stomp his way through the underbrush into a large thicket of trees. I went to go after him, not wanting him to leave, but Theo grabbed my shoulder to stop me. He let out a long breath through his nose.

"Just let him go, Brae. He needs to cool down."

So, I watched him blend into the darkness, consumed by the arching and curling trees, not knowing if he would come back.

Seventeen

J ulien had been gone for what felt like hours, but I couldn't be too sure as time didn't seem to pass the same way in the Ironwood. The branches and leaves of the trees were so tangled together, nothing could break through their mangled barrier.

Theo looked around helplessly while he sat on the knotted roots of the tree Grugo had perched on. He hadn't moved since Julien stormed off into the dark, and I suspected he was feeling somewhat responsible for the situation we were in. As silly as he was for bringing a grimoire into the Ironwood, I couldn't blame him for what had happened. It was my fault. I should have listened to Julien before running off. The weight of my recklessness hung heavy over my head as I realised I may have ruined any chance we had of reaching Ellesmere Castle in time to help my mother. The pain I felt was all-consuming and it tore at my heart, leaving me breathless. Seeing Theo was occupied—digging through his backpack—I slipped behind the first row of trees and let my pain take hold of me. Bile rose in my throat, and I doubled over, hands on my knees, struggling to catch my breath as the image of Morrigan's floating orb appeared before me. My mother was rotting in a dark and dirty prison cell. Closing my eyes, I tried to block out the image, remembering Maeve's technique when it felt like the world was crushing down on me.

It seemed like forever ago, but it had only been just before my induction ceremony. I had finished a lesson with my mother in the cramped back room of our apothecary when Maeve found me on the floor of the room, hugging my knees tight to my chest, as if letting go would cause me to fall apart entirely. The lesson had passed without issue, but it was what happened afterwards that had caused the attack. She had told me that, after my induction ceremony I would need to learn how to be the head of the Coven. It was my birth right and everyone would be counting on me when the time came for my mother to step aside. I'd nodded along to what she said, but when she left the room—a smile on her face at how happy she thought I was—this was when I had spiralled. The pressure of her expectations had weighed heavily on my shoulders.

Maeve had come into the room and pulled me into her arms. She'd brushed the hair back from my sweat-slicked face, and, taking my cheeks in her steady hands, she'd told me to take a deep breath and focus on letting the breath out. As I did this, the tension had left my shoulders and the weight that had settled on my chest seemed to slowly ease away.

Hearing Maeve's strong and steady voice in my head now, I kept my eyes tightly shut and took a shaky breath in through my nose. My chest felt close to bursting as I let my lungs empty, breathing out through my mouth and focusing on the small whistle as it passed my lips. I repeated this a few times before I began to feel the tell-tale signs of my panic subsiding. I rubbed my hand over my face, feeling the beads of sweat disappear. I couldn't spiral. We needed to find a way out of this place and save my mother. I wasn't going to give up and let King Elias win.

Stepping back out from behind the trees, I found Theo frantically looking around him as if he had misplaced something. His eyes looked wild with panic, and I felt a sudden spur of guilt for leaving him and not telling him where I had gone.

"Theo," I yelled out.

He spun in the direction of my voice, kicking up the scattered leaves around him. The minute his eyes met mine I saw the instant relief upon realising I hadn't been lost somewhere, consumed to the darkness of the Ironwood.

"By the elements, Brae. You scared me half to death." His hand rested over his heart. "Where did you go? I thought I had lost you to this creepy place."

Theo shuffled his things over a few inches to give me some space to sit down. My feet throbbed as I sat, immediately relieving the pressure. We had been walking for so long, my boots were covered in filth and seemed to be melded to my feet now. I turned my ankles slowly, feeling my muscles stretch and sighing in relief.

"I'm sorry for panicking you, Theo. I just needed some time to get my thoughts together." I shuffled my feet in the dead leaves littering the ground, watching as my boots carved deep crevices into the mud. "I want you to know that I don't blame you for being in this situation."

Theo fidgeted beside me, his kind blue eyes welling with tears. I turned my gaze away, not trusting myself to keep my own tears from overflowing .

"I would blame me," he whispered.

I placed my hand over his. "Well I don't, and I never will. It's my fault we are in this mess. I should have listened to Julien before I ran off." I gave his hand a squeeze.

Despite my trying to make him feel better, his shoulders were still slumped and it was as if a light had been extinguished behind his usual bright eyes. I knew he was punishing himself, that he thought he was a terrible warlock. I sighed, wishing I knew what to say to make him feel better, but every thought died on my lips. It didn't seem enough. I may not have understood what it was like to not be able to use magic—I had always been good with potions and my spirit magic seemed to come naturally to me—but I knew what it felt like to not live up to the expectations of others. Instead of trying to offer him advice, I gave his hand a simple squeeze.

"I'm here for you whenever you want to talk." Standing and stretching my aching back—tree roots did not make good resting places—I looked around, trying to find a way to get ourselves back on to the path.

"Now, let's try to find a way out of this hell hole."

While we waited for Julien to return, Theo and I planned a way to get back on to the small path that had become our tether to the king and my mother. We agreed to make our way through the first layer of trees caging us in, always making sure we still had the giant tree in sight. I wound my way through the maze of trees, trying to squint into the blackness that extended farther into the Ironwood, but I could never see much more than a few metres ahead of me. Looking back to make sure I could still see the large tree, I went a little deeper. Keeping the clearing on my left-hand side, I ran my hand along the trunks of the trees, feeling my magic sputter to life. The bark felt damp beneath my fingers and a sad, desperate feeling dripped off the trunk almost as if it was crying. My lip trembled. These woods were dying. I could sense the life that had once grown here, but it was almost like a distant and fleeting memory. This part of the Ironwood seemed to be heavy with magic and, the longer we stayed here, the more I felt drawn to it. My eyes darted to the giant tree often as whatever dark magic riddled the Ironwood drew me near it. The thought of dark magic spurred a memory inside me from the night I received my rune, remembering my mother's terrified face and that spirit witches were drawn to black magic. They *craved* power. *Could this be the reason my magic came to me so easily here?*

A faint sound back near the giant tree pulled me from my thoughts. Leaving the sad trees behind, I stepped around the twisting tree roots and found Julien sitting in the dirt, looking worse for wear.

His dark hair was dishevelled, leaves and twigs sticking out of it at every angle. I could see he was damp with dew. His face was slick with sweat, and mud caked the bottom of his heavy boots. Sitting in the damp dirt, Julien rested his forearms lightly on his knees, a hopeless expression on his face as he stared at his dirty hands. The soft ground muffled my footsteps, and he didn't hear me approach. I watched quietly for a moment as he ran both his hands through his hair, dislodging some of the debris entangled in his curls. Looking up, Julien spotted me watching him and our eyes locked for the briefest moment. His dark eyes blazed with the fire running through his veins and I blushed at being caught staring at him, that same fiery gaze heating my skin as he stared back. Giving me a small, lopsided smile, Julien pulled himself up from the ground, brushing bits of dirt and leaves from his trousers.

I had been so relieved to see him, I didn't notice the rush of anger now flooding through me as he closed the distance between us. While I was glad he was safe, I was annoyed he had just taken off after raking me over the coals for doing the exact same thing only hours before. I could see his smile begin to falter as my eyes narrowed at him. Stopping just in front of me, my hand balled into a fist, I punched him as hard as I could in his arm.

"Ow! What was that for?" Julien stiffened, his eyes wide at my lashing out at him. He rubbed the spot where my fist had connected with his arm, a small frown creasing the spot between his brows.

"Where the hell have you been?" I yelled at him.

It hadn't dawned on me until this moment but, seeing Julien stand in front of me, I couldn't deny I had been terribly worried about him. A deep, dark part of me had honestly believed he had simply left us here. An immense sense of relief flooded through me at having him back and my emotions bubbled out of me in a high-pitched giggle. I laughed hysterically as tears blurred my vision. Julien stood in front of me, not knowing what to do. As I blinked back my tears, Julien stood frozen in front of me, his eyes wide in pure astonishment.

I wiped a hand over my tear-stained cheeks, suddenly conscious I probably looked a real mess myself. Folding my arms across my chest, I waited for Julien to reply as my hysteria vanished.

"Good to see you have kept your sanity while I was gone." He waggled his eyebrows and a smile tugged the corner of my mouth but, instead of saying anything I remained silent, not sure if I was still angry or too relieved to care.

Sighing, he continued. "I'm sorry I was gone for so long, but I was trying to find a way back to the path. I thought I could map one out and make my way back to you, but I couldn't find any semblance of the path we had walked along."

Shaking his head, a few stray leaves fell from his hair. Guilt surfaced inside me. Despite his annoyance at me, he had still tried to help by putting himself in danger and trying to find a way out. A small part of me felt disappointed that he hadn't found an escape route. I'd thought if anyone could find one it would be Julien, but it seemed even he had his limitations.

I let out a frustrated sigh. "How are we going to get out of here?"

After Julien returned with his grim news, there wasn't much left to do but delve ever deeper into the trees to see if we could find a way out of this dark prison. While Julien and Theo continued to walk laps through the trees, I occupied myself with the giant ash tree, which still seemed to hum with the language of dark magic. Walking around the large base of the trunk, I gazed up into the lifeless branches as they stretched towards the sky. It seemed like it would have been a beautiful place had everything not been slowly dying around me. I couldn't help but wonder why there was so much death and decay in this part of the Ironwood while the rest of the wood seemed fine, despite its eerie feeling. The tell-tale sign of magic rippled through me as I stepped towards the trunk. It crackled like static, loud and harsh as I felt the pull of the ash trees magic thrum through me. It was a powerful witchcraft—one I would never truly understand—but it pulled me ever closer, making me want to reach out and feel the tingle of magic beneath my fingers. As I rounded the tree, the bark blackened, like someone had tried to burn the tree down. Reaching out to touch it, I half expected my hand to come back covered in soot but, as I pulled my hand away, something else caught my attention.

A brown shape darted from the opening between the tree's roots, startling me out of the magical trance. It had been too quick for me to see exactly what it was, but my heart beat rapidly in my chest, my mind racing with all the terrible things it could be. *What if Grugo had come back for the grimoire?* The image of his long claws glinted in my mind as I spun around, facing the wall of spindly trees. Julien and Theo stepped back into the darkness of the giant tree, whispered words passing between them. I made a mental note to ask them what they were talking about as seeing the two of them seemingly plotting concerned me. Motioning at them to stop where they were, their eyes met mine as they seemed to understand my hesitation. They stood frozen in place, as if we were children playing musical statues and they were waiting for me to start the music.

I searched the clearing desperately for whatever had slipped past me. If we had to stay in the shadows of the Ironwood, I was taking no chances of something ripping me apart while I slept. Feeling more foolish by the second, I made my way quietly to where Julien and Theo waited for me. Treading lightly on the slick ground, making sure not to make any sudden movements, I closed the distance between us as the brown blur made another appearance. This time, I wasn't the only one who saw it.

"Did you see that?" Theo breathed softly.

I nodded. "I saw it just before too, when I was standing over by the ash tree. I thought I was losing my mind like Julien had said."

Julien snorted softly at my comment as Theo looked between us, freckled nose creasing. Opening his mouth to shoot back what could have only been a snarky retort, I held my finger up to silence him. The action reminded me of Hazel, and my heart sunk a little in my chest. Despite her harsh manner and chastising words, I missed her terribly. Theo's words died on the air as I squinted into the darkness between the trees. A small movement in the underbrush made me jump back a little and I felt Julien's warm hand touch the small of my back as he steadied me. It was at this moment a small creature stuck its head out between the roots of the trees, sniffing the air in front of it. My eyes widened in surprise, and I heard Theo's sharp intake of breath behind me.

"By the elements," Julien whispered. "Is that what I think it is?"

Watching the creature closely, I couldn't help but smile and silently say a prayer to the elements for Hazel's intuition.

Eighteen

Taking a tentative step forward, I tried to be as silent as possible, not wanting to scare the jackalope away. It snuffled around in the dead leaves for a few seconds before its head shot up and two large, owl-like eyes gazed at me from the dark.

Hazel had been right about my father—he did have a remarkable talent. The detail he had managed to capture in his wooden carving was incredible. As I stood, eyes locked with the jackalope, I could see the likeness could only have come from seeing the real thing. An overwhelming sense of closeness to my father threatened to consume me, but I couldn't let the feeling take hold. I needed to remain level-headed.

The jackalope continued gazing at me—sitting almost as still as we were—then, ever so slowly, it began to inch its way out of the shadows. Each paw hopped one after the other as it cautiously approached. Its fur was a deep brown—almost the colour of mud—making it blend beautifully into the shadows of the Ironwood. Its ears stood tall, twitching slightly as it listened, and there, in the middle of its head, were the strong antlers distinguishing it from a normal rabbit. They were lighter than its fur and I doubted much could stand a chance against them.

Hazel's words began to echo in my mind. *They aren't friendly. Keep your distance.* Despite what she had said, the creature continued to edge closer, its small pink nose wiggling as it sniffed the air.

"Brae, why don't you see if you can speak with it the same way you did with the gremlin?" Theo's voice was eager in my ear.

My mind had drifted to the same thing. If I could speak to the jackalope, it might be able to tell us a way back to the path. It was a long shot, but we had tried searching for hours and we were no closer to finding a way out.

I knelt in the underbrush, studying the creature. At first, it had looked no bigger than a normal rabbit, but now that it sat close enough to touch, it looked to be around the size of a small fox. I leaned back on my knees, and it stiffened, wary of danger.

"Hello. Can you understand me?"

The moment the words came out of my mouth, I felt foolish. Theo and Julien's gaze burned into my back, and the longer I waited for the jackalope to respond, the sillier I felt. I waited a few seconds before asking another question.

"Can you hear me?"

Again, there was no response. Was I doing something wrong? Unlike Grugo, the jackalope seemed unwilling or unable to answer. Rocking back on my feet, I slumped to the ground crossing my legs underneath me, feeling despair creeping back in. *This is hopeless.* There was no chance of us making it to the castle. We had wasted so much valuable time already and I didn't know how much longer we had left to make it to the castle in time.

"Nothing is hopeless as long as your heart stays steady."

The voice echoed in my mind as if it was one of my own thoughts. My head snapped up as I met the eyes of the jackalope. Its head was tilted to one side as if considering what it had just said. Its eyes glistened such a deep brown they looked almost black. I went to speak aloud again when realisation struck me. It had replied to my thoughts and not my words. My heart fluttered in excitement, and I shot a smile back at Julien and Theo, who were looking down at me with odd expressions on their faces. They probably thought I was going mad.

"You can hear what I'm thinking." It was more of a statement than a question, but the jackalope answered anyway.

"Yes."

I never imagined that one simple word would be able to lift my spirits as much as it did, but I could feel the happiness radiate through me as if one of Julien's flames had been lit inside my chest.

"Why are you so deep in the forest? It is not a good place to be." The jackalope's words were thick with fear as its sweet, soft voice echoed in my mind. It was sitting back on its large hind legs, more at ease now. Its fur was lighter underneath its chin—almost like the colour of caramel. It really was a beautiful creature.

I leant forward slightly. *"We weren't meant to be in this part of the Ironwood, but got pulled away from the path because of a gremlin."*

The jackalope continued to watch me, a contemplative look in its large dark eyes. *"Yes, they are mischievous creatures."*

I nodded in agreement and thought the one question I had almost wanted to shout upon hearing the jackalope's voice in my head. *"Will you show us the way out?"*

I pushed every ounce of emotion into my question, leaning forward in anticipation of its answer. It didn't come quickly, and I grew nervous the longer I waited. Feeling the knowing tingle in my fingers as my magic reacted to my ever-changing emotions, I stuffed my hands under my armpits and tried to calm the jittering feeling in my stomach, but it was no use. My hands trembled beneath my arms as if I had drunk too many cups of coffee.

"I will help you find your way back, young witch. This is no place for a spirit witch to be, or any type of magical being for that matter."

My body relaxed, a slow smile spreading over my face. We would finally be free of this place. The jackalope looked up towards Julien and Theo. It was the first time it had paid any sort of attention to them. It gazed at both with a strange expression in its eyes, one that I couldn't make out.

Lifting myself off the damp ground, I brushed the leaves from my trousers and explained to Julien and Theo that the jackalope would help lead us back to the path. They looked astounded and a little impressed with my newfound talent, but I could see they wanted an explanation.

"Braelyn, how can you speak to these creatures?" Julien's voice was low, his eyes fixed on the jackalope.

"I don't know." I shrugged. "It's never happened until now."

"Maybe it's your spirit magic," Theo exclaimed. "It's the only explanation."

I had to admit, what Theo was saying did make a lot of sense, but in all my learnings I had never come across anything like this. There had always been a considerable amount of mystery around spirit witches and what we could do given how rare it was to be one.

"Come, my friend. Dark is not a good time to be in this place. We must go."

I didn't need telling twice. Gesturing to Theo and Julien that we needed to go, Theo shouldered his backpack and I made sure my small satchel was secured tightly over my shoulder. Julien simply shoved his hands in his pockets, a dark look smouldering in his eyes.

We followed the jackalope past the tall ash tree, its menacing presence looming over us. As Theo and Julien stepped through the trees, following the rustle of the jackalope's footsteps, I threw a quick glance behind me at the mysterious clearing. I could still hear the same low hum in my ears, the feeling reverberating through me.

"Braelyn, make sure you keep up."

Julien's voice sounded from up ahead. They had disappeared into the shadows of the trees, but I spied them just a short distance ahead, waiting for me. As I turned from the ash tree, a tall shadowy figure caught my attention. It appeared almost like a whisp of clouds, floating near the gaping hole at the base of the great tree. Drawing back towards my friends, I kept my eyes trained on the ghostly figure. It could have passed as the shadow of a person if it wasn't for the dark tendrils of smoke wafting around it like a murky halo. My mind told me to turn and run, but a small part of me, deep down, felt connected to whatever this shadowed creature was. A light touch on my elbow startled me out of my trance. Whirling around, my fingers tipped with fire, I came face-to-face with Julien. His head was tilted to one side as if trying to understand what it was that I was doing.

"Planning to use that against me?" He nodded in the direction of my still flaming fingers, his lips quirked in a half smile. My heart fluttered like tiny butterfly wings in my chest at seeing that expression.

"It wouldn't be much use against you," I teased.

I closed my hand so the fiery fragments burnt out. Julien's fingers still lingered on my elbow lightly, his touch heating my skin through the thick fabric of my jacket.

"Is everything okay? You look as if you've seen a ghost."

I glanced around to see if the shadows still floated near the bough of the ash tree, but there was nothing there. Pushing it to the back of my mind I gave Julien a half smile.

"Yeah, everything is fine, just thought I left something."

Julien raised an eyebrow as if seeing straight through my lie, but he didn't press the matter.

"Okay, let's get moving. We still have a way to go before we reach King Elias's Castle."

Taking my hand in his, Julien pulled me gently in the direction of the others. My mind still whirred, trying to figure out what exactly seemed to be following me throughout the Ironwood.

Finding our way back to the path was difficult. Stumbling more than once over winding tree roots lying half-hidden in the deep underbrush, I was starting to curse my short stature. Julien and Theo had no problems climbing over the obstacles in our path. Theo brought up the rear of our troupe, and Julien took the lead with the jackalope whose name he had told me was Alpheus. Although larger than a normal rabbit, Alpheus, was able to weave through the maze of trees and roots with ease. Even with his long antlers, he never seemed to get caught. Heaving out a frustrated sigh, I slumped down next to a spindly tree, gulping down the cool air. My feet ached in my boots, and I felt overwhelmed with exhaustion. I didn't think I could go any farther without taking a small break.

"Can we stop for a minute?" I called out to Julien.

He was well ahead of Theo and me, barely noticeable in the shadows as he followed Alpheus at a close pace—almost like he was terrified to lose sight of the creature. He hadn't spoken to me since we'd left the clearing and I was beginning to think he was regretting coming along with us. Between his dislike of Theo, my chase through the woods and now my slow pace, he probably thought this whole endeavour was a failed cause. If I was being completely honest with myself, I had thought the very same thing when we had been stranded by the ash tree. Still, with the jackalope's appearance, I *had* to believe things were going to be okay. I settled on a small, solid rock close to one of the many trees and instantly felt relief in my feet. Leaning back, I could feel the crisp bark digging into my spine, but I was too tired to move or care. Instead, I closed my eyes and thought of my mother. Hoping she was okay.

Julien's voice sounded from behind the tree I leant on, startling me out of my thoughts. For someone who was so big, he was as silent as an assassin.

"Not too long, Braelyn, we need to keep moving."

There was an edge to his voice, and I could see the same look in his eyes that had been there when we left the clearing. *Could he sense something we couldn't?*

"Your friend is wary about this part of the woods, and he is right to be. Dark things lurk in the shadows here."

I couldn't see where Alpheus was, but the tether in my mind indicated he was close by, his dark eyes probably watching the shadows.

Twisting around to see if I could spot him, I saw Julien standing just a few trees away from where I sat. Lifting myself up, I came to stand beside him, looking into the sea of darkness rolling out in front of us. It was an eerie feeling, looking out at something you knew was there but couldn't see. I conjured a small flame in the centre of my palm. Still feeling a little apprehensive to conjure any fire magic after my failed attempt back at Hazel's cottage, I seemed to be okay when the flames were small. Anything bigger than my palm, though, I struggled to control. The light didn't stretch far in the darkness, but it made me feel safer. It was short-lived though, as Julien flung his hand out towards me, wrapping his fingers around mine. He closed my hand into a fist, snuffing out the flame as quickly as it had come.

"This is not the place to use magic, Braelyn." His words were sharp, but I knew he meant well.

"What is it about this part of the Ironwood that scares you?"

His hand was still clasped around mine and, despite the chill in the air, the warmth radiating from him managed to keep the cold away. He was still gazing out into the dark, a frown pulling his brows over his eyes. I couldn't help but notice that even, with leaves littering his hair and dirt smearing his bronzed face, he was still incredibly handsome. Unbothered by the cold, he had removed his long black coat and pushed up the sleeves of his sweater, revealing taut muscles. Julien peered down at me, that shadow still in his eyes. My heart fluttered in my chest.

"It's not a certain part of the Ironwood that scares me, it's this whole journey that doesn't sit well with me. Since we encountered the gremlins, I've felt like we were never meant to find our way out."

His voice was sombre, and in the tiny flickers of light breaking through the canopy I could see the raw emotion on his face—the grim look shadowing his brown eyes.

From the moment I'd met Julien, I had always considered him to be strong. Despite the fire running through his veins, I believed there was a lightness to him that others either couldn't see or chose to ignore due to his family's terrible past. For the short time I had known him, I had come to find that nothing seemed to ever bother him. Not the whispers that were often spoken behind his back or even the scathing looks that I caught Theo throwing him. So when he didn't deny that the Ironwood frightened him, I couldn't help but feel terrified myself. Julien's hand still grasped mine in a vice-like grip, as if letting go would mean certain death. I tried to think of something comforting to say to him, but my mind kept coming up blank. As we stood in the shadows, it was Hazel's words that sounded in my head.

"I can understand why you might have thought this journey was doomed, Julien, but we don't need to worry now. Hazel told me that to see a jackalope is a good omen. We will find our way back to the path. I know we will."

My voice sounded stronger than I felt, and I chewed on the side of my lip, hoping Julien would take what I said and turn it into something positive. I needed the old Julien back. The one who laughed loudly, whose strength gave *me* strength. The Julien who seemed to believe in me undoubtedly and without question. I needed him now more than ever. He let go of my hand, allowing it to drop softly back to my side and I instantly felt a chill settle back into my chest. He ran a hand over the back of his neck and let out a cold laugh.

"That is just old women's superstition, Braelyn. You can't honestly believe that nonsense."

In my head I knew it was just superstition. Many older witches and warlocks in our Coven were exactly like Hazel and believed all the old stories. Old tales that said if you dropped salt you needed to throw it over your left shoulder, or hanging a horseshoe by your door warded off evil spirits. While I had always pushed these aside as silly superstition, I couldn't help but feel in my heart this was different. Hazel had said a jackalope would help those in need and we were desperate in the clearing. Superstition or not, I believed Alpheus showing up when he did was no mere coincidence.

"*You* might think it's nonsense," I said, mimicking the coolness of Julien's earlier words. "But *I* believe what she said. Alpheus showing up when he did gives me hope there is still time to stop King Elias and help my mother."

I could feel the sting of tears in my eyes, but I refused to let them fall. I had done all my crying back in the clearing and now I was determined not to let my journey be in vain. I would save my mother and stop King Elias, but I knew I couldn't do it alone. My stubbornness prevented me from telling Julien this, as I had gone my entire life not relying on the help of others, but I hoped Julien understood the message behind my words.

He rubbed a hand through his deep brown waves, his eyes dark and thoughtful. He let out a long sigh. "Believe what you want, Braelyn, but I'm telling you there is something else at play here."

We walked for a few more hours before the jackalope found us a spot to rest. It had been a quiet journey for the most part. A full day had passed and, apart from our brief break earlier in the night, we hadn't stopped. Julien's earlier words continued to echo in my mind, but I pushed the thoughts quickly aside, instead using the time to think about how we would get my mother out of the dungeons. Most of my plan involved using my magic to blast the door away from the hinges or finding another way to break down the dungeon door, but none of my ideas were useful in any way. I had no idea where the dungeons were located, and even if I did have the faintest idea where to look, all my plans involved loud noises that would surely alert the guards to trespassers in their midst. Realising how in over my head I was, I breathed out a frustrated sigh and pushed my plans aside for the time being.

My legs folded underneath me as I sat down, looking around the part of the Ironwood we had stopped at for the night. Taking in our surroundings, I realised how different this part of the forest looked to the section we had just come from. The trees weren't bunched as closely together here—the branches were fat with growth, not twisted and gnarled like they were in the ash tree's clearing—and the rustle of leaves sounded above me. Burying my hands in the soft mossy earth, the ground wasn't damp like the rest of the Ironwood had been. And there was light. Stars winked down at me from above. I smiled to myself. It had felt like days since I had looked upon the open sky. A full day had passed since I'd left Hazel's cottage and was thrown into the pages of the prophecy. Checking to make sure no one was watching, I pulled out the small book I had taken from the Forest Festival. After showing it to Hazel the night it had come into my possession, I had buried it in one of the drawers in my mother's old room, trying to forget about it until the night we left for the castle. Leafing through the old, worn pages, my mind began to wander. A week ago, I had been standing in the apothecary, whispers flying around the room about my spirit magic. I'd been afraid of what my magic had meant, but now a strange sense of power coursed through my veins. And despite the journey ahead, I felt I was ready to face whatever danger was to come. If it meant saving my mother and putting an end to King Elias's cruel reign, I had no choice. But one thing remained unclear. How was I supposed to stop him? My eyes skimmed the foreign script scrawled within the book's pages. There was no knowing what information lay within without being able to read the old language.

"What have you got there, Brae?" Theo's voice startled me out of my reverie.

Sitting beside me, he looked over my shoulder at Althea's old book. I watched him carefully as his blue eyes roamed over the page, drinking in each word that had been scrawled messily on the worn parchment.

"It's a book, written by the Wise Witch Althea. It speaks of the prophecy and how I am destined to be the one who finally destroys King Elias and reunites Ellesmere, but I have no idea how to do that."

Letting out a frustrated sigh, I tossed the small book to Theo, who caught it mid-air.

Leafing through the delicate pages with a touch as soft as a feather, he scanned them quickly until he stopped at one that seemed to have a few scribbled drawings and more words written in the language of old.

"Wait, can you read that?" I asked, my eyebrows raised.

A small glint sparkled in his eye as he grinned at me. "I can read some of the text, but it seems a bit muddled. It speaks of the king having an object of great strength, which he will use to help him reach a great power." Theo's brow furrowed slightly.

"What?" I asked. My stomach churned as I waited for him to respond.

"I can only decipher a few words, but it basically says only a certain great and powerful magic will be able to stop him."

I felt my heart sink to the bottom of my stomach. The overwhelming reality of what I needed to do made my ears ring and my hands tremble. I stared down at my hands, studying my spirit rune, wondering how I would ever be strong enough to defeat someone as powerful as King Elias.

Feigning tiredness, I told Theo I was going to get some rest. Giving me a small smile, he handed me back Althea's book and left me to my thoughts but, as I settled back against the trunk of a nearby tree, something caught my eye. Just off in the distance, strange plants lay scattered around the base of the trees. They swayed gently in the breeze and, standing, I bent over the closest. It was unusually tall—the top of the plant coming to the middle of my chest. Its long leaves ran all the way up the plant's stem, curling over at the tip. At the very top of the stem was a huge green bud. Tiny black spores covered the plant. They felt oddly soft as I touched one, but it left a sticky residue on my finger. Wiping the ooze on my trousers, I peered back up at the plant, my eyes widening as I took in what now stood before me. A flower the size of a dinner plate had bloomed from the green bud. The lilac-coloured petals gleamed in the moonlight, almost as if it was glowing. I was mesmerised as the petals gradually turned from a deep purple into a light shade of lavender in the middle, with what appeared to be small antennae fanning out around the petals. I reached up to touch one of the long buds, but before my finger touched the round yellow tip of the antennae, Julien's rough fingers grasped my wrists tightly, pulling me away.

Stumbling back, I felt dazed, as if I had drunk one of my mother's strong sleeping draughts. Julien's face hovered in front me, his features slowly becoming clearer. His voice echoed at the back of my mind as he called my name.

"Braelyn... Braelyn, look at me." Julien's voice was tinged with worry and I could vaguely make out a frown furrowing his dark brows.

"What's wrong?" I breathed out.

I still felt dizzy, but my vision no longer swam before me. Julien propped me up against the large tree trunk where I'd been sitting before. He crouched in front of me.

"Braelyn did you touch the purple flower you were looking at?"

I shook my head. "I only touched the stem, why?"

Relief flooded Julien's face, the small crease between his eyes flattening out, but concern still filled his dark eyes. He let out a long breath. "Oh, thank the elements." He ran a hand over his face. "Braelyn, that flower you were just looking at is called Lilithium Mortiferum. It was previously used to torture witches and warlocks who were convicted of standing against the king."

Looking back at the elegant plant, I flinched as the antennae continued to sway menacingly in my direction. *How could something so beautiful be used for something so callous and evil?*

"What does it do?" I asked softly.

"I don't know exactly what happens to someone who touches it, but it causes severe pain. It must be handled with extreme care." Julien looked over my head towards the lilac petals, still glimmering in the moonlight. "I'm surprised there are still Lilithium Mortiferum plants growing in this part of the Ironwood. I thought they were all destroyed."

"Who ordered them to be destroyed?"

Julien shrugged his shoulders once. "I don't actually know, but I'm guessing King Elias overruled the decision."

Julien's voice grew quiet, and a thought struck me like a bolt of lightning.

I remembered being in the back room of our apothecary one blustery winter's day, waiting for my mother to finish serving a grey-haired warlock in the shop. He had come in a few times over the years and loved to chat with anyone who would listen. Unfortunately for my mother, she'd been stuck with him that day and, as a result, our lesson had started late. Usually, I was eager to start our magic lessons right away. Before witches and warlocks received their runes, we learned about the history of our kind, as well as how to brew potions, salves and moon water. We also learnt how to distinguish helpful herbs from poisonous ones—that had been one of the first lessons my mother had ever taught me. I always loved learning from my mother's grimoire and our lessons were the only time she would allow me to use it, but that day I hadn't minded that our lesson was running late. Seated on the soft armchairs by the fire, I had relished in the warmth after being out in the bitter cold. I'd sat and listened to the fire spit and pop in the hearth as my eyes roamed our bookcase, trying to find another book to pour over. I'd read so many of them growing up that the familiar spines stuck out at me, worn and frayed from being opened so many times. As I'd searched the shelves, I spotted one I hadn't recalled ever noticing until that moment. Pulling myself away from the warmth, I had picked the book from the shelf, turning it over in my hands. The edges of the leather were slightly frayed and peeled away in the corners to reveal the hard cardboard underlay. After opening it up to the front page, I had quickly realised it wasn't an ordinary book, but a grimoire. It hadn't appeared to be one of my mother's family grimoires, but belonged to a witch by the name of Lilith—seemingly one she had created herself. As I'd flipped through the delicate pages, I came upon recipes for potions I'd never heard of before. Diagrams of objects I had never seen were hand drawn onto the light pages and my interest in the book had piqued. Sitting back by the fire, I had just opened it to a page of a beautiful hand-drawn flower when my mother yanked the book from my tight grasp. Her face flushed a deep red and her eyes narrowed in my direction—anger rippling off her in waves. Without a backward glance she had left the room, the small grimoire tucked tightly under her arm. My mother and I had never spoken about the incident again. I had rummaged through every part of the apothecary looking for the small grimoire, but no matter how hard I tried searching, I'd never been able to find the book again.

I wondered now if the same Lilith who had started writing her own grimoire had been the same witch whose name resonated with the deadly flower still swaying in the breeze before me. Gazing back towards the Lilithium Mortiferum, I had an overwhelming feeling that I had infact seen it before tonight.

After my near death experience I struggled to relax enough to be able to rest. My mind continued to wander to my mother, wondering if she was truly okay, then to thoughts of Hazel back at her cottage—left to deal with the wrath of the elders over me disobeying their orders. Julien kept a watchful eye on me for a while. He checked on me numerous times to make sure I wasn't suffering any pain from touching the Lilithium Mortiferum.

"Julien…" I said, letting out an exasperated sigh. "Please stop watching me. I'm fine. I didn't touch the flower."

It was about the fourth time Julien had come to check my pupils for dilation and feel for my pulse, making sure everything was normal. My heart fluttered despite my annoyance. It was the most attention he had shown me since we'd entered the Ironwood.

Julien ran a hand through his dark hair as he continued to watch me carefully, concern still reflecting in his beautiful eyes. "I know what you said, Braelyn, it's just…" He trailed off as he tried to look anywhere but at me.

I watched him closely as his brows pulled down once again into a deep frown. He appeared to be at war with something, not knowing whether to speak the words aloud or not. Eventually, he turned his eyes back to me.

"I feel very… protective of you. Ever since we stepped foot into this forsaken wood, my mind has been so preoccupied with keeping you safe. When I saw you by the Lilithium Mortiferum, it was like living in a nightmare. I thought I had failed you."

My heart beat a light rhythm in my chest as I stared back at Julien, my eyes widening. Coming over to sit in front of him, I reached a tentative hand to his cheek, turning his face to meet my gaze. His skin was warm beneath my touch, and a light stubble had begun to grow over his face, but the intensity of his stare was what made my breath hitch. His brown eyes blazed warmly as they searched my face.

"I'm okay, Julien. Honestly." I gave him a warm smile and watched as the corner of his mouth pulled up slightly. "But you don't need to keep me safe. I appreciate it more than you will ever know, but growing up and being the only young witch in our town, I've grown used to keeping myself safe."

Placing his hand over the top of my own, Julien gently pulled it from his cheek. Our fingers entwined together for the briefest of moments before he pulled his fingers from mine, shaking his head. A small grin playing on his lips.

"Braelyn Grey, every time I think I have you all figured out you say something that intrigues me even more."

My stomach fluttered like butterfly wings as Julien's grin broadened into a smile. He made to ask another question, but Theo's footsteps in the underbrush made him jump to his feet, a flame in hand. Theo glared at him before Julien turned his back, giving me a wink as he returned to his vigil.

After our conversation, Julien seemed to accept I was okay. He lay on a soft mossy spot beneath the trees—his head pillowed on his hands—and soon began snoring quietly. I wished I had the same ease of falling asleep. My bones hurt, my muscles ached and, mentally, I was exhausted. Unfortunately, my mind would not shut off. It seemed to whirr and spin, like one of the old spinning tops my mother would make dance with her air magic. Never stopping. Never stilling. With the idea of sleep completely off the table, my mind ticked over to my earlier conversation with Julien, his voice echoing around my head about how doomed this journey was—the Lilithium Mortiferum was just another example of how he strongly believed we were being railroaded at every turn. Thinking on it now, I couldn't deny how many things had steered us from our travels, but I had to believe it was all for a reason.

Leaning back on the tree behind me, I closed my eyes, trying to force myself into a world of dreams and rest. I felt the irritated, scratching feeling of tiredness behind my eyes and, trying to clear my mind of the day's events, I slowly began to feel the heaviness of sleep drop over me like a warm blanket. As I drifted, my dreams were filled with darkness and shadow. Stuck in the dark and twirling like the spinning top, I tried conjuring my fire magic to help me fight off the darkness, but nothing came. My magic refused my call. I could hear my mother and Hazel calling out my name, but no matter how hard I tried I couldn't find them in the dark. Theo's and Julien's voices came next as I continued spinning in the darkness, trying to find them. Just as quickly as their voices sounded, they stopped, throwing me into silence. That's when I heard the growl. A loud rumbling sound that shook the darkness around me, sending me into the blinding light.

Nineteen

I felt a hand on my shoulder, the shake startling me awake.

As my eyes adjusted to the warm light flooding in around me, Julien's face came into view—hovering only inches in front of my own. He was holding a small flame in the large palm of his hand and my heart beat a steady rhythm in my chest. The only other time he had used his magic since we came into the Ironwood was when we came across the gremlin on our earlier path. I knew instantly something was wrong.

Theo was standing just behind Julien, his backpack already slung over his shoulders, ready to go at any given moment. His face was partially hidden in the dim glow of Julien's flame, but what I could see was his usual worried expression.

"What's going on," I croaked, but no one had time to reply.

Behind me, a low growl rippled from the shadows between the trees. Starting at how close it sounded, I spun around. My eyes roamed the darkness as I tried to find whatever was making the low rumbling vibrations, but it was no use. The darkness hung like a thick veil around whatever it was that watched us. I spotted Alpheus near Theo's feet—his long ears tall and alert—listening for any other sound. Alpheus's whole body was tense, turned in the direction of the growling creature. I felt the gentle pull in my mind.

"My friend, we must leave. There is something out there that smells of death."

The jackalope's usual soft, lilting voice was riddled with

concern, which only terrified me more. Julien's free hand was wrapped tightly around my wrist, the pressure of his grip causing my fingers to tingle not with magic, but lost sensation. I tried pulling my hand out of his iron grip, but he merely shook his head at me.

Another loud growl echoed around us, coming from somewhere between the trees. It sounded as if it was only metres away and my blood ran cold at the thought of what it could be. Alpheus inched forward slightly, his entire body still rigid as he sniffed the air, trying to locate the scent of whatever animal stood hidden in the dark. A second later a loud thud shook the ground around us, making me grab hold of Julien's arm for support. The earth shuddered beneath us, almost like an earthquake had occurred exactly where we stood, but in the glow of the firelight I saw Alpheus lift one of his large back feet, slamming it down on the ground. The earth trembled, and astonishment washed over me at what I was witnessing. The same as a rabbit signalling danger, he was trying to deter the creature from coming near us. My throat grew thick with emotion as a wave of admiration came crashing over me. The small creature was trying to defend us. Julien inched slowly from where we still stood, his grip never faltering as he pulled me along with him. We reached Theo in a few steps, Alpheus, only an arms-length away. As we stood in the dark, a silence descended over us. It was like the Ironwood was holding its breath, then all I heard was the terror in Alpheus's voice as it sounded in my head.

"Run!"

My arm felt as if it had almost been ripped from its socket as Julien pulled me along after him. Theo's loud footsteps pounded along behind me and I heard the rustle of Alpheus beside us as he skittered through the underbrush somewhere to our left. Turning my head in every direction, I tried looking around to find everyone—my mind frantic at the thought of us getting separated—but it was no use. Julien continued to pull me after him and all I could do was focus on running and making sure I didn't fall.

My heart pounded in my chest as my lungs strained to pull in enough oxygen to keep me going. I still couldn't see what it was we were running from, but the sound of heavy footfalls behind us determined it was big. Stumbling over a tangle of thorns that clutched at my legs, I felt Julien slow his pace to match my own. My chest constricted with pain as I sucked in air while still running. Fear of the creature pursuing us pushed me onward, causing my breath to come in ragged gasps.

Julien came to a sudden stop in front of me and he let go of my wrist. Whirling on his feet, a flame instantly appeared in his hand. It flickered menacingly as he curled and flexed his fingers, eyes intent on the darkness. It was now, after the noise of our footfalls had fallen quiet that I realised the heavy tread behind us had come to a halt. Slowly, I turned to face the creature. Theo stopped beside me, doubled over, his hands on his knees as he tried to catch his breath. The Ironwood was thick with silence, as if the entire wood had been frozen in time. I could hear the low rustle of Alpheus beside me and, reaching down, I placed a trembling hand on one of his antlers. Feeling him gently nudge the tips of my fingers, a wave of ease passed over me, as if the jackalope had the ability to control my emotions, but whatever magic he used on me was short-lived.

The same low growl sounded in front of us and terror coursed through me, sending my blood running cold. In the small light of Julien's flame, I saw his muscles tense ever so slightly as he brought his other hand up to conjure another set of flames. Bringing his hands together, the light in the woods grew, illuminating the path in front of us. As my eyes adjusted to the light, I felt my breath hitch in the back of my throat as we finally laid eyes on what was chasing us.

My earlier thoughts of the creature being big had been a massive understatement. The gruesome creature standing before us now was enormous. In the low light of the woods, it almost looked like a very large dog but, as it took a small step forward into the glow of Julien's flame, I realised how wrong I was.

Standing on four muscled legs that ended in long razor-sharp clawed paws, the beast was entirely covered in long, thick black fur. It was no wonder we couldn't see it in the dark. Its fur blended so well with the darkness, it could have passed as a shadow itself. It produced another low growl in our direction as the thick fur on its back rippled in response. An overpowering odour filled the air as the beast continued to watch us with blood-red eyes.

Julien stood only metres away from the terrifying creature, his gaze never drifting from its face. I had been so preoccupied by the animal's size I hadn't even noticed its head. Long bat-like ears sat on either side of its skull—perfect for tracking prey—while long daggers for teeth dripped a foul-smelling drool at its feet. Tiny beads of sweat gathered on my forehead as fear rippled over my entire body. I could feel the tingle of magic in the palms of my hands as I stood frozen, not daring to take my eyes from the creature in case it attacked. I wanted nothing more than to run.

"What is it?" I asked Alpheus in my mind, my eyes still holding the creature's gaze.

"It's called a barghest. A dog of death. They occasionally wander the Ironwood, but they are usually kept at the castle under the king's command."

My blood turned cold, and I shifted uncomfortably at Alpheus's response. *"What is King Elias keeping these creatures for?"* I thought.

"For one thing only. Murder."

The soft lilt in the jackalope's voice was gone, replaced by a wavering fear of the barghest that looked at us hungrily. A dog of death. It was a fitting name. The mere sight of it was enough to scare the life from anyone. The fire in Julien's hands had grown larger as he continued to summon more magic. The flames flickered around his hands, dancing in the soft cool breeze of early morning. The barghest watched him closely, its beady little eyes glowing like rubies in the firelight. Licking its serrated teeth, its eyes turned on me. An almost sinister smile spread across its flat snout, sending a shiver down my spine.

"Little spirit witch, we meet at last." The barghest's voice was as deep and dark as the shadows it had appeared from.

My eyes grew wide. *How did this creature know what I was?* Julien turned his gaze towards me, and I knew in that moment he had understood the words which had come out of the barghest's pig-like snout. It was the first time since the barghest had appeared that Julien looked at anything but the giant beast.

"What do you want with her?" Julien ground out between clenched teeth.

The barghest snarled in Julien's direction. It was low and menacing. A warning.

"I was not speaking to you, traitor."

Julien's shoulders tensed at the word. Confused, I glanced between Julien and the barghest, not understanding what the creature meant, but whatever it had implied made Julien angrier than I had ever seen him. His flames blazed higher, glowing a molten red. I felt the heat from where I stood still frozen to the spot. I needed to do something before he burnt this creature to a crisp, leaving me with no answers. Pushing my fear and confusion aside, I closed the short distance between us, laying a tentative hand on Julien's arm. Feeling his muscles relax slightly, he stood rigidly beside me as I considered the barghest.

"What is it you want from me?"

The barghest turned its giant head towards me, its lips pulled back in a grim smile. A cold shiver ran down my spine. It was even more terrifying up close.

"I don't want anything from you spirit witch, but there is someone who wants you dead."

"Who?"

Feeling a sense of confusion wash over me, a frown formed between my brows as I tried to consider who wanted to murder me. While I knew Victoria disliked me, I was sure it couldn't be her, and Balor—the silver-skinned elf prince—while arrogant, didn't seem like someone to commit murder over a mere disagreement.

There was only one other person who came to mind. Feeling Julien step closer, his hands still flaming balls of light beside him, I doubted he would extinguish them until the beast was either dead or far behind us. I felt the tingle of my own magic in my fingertips as the barghest began to pace in front of us. Its large paws were silent on the leaf strewn ground. My heart continued to race in my chest, but I kept my hands steady, ready to call my magic if the situation called for it.

Before the barghest's words had left its toothy mouth I already knew what its answer would be, but I needed to hear the creature say it.

"The king, of course."

The barghest ran its serpent-like tongue over its lips, tasting the air. I shuddered to think about what its sharp teeth would feel like cutting into my flesh.

"I don't understand," I heard Theo mumble behind me. "Why would the king want you dead? He was the one who invited you to the castle in the first place."

Julien rolled his eyes, scoffing at Theo's comment, but I ignored him. Up until a few moments ago I had been thinking the same thing, but once again Julien's voice sounded in my head. How he'd thought this entire journey was doomed from the beginning. The barghest showing up only confirmed my deepest fears.

"The king never wanted us to make it to the castle, did he?" I said to the barghest, my voice soft as all the pieces began to fit together like a jigsaw puzzle inside my head.

The barghest snapped its jaws together as if laughing at my dismay. "Very good, little spirit witch. King Elias never meant for you to leave the Ironwood, he just needed a way to get you in here so he could dispose of you."

Pacing in anticipation, the barghest's large paws pounded the mossy earth in time with my racing heart. Dirt flicked up from its claws as they sliced into the ground.

My fear had long disappeared, replaced with burning anger at the king's deception. I'd never expected this journey to be easy, but

I had hoped he would at least keep his word as Ellesmere's King and as part of my family, no matter how cruel that part may be. My anger surged through me, blinding and unstoppable. My magic rushed through my veins—reacting to the growing intensity of my anger—my hands tingling violently as the once silent breeze increased in strength. The wind tangled my hair as the strong gusts blew the leaves along the ground, making Julien's flames flutter and dance.

The barghest's beady eyes darted around at the chaos, but if my growing air magic bothered the creature, I would have never known. Its thick, greasy fur ruffled in the wind as it continued to pace back and forth in front of us, its eyes narrowed and never leaving my face.

"It is herding us closer together so it can attack us all at once."

I started at the voice in my head, almost forgetting the jackalope was there. Alpheus had been so silent through this entire ordeal that I half expected him to have darted off into the woods to safety. I wouldn't have blamed him if he had decided to leave—the barghest looked to be ten times the size of the jackalope—but a small, selfish part of me was glad he had decided to stay. Alpheus's soft voice helped sooth my anger, but only slightly. Tearing my gaze away from the barghest, I looked at both Theo and Julien and saw that Alpheus was right. All four of us had huddled together without even realising what we were doing. I looked over my shoulder at Theo. Without magic, he was vulnerable. I needed to protect him at all costs. His blue eyes were wide, his skin pale with terror. Julien was quite capable of using his magic to defend himself, but we needed to be able to work together if we were ever going to get out of here alive.

"I'm not going to let you hurt my friends, so I would suggest you step aside and let us be on our way."

I had hoped my words would sound strong and powerful, but my fear at what was to come overpowered me, making my words sound shaky.

The creature gave me a menacing toothy grin. "You drive a

hard bargain, little spirit witch, but I can't let that happen. The king wants you dead and his word is the law."

Eying the four of us, the barghest licked its lips menacingly. Despite the fear roiling in my belly, I refused to let this beast hurt the people I cared about.

"Take one step closer, dog, and I will burn your flesh until you *beg* for death." My voice was steady, and my hands trembled with power.

Fire engulfed my hands—burning hot like the anger radiating through me. The barghest let out a low snarl, baring its teeth in my direction.

"I will make your death slow, spirit witch. I will make you watch as I tear the flesh from each of your friends. The Ironwood will run red with your filthy blood."

My stomach jolted at how easily this creature spoke of killing. My earlier terror began creeping its way back in, the flames licking my hands sputtering slightly in response to my fear. I had always suspected there would be other witches and warlocks out there who would not be kind to me because of my magic, but to hear they wanted me dead sent a shiver down my spine. I hadn't asked for any of this, and the weight of what lay ahead was pressing down on me.

The jackalope nudged its antlers against my fist in a reassuring gesture. *"Breathe,"* he whispered softly. I let out a ragged breath, almost falling to my knees.

Leaning on a nearby tree, I managed to steady myself enough to avoid crumpling to a heap on the leafy ground, but before I even had the chance to take another shaking breath, Julien was at my side. His hands felt hot on my sweat-soaked skin, but I leaned into his warmth, letting it take hold of me, easing my rapidly beating heart.

I didn't know if we would be able to get past the barghest, but I knew if we used our magic together, we would have a much better chance of surviving. Recalling the strength of his magic at the Forest Festival the first time we'd met, I prayed by combining our magic, we could beat the barghest at its own game.

I touched Julien's palm, my fingers grazing his elemental rune. Placing my own rune on top of his, I hoped he understood the silent message I was trying to convey.

"Ah, what a touching sentiment, but your time has run out, spirit witch. I've had enough of talking."

Snapping its jaws, a loud snarl rippled through the barghest as it launched at us. Spinning in a movement so quick I barely had time to move out of the way, Julien conjured a large fireball in front of him, the fire licking up his arms. The barghest had almost closed the distance between us and, quick as lightning, Julien sent his fire soaring through the air towards the creature. The barghest was too quick. The flames missed their target by mere inches, crashing into the dense trees behind the beast. Raging flames ignited the dry bark as Julien cursed under his breath. I watched helplessly from the side as the creature charged, its sharp teeth snapping in his direction. If I didn't do something fast, Julien would be dead in minutes. I searched the woods frantically for something to stop the barghest. There wasn't much in the way of weapons, but I was a spirit witch, and my magic was powerful.

Clenching my jaw, I looked down at my hands. "Spiritus!" I roared.

I felt the rush of magic in my blood, coursing through me like a raging river. The cool breeze tickled the small hairs on the back of my neck and I smelt the damp decay of mouldy leaves underneath my boots. Clenching my hands together, I let the magic build within me. The trees groaned as their life force reacted to my magic and fire bubbled in my veins, waiting to be released. I could feel the thrum of water beneath my feet as the breeze picked up its pace. Even looking death in the eye, I had never felt so alive. My magic reacted as I called to each element, beckoning with open arms. As the barghest's jaws came within inches of closing around Julien's chest, I opened my hands. The leaves littering the ground shot up towards the night sky, shifting to form a wall between us and the barghest. While I knew the leafy wall wasn't much for protection, it gave Julien just enough time to dart out of the way as the creature's attention faltered. In the split second the beast was distracted, I thrust my hand out to the side, the wind around us picking up speed and bringing our next line of defence. Small needle-like thorns hovered around me as the barghest's beady red eyes found my face amongst the flurry of leaves. A terrifying snarl pulled its jowls up in a dangerous smile.

"Give up, witch, you will never beat me. I am already dead."

The barghest leapt just as I let the thorns around me fly. They speared through the air like tiny arrowheads, plunging deep into the barghest's black fur. A loud roar burst from its foul-smelling jaws as it tried to free itself from the net of thorns I had pierced it with. I whipped my head to Julien, seeing his hands were aflame once more. I relaxed my own, letting the remaining thorns fall to the ground. The barghest spun around, snapping its jaws, looking more like a dog chasing its tail than the deadly creature trying to kill us. It stopped circling, setting its rage-filled eyes on me.

"Clever trick, witch, but it is going to take more than that to stop me."

Fear threatened to overpower me as it stalked closer. I wanted nothing more than to wrap my arms around myself and disappear, but instead I let my fear consume me. My magic always seemed to work best when my emotions were heightened.

"I'm counting on it," I spat.

The trees around us began to creak, like eerie spectators watching fighters in a ring. Focusing on the sway of the branches, I pulled them towards me—hearing the crack and splintering of the bark as I readied myself to pull the spindly branches to use.

Waiting until the barghest was close enough to smell its horrid, decaying breath, the moment I felt my fear heighten, I let my magic loose. The branches shot out like swords being pulled from their sheaths as I tried to create a twisted wall of armour between us, but the barghest was too quick. Batting the first few away, the branches snapped like kindling. I felt the crack of wood reverberating through me as if it were biting down and breaking my bones.

Pulling thicker branches towards me, I began to snake them along the ground, moving them in every direction as I forced them up and around the barghest's body, eventually pining it in place. The beast's low snarl rang in my ears.

Julien stepped towards the creature, fire burning like molten rivers up his forearms. My breath hitched as he stood right in front of the creature's face, and I threw all my strength into maintaining my wooden prison.

With the barghest trapped, I took a moment to seek out Theo's tall, lanky frame. He stood frozen by the nearby trees, the jackalope close by his feet. The tendons in his long neck stood out against his bloodless face, a look of pure terror in his blue eyes. I wanted nothing more than run to him, to throw my arms protectively around him and tell him everything was going to be okay, but I couldn't promise that. The barghest pulled against my restraints, and I gritted my teeth against the fight it was putting up. *At least Theo was safe.*

Turning my attention back to the creature, I noted its blood-red eyes were narrowed in Julien's direction. I could almost see the anger rippling through its fur as Julien stared at it, a smirk pulling up the corner of his mouth. Holding the branches as steady as I could, I focused on creating an iron grip to keep the creature imprisoned, but it had a strength beyond my own. It strained at my bindings, and the slightest drift in my concentration would mean certain death for us all.

Julien's hands burned hot beside him, the heat radiating from him like waves crashing onto the sand. Beads of sweat dripped down the sides of my face despite the coolness of the night.

"I will kill you," Julien said as his lips pulled back against his teeth. His voice was soft and even, as if the very thought of seeing this creature dead excited him. "And you will suffer painfully."

Placing one of his flaming hands around one of the barghest's bat-like ears, I expected to see the creature burn under the flame. To anyone else, this action alone would have been enough to bring them to their knees, but the barghest simply let out a low snarl.

Julien's shoulders tensed as he tightened his fiery grip on the creature's ear, but there was no howl of pain or whimper of agony, the creature simply stared back at Julien, a mocking grin lingering on its face.

"You think you can use your magic to cause me pain, traitor? I am not of your world. I was created in the depths of the underworld, and nothing will stop me from fulfilling the orders of the king."

Before my brain could decipher what was happening, I felt my magic falter, the wooden prison trapping the barghest splintering open. Broken branches burst around us in a small explosion. Thrown backwards by the sheer strength of the barghest's power, I crashed into one of the trees behind me—the air knocked from my lungs as I lay half sitting in the dirt, trying to catch my breath. Tears filled my eyes at the pain surging in my back, but it wasn't my pain that made me scream in agony.

Julien had been knocked aside by the barghest and lay face down on the ground, half covered in dirt and debris too far away for me to get to. Watching him push himself up I barely had time to scream out his name before the barghest's large paw was on his back, pushing him back down. Julien was pinned under those blades, which were only inches from piercing his heart. In a quick flick of its claws the barghest could end his life. As if sensing my terror, it turned its dark, dead eyes on me, a roaring snarl tearing from its chest. I tried conjuring the same magic that had trapped the creature only moments before, but the impact of being thrown into the tree trunk had left me dizzy and unable to concentrate.

"Foolish girl. Did you really think you were strong enough to overpower me?" Its voice was low and cruel. "Now you will watch as your friends die."

Before I had the chance to scramble to my feet, the barghest bent its head, clasping Julien's shoulder between its teeth. Julien yelled out in pain as a scream ripped through me, threatening to tear me apart. Blood pooled where the creature's teeth pierced Julien's skin, running like tiny rivers down the front of his shirt.

The creature watched me with grim satisfaction as it picked up Julien's limp body, dangling him in front of me tauntingly. My eyes went wide and my hands trembled violently as Julien's fate was dangled before me. I glanced over to where Theo still stood, his shoulders hunched forward, his freckled hand clutching his shirt. Alpheus's body trembled in fear as his breath came in quick bursts. Turning my gaze back to Julien's limp body, I locked my hazel eyes with the barghest's ruby ones.

"Please," I whimpered. "Take me instead. It's me you want, not them."

I tried to move forward, to conjure any type of magic, but nothing came. As I took another wobbled step, the creature sank its teeth deeper into Julien's shoulder, and he screamed out again. His face was a portrait of agony and my heart almost shattered into a million pieces knowing I had contributed to it. Watching in sheer horror as Julien's face turned a sickly grey, I opened my mouth, ready to plead with the barghest to let him go, when the creature simply tossed him aside like a discarded bone. Julien's body skidded along the ground, coming to a stop not far from where I stood. I tried to make a run for Julien, but before I managed even a few steps towards him, the barghest knocked me to the ground with a bone crushing thud.

My head hit the ground so hard I thought I was going to be sick. My stomach churned violently, and my vision swam before me as I tried to sit up, but the beast's large paws held me in a deathly grip. Its flat snout hovered only inches from my face, its hot breath on my skin leaving the smell of death and decay in my nose. I squirmed underneath the creature's claws, trying to free myself, but there was no point. The barghest's strength was too much.

"Your time has come spirit witch. Long live King Elias."

Twenty

My heart hammered in my chest as a menacing rumble sounded from the barghest's throat. It lowered its teeth towards my neck, Julien's blood still dripping from its jaws. I squeezed my eyes shut and waited for the pain to come, but to my surprise it never did. *Was I already dead? Had my death been so quick I never felt the searing pain or sharp stab of the barghest's teeth on my skin?* Laying on the ground, I felt the weight of the creature lift from my chest and the air flow through me. Rolling to the side, I gasped and slowly opened my eyes. Shock spread through me. The barghest was slumped on its side, a sharp branch protruding from the thick fur of its chest. Theo stood over the beast, his hands shaking and covered in blood. He stared, wide-eyed and trembling at the barghest's limp form as I scrambled to my feet. Rushing over, I patted his arms and chest, frantically searching for a wound, but I couldn't find a mark on him.

"It's not my blood," he breathed.

Realisation dawned on me as I looked back at the creature. Theo had been the one to bring the beast down. There was no movement in its chest, and a thick black liquid oozed from where the branch protruded, knife-like, from its torso. My heart swelled as my eyes darted back over to Theo.

"What happened?" I asked softly.

Theo fidgeted where he stood. His eyes were still focused on the corpse of the dead monster. Theo cleared his throat, his voice still raspy. "I don't know what came over me. I had been so terrified watching that thing attack Julien, when I tried to summon my magic, nothing happened. I could hardly think straight, but when it came for you, it was like something clicked inside me." His eyes darted quickly to the barghest, as if checking the creature was still dead.

"I knew if I didn't do something you would be killed right in front of me, so I tried conjuring the branches like you had done. I was so terrified and confused, they came shooting down towards the barghest and stabbed it through the chest."

Shaking my head in bewilderment, I gave him a warm smile. "Theo, you saved my life, whether you meant to kill the barghest or not you still managed to get your magic to do what you needed it to." I put my hand on his shoulder, giving it a light squeeze. "Thank you."

Theo's face turned beetroot red. Turning his eyes away from me, the scar on his cheek puckered, and I knew he was smiling to himself.

Knowing Theo wasn't hurt, I turned my attention to Julien. He still lay motionless on the ground where the barghest had discarded him like a piece of forgotten meat. Cautiously, I walked over to his limp body, holding my breath. My heart constricted, and my lungs seemed to close as panic set in. I didn't know what I would do if I found him dead. Sinking to my knees, I gently rolled his body over, so he was lying on his back. My eyes roved over him, trying to find any sign he was still alive. After a moment I saw the slight rise and fall of his chest. Crumpling against a nearby tree, I let out a sigh of relief. He was still alive. Barely. The wound in his shoulder was still bleeding badly, but the claws must have missed any vital organs. We needed to find help, if only we could just get out of this damned forest. Looking back towards Theo, I beckoned him over. There had to be something in his grimoire that would help stop the blood from oozing out of Julien's shoulder.

Theo reached me in a few long strides, sinking down to his

knees beside me, his face still pale.

"Is there anything in the grimoire that can help with the bleeding?"

It took Theo a few moments to answer, but his eyes widened as he stared at Julien. "There is a poultice that can help with preventing infection. It may be thick enough to help slow the bleeding."

"Can you make it?" I asked. I heard the desperation in my voice.

Theo nodded his head before jumping to his feet. Bringing his bag over, he tipped the contents out beside Julien and got to work searching through the numerous jars of herbs and crushed flowers he had bought with him. He pulled the stoppers from a few bottles, tipping out the contents into a bowl. The spicy smell of yarrow wafted from the mortar bowl, and I spied the long green leaves of calendula in another. Grinding them down with a pestle, Theo added a few drops of rosemary oil, making the herbs turn thick and fragrant. The last thing he added to the mix was moon water. It diluted the gooey poultice, turning it into a thick orange paste. Despite what Theo had said to me about his magic, I was in awe of him. He was a natural. It was like watching my mother prepare her jars of healing herbs and tea mixes. I knew Theo's inability to summon his magic weighed heavy on his mind, but watching his steady hands prepare the salve for Julien's shoulder, I believed he was destined for something far greater than elemental magic. I was glad Theo had been the one to save us.

Handing me the small bowl filled with mixture, Theo lifted the sweater from Julien's arm, careful so as not to cause him more pain. As Theo managed to get Julien's arm out of his sweater, I could see the once white shirt underneath was now stained a deep red, the metallic smell of blood wafting up from his shoulder as Theo pulled away the tattered material to apply the salve. My eyes widened as I saw the full extent of the damage the barghest had caused. Three long gashes ran diagonally from under Julien's arm to the top of his shoulder. The initial puncture wounds were still open and oozing little rivulets of blood down his arm.

Pulling a piece of cloth from his backpack, Theo poured out a few drops of the moon water and gently placed it over the top of Julien's torn skin. I heard Julien's intake of breath as his eyes swam in and out of consciousness.

Watching with rapt attention, Theo administered his care to Julien's shoulder with absolute precision. He cleaned off the dried blood sticking to Julien's skin with a little of the moon water he had used in the poultice. His movements were soft and gentle as he cleaned up most of the dried blood, leaving us to see the wound for what it was—a terrible mess of shredded skin and muscle. I swallowed back the bile in my mouth.

"Will he be okay?" I whispered.

Theo continued his ministrations, scooping the dark orange mixture and applying it thickly to the open cuts on the front of Julien's chest.

"He should be okay," he murmured as he gently turned Julien on his side, applying some of the poultice to the three round teeth marks lining the back of his shoulder. "As long as we can prevent infection, the magic in this poultice will restore the damaged tissue. He will need to see a Wise Witch though, as it will need stitches."

A grimace had formed on Julien's pale face, and he was shivering almost uncontrollably. The temperature had dropped considerably as dawn grew closer and I found myself pulling my jacket tighter around my shoulders. Theo finished covering Julien's shoulder in the healing salve, placing a thick, square piece of bandage over the top to protect it from infection. Pulling Julien's shirt back to cover most of his exposed skin, my fingers brushed the flesh of Julien's shoulder, and I felt goosebumps rise on his skin. I pulled his sweater around his shoulders, but his body still tremored from shock and the coolness of dawn.

"Maybe I could be of assistance?"

I had forgotten the jackalope was still with us. He was sitting just behind me, watching us with careful eyes. After a moment's hesitation, Alpheus hopped over to Julien's good side, stretching along the length of his body. Instantly, his features relaxed and his breathing slowed.

I had felt the same calming effect when I reached out to the jackalope only hours before, and I was glad he was helping ease Julien's fever.

"Thank you." With a slight nod, Alpheus rested his head on his front paws, closing his eyes.

With Julien's breaths coming steadily now, I picked up the small vial of healing elixir that lay discarded with the unused herb jars. Unstopping it, I placed a few drops over Julien's hands, which were riddled in red veins after using his fire magic. Seeing the tiny rivers of his magic start to recede, I turned my attention to Theo. He had packed up the remaining jars and was scraping the rest of the poultice into the empty moon water bottle. The remaining mixture didn't even fill half the jar and I worried, silently knowing it would only be good for another dosage. We would need to find a Wise Witch soon if Julien would have any chance of making it with his wounds.

Sitting in front of Theo, I pulled my legs underneath me and waited for him to finish repacking his bag. He placed the grimoire at the very bottom, the jars and mortar and pestle sitting neatly on top of it. Keeping it safe. Clipping the bag shut, he turned his light eyes to me, a sad smile playing on his lips. Reaching out, I took his hands in my own, gazing down at the faint green lines.

"It's your turn," I said to him as I shook the little vial of healing elixir.

As dawn slowly melted into morning, Julien still lay in a restless sleep underneath the sunlit trees. Alpheus was still curled warmly at his side as Theo and I took it in turns to sit on watch while the other slept.

After our run-in with Grugo and then the barghest, we didn't want to take any chances that King Elias wouldn't send any more deadly surprises. Theo offered to take the first watch, letting me rest for a much needed few hours. I felt like I'd only just closed my eyes when Theo gently shook me awake. I jumped at his touch, still wrapped in dreams of shadow and blood. Theo made a soft shushing noise as I realised where we were.

Letting Theo sleep, I found a patch of sun that had broken through the canopy of the trees. Sitting on a patch of mossy earth, I relished in the feel of it on my skin. It had been two days since we left the Ironwood Village, and I hadn't realised until now just how much I had missed the light. Closing my eyes and turning my face towards the sun, I hadn't felt this at ease since before we had entered the Ironwood. Taking a deep breath, I ran my hand over the small patch of moss in front of me—feeling it tremble beneath my fingers, its life force ebbing and flowing like a steady heartbeat beneath my hand. Smiling to myself, I opened my eyes and placed both my hands on the spot where the moss finished and hundreds of dead, decaying leaves began. In a slow arching motion I swiped my hand along the ground, watching as more moss sprung up from between the dirt and leaves.

The dirt underneath the debris of leaves was damp and, placing my hand a few inches over the ground, I focused all my attention on the tiny droplets of water deep within the soil. Concentrating hard for a few minutes—my patience growing thin when nothing happened right away—I pulled my hand away with a huff as I realised my hand was damp. The tiny drops of water had beaded on the palm of my hand like metal fragments drawn to a magnet. Staring in astonishment, I brought my other hand up over my palm, and in a small circular motion, turned my wrist, watching as the tiny droplets floated as if suspended on an invisible string between my hands. Tilting my palms horizontally, I curled my fingers around the droplets, watching as they formed a ball of water no bigger than the size of my fist. I held the watery orb between my palms like a child about to throw a ball, and it glistened in the morning sun, rippling and distorting the view through it. Watching my little ball of water float before me, my mind turned to Maeve and the way she could manipulate water in the most incredible ways. My heart lurched a little as memories of her cheeky smile and gentle eyes played out before me. I missed her terribly and hoped I would eventually see her again once this part of my journey came to an end.

"Neat trick."

Julien's voice startled me out of my reverie and, losing my concentration, the ball of water evaporated into a fine mist. Holding my hand over my chest, I tried to steady my racing heart. Julien's head was tilted slightly in my direction, his eyes dark and thoughtful.

"How long have you been watching me?" I asked, suddenly feeling self-conscious.

He smiled. "Not very long, but I can see you've learnt some new skills with your magic."

"I had some spare time while you lazy sods slept. I thought I could use the time to practice." I smiled softly, winking playfully.

"Well it seems like you're learning lots of new things on your journey through the Ironwood."

I watched him closely as his eyes sparkled a little mischievously in the glistening morning sun, highlighting the small golden fragments that were often hidden in his usual chocolate eyes. I knew he was talking about not only my growing spirit magic, but also my new ability to speak to other creatures who dwelled within the Ironwood. I knew eventually someone would ask, but I didn't have the answers as to why this was happening to me.

"It seems that way," I said back.

Julien laughed softly. "I take it you weren't aware of your newfound ability to talk to other creatures before we entered the Ironwood?"

"Unfortunately, no. It's a little hard to comprehend. I didn't even know such magic was possible." I tried to remember all the books I'd read over the years, sifting through the pages to see if I recalled ever hearing about this type of magic, but it was useless. Nothing came to mind.

"I remember when I was a child there was a Wise Witch in the village who had this type of ability, but I don't recall how she ever came to obtain it. My mother had always said she was blessed by the elements, but I'm not too sure what to believe."

Julien's voice broke through my thoughts at the mention of knowing someone else who had this ability, but what intrigued me more was the mention of his mother. In all our stolen conversations over the last few days, he had never brought up his family, and I was eager to know more about the mysterious Thorne family.

"Did your mother know the Wise Witch who had this ability?"

Julien's brow creased in thought before he replied. "I think her name was Althea, but I can't be entirely sure."

My breath hitched in my throat at hearing Althea's name. The same Wise Witch who had prophesied my future. My mind whirled at this information and I was eager to see if there was anything written in Althea's book about the ability.

"Are you okay, sweetheart? You look like you've seen a ghost."

I could see the worry written all over his face as he gazed at me, his bushy brows deepening into a frown.

"Yeah, sorry, just got lost in my own thoughts for a moment. I've never heard you talk about your family before. Would you tell me about them?"

Julien's lips pursed at the mention of his family, and I waited with bated breath, wondering if I would finally hear if the rumours were true. Over the last few days I had seen a side of Julien that made me truly believe he wasn't a bad person, but there had been flickers of darkness, too. Shadows of a haunted past, perhaps.

"There isn't much to say about them. My father died when I was really young, so my mother raised me on her own at the apothecary until she died of illness just before my rune ceremony."

His voice turned sad at the mention of his mother's passing, but a small smile pulled up one corner of his mouth in fondness.

"Oh, I'm so sorry, Julien. It must have been so hard for you."

He gave a small shrug before wincing in pain, the movement causing his shoulder to shift slightly. I knelt by his side, lifting the bandages to check his wound. I was aware of his eyes watching me as my fingers gently pulled back the bandages, my soft touch sending goosebumps rippling over his exposed skin.

Looking at the shredded mess of his shoulder I could see the salve was doing its job. The bleeding had slowed almost to a stop and there was no red blotching signalling infection. I re-covered it with the cloth bandage.

"How does it feel?" I asked.

"Like I've been mauled by a death dog."

There wasn't any malice in his words and I was glad to see his injury hadn't affected his sarcasm.

I gave him a weak smile. "I'm sorry about your shoulder, Julien."

A heavy weight settled in my chest. I was the reason he was injured and I lowered my gaze, not wanting to see blame in his eyes. Reaching out his good arm, Julien tilted my chin to face him. His hand was rough and, despite the amount of blood he'd lost, his touch still held its usual warmth.

"None of this is your fault, Braelyn. I was stupid and reckless and I shouldn't have taunted the barghest like I did. I provoked it into attacking me."

His eyes were like golden honey in the sunlight, pleading for me to not blame myself, but as much as Julien said it was his fault, a small part of me would always feel responsible.

"Julien, if it wasn't for me, you wouldn't have been out here."

Julien shook his head. "I don't blame you for any of this, I'm just glad you weren't injured."

I searched Julien's face for any sign of his usual joking or sarcastic behaviour, but there was none. Ever so gently, he grazed my cheekbone with his thumb, making my heart flutter in my chest. I wasn't sure what had happened between us before, but all I knew was something had shifted. Julien's hand slid behind my head, his fingers tangling in my messy, windswept hair. Bringing my head closer to his, I leant in towards him, our faces only inches apart. Julien's eyes burned like molten lava as he searched my own. I hadn't felt this nervous since my rune ceremony. My cheeks blazed and, biting my lip, I tried to turn my head away, not used to this type of attention and unsure what to do with it now. In Pryhollow, most people stayed away from us. I had never caught the attention of anyone in the town. I had never even had a first kiss.

Julien's grip in my hair tightened ever so slightly, preventing me from turning my gaze away. "Please don't look away." His voice was low, his breath tickling my cheek.

Leaning his head towards me, I mimicked his movement, our lips only inches apart. His usual smell of burnt wood and smoke was mixed with the tangy scent of blood, but it didn't faze me. Nibbling on my bottom lip as the nerves bubbled up in my stomach, Julien's eyes burned with a need I felt deep within my chest. His hand pulled my face even closer, our lips almost touching, but a sound came from behind me, making me jump away from him as if an electric current had passed between us.

Theo's head had slid off the bag he had been using as a pillow, startling him awake. Sitting up, his arms floundered in the air like large balloons being let go. He had dried brown leaves stuck to his face and the sheer sight of him made a laugh burst from my chest. I even thought I heard Julien's deep chuckle from behind me.

Startled, Theo looked at us both with an annoyed expression, but it only lasted a moment—a large grin spread over his face as Theo's loud laugh echoed around us.

"Maybe that's a sign we should get moving," I said through small snorts of laughter.

Sighing, Theo rubbed a hand over his face, brushing the leaves from his cheek. "Julien, will you be okay to move with your shoulder?"

"Yeah, I should be okay." He tried pulling himself into a sitting position.

I stopped laughing and stared wide-eyed between the two of them. It was the first time they'd interacted without a snide comment or sarcastic retort. My heart soared. Maybe there was still a chance they could get along and I wouldn't feel like my heart was being pulled in two separate directions.

"Brae, why are you staring at me that way?" Theo raised a curious eyebrow in my direction.

"It's nothing, I'm just…I'm just glad you're both with me." Giving him a bashful smile, I turned my attention to Julien.

Helping him get to his feet proved to be more of a difficult task than I had originally thought. I could only lift his one good arm to pull him up, and we kept toppling over which only made things more awkward between us. After a few grunts and unsavoury words from Julien, we managed to get him leaning against the tree he had been laying under. The effort of trying to get him up one-handed had spent a lot of his energy—his face was now a chalky white and pinched with pain—so we waited a few more minutes until he felt stable enough to walk.

"Are you sure you will be okay?" I whispered as I tied his sweater into a makeshift sling around his shoulder.

He put his good hand out and lightly brushed my hand in a lightning quick movement. Goosebumps spread over my arm and a blushing heat rushed to my cheeks again.

Julien smiled. "I'll be fine, as long as I have you to take care of me."

Feeling the heat in my cheeks intensify, I watched as Julien's smile broadened into a gorgeous toothy grin before he stepped away from the tree, leaving me hot and embarrassed.

Theo's voice yelled out to me from somewhere up ahead that we were leaving and, with a quick smile to myself, I followed them through the trees towards what I could only hope would be the end of our tumultuous journey.

Twenty-One

The cool morning quickly turned into a magnificent autumn day and the sun continued to warm my skin as the crisp dried leaves crunched under my boots. I soon felt myself beginning to overheat in my thick jumper and coat, and quickly stripped both off, feeling the instant relief of just being in my thin blouse.

The trees in this part of the Ironwood were sparser and, despite having more room to move around, our walking continued to be slow. Julien's injury had weakened him considerably and we found ourselves needing to take more breaks than usual to let him catch his breath. At first, I didn't mind the constant stopping. Now that we were reaching the end of the Ironwood, it was alive with sound. Small forest creatures skittered in the underbrush and birds warbled to each other in a chorus of chatter. If I closed my eyes, I could almost imagine being back in the woods near Hazel's cottage. Even the jackalope seemed to be less cautious in this part of the woods. Ever since the barghest attack, Alpheus had been on alert every time we stopped. Sitting tall and rigid, he constantly searched the trees around us for any sign of danger, but now simply sat in the slivers of sun burning through the canopy of the trees—his eyes closed in peaceful thought. I found myself wishing I was able to do the same.

As our journey brought us closer to the castle, an

overwhelming sense of anxiety had been churning inside me. After the hurdles we had faced, I didn't know what to expect from King Elias. Knowing he wanted me dead put a pin in my plan to simply meet him at the castle and ask for my mother's freedom. He was likely to strike me down the minute I stepped through the castle doors. We needed to find a way in that would prevent the king from knowing we were there, giving me time to find my mother and escape.

As I sat sifting through my many thoughts, a low growl sounded from behind me. I spun, hands surging with fire magic—ready for whatever foul creature had come to try and kill us this time—but it was Julien who had made the grumble. Letting out a shaky breath and extinguishing the fire in my hands, I brought them down to relax by my side.

Theo was standing in front of Julien, his brow creased in silent thought. Standing back, I watched as Theo's deft hands removed the sling and the sodden bandages that had crusted with old blood. As Theo pulled the bandage away, Julien grunted in agony. It was obviously still causing him immense pain as, each time Theo would pull the bandage away from his wound, Julien's jaw would tighten, his teeth clenched in agony.

"Will you stop moving?" Theo said crossly. "The more you move, the more it's going to hurt!"

Julien's eyes burned into the top of Theo's sandy blond head as he bent over to pull away the bandage.

So much for them getting along.

When Theo finally got the bandages off, my breath hitched sharply at the sight of Julien's chest. The puncture marks where the barghest's teeth had sunk were a deep red. The bleeding had stopped and dried blood still covered his chest, but it wasn't what caused my eyes to widen. Snaking out from the bite marks were dark inky lines spreading like a spiderweb across Julien's chest. From where I stood it could have almost passed as a bruise, but as I looked closer there was no mistaking the dark ebony colour of Julien's veins.

"What's wrong with him?" I asked, coming over to stand next to Theo.

"He's been poisoned."

I looked at Theo, eyes widening in alarm. "What do you mean he's been poisoned?"

Theo let out a long breath before he replied. "I remember reading that when a barghest bites its prey, sometimes it's able to release a poison into the blood stream. They do this in the small chance the prey does manage to escape. This way, if the barghest doesn't finish the kill, the poison eventually will. I thought it was just a myth, but clearly not, looking at the state of this." He pointed to Julien's darkening chest.

"Can you stop it?" I asked, feeling anxiety begin to bubble up inside me again.

"The poultice I made will slow the spread of poison, but only a Wise Witch will be able to cleanse his blood."

My hands began to shake and I shoved them beneath my arms so neither Theo or Julien could see how much this was breaking me. I peeked at Julien. His face was contorted in pain and anger, but he gave me a small, one-sided smile.

"I'll be fine, Braelyn. Let's get moving, the sooner we get to the castle and find your mother, the sooner I can get this wretched shoulder fixed."

He shrugged his shirt back over his chest, reluctantly letting me help fix the buttons. Pulling the sling over his head, I let my hand linger lightly on his arm. Feeling the slightest touch of his fingers on my hip, I met his fiery gaze, trying to silently tell him everything on my mind. I wanted to tell him about the anxiety clutching at my heart the closer we came to the castle and the fear of finding my mother dead before I had the chance to save her. I wanted to tell him that talking to him made me feel at ease—like I finally had someone who understood me—but instead I gave him a shy, fleeting smile and stepped away from him, following behind Theo as Alpheus lead us onwards.

We finally arrived at the edge of the Ironwood at dusk. My pulse quickened as I spied part of the castle in the distance. The weight on my chest lightened at the prospect of knowing we were going to reach my mother within the time frame. The trees were fewer and far between now, so we stuck to the shadows to avoid being seen by any passers-by.

Peering around the safety of the few trees still around, I had a perfect view of what lay before us. A few metres ahead, the trees had thinned out completely into a large clearing. The entire grassed area had been thrown into shadow as the sun continued to sink lower on the horizon, turning the once bright blue sky into magnificent shades of orange and pink. What caused me the most concern was the giant stone wall towering over the Ironwood, separating us from accessing any part of the castle grounds. Looking in both directions, the wall ran almost the full length of the Ironwood. I squinted through the scattered trees for a ladder or break in the stone that would allow us to the other side, but there was nothing. Huffing, I sank to the ground, my back facing the castle.

"How are we going to get through that?" Theo asked, his eyes staring up at the bulk of stone and rock. "There is no way Julien will be able to climb that with his arm."

His voice was so matter of fact, I stared at him at a loss for words. Apparently, he was under the impression we would have had a chance at getting to the top of the wall.

"You're delusional," Julien muttered.

Theo shot a dark look in his direction. "I don't see you coming up with any plans to get over it."

My head pulsed with an oncoming headache. Rubbing my temples, I closed my eyes and tried to think of something, anything, that would get us through the outer wall of the castle. I wondered if I could use my earth magic to create a hole in the wall? It was a terrible plan. King Elias would surely have guards patrolling the outer areas of the castle, and a gaping hole in the stone would create far too much noise. Perhaps I could move the earth under the wall just enough to create a space big enough for us to squeeze through?

I had great control over my earth magic and tunnelling under the wall seemed like the stealthiest option. It was quiet and we could use the shadow of the wall to shield us from being seen. But would I have the power to be able to pull off something as miraculous as this?

I shifted to narrow my eyes at the large stone structure standing between me and my mother when the jackalope's voice sounded in my head.

"I might know a way through the wall."

Alpheus's voice was soft and sure, and I felt his instant calming sensation wash over me. Julien and Theo continued to bicker behind me, their voices growing louder as they tried to assert their dominance over each other. I shook my head. *Would these two ever learn to just get along?*

The pounding in my head had grown considerably despite the soothing sound of the jackalope's voice. My anger flared like wildfire and I lashed out.

"Will you both be quiet!"

Julien and Theo both stopped their arguing and looked at me with raised brows. Theo's cheeks blushed a soft pink and Julien rubbed a hand over the back of his neck as they mumbled a quiet apology. I felt bad for snapping at them, but I was tired of their bickering. Being so close to saving my mother yet still so far bothered me more than I cared to admit.

Taking a deep breath, I mumbled a quick sorry before continuing.

"Alpheus knows a way into the castle and if you would be quiet for just a few seconds I can tell you what he knows!"

Neither of them said a word to me, but nodded their heads in agreement. Not used to having this effect on people, I felt a little rush of power at the ability of being able to stun them into silence.

Alpheus launched into a plan. *"There is a small hole in the wall towards the western section of the castle that is used to drain water. It will lead you through to the castle grounds."* He nudged his head to the left of where we stood. *"It is only small but should be big enough for you to get through.*"

I gifted the jackalope a broad smile. This creature had been our guiding light and I was beyond grateful for its help. I touched a tentative hand to the top of his head, my palm resting on the soft fur between its antlers.

"Thank you," I whispered. "For everything."

Alpheus's nose twitched slightly as I withdrew my hand. *"It has been my pleasure, friend."*

Getting to my feet, I looked out towards the castle wall. The sun had sunk lower in the sky, casting this side of the Ironwood in shadow. It was the perfect time to make our way towards the drainage hole.

"What did he say?" Theo stood at the ready, looking more like a soldier waiting for his instructions than the gangly teenager I had met only a week ago.

"There is a hole we can get through that will take us to the castle grounds. If we make our way there now, we can keep to the shadows of the Ironwood and pass through at nightfall."

"Sounds like a plan," he replied seriously.

He busied himself with adjusting his backpack—a task he often did after the gremlin attack. Julien was still lounging against a nearby tree, looking a little worse for wear. His face was creased in pain, his colour still tinged a pale grey.

"Will you be okay?" I asked softly.

Despite the pain I knew he was in, Julien's eyes shone a deep golden brown as he explored my face. An overwhelming feeling to reach out and touch his warm skin came over me, but I restrained myself. I had never experienced feelings like this towards anyone before, and it made me feel a little breathless. My feelings towards Julien had only grown in the time we had spent together in the Ironwood—especially since our near kiss—but there was still so much I didn't know about him. He seemed to have a shield in place that stopped people from getting too close—stopping *me* from getting too close. And something told me it had to do with his family's history.

He let out a heavy breath. "I'll be fine."

The tightness in his voice concerned me and I gnawed at my lip, worried about how the poison was affecting him. His face was pinched with pain, and I tried to give him a reassuring smile, but his gaze pulled away from me before I was able to see his expression. A thought niggled at the back of my mind that something seemed off about him, but I couldn't quite put my finger on what it was. Something told me it wasn't just his injury. Running my hands over my mess of hair, I took a deep breath and turned back to Theo, who stood patiently waiting next to the jackalope, his eyes lingering between me and Julien.

"Lead the way."

Twenty-Two

It didn't take us long to find our way along the edge of the Ironwood and over to the western section of the castle. Sticking to the shadow of the trees, I peered out at the looming castle wall—trying to get a better picture of what we were up against. The small drain was set low to the ground and away from the main gate. It was the perfect route to get into the castle grounds unseen. Shifting my gaze up to the massive blocks of stone, my stomach rolled as a handful of guards patrolled the top of the wall. If we stepped out of the shadows now, we would be spotted immediately. Turning my back on the castle, I looked into the faces of my friends. Julien was growing paler by the minute and he had settled himself against an exposed tree root, Alpheus close by his side. Theo stood next to me, his round eyes glistening a brilliant blue in the dying light.

"There are too many guards for us to get across the clearing unseen. We will need to wait until nightfall, so it's probably best we all get some rest."

Julien closed his eyes, his injured shoulder still hanging limp in the makeshift sling. Dark circles had begun to show under his eyes and he was growing more agitated as the afternoon wore on. His declining health worried me and I was glad when he finally fell into an unsettled sleep, the jackalope still tucked beside him.

Theo had found himself a patch of lush grass, sitting cross-legged, his bag laying in front of him. Ever since the gremlins had stolen his grimoire, he never let it out of his sight.

Coming to sit next to him, I could see he was dragging his palm lightly across the grass. Leaning around his bulk of a bag, I noticed the little green blades were swaying lightly, as if a soft breeze had tickled their stems and made them dance. Looking up into Theo's face, I smiled.

"I'm trying to make it grow," he said miserably. "But it doesn't do anything other than wiggle back and forth."

Theo yanked his hand away, letting out a frustrated huff. He ran a hand over the back of neck, his eyes bright with frustration.

"You're thinking too hard about what you want your magic to do. Hazel told me you need a clear mind and to focus solely on what you're trying to summon."

Placing my hand over the blades of grass, I focused my mind on making them grow, imagining the thin, feathery blades sprouting beneath my fingers. Feeling the silky blades of grass flutter against my palm, they began to shoot their way upwards, pressing between my opened fingers. Theo's brow creased dramatically as he watched my hands intently. Shaking my head and stifling a small chuckle at the concentration on his face, I moved aside to give him some more space. A small smirk pulled at the corner of my mouth.

"Now, I want you to make this area grow." I pointed to a spot where the grass hadn't reached the shadows of the trees. "Just relax your mind and listen to your magic. Feel it flow through your veins like water running through a riverbed."

He closed his eyes and I tsked at him sharply, sounding exactly as Hazel had when she taught me. *The apple doesn't fall far from the tree.*

"Magic requires all of your senses, so make sure to leave your eyes open."

Amused, Theo raised one of his eyebrows at me.

"Just try it," I said, nudging his shoulder playfully.

With his eyes now open, Theo looked down at the soil covered in orange-yellow leaves and dried tree bark. Taking a deep breath and letting it out through his nose, he relaxed into a sitting position. Copying my earlier movements, Theo waved his hand slowly over the ground, his fingers trembling. I held my breath, crossing my fingers in my lap in the hope something would happen. After a few anxious minutes, Theo moved his hand away, and my breath caught in my throat. Where there was once only dirt and sodden leaves, there now stood tiny blades of grass. Bright green and fluttering happily in the light breeze. I swallowed back the shout of glee threatening to bubble out, too nervous that the sound would attract unwanted attention from the guards patrolling the castle's outer wall. Instead, I threw myself at Theo, wrapping my arms tightly around his slim torso. Theo's face glowed a bright red at my reaction, but his smile spread from ear to ear. My entire body felt like it glowed with pride.

"See, I knew you could do it."

Theo's face beamed with happiness as he let out a loud laugh, startling Julien who still dozed uneasily. Theo's hands flew to his mouth as I held my breath, hoping we hadn't alerted any of the guards nearby. No alarm sounded and I let out a small breath before turning to Julien. He still appeared to be snoring lightly—his chest rising and falling slowly. I saw Theo staring out of the corner of my eye. He leant forward, his elbows resting on his knees as he raised a questioning eyebrow in my direction.

"What?" I asked defensively. I sat back, staring down at my clasped hands, not wanting to meet Theo's crisp blue gaze that seemed to see right through me.

"What's going on between you two?" he whispered.

I shrugged my shoulders. "Nothing, we're just friends."

"'Pffft." Theo rolled his eyes. "As if. I'm not blind, Brae! I see the way Julien stares at you when you're not looking and the way you turn as red as a tomato the second he gets close to you."

"I don't do that," I retorted, crossing my arms defensively over my chest.

Theo had been more observant than I'd realised. All this time, I thought he hadn't taken much notice of me or Julien when, in fact, he had been watching us both like a hawk.

"Don't lie to me! I'm supposed to be your friend and I told you to stay away from him. He's dangerous." Theo's voice rose a few octaves as his temper began to boil over, but I wasn't going to let him yell at me about who I could speak to. Especially when it was just a little bit of harmless flirtation with Julien.

"You keep saying that, Theo, but I don't think he's dangerous at all. He has done nothing but help us on this entire journey, nearly killed himself protecting us. I just think you don't want me to have another friend aside from you!" Regretting my words the second I blurted them out, my hands flew to my mouth as my chin trembled.

Theo stared at me with wide eyes. The colour drained from his face as his lip began to quiver.

"I'm sorry," I said, my voice tearful. "You keep saying he is dangerous, but you have never told me why."

Busying myself with the dead leaves that littered the ground, I avoided Theo's sad gaze, but the silence stretching between us forced me to look up. His face was blank, his eyes distant as if lost in a memory.

Theo let out a long, slow sigh. "Fine. You want to know why I keep telling you he's dangerous, it's because of this!"

He pointed at the long pink scar running across his cheek. His eyes burned as he looked at me.

"Julien and I used to be friends. We grew up together in the Ironwood Village and at one point we were inseparable."

I stared at Theo, my mouth hanging open, not expecting him to say anything like this. Hazel had told me on my first day in Ellesmere that the witches and warlocks occupying the Ironwood Village had lived there most of their lives. That everyone knew one another. But from the constant sourness between Theo and Julien, I had always assumed they had been enemies since childhood.

"What happened between you both?" My voice came out soft

and shaky as I tried to wrap my head around Theo's earlier words.

"It was the night of our rune ceremony. We had just received our elemental runes and thought we were invincible. We decided to play a game of dare devil—a game we had made up as kids where we dared each other to do stupid things."

I rolled my eyes at the silliness of boys as Theo continued.

"I went first and dared Julien to sit in the gravedigger's shed that stood at the back of the cemetery near the elders' hall. A few of the other kids from the ceremony were there, as well as Julien's older brother."

My eyebrows shot up at the mention of Julien's family. In all the times we had spoken, he had never mentioned anything about having a brother. While I didn't think it was unusual, it did make me curious as to why he never spoke of him. Leaning a little closer to Theo, I waited for him to go on.

"He seemed a little nervous when we entered the cemetery, but when we got down to the gravedigger's shed and he saw the crowd that had gathered, he went inside without saying a word. He stood in the tiny shed while everyone watched from the open door. When his time was almost up, he went to leave, but the shed door somehow slammed closed before he got out."

Theo stopped for a minute, running a sweaty hand through his hair. It was like he was reliving the night all over again. I felt bad for asking him to tell me what had happened, but I needed to know why there was so much bad blood between them.

"I tried to pull it open, but the door was too heavy. It felt like an invisible force held it closed. I could hear Julien yelling from inside and I kept trying to get the door unstuck, but nothing worked. As I screamed out for the others to help me, I heard a low crackle coming from inside the wooden walls. The air around me had grown hot and, before I had the chance to move away, the gravedigger's shed exploded into a cloud of fire and broken wood. Julien had managed to conjure a ball of blue flame—the rarest form of fire magic—without any training. It had grown so hot in the shed that whatever had been inside reacted with his magic, causing an explosion. I managed to get far enough away to avoid any further injury, but a piece of heated metal from the explosion hit my cheek and, well..." He paused for a minute, his freckled hand reaching the scar on his cheek—a mark of Julien's actions. "The Wise Witch in the village tried to mend it as much as she could, but I still have this scar to remind me what happened."

Theo's eyes were rimmed red as he stared at Julien's sleeping form. The sadness there almost broke my heart in two, but something didn't seem right. I still couldn't understand why Julien would behave so terribly towards Theo, who was only trying to help him.

"What did Julien say to you after all this happened?" I asked quietly.

Theo shook his head. "When he walked through the thick columns of smoke it was like he was in a trance. His eyes were glazed over, staring at nothing as he walked towards me, his hands still flaming balls of fire. I tried to help him. Release him from whatever magic had taken hold of him, but rather than taking comfort in my words, he attacked me. The sleeves of my shirt were in flames in an instant. The skin on my arms burning as he walked away." Theo pulled up the sleeves of his jumper. Mottled pink scars covered most of his forearms. "That's what upset me the most, Brae, he never said anything—didn't even try to help me. He just stalked past me and walked directly into the Ironwood. We hadn't spoken until this trip."

We sat in silence. I didn't have the words to comfort him. I could see the hurt he had felt back then still reflected in his thin face. Bending forward, I placed a hand over Theo's feeling the softness of his fingers as he brushed soothing circles over the top of my hand. I couldn't help but notice the difference between Theo's soft, smooth touch and Julien's rough one. A testament to their personalities, it seemed. Theo was soft, kind—a comfort I couldn't live without now. Whereas Julien was wild, confident and, despite his stubbornness, I could see a kindness in him others seemed to look past.

"I'm so sorry," I said. "If I'd known about you and Julien—"

Theo didn't let me finish. "It's okay, Brae, I should have told you sooner, but I was ashamed. I didn't want you to think less of me." He gave me a weak smile.

I shoved his shoulder lightly. "I could never think less of you, Theo. You are too kind to have a bad bone in your body." Getting to my feet, I held my hand out to him. "Come on, we should probably make a move now that it's dark."

Taking my hand, Theo rose clumsily on his feet, knocking his bag over in the process. *That bag will be the death of him*, I thought, shaking my head. I wandered over to where Julien still lay asleep, his injured arm still cradled against his chest. Shaking him lightly to not cause him pain, I felt my heart flutter a little in my chest as my fingers brushed the skin along his neck. Even after everything Theo had told me about him, I still couldn't deny that I cared for him deeply. When Julien didn't immediately respond to my gentle nudging, I pushed him a little harder, my heart beating rapidly as panic spread through me at the thought of the poison having spread too far. He startled awake, wincing as the movement jolted his shoulder.

"I'm sorry, I didn't mean to startle you, but it's time to leave," I said, helping him stand.

"How long have I been out of it?" he asked as he ran a hand over his face, dark eyes turning down towards me. He grimaced at the movement in his wounded shoulder, making me a feel a little bad for waking him so abruptly.

"A while," I replied shortly.

I didn't want to stand around talking to him. The longer I was near him, the more I sensed my feelings coming to the surface… and after what Theo had told me, I *couldn't* have feelings for him. I couldn't betray Theo like that. Turning my back to him, Julien grabbed my arm and spun me so we faced each other again. I felt my heart betray me as its beat quickened.

"What's going on? Why are you being so short with me?" His bushy brows drew together, making my heart constrict.

"I'm not being short with you. We just need to leave."

I turned, knowing I was a terrible liar, but he was too quick for me. He reached out, pinching my chin gently between his fingers. His thumb rested inches from my bottom lip, sending a thrill over my skin.

"Braelyn, if this is all because of our near kiss earlier, I'm sorry. I didn't mean to overstep or make you feel uncomfortable, it's just…" He ran his hand through his hair, making it stand up on end. "It's just when I'm with you I feel different, like my heart is going to burst if I'm not near you."

He was standing closer to me now and in the moonlight I could see a slight flush to his cheeks. He cupped my cheek, brushing his rough thumb over my cheekbone. Closing my eyes for a second, I leant into the touch of his warm hand on my skin. The roughness of his fingers. When I opened my eyes, he was still looking at me, searching for a response to his earlier statement. Reaching up and lacing my fingers through his, I pulled his hand gently from my face, letting it slowly fall between us. A lump formed in my throat as tears threatened to spill over my cheeks.

"We should go," I murmured.

Turning away quickly so I couldn't see the look on his face, I felt the tears finally spill over as I walked away from him. Not knowing if I had made the right or wrong decision.

Twenty-Three

As I surveyed the castle wall, I tried to figure out the best way for us all to cross safely. The wall was a few metres from our hiding spot amongst the shadows of the Ironwood, and if we took too long out in the open, we would be seen by the two guards patrolling the perimeter. They walked back and forth along the top of the wall with a perfect bird's eye view of the terrain below. As I watched their patrol, I studied their rounds, interest piquing as they paused at every corner before turning and repeating the run. This was when we would have the best chance of getting across the clearing unseen.

I told the others of my plan. While it may have been simple, we needed to time our dash perfectly. Theo offered to go first, followed by Julien and me, then Alpheus in the rear.

Once the guards neared the end of the wall—their backs turned in our direction—I gave Theo the signal, waving him across the clearing to the safety of the towering stone. He darted out of the trees, loping his way over to the other side. His long legs carried him swiftly in the dark and he managed to make it across without so much as a glance from the guards above.

Letting out a long breath, I wiped away the small droplets of sweat beading on my forehead. Pivoting, the guards made their way back across the top of the wall, and I watched closely, readying to give Julien the signal to move.

While I couldn't see him among the shadows, I knew he was close by. We hadn't spoken to each other since I walked away from him and a part of me wished I could go back in time and do things differently, but he'd never felt further away.

The guards reached their spots and I waved for Julien to make his way across. He wasn't as quiet as Theo had been, but the darkness kept his broad form shielded from sight as each of the guards spun on their patrol. As I watched him stumble across the grass, I felt the rising sensation something was off about him. About halfway across the clearing, he stopped. My breath caught as he took a few steps forward and fell to the ground. The guards still patrolled unawares and I let out a shaky breath. I needed to get to him, but the guards were only halfway through their repetitive march and leaving the shadows now would surely get us caught. Feeling the jackalope tug at my consciousness, I peeled my eyes from Julien as Alpheus spoke.

"We need to be quick, my friend. The dark-haired boy is not well, and I fear what may happen if we delay much longer."

My eyes flashed back to Julien's limp form and my heart thudded heavily in my chest. I needed to move now. My legs quivered as I let out a short breath and a few seconds later I was running from the comfort of the trees across the wide opening, like prey running from a hungry predator. My heart hammered in my chest as I sucked in a breath, scrambling to Julien before the guards could notice us. My legs burned, but I pushed myself faster across the wide expanse of grass until I came to a screaming halt by Julien's side.

Alpheus fidgeted beside me as I dropped to my knees. His ears turned to the wall, listening for the slightest sound of trouble. Julien lay face down in the grass and, placing my hands on his good shoulder, I used all my strength to roll him over onto his back. What I saw made me pull my hand back quickly. The barghest's poison had spread from Julien's bandage and now snaked its way up his neck. The dark venom stood out stark against his pallid skin, and Julien clenched his teeth at the growing pain. Gnawing on my lip, I tasted metal in my mouth, realising I had ripped the skin off my bottom lip out of anxiety. Cursing under my breath, I wiped the sticky blood from my mouth.

"Brae, what's going on?" Theo's voice sounded from beside me, making me jump. I hadn't seen him come to us.

"The poison in Julien's shoulder has spread and he fainted on his way over." I spoke quickly and quietly, all the while trying to figure out how we would get Julien to the drainage hole.

"It's not that far to the wall. Theo, grab Julien's shoulders and I'll take his feet." It wasn't the greatest of plans, but it was the best I could do given the circumstances.

Julien slipped in and out of consciousness as Theo and I readied ourselves to lift his muscular body. As Theo placed his hands on Julien's shoulders, he let out a loud scream that echoed into the once silent night. Immediately, a bright light shone down on us from the top of the wall, banishing the shadows hanging around us like a cloak and throwing us into a golden glow. Squinting up into the brightness as my eyes adjusted, I noticed the light came from the hands of a rather large fire warlock. Both his hands were engulfed in flame as a sickening smirk spread across his face.

"It's the spirit witch," he bellowed to his fellow guard, who had now turned and was running in the fire warlock's direction. "Tell the king we got her."

My hands began to tremble as an overwhelming feeling of dread made my blood run cold. Turning to Theo, I grabbed his arm. "You need to take Julien and Alpheus and get to the wall."

Theo shook his head. "Not without you Brae."

"I have a plan, but you need to trust me. Please." I gave his arm a tight squeeze before spinning on my toes and running in the opposite direction.

Startled, the large fire warlock took off running along the wall. Surprisingly, he kept pace with me. Stopping abruptly, I threw a quick glance back at the clearing to where I could just make out Theo pulling Julien's arm around him. They stumbled a few times but managed to reach the safety of the wall. I just needed to preoccupy the guard long enough to allow them time to crawl into the drain. There were now four burly guards glowering down at me from their pedestal upon the wall.

"There's nowhere to run, little spirit witch. We got you now," the large warlock bellowed as the other guards chortled along with him.

"That's what you think," I spat at them.

Whether they heard me or not, I didn't know, but they would feel the wrath of my magic. Allowing myself to feel all the emotions of the last few days, the magic bubbled up inside me. Feeling the tingling begin in my fingers, I called out to the power within. Fire blossomed in my palms, and I watched with glee as the smirks disappeared from the guards' faces, replaced with looks of utter surprise. One of the guards made a break for it along the wall. He sprinted from the others, yelling into the castle grounds to alert more guards or signal an alarm. Summoning my earth magic, the branches of the trees behind me began to creak and groan in an eerie warning. The thick branches snaked up my arms and, with a quick flick of my wrist, a branch soared through the air like an arrow being shot from a bow. It reached its target, piercing the running guard through the neck as blood oozed from the deathly blow.. Within seconds, the fire warlock had two balls of fire glowing red in the palms of his hands and he hurled them in my direction. Darting out of the way of the first one, I barely managed to escape the second as it struck a large tree behind me, causing it to burst into flames. Baring his teeth in an animalistic snarl, he made to conjure another flame, but I was too quick. Flames licked up my arms and I threw my hands out in front me. A scalding stream of fire spiralled through the air with such force it struck two guards directly in the chest. They fell over the edge of the wall and out of sight onto the ground below. Only one guard remained. Tall and thin, they stood above me, a large vortex of water spinning before them. My arms felt heavy as exhaustion settled over me. I needed to end this now or I'd never make it back to my friends. As the water wielder moved their hands closer together, the vortex began to freeze. Tiny shards of ice started to form and, with a turn of their hand, the icy fragments rained down on me. What seemed like a million daggers soared through the night sky, all trained to impale me. I managed to avoid the first few icy shards, but one skimmed my arm, slicing my skin in a sharp slash. The stinging pain brought tears to my eyes. Embracing the tingling in my fingers, sparks flickered menacingly from my hands as lightning gleamed in the darkness. Clenching my fist tightly, I focused all my remaining strength into my magic. Summoning my air magic in a last-ditch effort to bring down the final guard, my hand now flashed with electricity. A jagged stream of lightning shot from my fingertips, hitting the guard with such force they stumbled back a few steps. The tall guard swayed where they stood for a moment before falling lifeless on the stone.

My hands hung limply by my sides as I stared at the place where the guards had once stood. Every muscle in my body seemed to ache with exhaustion and I could feel the slow trickle of blood running down my arm from my wound. I couldn't believe what had just happened. My shaking hands didn't look like my own. I had never hurt anyone in my life, yet I had just killed four guards without a second thought. I hadn't meant to. My initial thought was to knock them out to prevent them from alerting any more guards, but the moment my magic had spurred to life it was as if it had taken over. *What was my magic doing to me?* A wave of nausea rushed over me as I imagined the guards' lifeless bodies. Bile climbed the back of my throat as I retched at the image materialising behind my eyes, but I needed to remain calm. I couldn't think of these things right now. All that mattered was getting into the castle grounds.

Stumbling to the shadows of the wall, I made my way back to the western section where Julien and Theo would be anxiously waiting. Taking the last few shuffling steps towards the drain, I felt arms wrap around me, steadying me on my feet. Looking up into Julien's face, his brown eyes gazed down at me, half shadowed in moonlight. My head wobbled as I dropped on to Julien's strong arms.

"Braelyn," I heard him whisper before everything went black.

Twenty-Four

My eyes fluttered open as a spicy aroma made my nose crinkle in distaste. Theo's face hovered above me—the silver glow of the moon creating a cool halo around his face. My head throbbed painfully as I slowly sat up. Massaging my temples, I observed my surroundings, realising we were still sitting by the edge of the castle's outer wall.

"How long have I been unconscious?" I asked. Stretching out my limbs, I could still feel the dull ache from using my magic.

"Only a few minutes," Theo replied. "Here, you need to take one more sip of this. It will make you feel better." He held out a small vial filled with a brown elixir. The same pungent smell from earlier climbed my nostrils.

"What is that?" I asked, scrunching up my nose at the smell.

"It's called convaluisset, a recovery potion. It will help with the exhaustion." Theo pushed the vial closer and, reluctantly, I took a sip.

The flavours were overwhelming and a strong spice burnt my tongue, but as soon as the potion slid down my throat, my muscles relaxed and my head cleared from the haze of my headache.

"Thank you," I said. Handing the vial back to Theo, he placed it back in his bag and I asked the question that had been nagging at me since I woke. "Where's Julien?"

Theo glanced behind me, and turning around, I spotted Julien a few steps away, leaning against the wall.

"I'm here sweetheart. How are you feeling?" His voice was soft and lacking his usual humour.

Getting to my feet, I closed the short distance between us, coming to sit by his side. His face was still deathly pale. The barghest's poison didn't seem to be progressing any further up his neck, but unease still spread through me at just how long he would be able to keep going.

"I should ask you the same question. Are you okay?" I moved closer to him and brushed away some of the hair plastered to his sweaty forehead. My hand lingered momentarily on his neck as Julien brought up his hand to rest tenderly over mine.

"I'll be okay, Braelyn." Lacing his finger between my own, he gently pulled my hand away, still clasping it in his lap. "Speaking of which, you almost killed yourself using that much magic. What is it with you and throwing yourself into harm's way?" He quirked an eyebrow at me, but seemed too tired for playfulness.

I felt my cheeks begin to warm and, ever so gently, I squeezed his hand. "If it wasn't for my recklessness, we would all be holed up in one of the king's dungeons, no use to anyone."

An amused smile spread across Julien's face as he shook his head at me. "Yes, can't argue with that logic, but on that note we should probably get going before anything else threatens to forsake this journey."

The drain appeared to be wide enough for us to fit through in single file but would require us to walk hunched over. Moving into the opening of the drain, I tread carefully in the dingy hole, not knowing what could be down here. As my eyes adjusted to the light, I felt my stomach drop. Only a metre or so inside the drain, thick iron bars closed off the rest of the tunnel, stopping anyone or anything from getting through to the castle grounds.

"By the elements," I ground out. Rubbing a shaky hand over my face, I looked back into the tunnel. This couldn't be happening.

"What's going on, Brae?"

Theo was almost doubled over beside me. It was such a strange sight that, despite the dreadful situation, I almost found myself laughing. Theo peered past me, a frustrated breath escaping his lips.

"How are we going to get through those?"

"I don't know, but we need to come up with something soon." I had no idea what the time was, but with all the obstacles we had encountered we couldn't have much time left. Once the sun started to rise, it would all be over.

Coming out of the hole, I relayed our findings to Julien, who cursed angrily.

"Could you melt it with your fire magic?" Theo asked.

The hope in his voice was contagious, and I waited anxiously as Julien shuffled around to lean against the stone.

"My fire isn't hot enough to melt iron. You would need to conjure a blue flame to be able to attempt it." He ran a trembling hand through his hair again.

I wracked my brain, trying to think of something when an idea dawned on me. Stepping back into the darkness of the drain, I placed my hands on the iron bars, wriggling them a little. They didn't come out—it couldn't have been that easy—but they slipped around in the holes they were fitted into just as I had hoped. They hadn't been fixed into the wall. Hope blossomed in my chest and, kneeling, I ran my hand over the roof of the drain. The stone was smooth and damp, and I knew what it was I needed to do.

"Spiritus," I murmured.

Placing both hands on the stone above the first iron rod, I made a diamond shape around the top of it, making sure I wasn't touching any part of the iron—knowing if I did my magic would be useless. Taking a deep breath, I cleared my mind. Pushing my hands into the stone, I imagined it falling away beneath my touch. Digging the tips of my fingers into the rock, I began to feel the stones loosen beneath my palms. The roof of the drain creaked beneath my hands, slowly cracking and crumbling into the muddy water by my knees. A wide grin pulled at my lips as I moved my hands away and shook the first of the iron bars. It fell away easily with a loud splash. Getting to my feet, I shimmied my way past the other bars, making sure the gap was big enough to fit through.

Coming back out to the others, I let them know the good news.

"Wait, so you just melted the rock away?" Theo asked, awestruck.

My chest swelled with pride at Theo's reaction. Ever since my interaction with the ash tree in the Ironwood, I'd felt stronger, more capable.

I shrugged. "We should be able to fit through now, and I think the gap should be big enough for your antlers to fit through as well."

"Thank you, friend." Alpheus replied. *"But I am afraid I cannot follow you. This is where we must part ways."*

I stared at Alpheus, not knowing what to say. He had been with us for almost half our journey, and I didn't think I was ready to say goodbye. Kneeling so I was the same height as the beautiful creature, my shoulders drooped forward as an overwhelming sadness filled my chest.

"I'm not ready for you to leave." I said. My voice wavering with emotion. Placing my hand between the jackalope's antlers, I gave its soft fur a light pat and it leant into my touch as if trying to savour the memory.

"You have come a long way, and I am pleased to have met you, but I cannot go in there. Stories have reached my ears of terrible happenings to creatures like me." Alpheus pulled away from me, his beautiful almond eyes staring into my own.

"But if you should ever need me, simply call and I will be there."

With a slight bow of his head, Alpheus turned away, bounding elegantly into the shadows of the Ironwood. Watching the spot where he had disappeared between the trees, I wondered if we would ever see each other again. Feeling a steady hand on my shoulder, I turned to see Theo standing behind me. A sad smile tugged one side of his mouth.

"Come on, Brae, we better get moving if we are to reach your mother in time." He steered me towards the entrance to the drain.

With one last glance back, I turned my back on this part of the Ironwood for what I hoped would be the last time.

Stepping into the mouth of the tunnel, I lit a small flame to help light the way. Julien's face was illuminated in the orange light, causing a grim feeling to spread over me. He shuffled awkwardly along the wall, his elbows pulled into his sides, making the muscles in his shoulders and neck bulge. His face was slick with sweat.

"Julien," I said quietly, not wanting to startle him. His eyes jammed shut, his chin trembling. "What's wrong? Is it your shoulder?" I moved to inspect his wound—concerned the poison was making him feverish—but as I touched the make-shift sling, his hand shot up, grabbing my wrist tightly. His eyes were overly bright as they stared down at me.

"I… I can't go in—in there, Braelyn." His words were barely more than a whisper. His breaths rasped from his chest, hands trembling by his sides.

Glancing at the tunnel, then at Julien's face again, something dawned on me. I thought of his actions on the night of his rune ceremony, when the door on the gravedigger's shed had slammed shut. It suddenly clicked… his outlandish behaviour towards Theo, and now his reaction about the tunnel? He was claustrophobic.

Closing the small distance between us, I placed my free hand on his cheek, turning his face towards mine. My flame still glowed brightly in my other hand, making Julien's eyes glisten a deep amber.

"It's okay," I said soothingly. "I will be with you the whole way." Running my hand down his arm, his muscles tensed. Taking his good hand in mine, I squeezed it tight.

"We are in this together," I whispered.

As I pulled his hand lightly, he took a few shaky steps towards the opening of the tunnel.

Traversing the tunnel wasn't as hard as I'd expected. The light from my flame illuminated the path just enough for me to see what lay ahead, allowing us to pass through the dingy passage without injury. Julien still held my hand in a tight grip and, after a while, I began to lose feeling in my fingers. His rapid breathing would intensify and he would murmur encouragement to himself. I couldn't make out the words, but assumed he was trying to keep his mind occupied. Theo brought up the rear, grumbling about our slow-moving train of bodies. We had been hunched over in the tunnel for only a short period of time, but I could feel Theo's annoyance starting to build.

"What is the matter with him!" Theo said between clenched teeth as Julien stopped abruptly, causing my arm to feel like it had been torn from the socket.

Shuffling around to check on him, I found Julien leaning against the grimy wall, his hand cradling his wounded arm. His eyes were squeezed shut as his head rested on the slime covered stones. My flames flickered with my movement as I brought the warmth around him, trying to warm his damp skin as he continued to shiver and mutter to himself. Reaching out a tentative hand, I tried to brush away the tendrils of hair stuck to the sweat lining his face but, despite Julien's fear, his reflexes were quick. Letting go of his wounded shoulder, he caught my wrist mid-air, his grip tightening. A small grunt of pain escaped me and, in an instant, Theo had his fist raised. Before I had time to stop him, Theo threw a punch at Julien's jaw. As his fist connected with Julien's lip, he let go of my wrist, almost crumpling to the floor.

"What are you doing?" I hissed at Theo.

Dropping to my knees by Julien's side, I pulled his face into the light of my flame. His lip was split down the middle, with one side already swelling. As I tried to pull my hand up to tilt Julien's face closer to the flickering light, Theo pushed in front of me, his eyes frosty.

"What am I doing!? What are you doing? Why are you trying to help him!? He literally just lashed out at you."

"He's claustrophobic. That's what the matter with him. He's terrified of being in here, just like he was terrified of being locked up in the gravedigger's shed."

I met Theo's steely gaze and, in the small orange glow of my flame, I could see him fighting his own internal battle of whether

Kirsty Inic

to believe me or not. His eyes turned back to Julien, who was still pressed against the wall, his hand held up to his bleeding lip.

"But you're not afraid of anything," Theo whispered in disbelief. His eyes remained locked on Julien's limp body. "Every time we played dare devil you always won."

"Everyone is afraid of something, Theo," Julien replied softly.

In the wavering light I could just make out Julien's sad expression. He stared at his feet, and when his eyes met mine, they were dark and distant, as if remembering something he longed to forget. Bringing my hand up again, I took his calloused one in mine, squeezing gently.

"What happened?" I asked, thinking it might help him overcome his fear if he talked about it.

Julien sighed deeply. "It happened when I was a child. My brother and I were playing in the apothecary while my mother worked. She was getting cross with us because we kept getting in the way, so she told us to go and play in the stock room. Somewhere we weren't going to be under her feet." Julien paused for a moment, running a hand through his hair before he continued. "We had a small cellar beneath the shop that my mother used to keep some of her more unusual mixes in. My brother loved going down there. He used to try and scare me with stories of the warlock who owned the shop before us. The stories would say he was into dark magic and liked to try and summon the Wraiths of Umbra to come and terrorise the village."

The stories of the dark spirits from the underworld were known by every witch and warlock child, told as ghost stories to terrify people into never choosing dark magic.

I shuddered, wondering why his brother would be so cruel as to torture Julien this way.

"One day, my brother went down to the cellar and, stupidly, I followed. We got into an argument over something I don't even remember anymore, but whatever it had been about, it made my brother extremely mad. He shut me down there, leaving me in the dank cellar. I was so terrified about the stories my brother had told

221

me, I was certain I had seen one of the Wraiths that haunted my dreams."

"You saw one of the Wraiths?" Theo exclaimed.

Julien nodded once. "I believed I did. I was crouched in the corner of the cellar, terrified, when a dark shadow flickered in the opposite corner. I thought it was just my eyes playing tricks on me, but when I saw two glowing red orbs, I knew something was down there with me."

My entire body went rigid as a knot formed in my stomach. What Julien spoke about seeing in his apothecary cellar almost matched the description of the shadows I had seen on the day we came across the ash tree. But surely the Wraiths of Umbra were just an old superstition.

"I screamed until my mother came to find me."

My heart ached as I tried to imagine Julien as a small boy, alone and afraid as he sat waiting for someone to find him. I looked sidelong at Theo. His face was half concealed in shadow, but in the little light that did illuminate his features, I could see his mouth opening and closing, trying to say something. Every word died on his lips.

Julien's dark eyes roamed over my face. He reached out his hand towards me and, looking down, I could see his fingers trembling. I knew it must have taken a lot for him to reveal what he had to us and a small part of my chest swelled with pride for him having the courage to do so. Placing my hand on top of his, I gave it a light, reassuring squeeze.

As he looked at Theo, I wondered what might happen between them now that Theo knew what caused Julien's outlandish behaviour at the gravedigger's shed.

"I'm sorry for what I did to you that night, Theo. I never meant to hurt you." Julien's voice hitched on the last word. Running a hand over his face, I thought I saw the faint glisten of a tear running down his cheek. "I was just so terrified and overcome with fear that I can barely remember even conjuring my magic. It was like I was consumed by the fire that flowed through my veins.

After that night I heard the whispers that spread around the village of what I'd done to you. I couldn't stand that I had been the one that caused you so much hurt, so rather than apologise I took the cowards way out." Shaking his head, he let out a deep breath. "And I hope one day I might be able to earn your forgiveness." Julien's chin quivered as he stared unseeing at the floor of the tunnel.

Theo shrugged his shoulder, "I don't know if I can forgive you at the moment, Julien, but your apology is a good start."

Nudging gently past me, Theo turned his back on us, continuing through the tunnel, still hunched over. As I held Julien's hand to help him to his feet, our palms remained touching, neither one of us quite ready to break the tether between us.

My back had begun to ache from being stooped over for so long, and I didn't know how much longer I would be able to stand the smell. The dank stench of stagnant, mouldy water wafted up my nose, making me gag more than once. As I was just beginning to worry this nightmare would never end, we came around a small bend and a circle of light beamed in front of me. At first glance I thought it was daylight, and my heart beat rapidly—worried we were too late—but dimming the glow of my flame, I could see that it was just the lights from the castle. My muscles relaxed, and we made our way hurriedly through the grime and muck to leave the horrid place.

Reaching the end of the drain, I was thankful to see there were no iron bars blocking our way. Clearly the king only thought it necessary to block the entrance from the outside of the castle wall. Standing within the shadows inside the tunnel, we were hidden enough to avoid the attentions of any guards patrolling nearby. Taking a short break, we stretched our aching muscles, inhaling the fresh, crisp night air.

Crouching to better see out the drain, I cast a quick glance around, realising we had come out to a cobblestoned courtyard. A large stable stood to the left, which could prove useful if we needed a quick getaway. Bringing my gaze back to the right, I barely had enough time to pull my head back into the shadows before a tall guard sauntered past. Poking my head back out, I watched him make his way to the stables before turning on his heel and marching past our hiding spot. The courtyard was poorly lit by two tall lanterns set either side of a sturdy looking wooden door. That was our way in. The lamplight flickered, creating wavering shadows on the ground, and I shuddered, reminded of the Wraiths of Umbra. I didn't have a clear view of the sky, but from the parts I could see, it didn't look like any guards had been stationed to replace the ones I had disposed of. *Thank the elements.* But despite my elation at finally having some luck on our side, a slight chill ran down my spine as I thought of the guards I had killed. While I knew it was either them or me, I couldn't help but think I was turning into a monster. Since my encounter with the ash tree, my power had been overwhelming. When the guards had spotted me, my only thought had been to remove them. It was this type of thinking that terrified me. How many more witches and warlocks would I need to kill in order to save hundreds of others?

"I think we should take our chances with whatever lies on the other side of that door," I whispered to the boys.

"Whatever gets me out of this place," Julien replied quickly.

He grimaced at his shoulder and I worried about how far the poison was spreading. He looked terrible.

Theo glanced at the door, his back still hunched as he stood in the dirty water. "What if there is someone behind there? We could get caught straight away."

"It's better than staying in this grimy hole," Julien muttered back.

"We don't really have another choice, Theo. We can't move around the grounds without being seen."

Theo let out a long sigh. "Fine, but if we get caught, I will not hesitate to say I told you so!"

A hint of a smile lightened Theo's eyes and I shook my head, turning to the courtyard. First, I needed to take care of the guard.

Taking one last look around the tunnel, I found a large stone and waited at the opening.

"What's that for?" Theo asked.

I whispered a quick shush as I waited for the guard to pass. Once he was past the tunnel opening, I stepped into the light, raising the stone above my head. The guard didn't see me coming. Bringing the rock down hard on his head, he collapsed in a heap on the cobblestones—the iron armour he wore clattering loudly around the courtyard.

I motioned for Theo and Julien to move towards the door as a thought struck me. I conjured thick twisting vines that wrapped around the guard's ankles in a tight grip. He was only a few years older than me and I felt a pang of guilt deep in my chest. At least he was merely unconscious. My earth magic continued curling around the guard's body like a giant serpent consuming a meal. Once the twisted vines were secured, I brought my hands up and watched as the guard's limp body floated a few inches off the ground. I pushed him against the wall, out of sight from anyone who would be walking past.

Julien and Theo had managed to make it across the courtyard and, after disposing of the guard, I met them at the small alcove where the door was situated. It was set into the stonework of the wall atop a set of stone stairs. It was a tight squeeze, but I felt a little more at ease as the three of us shoved ourselves into the small alcove.

"What if the door is locked," I heard Theo whisper from behind me.

It was a logical question and something I cursed myself for not thinking of sooner.

"It's okay, this lock isn't iron, so I'm sure I'd be able to melt it enough to pull the door free." Julien's voice was close, our bodies almost touching. I felt my cheeks flush and, despite the shadows, I knew it was light enough for both Theo and Julien to see me. Rushing forward, I jangled the handle loudly, the noise echoing around the once quiet courtyard.

Theo shushed me, but relief flooded through me as the door

easily pushed inwards, letting us fall into a small corridor. Stepping into the narrow hallway, the same cobblestone covered most of the floor and walls, making the space smell damp. I shivered slightly at the cold clinging to the stone. Feeling a slow warmth bloom from behind me, I knew Julien had summoned a flame to help us find our way.

"What do we do now, Brae?"

"We need to reach the lowest level of the castle. That's where the dungeons will be."

A set of stone stairs twisted downwards into the depths of Ellesmere Castle. Conjuring a small flame of my own, I led us down the steep stairway, all the while listening for the faint footsteps of an approaching guard. We followed the spiralling staircase as it twisted deeper into the belly of the castle, each step past a locked door or empty room heightening my distress. My chest grew heavy with the fear of running out of time, but still we pushed on. After what felt like an eternity of walking into the belly of a beast, I stopped by the last door at the bottom of the stone stairs. The wood was old and peeling, with a large iron handle. My stomach fluttered lightly as I reached out a trembling hand and pushed open the door. Stepping inside the dimly lit room, my stomach turned to stone. We had walked not into the dungeons, but what appeared to be the castle apothecary.

It was only a small room, cramped with a large shelf displaying jars and vials of all sorts. A large table occupied the middle of the room and dozens of herbs hung from a metal structure above—the drying practice already under way. Slumping in one of the hardwood chairs by the empty fireplace, I pressed my hands to my temples and closed my eyes for a moment. Disappointment clawed at my heart and I breathed a heavy sigh.

Theo placed a steady hand on my shoulder. "Don't give up hope, Brae. We will find her."

Theo was right. We hadn't come all this way just to give up now. My mother's life and the fate of Ellesmere rested on my shoulders, and I was determined not to let them down. Pressing my lips together, I rose, squaring my shoulders. A sound from outside the door startled me and, rushing back to the corridor, I sagged against the stone door frame as I realised it was only Julien. My relief was short lived; he was growing sicker by the minute. His skin was sallow and his face was slick with sweat. His fire magic had dulled—the once bright and brilliant flames now a mere glimmer in the dark. I placed a gentle hand on his chest, feeling the slow beat of his heart. The poison was spreading and I wondered if there was anything in the apothecary that would help slow the spread of the poison. Julien must have seen the light in my eyes as I considered this, but he simply shook his head.

"Only the magic of a Wise Witch will be able to stop the poison, sweetheart. Besides, I think I found a way further down." Despite the pain he must have been in, a slow smile spread across his beautiful face.

Julien's good hand came to rest on my neck, his thumb tenderly brushing my cheek. I could feel my heart beating rapidly in my chest and I knew, in this moment, whatever feelings I had for Julien were not going away. Rising on my tiptoes, I bent my head towards his, feeling his grip tighten ever so slightly on my neck. Our faces were inches apart and I could smell the heady scent of smoke and fire on his skin. A smell I now could only associate with him. His lips parted as he whispered my name. "Braelyn…"

I didn't let him finish.

My entire body felt enflamed as I pressed my lips to his in a small, soft kiss, too nervous to do much more. My breath came in quick bursts as I pulled away. I glanced up through my lashes at Julien's face and his eyes burned deep and dark before he pulled me close and pressed his lips to mine again. We were suddenly lost in each other's embrace, our kiss no longer soft, but urgent and pleading. All our unspoken feelings felt concrete in this moment. We both eased out of our kiss at the same time, Julien's forehead resting lightly on my own.

"I have wanted to do that since the moment I met you, Braelyn."

I smiled, cheeks burning from the heat of our embrace, not wanting to say anything and simply stay in this moment. I could hear Theo rustling around in the apothecary behind me, which brought me back to the matter at hand.

"We should probably get moving before we attract unwanted attention." I felt Julien nod and, despite my reluctance to leave his warm embrace, we pulled away from each other slowly. Theo appeared in the large doorway, a strange look on his face. His eyes flicked between Julien and me as if he knew what had happened between us, but he remained silent, a knowing glint in his blue eyes.

When Julien told us about the secret passageway, I almost wept in relief.

The corridor was narrow and twisted slightly to the left through the castle. Summoning my fire magic again, I took a tentative step down into the dank stairway, but it didn't take us long to come out the other side.

Twenty-Five

Stepping down into a large square room, my flame sputtered out as light flooded in around us. Doors stood metres apart from each other with iron bars lining each of the openings. We had finally found the dungeons. Every emotion I had felt on our journey through the Ironwood flooded over me and I found myself scrambling around, looking in every door to see which one kept my mother locked away. While the room we stood in was well lit, the cells were still too dark for me to see all the way in and I struggled to find anyone resembling my mother. Trying to steady my racing heart I looked from one cell to the next, it was no use. I could feel the panic begin to bubble up as I tried desperately to find her.

Theo placed his hands on either side of my arms. "Brae, you need to calm down. Otherwise you are going to spiral and be no use to anyone."

Encouraging me to take a few deep breaths, I followed Theo's deep inhalations, counting to ten as I did so. Feeling my mind slowly relieve itself of the fog clouding it, my heart eventually slowed to its normal rhythm.

"Sorry, you're right. It's just we are so close to her, Theo! I don't know what I'll do if she slips through my fingers."

It was the first time I'd said this to anyone. These thoughts had occupied my mind for days now and saying them aloud to Theo made me feel a tiny bit better.

"We are going to find her, Brae. I promise!" He squeezed my forearms in encouragement and I took another deep breath.

Turning back to the cells, I made my way to the first one, wanting to search each cage more thoroughly. The first cell was the closest to the hallway we had just come from, and the lantern light managed to seep into all corners of the stone room. It was empty. *Of course*, I thought angrily. Making my way to the next one, I tried to summon a flame so I could see right to the very back, but nothing came. Moving my hand further from the bars, I tried again, but only a few sparks appeared.

"There is too much iron in the room for any magic to be conjured. I suspect that's King Elias's doing, to prevent anyone trying to escape." Theo's voice sounded from somewhere in the shadows.

Stepping back towards the stairs, I pulled the lantern off its stand—my arm wavering a little at the heaviness of it. What I saw inside the second cell made me stumble back.

Swallowing the bile rising in my throat, I stepped closer to the cell bars, holding the lantern higher to inspect the person sitting on the damp, mouldy floor. There was no mistaking the silver starlight skin, still shimmering brightly despite the darkness of the cell. Balor sat hunched in the corner of the damp dungeon, his knees hugged to his bare chest. He still wore the same light trousers he had donned at the Mabon Festival, except instead of being clean and beautifully pressed, they were now tattered and covered in filth.

I tried calling out his name, but the once grand Prince of the Elves simply sat with his head rested on his knees, not even sparing me the effort of a glance.

Continuing between the other cells, the lantern held in front of me, I noticed most cages were occupied. A group of gremlins were huddled together in one of the grimy cells, their large yellow eyes glinting in the light of the lantern. The next one was the home of a grey-haired witch whose bandaged hand lay open on a dirty, woven hessian mat. The filthy covering was stained with blood and dirt, and I heaved a little at the rotten smell wafting from her chamber.

"What is all this?" I asked quietly as Julien and Theo came to stand by my side at the door to the witch's cell. The smell of decay and rot only grew more pungent as I moved farther down the dungeon corridor.

Neither of them could answer me. Theo kept inspecting the iron bars as if looking at them would cause them to magically break open. Julien scowled around the room, his good hand clenched in a tight fist by his side.

The answer I was looking for came only a moment later from a cell a few paces up from the old witch. Shining the lantern into the chamber, a dwarf stared out at me. He was as tall as my chest, with a once white beard—now filthy with grime—hanging knotted to his knees. From the soiled clothing and the terrible odour wafting from his breath, I assumed he had been in here a while.

"We are prisoners of the king, my dear. Hidden away for him to siphon our powers whenever he sees fit."

The elderly dwarf had a deep, monotonous voice and was slightly hunched from old age.

"I don't understand," I replied, dumbfounded at what the dwarf was saying. "I thought the king could use spirit magic, like me."

While I had never seen the king use his magic, I assumed he must have been the one I had inherited my spirit magic from, considering no one else in my family had the ability to wield all the elements.

The dwarf shook his head, his beard swaying. "The king is no ordinary spirit warlock. He was once just a normal air wielder, but he used dark magic to suck the powers of others and claim the title of the most powerful king to ever rule over Ellesmere."

I couldn't believe what I was hearing. All this time, I'd assumed King Elias had the same magic as me. A small part of me had thought I'd finally find some answers about where my spirit magic came from, but it was all a lie. He was stealing the magic of others, leeching their energy and tossing them aside like trash. He was a murderer.

I didn't have much time. If I didn't find my mother soon, the king would steal her power, leaving her an empty shell of the witch she had been. My mother was proud of being a witch and she would see it as a fate worse than death if her power was taken from her. I couldn't let that happen.

"Excuse me, but what is your name?" I asked.

One of the dwarf's eyes was swollen shut and my heart surged with sorrow. The other one shone a deep forest green in the light.

"My name is Lorcan, my dear. Lorcan Lightbeard, master of weapons for the dwarves of the Ironwood Mountains." Despite his gruesome appearance, Lorcan's voice was strong and proud.

"Lorcan, how did you come to be the king's prisoner?"

To my surprise the bearded dwarf smiled sadly. Half of his teeth were missing—no doubt a result of the king's guards.

"I don't know how much time has passed, but I remember it was a fine day during the spring equinox. I was out in the Ironwood, on my way to one of our mines to collect more magnetite, when I happened across a convoy of king's guards." Lorcan paused for a moment, rubbing a large grubby hand over his face, wincing as he touched his swollen eye.

"They asked me where I was headed and if there were other dwarves nearby. I answered truthfully, telling them I was alone, and that's when they attacked me. They brought me before the king who spoke favourably of my work. You see, we make the iron weapons and armour that's used throughout the kingdom." Lorcan held his chin high, his one green eye gleaming with pride as he discussed his life's work. I nodded once in acknowledgment, waiting for him to continue.

"The king commanded I forge him a great weapon. One that would protect all of Ellesmere against an awakening force."

My hands shook slightly, the lantern light wavering as I processed Lorcan's words. What force in Ellesmere needed more than magic to defeat it? My mind flashed to the vision I had at the

Forest Festival and a shiver ran down my spine.

"What weapon did he want you to make?" I asked urgently.

"He said it was called a circulum. A pointed ring forged with iron and magic. I didn't understand the magical properties but I knew how to work iron, so I made the circulum exactly how he told me, with the equipment provided." The dwarf's voice softened as he paused.

"The first few times I made it for him it would crack under the power each element held, but a few days ago he came to me with a new set of instructions that seemed to work favourably when he used it."

Emptiness hollowed out my stomach, and I asked the question playing on my mind since Lorcan told me of the circulum.

"What exactly did King Elias give you to make this weapon?"

Lorcan closed his eye and took a long, deep breath before he replied, as if speaking the words aloud troubled him. "The runes from each of the elements, the strength of the elves, and the workings of a dwarf."

I didn't need any more explanation. Rushing back towards the stairway, I shone the lantern into the chamber where Balor still sat, hunched and frail. Tilting the light, I saw what I needed to confirm my suspicions. One of his magnificent antlers that had once stood tall and proud was missing—cut away like a tree branch. Spinning around, I emptied my stomach in the corner of the dungeon corridor. Wiping the sick from my mouth, I moved back to Lorcan's chamber. His green eye studied my face carefully, and I could see the pain it had caused him to make such a thing. The circulum was how the king was stealing magic. He didn't need it to destroy an evil force, he needed it to make himself powerful. *He* was the evil force. Fear for my mother's safety bubbled up inside me.

"Do you remember seeing a dark-haired witch in here? She was brought to the castle a few days ago. She was wearing a black dress."

Lorcan's one green eye gazed up at the ceiling as he stroked his beard with one hand, deep in thought. "Now that I think on it, I do believe there was a witch of that description in here."

I leant forward, my nose inches away from the bars, eager to know which of these cells held my mother.

"The king's personal guard took her a few hours ago."

Slumping against the bars, I let out a frustrated sigh. Running my hand aggressively through my tangled mess of hair, I tried to imagine where in this maze of a castle she would be.

"Do you know where they took her?" I asked desperately, voice cracking.

Before Lorcan could answer my question, a loud crash startled me, making me jump. A coldness settled over my entire body as I saw the source.

Julien was lying in a heap on the hard stone floor, a pile of broken old lanterns shattered on top of him.

"Julien," I gasped.

I threw myself to the floor, my knees smashing on the stone. I bit back the pain, pushing aside the heavy metal lanterns lying broken in hundreds of pieces all over Julien's chest. Theo was at his other side, peeling back the sodden bandages, checking on his wound. A small cry tore through me. The black web-like poison had now snaked its way through his veins, covering almost the entire left-hand side of his chest. It had begun to wind its way up his neck, making the tendons stand out hard as he strained against the pain coursing through him.

Covering my mouth with my hand, I tried to stifle the sobs threatening to erupt. If we didn't get Julien help soon the poison would kill him. His eyes were squeezed shut, but his good hand searched for something to hold. Taking his hand in mine, I could feel the clamminess of his skin, his hand trembling.

"Braelyn." His voice was soft, like a whisper on the wind. "You need to leave me here. Go find your mother. You're running out of time and you will move quicker without me."

I shook my head. "No, I'm not going to leave you. We're in this together, remember."

Tears gushed down my cheeks as Julien's hand went limp in mine. For a second, I thought the poison had consumed him, but

I could see the slight rise and fall of his chest. He had fainted from the pain.

"Well, well, well, what do we have here?"

A shiver ran down my spine as I recognised the leering voice behind me. One of the castle's guards stood in a doorway just above us, staring down with a sickening smile. Her long hair was pulled back in a slick ponytail, the white-blonde strands bright even in the orange glow of the lanterns.

Twenty-Six

Victoria stood at the top of the ledge, looking down her long nose at us, her eyes glowing with satisfaction at her catch. Theo's eyes were wide, rimmed with the same shock I felt as he took in the sight before him. I had always known Victoria's motives would be bad, but this was just insane. There was no way she was working with King Elias.

"What are you doing here, Victoria?" I said through clenched teeth. My hands tingled slightly by my sides, but my magic was useless surrounded by all this iron.

Victoria cackled as she stared from her ledge of superiority. She leant back against the stone wall, her pointed chin turned down as she raised a perfect eyebrow at me.

"I would love nothing more than to torture your tiny mind with the reason I'm here, Braelyn, but I have orders from the king to bring you and your companions to meet him without delay."

My brows pulled together in dismay. How did he know we were down here? Seeing the confusion linger on my face only made Victoria's smile widen with satisfaction.

"You honestly think your little encounter with the guards went unnoticed, Braelyn? The king knew you were here the moment you stepped out of the Ironwood."

I shook my head. "Then why would he let us break into the

castle? Why not capture us when we arrived?"

Victoria rolled her icy eyes at me in displeasure. "I don't question the king's decisions, Braelyn, I simply do what he bids me. Now, let's get a move on, the king doesn't like to be kept waiting."

I didn't know what Victoria's relationship was with Elias, but she clearly admired him more than she feared him.

Two beefy guards stepped past Victoria, jumping to the floor with ease to where we still knelt beside Julien's limp body. The smallest of the two took Theo and me by the arm, tugging us to our feet. The second scooped Julien into his arms as if he weighed nothing but air. His blond beard and shaggy hair caused me to step back an inch. Blight stood before me, half hidden in the shadows, but there was no mistaking him. A ghastly smile disfigured his face.

I could hear Julien's low groans as Blight's movements jostled his wounded shoulder.

"Be careful you idiot," I spat. "He's injured."

I fought to loosen my arm from my captor's firm grip, but it was no use. His fingers pinched painfully into my skin and, the more I moved, the tighter his hold became. Gritting my teeth, I let him lead us up to where Victoria still waited, her arms folded across her chest impatiently.

When we reached the ledge, she gave us a menacing smile before spinning on her heel and leading us towards the king.

The castle was plainer than I'd expected it to be. I had always thought castles were meant to have grandeur. Chandeliers, marble floors and ceilings made of glass, but Ellesmere Castle had none of these things. Instead, it was made from the same stone lining as the dungeons and was lit by long iron sconces. Following Victoria through the main foyer, I glanced around, trying to take in as much of the large room as possible. If it came to a fight with the king and his guards, we would need a way out. The foyer was grand in size, but that was where the grandeur stopped. Two large stone staircases loomed in front of us, crossing over each other in the middle, creating a small landing towards the back of the foyer. Light streamed in through a large round window, intricately designed by someone with exceptional talent. It was probably the most beautiful thing in the entire room.

Pushing us up the staircase that snaked to the left of the foyer, I was able to get a better look at the design on the window. It had been welded using a beautiful silver metal that sparkled in the early morning sun. Its long lines and jagged edges formed tiny metal leaves of exquisite detail. As I admired the craftsmanship, I realised the artist had created their own rendition of the four elements. The small leaves connected to twisting vines as metal fire spewed flames entwined with the beautiful flowing lines of the element of water. Curling, twisting metal represented air as all of them wrapped and curled around each other in a perfect circle. The rune for spirit magic.

Pulling hard on my arm, the burly guard—whose name I learned was Zuko—continued to push me and Theo down a small passageway, his beady brown eyes trained on us. The passageway came to a fork and we took the hallway leading to the left. I tried to remember each turn we took, imagining a trail of breadcrumbs to lead us out. Zuko stopped in front of a set of dark wooden doors ingrained with the same swirling pattern set into the window. Victoria was already standing there waiting, her smiling merely a mask I was sure she was readying for the king.

Placing her hands in the middle of the wooden doors, Victoria pushed them open with a small grunt, opening to a large rectangular room. It was quite sparse, with a wide set of stone stairs leading up to a wooden dais housing a large, plush red throne. It had been draped in black silks glittering with speckles of gold to match the large arms either side of the ornate chair. We had been brought to the king's throne room.

My eyes darted around the room quickly, searching for my mother, but to my disappointment she wasn't there. Neither was the king.

"Leave him there." Victoria's voice was sharp and icy as she pointed to a spot for Julien to be set down.

As soon as our captor had released our arms, I rushed over to Julien's side, making sure he was still breathing. To my relief, his breaths came in short, rapid bursts, but they were there. I closed my eyes briefly, thanking the elements he was still alive. Theo had come to stand by my side, his hand placed protectively on my shoulder.

"How sweet," Victoria crooned, her voice still hard. "The magic-less warlock, the traitor, and the deceiver."

I watched as her eyes flickered between Theo, Julien and myself as she studied us closely. Her face contorted with loathing.

"Why are you here, Victoria?" I hissed.

My muscles quivered as anger surged in my veins. Magic tingled in my fingertips for the first time in what felt like forever now that we were away from the warded iron of the dungeons. I welcomed it like an old friend.

She cackled, her body shaking with laughter. "I thought even you could have guessed that by now, Braelyn."

I didn't answer but continued to scowl in her direction as I held tight to Julien's hand, taking comfort in the rise and fall of his chest and knowing he was still alive. Barely.

A whispered murmur came from Julien's lips as Victoria and I continued to stare each other down. At first, I couldn't understand what he'd said, then he murmured my name more clearly. I watched as Victoria's face morphed into rage. I knew she had feelings for Julien but, given the current situation, I'd thought she had found a way to move on from her obsession with him. I was clearly wrong.

"You want to know why I'm here?" she ground out between her teeth. "Power!"

The weight of that word hit me in the chest and, in that instant, I almost felt sorry for her. What promises had King Elias given to make her turn on someone she supposedly cared about only days ago? On her family and friends back in the Ironwood Village?

"Is being a witch not powerful enough?" I asked. "You would harm your friends and family just to be able to use more magic?"

Victoria laughed loudly. "I'm an air witch, Braelyn, the weakest of all elemental magic. And I have no family. My father left when I was a girl and my mother died years ago, leaving me to fend for myself. I was meant for more than my gift allows. King Elias has promised me power beyond my wildest dreams. It was an easy decision." She flicked her long ponytail over her shoulder in a swift movement.

Her cruel smile returned, all anger gone and, despite our differences, I felt sorry for her. King Elias would never give her the power she sought. He was using her and, once he was done, he would discard her like all the others.

"Now, Victoria," a smooth, crisp voice interrupted. "Is that any way to speak to our guest of honour?"

"Sorry, my king," Victoria replied, her head bowed.

I hadn't seen King Elias enter the room. Too preoccupied arguing with Victoria, I hadn't heard his footsteps on the stairs behind me.

Turning slowly, I could see the king now lounged upon the throne, his leg thrown over one of the gilded arms. He reclined in the chair nonchalantly as he watched me take in his appearance. As far as siblings go, my father and King Elias could have passed as twins and, as I gazed upon the man who murdered my father, my magic brewed in my veins like a growing storm. They had the same dark hair, but where my father's had been long, the king's was cut short. They were built the same—tall and lean with a rosy complexion. The only difference between them was the onyx eyes King Elias possessed. Settling back against his gilded throne, the king folded long, elegant fingers over his dark tunic as a smirk split his somewhat handsome face.

"Do you not have anything to say to your dear uncle, Miss Grey?"

He continued smiling at me, his black eyes deep and thoughtful. I felt a tempestuous anger slowly rise within. He was referring to me as *family*, not the spirit witch he had tried to derail every step of my journey.

"Where's my mother?" I said between clenched teeth.

My hands were balled into tight fists at my sides and Theo had now positioned himself to stand beside me. He towered over my crouched frame like a protective watchman.

King Elias's smile widened into a malicious grin. "Ah yes, the reason you have come. She is fine," he said simply, waving a dismissive hand. "Morrigan is keeping her company."

"I want to see her!"

"All in good time, my dear niece. All in good time."

Sitting forward on his throne, he steepled his fingers under his chin. He rested his elbows on his knees, looking down at me quizzically.

"Stand up and let me see you."

He watched me like a hawk, taking in every inch of the one family member he had left. The one person who could overthrow his power and ruin all his grand plans. I pressed my lips together and, instead of standing like he had asked, I simply returned his gaze with one full of loathing. I was hoping my defiance would ignite annoyance, give me a reason to use my magic, but instead he just stared back. His lips cracked into an amused smile, as if my disobedience perplexed him. With a deep sigh, he removed a hand from under his chin and simply waved it in an upward motion, like he was gesturing for someone to leave him. Feeling a small pull in my chest, I was forced to my feet without even twitching a muscle. Like a puppet on strings, he pulled set me to my feet as I looked to Theo with wide eyes. He gaped at me in horror.

"It's quite remarkable, isn't it?"

The king stared at his own hands in wonder. "My rune is air, so it will always be my most dominant element, but with the use of all four I am the strongest I have ever been."

"What you're doing doesn't make you strong, it makes you a monster." Theo's voice wavered slightly as the king turned his cruel gaze to him.

He stiffened beside me, but held his chin high. Not backing down on the truth.

"Ah, Theodore Edwards, the earth warlock who has no skill with magic."

Theo's hand trembled at his side and I placed it in my own, giving it a tight squeeze, hoping I could transfer some of my strength to him.

"H—How do you know who I am?" Theo stuttered.

King Elias stepped down from his dais, each footstep echoing around the cold, empty room. He leaned over us both with a cruel smile. He was thin, with loosely hanging trousers and a loose tunic, and his skin shone a glossy, pearly white. He stood only a few inches taller than Theo, but his menacing presence made him seem much larger.

"I make sure I take the time to get to know everyone who lives in my kingdom, Mister Edwards. *Especially* those who are a close acquaintance to my dear niece here."

Turning to face me front on, he gave me a quick wink before shifting his gaze to Julien, who I thought still lay unconscious on the cold stone floor. I had been too preoccupied by my encounter with the king to realise that he was awake. He'd propped himself up against the stone wall.

Elias knelt before him. "It's nice to see you again, Julien, but I must admit you look a little worse for wear. Is that a barghest bite I see?"

Julien grunted in reply. His face was drained of colour but, from what I could see, the poison hadn't spread any further. Julien grimaced as King Elias lifted his bandage and I knew if he didn't see a Wise Witch soon it would be too late for him.

"Hmm, nasty creatures, barghests. Their bites can be quite lethal unless you have the right treatment. It seems you were only lightly dosed with poison, otherwise you would already be dead."

King Elias straightened, making his way back to the throne in a few quick strides. Growing impatient, I fidgeted where I stood, my palms tingling madly by my sides. My magic ebbed and flowed with each emotion rolling over me. I was growing tired of listening to the king's slick voice. If he wasn't going to show me my mother,

I at least wanted answers to the questions that had plagued me since discovering the prophecy. As I stepped towards the dais, a dark-haired guard I hadn't noticed earlier stepped down, his hand blocking my path.

"No closer, decepitor, or I will not hesitate to cut you down where you stand." His voice was cruel, but it was the deep brown eyes glaring down at me that made me take a tentative step back.

They were eyes I had come to know so well—eyes that had stared at me in earnest and with loyalty. But now... they burned with hatred, despising every inch of me.

A large grin spread across King Elias' face. "I see you never told my darling niece about your family's ties to me, Julien. Braelyn, I would like to introduce you to Sebastien Thorne."

As I gaped at Julien, I recognised the sadness rimming his eyes—the defeat upon realising I'd learned one of his deepest secrets. I already knew his parents had once been loyal to King Elias, but when they had perished, I had assumed his ties to the king had ended.

"It's a pity, really. I could use another strong fire warlock by my side."

Julien let out a low growl that sounded more animal than human. He tried pushing off the floor, but he was too weak to do anything aside from sit and scowl in the direction of the king and his brother. I could see the hatred behind Julien's stare, but a small part of me still felt a twinge of betrayal that he'd hidden his brother's alliance with the king from me.

"I can see the barghest's poison has affected you greatly Julien. Normally, you are nothing but flame and heated words, but not today. I could fix it, you know. Have Morrigan draw the poison out and give you an elixir for the pain, but I would require something from you in return."

"I would rather die," Julien spat before he stiffened, clenching his teeth in pain.

He squeezed his eyes shut as his good hand shot to his forehead. Rushing over, I crouched next to him, taking his head in my hands. I stared wide-eyed as I watched the black poison climb his neck and over his jaw. It seemed the more energy he used, the quicker the poison spread. When the pain eventually subsided, Julien's skin was clammy and small beads of sweat trickled down the sides of his face. As his eyes opened, I was taken aback to see half his eye had gone black. The poison was consuming him.

Despite Julien keeping his brother's identity a secret, he still meant a great deal to me and I had to believe that he had kept this from me for a good reason. Brushing away a trickle of sweat sliding down his face, I turned my eyes to King Elias, who was lounging on his red cushioned throne in utter amusement. Feeling my fire magic bloom in my chest, I tried to calm my shaking hands.

"Fix him," I said, my voice dangerously low.

"I beg your pardon?" King Elias raised a perfect dark eyebrow, challenging me.

"I said I want you to heal him. I will give you whatever you ask for, but first I want to see my mother."

The king's eyes narrowed. After a moment of contemplative silence, he turned to Victoria, who was still standing near the open double doors. She hadn't said a word since he'd joined us and, truthfully, I had almost forgotten her as she no longer posed the biggest threat in the room. He nodded curtly and Victoria wrapped her knuckle on a wooden door to the left of the chamber. A second later, the door was pulled open, the hinges squealing loudly under the weight of the wood. I held my breath as the darkness behind the door rippled, revealing my mother.

Morrigan shoved her through the door, her hands bound in iron shackles and preventing her from summoning magic.

"Mother." My voice broke on the word.

Running towards her, I closed the distance between us in a matter of seconds, throwing my arms tightly around her neck. A loud sob broke out of me. I heard my mother's calming voice in my ear as she tried to soothe my pain.

"Okay, that's enough," Morrigan barked.

Despite how hard I tried to shake her off, Morrigan had an

unnatural strength that overpowered my own and, eventually, I stopped fighting, letting her pull me from my mother's embrace.

Just like the other prisoners we had seen in the dungeons, my mother's face was covered in grime, her tears creating clean lines down her cheeks. She still wore the black dress she had been wearing the night of my rune ceremony, but it was now torn in several places.

"Braelyn, you shouldn't have come here. It's too dangerous." Her voice was almost a whisper.

"I couldn't just leave you here." My tears were falling hot and fast down my cheeks, blurring my vision, but I didn't bother brushing them away.

"Such a touching scene to witness," Elias crooned. "But time is ticking, Miss Grey, Julien doesn't have much longer to live. Should I ask Morrigan to heal him now?"

Despair filled me as I looked at Julien. Theo had sunk to his side and was trying to keep his eyes from fluttering closed. Julien's face was half hidden, covered in the twisting black web of the barghest's poison. Feeling helpless, I nodded at the king just once and he waved Morrigan over to Julien's side. Rushing after her, I heard my mother calling my name, but I drowned out her voice. I needed to ensure King Elias wouldn't go back on his word like he had done earlier when setting the barghest on us. Morrigan ran her hands over the bite mark. "The traitor is strong," she crooned. "This volume of barghest poison would have killed anyone else hours ago."

She pulled back the bandages covering Julien's wound and a small whimper escaped his lips. I stroked his hair gently as Theo assisted Morrigan in tearing away the rest of Julien's shirt. He shivered as his skin touched the cold stone and I summoned a small ember in the palm of my hand—not enough to form a full flame, but enough to ease Julien's tremors. He turned his head to the warmth, a deep sigh escaping his dry lips.

Morrigan lowered her palm to hover over Julien's wound, a smile twisting her face. "Here we go."

She pressed down on the bite mark as her sharp, pointed nails dug into his skin like tiny needles. Julien cried out in pain. The noise tearing from his throat threatened to break me in two as I tried to push Morrigan's hands away, but Theo stopped me. He seized my wrists before I could break the connection.

"No, Brae, look."

Theo pointed to Julien's face. The dark web-like lines were retreating from Julien's eye as if Morrigan was sucking the poison from his body. She mumbled words I didn't understand, reciting an ancient magic I had assumed was long since forgotten.

Slowly, the poison receded entirely, leaving only angry red puncture marks in Julien's skin. His screaming had stopped and, at some point, he had collapsed into unconsciousness. Even he had his limits. I breathed a sigh of relief. Julien was going to be okay. His breathing had evened out and he was no longer trembling in feverish sweats. Letting the embers in my hand burn away, I smoothed Julien's sweat-soaked hair back from his face, waiting for him to wake.

"A deal is a deal, Miss Grey. Morrigan healed Julien for you, now it's your turn to hold up your end of the bargain." King Elias stood with his hands behind his back, looking like a dutiful soldier called to attention. He stalked towards me, holding his hand out expectantly.

"Braelyn, what is he talking about? Holding up your end of the bargain? What did you agree too?" My mother's voice dripped with concern, and I wished I could say something to ease her worry, but I couldn't without giving away my quickly hatched plan.

"It's okay, just trust me."

I tried to convey my confidence, but only terror filled her eyes. Placing my hand in the king's, I let him guide me to the dais. Placing me on the first step leading up to his throne, he turned me around to face everyone. My heart pounded as I waited for King Elias to tell me what I had bargained away. He bent so our faces were now level and I saw the storm brewing deep in his eyes. The same round eyes that might have looked upon me lovingly had he let my father live all those years ago.

King Elias flexed his fingers as a long, pointed metal ring glinted on his index finger. The circulum. It was the most elaborate ring I had ever seen and it shone a magnificent silver that sparkled like starlight in the fire from the hanging wooden chandelier. If the story behind its creation wasn't so menacing, I would have thought it was beautiful.

"The only thing I want, Braelyn, is your magic."

A look of pure hunger had taken over the king's face, sending a frosty shiver down my spine. I needed to try and stall him if my plan was ever going to work.

"Wait. You need to answer some questions for me first. I think it's only fair, don't you?" My voice sounded a little shaky, but I hoped it was enough to delay the king's actions.

Elias stared at me; his eyebrows raised. I felt my stomach quiver as a wave of unease washed over me. I knew what he was capable of. If I had misjudged his amusement at my behaviour, my life would be cut short in a matter of seconds, my magic drained.

"Well, I suppose I should give you the courtesy of a few answers given I am the reason you are in Ellesmere in the first place." His voice was light and teasing.

"What do you mean you're the reason I'm here? I stepped through a portal."

Elias tossed his head back and laughed arrogantly. "How do you think the portal came to be in your mother's apothecary? Granted, you weren't supposed to end up at the Redferne cottage, but a small mistake with Morrigan's magic turned out to be even more fun in getting you here."

My heart thudded as I remembered back to the night the portal had appeared, but something still didn't make sense. Hazel had told me my mother had fled Ellesmere after the Royal War so that I would be safe from the king's reach.

"But... I don't understand. How did you find me?" I asked, pursing my lips.

"Now that's an interesting story. The day you received your

element rune I felt something shift in the magic surrounding Ellesmere. I knew you were the one that stupid prophecy spoke about. I tried tracking your magic, but your mother had hidden you well amongst the dull and meaningless existence of humans. Eventually, it was the old ways of magic that helped me find you. I will admit it was no easy feat, but with a little help from your father and Morrigan's keen tongue for speaking the language of old, I was finally able to find you."

"What do you mean you had my father's help?" My voice quaked as I stared at King Elias with wide eyes. Theo had been right when he had told me there were old spells that could be used to track down witches and warlocks. My legs felt weak as I stood waiting for him to answer my question.

"Well, with a few drops of his blood—the same blood running through your veins, Miss Grey—Morrigan was able to trace your whereabouts to the woeful human town you had been residing in. She conjured the portal to bring you to Ellesmere." Sticking his chest out proudly, a smirk pulled at the corner of the king's mouth.

My heart sank at his confession. A small part of me had foolishly hoped my father might still been alive, perhaps hidden away in the depths of the castle. Despair filled my bones, and my stomach flipped. I watched Elias's face relax, his smile deepening upon seeing my anguish. Anger boiled as my fire magic ignited deep within me. *How could someone be so cruel?*

"Why didn't you just kill me when I first came to Ellesmere? You saw me at the Forest Festival, why wait?" I spat.

The king tilted his head in thought and I could see his smile waver ever so slightly. His patience was wearing thin with my continued barrage of questions.

"I had considered destroying you when you arrived, but seeing how frightened you became when I spied your spirit rune… I knew you were nothing to contend with at the time and, unfortunately, I still lacked one thing I needed for your demise." Holding his right hand up in front of him, the circulum shone magnificently on his finger.

"But you already had that," I replied gesturing to the pointed ring.

"Yes, but I did not have everything required to complete the circulum. Your father found me with the Book of Lilith once, you see—the grimoire written by one of the greatest dark witches of this century and the true creator of the circulum. I had always been fascinated with dark magic as a boy and had come across the tome digging around in the castle archives. I believed it to be a sign from the elements themselves that I was destined for greater things."

Elias paced over the stones in front of me and I could see his eyes were distant, lost in the memory of the day he thought his luck had changed. The hope glittering deep within his eyes almost made me feel sorry for him. Once, he was just a child, lost amidst the rules and regulations of royalty, but I knew the destruction was yet to come in his story, and the feeling dissipated rather quickly.

"As the eldest born son to the king, I knew one day I would rule over Ellesmere and vowed to use all I had learnt from Lilith's grimoire to cleanse the kingdom of those who did not deserve the magic they possessed." His eyes flashed with anger. "When your father found me trying to complete the circulum, he put a stop to it, pulling the grimoire from my grasp. I managed to rip free the pages I thought I needed. Our father was enraged and vowed I would never sit on the throne as long as he lived, so I ended his life and all those who threatened my claim to the throne. That is… until I found you, my dear niece."

I stared at the king's handsome face, unable to utter a word. The way he spoke so freely about killing sent chills over my entire body. My instincts urged me to run as far as I could from the warlock standing before me, but I couldn't. I needed to fulfil the prophecy and put a stop to his manic behaviour. So I asked one more question.

"Why did you need my mother?" My voice was soft, probing him for the answer I thought I already knew.

The permanent smirk on Elias's face wavered, shifting to a menacing scowl. His jawline hardened as he clenched his teeth and

I knew his patience had come to an end.

"When your father found me with the Book of Lilith and stole it from my grasp, he sent it away with your mother, knowing I hadn't secured all the pages needed to complete the circulum."

"But you have been stealing the magic of other witches and warlocks since before I came to Ellesmere. So why—"

The king held up his long slender finger with the circulum gleaming in the light of the sconces. It looked like he had a huge claw attached to his hand, ready to devour his prey. *Me.*

"Each time a dwarf tried to forge the circulum for me, I would use it to siphon the magic of another, but after a few uses the power would be too much for it to contain and so it would shatter. I knew then that I needed to find the remaining pages if I was ever going to cleanse the kingdom of those undeserving of magic. And now I have succeeded." He smiled a dazzling, toothy smile which, on any other person would have been infectious, but on the king it appeared deadly.

He stopped his pacing and stared up at me, tilting his head to one side as if considering my fate. As he approached me, he brushed away a strand of hair that had come loose—the tip of the circulum drawing a cool line across my cheek. I stood my ground, eyes narrowed as my heart thumped heavily in my chest.

"Call it what you want, you are still a murderer," I said between clenched teeth.

"Well it's a shame you think that, Braelyn, but unfortunately your time is up. I will be taking your magic because, with you out of the picture, there is no one else left to contest my right to the throne. I will rule over Ellesmere for years to come and anyone who does not bow before me will suffer my wrath." His face twisted into a look of pure hatred as he brought the circulum close to my chest.

Panicking, I glanced at my mother who was fidgeting within Morrigan's tight grasp. Her hazel eyes filled with fear as she watched Elias bring the pointed tip of the circulum closer.

"Elias, don't you dare touch her. How could you do this to your own family? Was slaughtering your father and brother not enough?!" My mother's voice rang loudly around the room.

I saw something flicker in Elias's dark eyes at the mention of family, but I could see it only made him angry. His head snapped to the side as he glared at my mother.

"A deal is a deal, Nora. The boy's life in return for something I wanted. Your daughter didn't even consider what I was asking when she agreed."

My mother's face turned ashen as she looked between me and Julien. My eyes stung with unshed tears. I hadn't expected things to escalate like this. I felt so useless now, but I had to believe this journey hadn't been in vain. Everything I had endured to get to this very moment had only made me stronger and I would be damned if I was going to let King Elias hurt anyone else in the kingdom I had grown to love.

"I'm sorry," I whispered to her. "It was my fault Julien was going to die and I couldn't let that happen."

My mother's face softened ever so slightly. I could see understanding dawn on her beautiful face as my eyes connected with hers, telling the silent story of a boy who I had come to love like she had loved my father. I desperately wanted to run to her. To have her wrap me in her arms and tell me everything was going to be okay, but instead I stood frozen on the stairs, too terrified to move.

My plan to stop King Elias required me to be as close to him as I could possibly get and, despite the fear of losing my magic, I knew there was no other way.

The king looked at me hungrily, eyes flashing. "Shall we begin?"

Twenty-Seven

My heart felt like it would burst from my chest. A constant pounding I tried to focus on to steady my heavy breathing. King Elias stood before me, his hand at the ready. The silver-taloned circulum sparkled menacingly as he brought the pointed tip so close to my chest I could feel the hum of magic forged inside it. I was so exhausted at this point—everything leading to this moment weighing heavily on my shoulders—that I wanted to close my eyes. To block everything out and accept my fate, but the satisfaction glinting in Elias's jet black eyes—thinking he had won—sent a wave of anger through me. I would *not* let him win. As the tip of the circulum touched my chest, my mother cried out.

"Stop, take my magic instead."

Her voice was desperate, pleading, but I knew Elias wouldn't fall for it. He didn't want just anyone's magic to be powerful, he wanted *my* magic. I was the only person left in his family who could challenge him, who had the power to destroy him and everything he had created.

"You know that isn't a fair trade, Nora. You are just an air witch—a powerful one, yes, but an air witch all the same." He turned his gaze back to me. "But Braelyn here holds the fate of my future in the palm of her tiny little hand."

Turning my hand to gaze at my spirit rune, a look of triumph filled his greedy eyes.

"Such a shame," he murmured, "that such power can be given to someone with no use for it."

As he released my hand, I let it fall to my side, no longer ignoring the tingling in my fingertips, the thrum of my magic rushing through my veins. I let my body succumb to the magic inside me, feeling it growing more potent as each second ticked into another. I waited for my moment to act, needing the king to think I would give him what he wanted for saving Julien.

As he placed the sharp ring to my chest, I felt the sting of metal biting into my flesh and held back a cry of pain.

"This may hurt a little," Elias crooned with a sneer, "but don't fret, it will all be over soon."

Before I had the chance to summon my magic or make a grab for the circulum, a searing pain erupted in my chest, making me scream in agony. My chest felt like it was being sliced open with a blade dipped in fire. Within seconds of the circulum touching me, a searing pain erupted in my skull. My hands flew to my head, clutching it in a tight grasp as if I could squeeze out the pain. Firm hands looped under my arms, holding me upright and preventing me from moving. Determined not to give Elias the satisfaction of seeing me faint, I forced my eyes open, tears blurring my vision. Where the circulum still connected with my skin, a thin line of gold pulled from the centre of my chest. Taking in a shuddery breath, I watched in horror as my magic was pulled from me bit by bit, flowing into Elias's veins, sending golden webs up his hands and arms. His chin was tilted to the ceiling, a satisfied sigh escaping his lips as my magic ignited within him.

My mother fought against Morrigan's hold, trying to pull her hands free of her shackles to get to me, but the dark witch's strength overpowered my mother's love, holding her firmly in place. I could see Theo being restrained by Victoria, his height not helping him win his struggle against her tight grip on his arms. Finally, my eyes settled on Julien. I expected him to still be sitting on the stone floor, but instead he fought against the restraints of Blight and Zuko as he tried to fight his way to my rescue. His face was contorted with rage, his mouth forming words I couldn't hear with the heavy pounding in my ears.

As I gazed at my mother and the two people who had been with me throughout this entire journey, I felt something stir deep within. I could feel my mother's love radiating through my veins like a furnace igniting in my chest. I felt the bonds of love and friendship I had made with Julien and Theo strengthen my mind as a power I didn't know I possessed threatened to consume me.

Closing my eyes, I let myself feel every emotion that had coursed through my body over the last few days. The fear over losing my mother and the possibility of never seeing her again, the terror I had felt watching Julien almost die because of me, my sadness at having to say goodbye to Hazel and the bond of friendship I had created with Theo. All these feelings bubbled up inside me like a cauldron ready to spill over. Opening my eyes, I met King Elias's steely gaze with a look that oozed utter hatred. I was done with being a pawn in his conniving scheme. I was the true queen and, by the elements, I was going to *end* the king's game.

"I am not as weak as you think," I ground out as the searing pain in my chest reached a new level.

My fingers surged with power. My magic answered my anger, fear and love like two magnets drawn together. My veins burned a brilliant gold with the magic blazing within me, setting my soul alight. The tingling that had once only been in my fingertips now ran through me like waterfalls, strong and turbulent. Magic brewed in my chest, threatening to erupt into a deadly thunderstorm.

My muscles quivered as I lifted my hands, trying to breathe through the pain still slicing through my chest as I brought them together in front of me. Electricity flickered around my fingers as streaks of lightning grew to a crescendo. Elias's eyes bulged as he stared at the white-blue lightning wreathing my clasped hands. Pulling my palms apart slowly, my magic grew in strength and size as the lightning sparked dangerously between us.

"This... this is not possible," Elias sputtered. For the first time, I saw fear in his eyes.

I gave him a tight-lipped smile. "This may hurt a little."

The lightning hit him straight in the chest. The sheer strength and power of the strike sent him careening backwards, his talon-tipped finger no longer sucking the magic from my chest. Spinning around to face Julien's brother, I let him feel the wrath of my air magic. His face was a mask of shock, his eyes darting from me to King Elias's body laying only metres away. With a quick flick of my wrists I sent him soaring in the opposite direction. He hit the stone wall behind the king's throne with a sickening crunch before he crumpled to the floor.

I doubled over, taking a second to catch my breath, my hand grasping at the cut in my chest. Glancing down, I could see it was only a small slice, barely making me bleed. As the searing pain began to subside, I looked up to find Elias had gotten back to his feet, his face a portrait of rage.

"Your magic is *mine*," he growled through clenched teeth. His features were animalistic. Frenzied.

Raising his arms, Elias summoned the same air magic he had used earlier to pull me to my feet. My boots began to slide inch by inch along the stone stairs, the wind roaring around me in gusts. Gritting my teeth, I clenched my fists together. Pushing my feet into the stone as hard as I could, the earth reacted to my magic, holding me in place against the brewing storm the king had conjured. This only angered him more.

Elias narrowed his eyes as he clenched his hands together, instantly engulfing them in searing flames. *Two can play at this game.* Summoning my own fire magic, my hands swam with the same flames Elias had conjured. My hazel eyes locked with the king's stormy ones as the first jet of fire left his hand.

The fireball soared through the air, spitting embers as it licked at the air. Rolling out of the way, the flames hit the crimson cushions of the king's throne, instantly sending it up in a blaze. My palms stung with grazes from the impact of sliding against the rough stone floor. I scrambled to my feet just as Elias conjured another ball of fire and tossed it in my direction. Too late, I realised I didn't have time move out of its path. My eyes grew wide as the flaming orb flew towards me. Feeling strong hands grasp my arms, I was pulled away just before the fire engulfed a tapestry hanging on the wall behind me. It devoured every thread of the intricate design.

Julien pulled me to my feet, his hands fluttering over every inch of my body to check if I'd been hurt.

"I'm okay," I gasped. "How did you…"

My voice trailed off as I spied Blight on the floor, half his face now the colour of charcoal from where Julien had touched a flaming hand to his skin. Zuko rolled on the ground, cradling his face as blood dripped steadily through his fingers.

"Magic doesn't always do the trick. Sometimes you just need to use good old brute force."

Giving me one of his usual winks, he turned his attention to King Elias, whose hands still flamed brightly by his sides. I wondered how he was even able to stand that type of heat when fire wasn't his natural element.

"What a touching scene that was, Julien, but I wonder how your little lovebird would feel knowing what you did for me?" A cruel smile spread across his face.

Turning my gaze towards Julien, I noticed his eyes widen slightly at the king's words. His hands trembled by his sides, causing his fire to flicker and dance. My eyes darted between the two of them.

"What is he talking about?" I said softly, looking towards Julien.

Julien narrowed his eyes at Elias before he turned his head toward me, his eyes rimmed red. I searched his face, trying to find answers.

"Braelyn, I—"

I held up a finger to silence him as something in the back of my mind clicked into place . The Lilithium Mortiferum. I knew I had seen it before, but it hadn't just been in the small leather grimoire at the apothecary—which I now knew to be the Book of Lilith. Julien had been holding some the night I saw him leaving the Ironwood. He had shoved it into his satchel upon seeing me in the clearing, but I distinctly remember the luminescent purple I had glimpsed ever so quickly before he pushed it out of sight. He hadn't only been foraging for mushrooms, he had been collecting the Lilithium Mortiferum for the king.

Betrayal sliced, sharp as knives, as my heart cracked in pain. "You're the one giving him the means to torture innocent people," I whispered.

My voice sounded strange to my ears. I felt empty, as if King Elias had taken my magic after all. Julien took a step towards me, but I held my hand out to stop him. Streaks of lightning wove through my fingers, surging menacingly, just waiting to be freed.

"Don't come near me."

My voice cracked, and I could feel myself beginning to fall apart.

"Please, Braelyn, let me explain," Julien pleaded, but I'd had enough of people lying to me.

First it was my mother keeping secrets about my lineage and now Julien. I felt like the only person who had been honest with me from the beginning was the one I was trying to destroy.

Turning my back on Julien, I looked to King Elias who now lounged against the stone wall, a delighted grin on his face. He would revel in telling me the truth.

"Why?" I said softly.

Elias stepped away from the wall, coming to stand in front of me. His hands were clasped behind his back, obviously at ease with a temporary truce.

"Everything has a price, Braelyn. Young Julien here didn't want to join me like the rest of his family, so I made a deal with him. The Lilithium Mortiferum for the price of his freedom. He was happy to oblige. That is, until a certain someone arrived in Ellesmere."

Gnawing on my bottom lip, I considered Elias's answer before

I turned back to Julien. He watched me carefully, his shoulders slumped.

"I haven't given him a single petal of Lilithium Mortiferum since the day we spoke in the clearing, Braelyn. You showed me that, despite what people expected, *I* was responsible for my own destiny, and I no longer wanted to be under his control." Julien gestured at Elias, who still looked at me with a bemused expression.

I wanted to believe him, but my apprehension at being made a fool of again made my chest feel tight. I opened my mouth to say something to him, but before I had the chance, I felt my head pulled backwards—my hair almost tearing from my scalp. Crying out, I hit the ground with a bone crushing thud that left my head spinning. As the room came back into focus, I saw Julien try to rush to my side, but Sebastien stopped him. Seeing them next to each other now, I was relieved to see their eyes and bronzed complexion was as far as the resemblance stretched. Where Julien was well built, Sebastien was lean. His hair fell in curls to his shoulders, which he wore pulled back from his long face with a piece of rope.

Victoria's black heeled boot pressed heavily on my chest, holding me down so Elias had time to reach me. He must have signalled behind his back while we'd been speaking.

"I have wanted to do that since the moment I met you," She sneered. Her face twisted in a malicious smile.

My eyes watered from the force of being yanked down and I could feel the warm ooze of blood from where she had ripped a chunk of hair from my scalp. Victoria's boot crushed my chest and my lungs burned with the need for air. King Elias knelt by my side, his face hovering above mine, eyebrows raised and a smug smirk pulling at one side of his mouth.

"The price of your treachery, my dear niece, will be a fate worse than death. To live the life of a witch with no magic. I'll siphon your power so only a tiny amount lingers in your veins, but not enough for you to conjure. Always there, but out of reach."

The light of the lanterns illuminating him from behind made the edges of his face glow gold. He looked almost like a mythical god one might read about in stories. As he brought his taloned finger towards me again, I knew this time it was over. I tried my best to struggle out of Victoria's hold, but her hatred of me fuelled her more than any strength I could muster. As Elias placed the tip of the circulum back to my chest, I let my lids droop. But, as they neared closing, I saw a flash of magic. Victoria flew backwards and I felt the instant relief of air rushing back into my lungs.

Coughing and spluttering, I scrambled to my feet, freezing where I stood. Theo stood a metre to my left, vines streaming from his palms as they wrapped around both Elias and Victoria, securing them in tight bindings. My chest swelled with pride as Theo unleashed his magic for the first time since the barghest attack. Coming to his side, I let my earth magic soar to the surface. Thick, twisting vines slithered from my fingertips like great serpents as they snaked along the stone, joining Theo's and entwining Elias and Victoria in a tighter snare. With a moment of breathing space, I looked towards my mother who, despite not being able to conjure her magic, was putting up a fight against Morrigan's water magic.

Julien was now in a fiery fist fight with Sebastien. Both were locked in an inferno of smouldering flames. Julien let loose a spiralling jet of molten fire towards Sebastien, who jumped and rolled out of the way with his arms still ablaze. Sebastien sent a flaming orb of blue flame soaring through the air like a blazing sun. Julien managed to side-step the fiery ball before it could hit him in the chest and it collided with the creeping vines entangling the king, devouring the green cords holding him captive. Theo recoiled as if burnt by the fire that had converged with his own magic. I stretched my climbing vines to slide over the stones and hold the king captive once again. He tried to conjure the same flames Sebastien had used to free him, but it was no use. I was a spirit witch, and the heat of the fire merely danced along the vines like a match being struck alight. My gaze then darted to Julien who was facing a barrage of flaming bullets. They rained down on him like meteors, preventing him from conjuring any more magic. My free hand fluttered at my side as panic threatened to overtake my thoughts. If I didn't do something soon, everything could unravel very quickly. As I held Victoria and Elias tightly bound by my earth magic, I conjured a flame in my free hand. I had never summoned more than one element before and I hoped with my entire being that my plan would work. Letting the flame engulf my hand, I watched it curl from my fingertips like long, fiery tendrils, reaching out towards Sebastien and ensnaring him in a fiery web. With his hands now pinned to his sides, Sebastien's magic extinguished, allowing Julien to recover his position. I could feel my magic constrict my chest as the exertion of conjuring two elements took hold of my body. I tried to focus my attention on keeping everyone contained in my webs of earth and fire magic, but my strength was fading fast. Fog began to roll into my mind, clouding my vision and causing my power to waver. I searched the room for the other guards when Julien's voice broke through the chaos.

"Unlock Mrs Grey's shackles or I will burn this wretched hag to a cinder."

Julien's words were fire and ice, sharp and dripping with the heat burning through his veins. He had one arm wrapped around Morrigan's throat as the other burned brightly with a scarlet flame.

King Elias's nostrils flared as he took in the scene before him, unable to do anything other than watch as his plans fell limp at his feet. We had managed to detain two of his best guards, while the others still lay unconscious and recovering from their earlier wounds. He looked blankly at Morrigan, before a cruel smirk twisted his lips. "Go ahead, Julien, kill her."

Julien's face wavered as he stared back into King Elias' dark eyes. The king letting out a harsh laugh. "You're weak Julien. Nothing but talk." Julien grit his teeth, letting out a low growl. Pulling Morrigan towards my mother he glared at the king as his once orange flame now blazed a magnificent blue, conjuring the rare and powerful blue fire. Placing his hands on the shackles that bound my mother's hands, the metal groaned under the heat before snapping in two like a broken twig. My mother rubbed at the raw skin of her wrists, before turning to Morrigan and punching her square in the face. The Wise Witch stumbled, as Julien released her from his grasp, falling to a crumpled heap on the stone floor. Rushing to my side, my mother took my face in hers. I stared back at her, my eyes wide with surprise at what she had just done. Giving her a quick smile to reassure her, I looked to Julien and the empty shackles lying discarded at Morrigan's feet. I could feel my magic fading as the flames holding Sebastien sputtered. The vines holding Victoria and Elias twitched as I scrunched up my face in concentration.

Seeing my gaze drift to him, Julien straightened his shoulders and scooped up the abandoned shackles. Turning to his brother, Julien pulled him close, their faces only inches apart. Hatred radiated off Julien in hot waves, his muscles tense and his jaw clenched as he secured the iron tightly around his brother's hands, preventing him from using any magic against us. I felt my fire magic finally break as the flames holding Sebastien fizzled into nothing but dying embers. I gave Julien a brief nod of thanks, not trusting myself to say anything. I knew we would need to speak to his part in all of this, but for now, King Elias was my main concern.

"So what now, my dear little niece? You lock me up and take over the throne, sending Ellesmere back to its weak little self?"

I shrugged as I tightened my hold on the vines twisting around his body. Victoria winced in response to their tightening grip.

"Something like that," I said evenly.

The king chuckled, his whole body shaking with the cruel sound. "You are such a fool. There are more powerful beings out there not even you can defeat on your own. Ellesmere will be thrown into darkness. The shadows in the Ironwood will grow, as will the darkness inside you."

A wave of cold dread washed over my face at Elias's words and, despite trying to keep my face neutral, the king saw through the cracks in my mask. He grinned broadly, realising he had struck a nerve buried deep within me since my encounter with the ash tree in the Ironwood. I'd felt the tendrils of dark magic reaching out to me ever since and a small part of me craved to feel that power again.

"Ah, you know what I speak of, don't you?" He watched me carefully, black eyes glittering.

"You don't know anything about me," I snapped, my voice wavering slightly.

"You might think that now, but you and I are more alike than you care to admit."

I shook my head, either in response to Elias's statement or to convince myself he was wrong, I wasn't sure, but I did know there was some truth to his words. What I had felt standing before the ash tree was something I struggled to describe even to myself. Using my magic made me feel more powerful than I had ever felt, but what I'd felt in the Ironwood was raw, as if my magic was controlling me instead of me controlling it. Despite what Elias told me, I would not let myself succumb to the darkness. Not like he had.

Elias shrugged his shoulders. "Whether you want to believe it or not, the dark power will come for you, Braelyn, and I will be there when it does."

With an almighty yell, Elias threw his arms out wide, catching me off-guard as the vines holding him ruptured. The force of his air magic made me stumble backward as the tie connecting me to him and Victoria severed. I felt my mother's hands steady me as Elias's wrath exploded around us. The stones covering the floor of the throne room began to crack and split as he lifted his hands up, the rock and rubble following the commands of his stolen earth magic. My mother and I darted out of the way, narrowly missing a rock hurtling into the stairs, causing them to crack and break away. Swearing under my breath, I summoned my own magic, trying to break the boulders down as Elias continued hurling them in my direction. Moving to the side of the room, I saw Morrigan had regained her composure and was mumbling under her breath, summoning the same ancient magic she had used on Julien. Her hands swirled in front of her in large arching circles.

"She is trying to conjure a portal," my mother yelled towards me.

Elias had already started making his way to the growing light swirling and rippling only steps away from where I stood. Whatever magic Morrigan was using now was a lot stronger than the power she had used to create the portal in the apothecary. A buzzing filled the room at an almost deafening rumble, and I clamped my hands over my ears to block out the sound. As Elias closed the distance between us, I saw the glint in his eye as he reached for my arm, trying to drag me through the portal with him.

Julien and Theo mouthed my name as they both bolted from where they stood. Theo's long legs closed the distance between us in seconds, leaving Julien a few steps behind. Pushing me out of the way, Theo took my place as Elias stepped into the portal, his hand clasping tightly around Theo's wrist. My friend was pulled into the wavering glow of the portal. The last thing I saw was a cunning smile disfiguring Elias's face before they disappeared.

Twenty-Eight

"**N**o!"

The guttural sound of my scream threatened to tear me apart. I stared at the spot Theo had just been, my body trembling with the shock of what had just happened. The last remnants of the portal shimmered in the remaining firelight. The deafening buzz had now stopped and where the portal had once been there was now nothing but empty air.

My chest heaved with pain, my voice raw as heavy sobs rattled my body. The weight of what had just happened settled over me like the first snowfall of winter, sending my body into a shivering frenzy. My vision blurred as the tears ran hot down my cheeks. I could just make out my mother's flowing skirts as they appeared at the edges of my vision. Kneeling beside me, she took me in her arms and rocked me gently, like she used to do when I was young.

I could hear Julien arguing with Victoria behind me, but I took no notice of them, instead letting the comfort of my mother's embrace ease my trembling body. My tears eventually dried out. I didn't know what to do with myself. I had promised myself I would take care of Theo—make sure nothing happened to him—and instead I'd pulled him into the most disastrous situation.

Wiping my nose on the back of my hand, I peered at my mother. Her face was slightly flushed and her hair fell in mussed waves around her shoulders. She gave me a sad smile.

"I'm sorry Theo's gone, honey."

The stabbing pain of loss pierced my chest as I stared back into my mother's caring eyes. "I never wanted any of this to happen."

I took in the damage of the throne room. King Elias's throne had been destroyed. The once ruby red cushions of his ornate throne now hung in tatters, the intricate designs on the arms now a melted pile of gold. Most of the floor had been destroyed in Elias's wrath. Rocky debris scattered the room and the dais now lay in pieces.

I spotted Julien still standing near Victoria, who was now sitting slumped on the floor. She stared at me with such hatred it made my hands tremble. I knew her dislike of me would now reach a new high. I had prevented her from getting the thing she wanted most. I'd lost sight of Morrigan in the chaos of the portal, but I knew she must have gone through with Elias. Sebastien's hands were still cuffed in the iron shackles, his eyes trained on his brother as Julien came to stand beside me. His hair was littered with dust and debris from the battle, turning his usual dark waves grey. His lip was still swollen from where Theo had punched him in the tunnel and a small graze bled above his eyebrow. My lip trembled as he took my hand in his, giving it a warm, tight squeeze.

"We will find him, Braelyn. I promise you. I will not stop until I bring Theo back." Julien's voice was hard, but I heard the sadness behind his brave facade.

I knew he meant the words he said and I didn't doubt for a second he would leave no stone in Ellesmere unturned in his search for our friend. Despite their differences, I knew Julien still cared for Theo deeply. Balling my hands into tight fists, I met Julien's deep eyes with a steely gaze.

"I know you will. We'll find him if it's the last thing I do."

After we had safely secured Sebastien, Victoria, and the other guards in the dungeons, we released the innocent prisoners, who, despite their disbelief of the king having fled, were thankful for our help. Lorcan danced around the castle, randomly breaking into songs and singing in dwarfish. They were deep and soulful sounds that would have others spinning and dancing with him. He was beyond thankful to my mother for taking care of his wounds and many were sad to see him leave the castle—myself—included, but he assured me we would see each other again.

My mother pulled Julien aside and administered the healing elixir to his hands. The extreme use of his magic had caused angry veins to twist and cross all the way up to his elbows. It took a little more than the usual three drops, but I was relieved when I saw them fade.

As Julien left the apothecary, my mother turned her bright hazel eyes on me.

"You care for that boy a lot, don't you, Brae?"

I turned to hide the flush of embarrassment creeping up my cheeks, but my mother reached out a delicate hand, tilting my face towards her.

"Braelyn, I just wanted to apologise for not telling you about all of this." She waved a quick hand, her sad eyes still roaming my face in search of forgiveness. "I was trying to protect you from anything terrible happening, but I can see now that you are a lot stronger than I ever gave you credit for."

Smiling warmly, she pulled me close, wrapping her arms around me in a loving hug. I closed my eyes and let the tension of the day's events drip away. Releasing me from her embrace, I saw tears in her eyes.

"You don't need to apologise," I replied softly. "I understand why you did what you did and I'm thankful I grew up away from all this. Coming here now has made me appreciate this wonderful place a whole lot more."

A beautiful smile lit up my mother's face as a peaceful silence settled over us. Taking a deep breath, she stretched out her hand and I watched as a small mortar and pestle floated through the air to settle lightly on her outstretched palm.

"Let's get you fixed up."

With the help of a few other witches in the castle, my arm—where it had been cut by the water wielder's ice magic—received a few stitches and the slice on my chest had a sweet-smelling salve applied to it, which instantly soothed the stinging. Julien returned to the apothecary with his arms full of herbs my mother had sent him out to get. I watched now as my mother's deft hands cleansed Julien's barghest wound with moon water before she stitched the long gashes and applied a mix of sage, witch hazel and calendula to the wound to help with the healing.

Balor had experienced some of the more terrible treatment in his time at the castle and my heart still ached to see one of his magnificent antlers missing. His usual arrogance was gone, leaving him withdrawn and moody. My mother insisted he stay at the castle so she could help heal him, but despite his gruff thanks for his rescue, he told her that he would prefer to leave the castle as quickly as possible.

Days had passed since the battle with King Elias and my mind continued to linger on the grief of losing my friend. My mother had sent word to Hazel, asking her to notify the elders about what had happened at the castle. They had arrived in a flurry of cloaks and horses just two days after her note was sent.

A council meeting was immediately arranged in one of the smaller rooms of the castle where the remaining guards were called up for questioning about their involvement in the king's rule. We had quickly discovered many of King Elias's loyal followers had fled the castle after he had escaped, and those remaining seemed to have followed him out of fear he would take their magic if they refused to obey him. They swore their loyalty was bound to my father and grandfather. Once the elders had deemed this information trustworthy, the discussion turned to who would rule the throne.

As the only remaining blood heir, many assumed I would take up my spot on the throne, but I wasn't ready to rule over the kingdom. Not when my sole focus was trying to figure out King Elias's plan and getting Theo back from the clutches of darkness. The elders seemed to believe otherwise, but before I would be crowned queen I needed to learn the ways of Ellesmere and gain full control of my magic. So the elders agreed they would be my royal advisers, assisting my rule over Ellesmere until I had shown I was responsible enough to take my place as queen.

Many weren't exactly happy with this decision—my mother included—but I was relieved. I wasn't ready to be a queen. I had barely learned how to use my magic and the thought of ruling a kingdom left me feeling a little queasy. Besides, having the elders help me with the kingdom's comings and goings left me time to plan Theo's rescue with Julien and not be overwhelmed with royal duties. A responsibility I wasn't ready for in the first place.

After the elders' arrival, rumours began to spread of King Elias's escape and the poor boy who had been taken with him. Most of the rumours I'd heard were close to the truth, but as the days wore on, they began to grow in extravagance. Things such as Theo only being friends with me to get close to the king, or worse, him being one of King Elias's followers. When I heard this rumour uttered by a few of the kitchen maids, I had been down by the stables feeding apples to the beautiful chestnut mare occupying one of the bays. The poor stable boy who was tending to the horses caught the brunt of my anger as I yelled at him for simply knocking the bucket of apples, sending them rolling in all directions. His eyes widened at my harsh tone, but Julien came to the boy's rescue, pulling me back towards the castle grounds. I instantly felt terrible and wanted to apologise to the poor boy, but Julien assured me it would be better if I left it alone.

"And what about you and me? We still haven't spoken about what King Elias told me."

My voice had lost its harsh edge as we took a seat on a wooden bench set into a small alcove along the castle's outer wall. It was the first time we had been alone together for longer than a few minutes since the battle. Between my meetings with the elders and Julien taking it upon himself to begin our search for Theo, we had barely had enough time to pass each other in the corridors, let alone talk. As we sat on the bench, I was aware of just how close together we were. Julien's natural warmth radiated from him and I breathed in his usual smoky scent. I'd missed him.

"Before you say anything, Braelyn, I just want to apologise for not telling you about the Lilithium Mortiferum. It was a stupid mistake, and I didn't want you to think badly of me." He pressed his chin into his chest and it trembled slightly as he took a shaky breath. "I liked that, despite the rumours, you never looked at me as a bad person, and I was too weak to tell you out of fear you would dismiss me as others do." Sniffing and wiping at his nose, Julien turned his eyes to me and I was surprised to see they were wet. He had poured his heart's deepest fears out to me and my own heart constricted at the pain it caused him. Reaching out a tentative hand, I brushed away a stray tear trailing down his cheek.

"I understand, Julien," I murmured back softly. "You're a good person. You wouldn't be sitting here now if you weren't."

Linking his fingers through mine, he pulled my hand from his cheek and brushed a gentle kiss along my knuckles.

"I don't know what I did to deserve your forgiveness, Braelyn, but I promise I will spend the rest of my days showing you just how thankful I am that you came into my life when you did."

A week had passed since Theo's disappearance and the castle was slowly starting to resume its normal rhythm, but it wasn't so for me and Julien.

Our days were spent huddled in the castle's small library, poring over as many books as we could fit in our arms, trying to find out where Elias could have possibly gone into hiding. Every book we flicked through didn't bring us any closer to the answers we were after and I grew more restless with each passing day, not knowing when or if I would ever see my friend again.

I spent most of my nights awake, staring at the stone ceiling of my room, pondering which books we would comb through the following day. If I did manage to close my eyes, my sleep was wracked with terrifying nightmares—filled with shadows and eerie noises.

I awoke one night soaked in sweat, my breaths coming in rapid bursts, leaving my chest trembling. Rushing to the window, I pulled open the light curtains and gulped in the cool night air as I tried to forget the darkness plaguing my mind. Every time I closed my eyes, the shadows would creep back in. The sounds of footsteps outside my door made my heart flutter wildly in my chest, but it was the tug at the edge of my mind that alerted me to who it was. Pulling open the door, I was overjoyed to see the jackalope waiting patiently in the dark hallway.

"I'm so happy to see you," I thought, a smile breaking my face for the first time in days.

Alpheus's nose twitched slightly as he bowed his head. *"It is wonderful to see you too, my friend, but I am afraid I come bearing bad news."*

My smile faltered as I stared into the creature's almond eyes, wondering what else could go wrong. I made room for Alpheus to enter. He hopped in slowly, his antlers fitting perfectly through the doorway. Closing the wooden door with a quiet thud, I turned towards Alpheus. The sun was just peeking over the horizon, casting his dark fur in a golden glow. A cool breeze rustled the sheer curtains hanging by the open window, sending chills over my arms.

"What's happened?" I asked silently as I rubbed my arms, trying to keep warm.

Alpheus contemplated his answer, dark almond eyes never leaving my face.

"There has been talk in the Ironwood about an evil growing in the shadows. One that, once released, will wreak havoc on all of Ellesmere."

Alpheus turned to face the window, tilting his head slightly as if beckoning me to follow. Tentatively, I stepped over to the open window, my hands worrying the bottom of my night shirt. I pulled back the sheer white curtains. The sun cast a beautiful golden glimmer over the kingdom, lighting the castle grounds and the edge of the Ironwood. Alpheus stretched himself up so his front paws rested lightly on the window ledge.

"Look to the west," he said simply.

Turning my gaze, I saw what appeared to be a foggy mist rolling in far from the west. Squinting, I tried to spot what Alpheus wanted me to see, but all I saw was a spattering of grey fog. The start of a growing storm, I expected.

"I don't understand," I replied.

"Look closer, my friend. It is the beginning of the end."

Turning back to the view, I focused my gaze on the shifting fog rolling over the western kingdom. I narrowed my eyes against the soft glow of the sun and, as I did, a shadow in the mist caught my attention. My breath hitched in my throat. I had seen something like that before. My mind returned to the day we began our journey through the Ironwood—to the ash tree in the clearing and the shadowy figure that had lingered at its long, curved roots. The power I felt there was intoxicating, and I knew in that moment it had to be where King Elias was hiding.

I watched the growing mass of fog, feeling the tell-tale sign of my magic unfurling within me. My hands tingled, the warmth of fire prickling my fingertips as I dug them into the stone windowsill. The stone shifted and groaned in response to my magic.

I knew where my search for Theo would begin and I knew deep down inside that it would need to end with the death of a king.

Acknowledgements

Where do I even begin… I cannot put into words the amount of love and gratitude I feel towards everyone who has been there for me and helped me along in my writing journey.

Firstly, to my wonderful husband, thank you for everything you do for me. From cooking dinner—even after you've worked a long day—so I could write, to always encouraging me to pursue my dreams no matter how hard they sometimes seem. For being my biggest fan since my very first draft, no matter how bad. I love you beyond measure and will never be able to tell you how thankful I am to have been blessed with such an amazing life partner.

To my beautiful Davis & Inic family who have cheered me on from the moment I started writing over ten-years ago, thank you for always believing in me and knowing I would one day fulfil my dreams and publish a book. Your belief in me helped me through some of the hardest times in my writing career and I will forever be thankful for your kind words.

I would like to thank my incredible editor, Chloe Hodge, without your wise words and encouragement I would still be writing this book rather than having people read it. Your incredible writing advice has helped shape me into the writer I am today.

To my amazing beta readers, Paul Pittas, Claire Urquhart, and Maya Sathiah, thank you for taking the time to read The Witch of Ellesmere and providing invaluable feedback. You gave me courage to put my book in front of more readers. To my wonderful cover designer, Sara Oliver, you created the book cover of my dreams.

Your guidance and vision for The Witch of Ellesmere has brought my book dreams to life and I will forever be thankful. Thank you to my gem of a friend, Tess Pollard, for designing my chapter headers. No matter how many times I wanted to add to the designs you took it in your stride and created something that added to the magic within the pages of The Witch of Ellesmere. To my book designer, Lorna Reid, thank you for turning my manuscript into the book I always dreamed it would be. You were an absolute pleasure to work with and I couldn't have done this without your expert knowledge.

And last, but certainly not least, to my wonderful readers. From the bottom of my heart, thank you, for all your encouragement and excitement for The Witch of Ellesmere. This book wouldn't be what it is today without you and I hope you love reading it as much as I loved writing it.

About the Author

Born in Sydney, Kirsty grew up writing from a young age. Ever the dreamer, she was forever writing creative short stories and could always be found with her nose in a book. Always day-dreaming about one day writing a book of her own, she fulfilled her publishing dream with her debut novel The Witch of Ellesmere.

Still living in Sydney with her husband and mini-lop bunny, Winston, she is a lover of tea, books, and all things magical. When not writing, Kirsty can be found sipping on copious amounts of tea and snuggled up with a good book. If the weather is nice, you may also find her outside in the garden tending to her many plant babies.

www.ingramcontent.com/pod-product-compliance
Lightning Source LLC
Chambersburg PA
CBHW030612120726
47904CB00006B/1873